Movement
Off
The
Dime

V. D. O'Connell

iUniverse, Inc.
New York Lincoln Shanghai

Movement Off The Dime

Copyright © 2004 by V. D. O'Connell

All rights reserved. No part of this book may be used or reproduced by any means, graphic, electronic, or mechanical, including photocopying, recording, taping or by any information storage retrieval system without the written permission of the publisher except in the case of brief quotations embodied in critical articles and reviews.

iUniverse books may be ordered through booksellers or by contacting:

iUniverse
2021 Pine Lake Road, Suite 100
Lincoln, NE 68512
www.iuniverse.com
1-800-Authors (1-800-288-4677)

ISBN: 0-595-33116-5 (pbk)
ISBN: 0-595-78912-9 (cloth)

Printed in the United States of America

For my daughter Alison, the best writer in the family.

Contents

Courtney

Chapter 1 3
Chapter 2 20
Chapter 3 37
Chapter 4 52

Nathan and Cecelia

Chapter 5 67
Chapter 6 79

A New Academic Year

Chapter 7 91
Chapter 8 110
Chapter 9 121
Chapter 10 136
Chapter 11 146
Chapter 12 156
Chapter 13 172

TO AID AND ABET

Chapter 14 181

Chapter 15 188

Chapter 16 205

Chapter 17 213

Chapter 18 238

Chapter 19 255

Chapter 20 263

RETURNS

Chapter 21 277

Author's Notes.. 283

COURTNEY

Chapter 1

▼

Courtney Brentwood hated Philadelphia. The city had an alienating mean streak, she thought—a deliberately malevolent attitude, which blended together with an unusually haughty aristocratic element that irritated her even more. And if given the opportunity, Courtney could easily fire off a rapid succession of additional grounds for maintaining her prejudice against all things Philadelphian. *You really want to know why I detest this city? How much time do you have?*

This uncharacteristic animus stemmed, at least in part, from the wearing effect of feeling constantly exposed to personal harm. Courtney had lived for three years in an area of North Philly near Ontario Street, a disadvantaged, run-down, slum-filled section of the inner city about which even champions of Philadelphia would warn their friends. There, she fell into a chronic survivalist mentality: ever-vigilant, self-protecting, always on her guard.

But truth be told, the real root of Courtney's disaffection stemmed less from wariness about the dangers around her, and more from a simple and quite natural fidelity she felt for home turf in metro New York. Courtney endured her time in Philadelphia like that of a stranger visiting from another land, the fiercely patriotic type who makes little effort to hide a general disdain for the indignities that need to be tolerated while away from native soil. *It isn't being in a city that I can't stand*, she would insist; *it's being in this city.*

Courtney played the role of disaffected foreigner with relentless, derisive vigor. She collected injustices all around Philly, like a cynic who saw the proverbial glass always half empty—and who cared little about the glass's actual contents in the first place. Every insincere, arrogant or small-minded behavior she experienced in the alleged City of Brotherly Love reinforced the negative opinion she held about the area. If a well-dressed but ill-tempered woman in front of her in line at an upscale department store caused a scene, doggedly insisting to the sales clerk that a trifling discount coupon she was holding had not expired or some free gift she felt entitled to was still hers to claim, Courtney would cringe. *Does every blue blood from the Main Line act this way?* Attending a sporting event at the Vet or Spectrum, she always seemed to draw boorish behavior from surrounding fans, who baited her for supporting the visiting team—usually one representing New York. *These are fans that booed Santa Claus, for God's sake*, she would explain to those in her company, pointing to the entire crowd in one circular motion, as if they were all the same.

Once, on a perfectly pleasant fall afternoon at the Philadelphia Zoo, she stormed out of the park vowing never to return when a food concessionaire ignored her order in favor of carrying on a protracted conversation with another employee—behavior she insisted would never occur at this zoo's counterpart in the Bronx. Even trips to the Museum of Art, a Philadelphia institution that should have held considerable appeal for Courtney, became imperiled by various grief-filled episodes, like the maddening experience she had unsuccessfully trying to find a parking spot on the access road that circled behind the museum, only to be thrust back on a major thoroughfare heading away from it with no safe means of turning around. *I can't take this,* she had screamed. *Who planned such a ridiculous arrangement, anyway? This place just sucks!* She said these latter four disparaging words so often, the phrase became a kind of personal mantra.

If asked to concede some attribute about the Philadelphia area, Courtney would note only that it was two hours closer to New York than Boston, the only other major northeastern city where she would ever consider taking up residence. But head to head? Big Apple versus Philly straight up? The comparison was absurd. New York was the driver of the pair, leaving Philadelphia in its aesthetic, cultural and culinary dust.

Longstanding local citizens with whom Courtney socialized heard about all the troublesome incidents she experienced in their hometown, over and over again. "Oh no, here we go," they would say, heads shaking and eyes rolling, as they were buttonholed into listening to some disastrous circumstance she had experienced or some irrefutable evidence she had uncovered about the inferiority of their hometown. Some would fight back, sharing their own harrowing tales of misfortune from trips to Manhattan. In response, Courtney would just shrug, acting like they had gotten what they deserved—the inevitable result of provincial naiveté, a total lack of New York street smarts. "Let me explain something to you," she would begin, in as patronizing a voice as she could muster, playfully provoking these friends as if they needed a thorough indoctrination into the ways of the world. "You just don't park your car on the street on the Lower East Side of New York to save the eighteen dollars it would cost to put it in a garage. Anyone knows that. You might as well have put a sign on your car that said, 'Hello, I'm from out of town; please break these windows, steal my loose change, and while you are at it, also take my new leather jacket and cassettes I left out so conspicuously.'"

Ultimately, Courtney's friends would be spared these frequent harangues. Not because of a fundamental change of attitude that Courtney underwent about her surroundings. Rather, the simple fact was that she was no longer obligated to stay. Having just graduated the prior evening from the Temple Medical College, she was set to put her personal Philadelphia Story behind her. It was 1990, a new decade had just begun, and Courtney was now a degreed medical doctor. Better yet, the residency placement to which she had been accepted was reasonably close to her parents' place in suburban Westchester County, just outside New York City. After three long years living away from familiar terrain, Dr. Courtney Brentwood was going home.

At the graduation ceremony and reception afterwards, Courtney vowed to all who would listen that she intended never to return to Philadelphia if she could help it. She begged a few fellow graduating students to join her in performing their residencies around the New York area, so they all could stay in touch. She tried particularly hard to twist the arms of some closer friends, many of whom were still toying with the idea of staying on at Temple or another local hospital for their post-graduate training. Showing less inhibition as a result of partaking in some celebratory champagne, Courtney informed them that this decision to stay on in the Philadelphia area was not just bad judgment, but probable madness—fully fitting the criteria that she, as a newly degreed physician, was now legally entitled to certify. She proclaimed that remaining in Philadelphia was ample evidence that these classmates had taken leave of their senses, and were a danger to themselves and other people.

But she began softening her vow as she engaged in more and more congratulatory hugs and heartfelt, tearful goodbyes. These classmates had been so much a part of her life over the past three years, it would be unfair to shun them forever simply because of their misguided plan to stay on in Philadelphia. *Well, maybe we can meet in Atlantic City or some place on the Jersey Shore. Just not in North Philly, please.*

With a prompt departure from Philadelphia at the earliest possible opportunity monopolizing her attention for some time, Courtney had most of her belongings fully packed well before her graduation, in preparation for the impending move north. The U-Haul truck she had rented earlier in the morning was parked outside her modest apartment near the hospital, poised to receive these possessions and facilitate her exodus.

It was early in the final week in June, and the only major responsibility Courtney had between then and the second of July, except for this relocation of her belongings temporarily back to her parents' home in Scarsdale, was to complete a final round of courtesy interviews with senior faculty at the Hunt-Fisher Psychiatric Hospital, a University of Connecticut teaching affiliate located in Norwalk. There, if all went well, the institution would be guiding her through the requisite four post-graduate years of residency training, preparing her to become a fully trained psychiatrist.

Because of scheduling difficulties, and to accommodate vacations her interviewers previously had planned for the upcoming extended Fourth of July weekend, Courtney's meetings at the hospital had been arranged for the very next day following her move back to Westchester. Once she was finished with this four-hour ordeal, though, she would have her first real time off—a bit less than a week of no studies and no hospital responsibilities—since she finished her undergraduate studies at Cornell in May of 1987.

Jason Burke was coming over to help her move out. Jason had been her savior more than once before. He regularly performed acts of kindness for Courtney, like accompanying her on a SEPTA bus ride across Philadelphia, or trailing her out of the city over the Ben Franklin Bridge in a separate car to make sure she connected to the New Jersey Turnpike at Exit 4 near Mt. Laurel at the start of a short getaway weekend. He served as her chaperone more than once, at departmental receptions or Saturday night parties at their mutual friends' places, events that she probably otherwise would have avoided. Courtney always remained very leery about venturing far from her apartment alone, especially at night when the ultimate destination lay anywhere in the scary neighborhoods around Temple.

He was also Courtney's closest ally in Philadelphia. Their friendship had been forged on common ground. Jason—a native Southern Californian who had never been further east than Texas prior to attending medical school—held as much disdain for Philadelphia as she did. One class behind Courtney at Temple, he had made his introduction to her in a hospital cafeteria line early in his first year. Moving his tray against hers in a less-than-subtle gesture to draw her attention, he had leaned down to her and uttered, with dramatic effect, the very words she loved to say but had never actually heard from anyone else around her—certainly no one associated with the medical school or hospital.

"You know," he stage-whispered to her in an earnest but semi-serious tone, "this place really sucks."

Here, Courtney had thought at the time, was a tanned, blond guy, standing next to her on a cafeteria line in an inner city Philadelphia hospital, sporting a colorful Hawaiian shirt under his requisite white lab coat, who certainly did not fit the visual profile of the typical Temple medical student. Courtney was highly impressed. His initial message had certainly hit home. It might have been that he was alluding to the medical school, or the hospital in general, or the cafeteria and its bad food, or any of a number of relevant negative experiences he had just endured. But Courtney did not want to buy that. He was talking about the whole Philadelphia environment, she was sure of it. In Jason, Courtney had found a soulmate, and one whose good looks just accentuated the engaging creativity he had shown in acknowledging their kindred spirit.

She had turned toward him during that initial meeting, feeling instant camaraderie. "You know," she replied, smiling broadly, "you're right. I say the same thing all the time." Courtney could never bring herself to ask Jason if someone had clued him in about echoing her oft-repeated mantra. She had preferred to believe that what had transpired was that rare, special, spontaneous bonding moment, best left unquestioned and simply savored.

From this point of introduction on, they had grown very close, pairing up with each other frequently. Jason had a serious girlfriend back in California, thereby negating any prospect of romance between the two of them. But the platonic nature of the relationship was fine with Courtney—or, at least, so she rationalized. If she felt any tug of disappointment when she first learned about Lara King, the yoga instructor and aspiring actress from Santa Monica to whom Jason had given his heart, Courtney quickly set it aside. She insisted to herself that having no likelihood for anything more than friendship with Jason was a far superior arrangement at this stage in her life. It was wonderful to have someone she could lean on without the distraction of the inevitable relationship entanglements, especially given the academic and clinical practice rigors of medical school. Maybe she was in denial, maybe it was all a huge self-delusion, but after two years of knowing him, Courtney felt like she could not have been happier with their relationship being safely placed in the "we're just friends" category. In private moments thinking about him, she would concede that she adored Jason in so many ways, but it felt to her more akin to the love a sister might feel for her favorite big brother.

Many classmates had assumed they were an item, until Lara appeared one weekend on Jason's arm at a party, just in from the "left coast," tanned, firm, dazzlingly beautiful and drawing admiring stares from men and women alike. When Courtney first witnessed the two of them together, she caught herself again feeling a slight pang of envy for Lara. It was not due to her attractiveness, since Courtney, while not owning movie star appeal like Lara possessed, had been graced with the kind of physical charms that consistently turned male heads most of her life. Rather, the twinge of jealousy centered on Jason's evident adoration for this gorgeous being from California.

Together, Jason and Lara exuded a mystical connection that was palpable. While Courtney believed that she and Jason had a meaningful friendship, one that transcended that of being merely medical school colleagues, she saw that Lara and Jason's relationship was on a far different and much loftier plane. Theirs was pure and utter devotion to each other.

But any lingering feelings of envy Courtney had about the pairing of Lara and Jason, at least the ones she was conscious of and owned up to, dissolved as quickly as they came. Courtney reminded herself how grateful she was for the personal liberty she had been able to maintain throughout medical school. It was a freedom that she had rarely enjoyed as an undergraduate at Cornell, when she had spent far too much time with the bright but ultimately insecure and pathologically needy boy from the UK, Colin Fastinger, whose European attitudes and manner of speaking had seemed so alluring to her at first but which grew increasingly tedious over time. Their breakup had been difficult and fractious, prompted by Courtney's insistence—but Colin's unwillingness to accept—that he not follow her to Philadelphia as she started medical school. He had done so anyway, and the results turned ugly: court-ordered protection from his stalking behavior; threats from her lawyers about revocation of his student visa should he not abide by the terms of the court order. Ultimately, Colin had backed off, returning to England, conceding defeat.

The distressing split-up had left Courtney very gun-shy about intimacy of any kind with the opposite sex. Even after three years, she acknowledged to herself that the trauma of her ex-boyfriend's scary behavior was still playing a role in her interpersonal relationships. The fact was that for the full time she spent in medical school, Courtney had managed to avoid any semblance of romantic involvement with classmates or any other men she met during this period. Many of her fellow students—and even a faculty member or two—had given it the old medical college try, but to no avail. After being quite sexually active with Colin throughout college, on the Pill for most of her junior and senior years, Courtney had moved into a more self-protective, single existence in medical school, associating intimacy with the possibility of having to endure the inevitable pain that results when intense relationships end acrimoniously. The threat of AIDS her generation guarded against only made celibacy more defensible, at least in her own mind.

Courtney grew to really like Lara. She had so many qualities that were sadly deficient in many of Courtney's fellow medical school students, like spontaneity and optimism and simply being fun to be around. She was exuberant and full of the life energy she evidently drew from the tenets of yoga. *Here,* Courtney thought, *was a woman born to make a fitness video.* Courtney envisioned Lara starring in her own infomercial: looking engagingly into the camera, Lara would implore others to share the excitement she felt, and the fitness results she had achieved, by simply following her half-hour-a-day workouts, guaranteed to rejuvenate the wonder and spirit just waiting to emerge from the customer's human temple. *"You too can find the harmony and great shape you see in me, Lara King, by purchasing my personal line of yoga-centered fitness audio and video tapes, now available for three easy payments of $19.95."* Lara would be perfect for that role—absolutely perfect!

Refreshingly, Lara's charm was genuine. If she was a caricature of the L.A. culture, Lara found a way to carry it off with grace. Her ability to form interpersonal bonds with those she met was very impressive. She was a dynamo, engaging with people of all types effortlessly. Certainly, Lara was a tad more narcissistic than most, and far more self-absorbed than Jason. But with a face and body like hers, Courtney thought to herself, who wouldn't be?

Jason adored Lara not just for her physical attractiveness, but also because she represented the California lifestyle he so sorely missed. And it was clear that Lara reciprocated this worship. They spoke to each other in low murmurs, gazing intently in each other's eyes as if the rest of the world was entirely irrelevant. Lara told Courtney how she loved the fact that Jason shared so many compatible views with her about life, and how he seemed always invested in raising her spiritual awareness.

Courtney witnessed these interactions. Often, Jason's role in their discussions involved cleverly and empathically asking just the right question to provoke an insight that had previously eluded Lara's consciousness. Lara would brighten, delighted by the opportunity to look beyond the more superficial and obvious interpretations of things. She called it peeling back the onion to see what was inside. It was a process, no doubt, that was part actor training—in which she had participated for several years—and part amateur psychology and philosophy. To

Courtney, Lara's interest in the underlying dynamics of human behavior seemed driven by a slight insecurity, since she lacked formal education in the psychological sciences. Unlike Jason, who had excelled in school throughout high school in Hermosa Beach, college at UCLA and now in medical school—he was near the top of his class at Temple after his second year—Lara had taken but a few evening classes at branch campuses of UCLA, never really pursuing a degree. Yet, even without the academic foundation to spur it along, Lara's mind was innately curious. And Jason was adept at helping to stretch her boundless interest in self-discovery. He was far more gratified eliciting insights and creative thoughts from his girlfriend, addressing some spiritual agenda about which she was absorbed at the time, rather than focusing on any need or desire he experienced. Discussions between them about medicine, or how his professional training was going, occurred very rarely, if ever. When they were together, the focus always tended to be on Lara, or on the two of them as a couple. It was the basis for a relationship that appeared to Courtney to be working beautifully.

Courtney often wondered, given Jason's evident natural gifts at helping others like Lara explore issues and find more inner meaning, why he was not thinking of pursuing psychiatry as she was, instead of leaning toward radiology as his expected specialty. When she finally asked him about this, he was ready with an answer. "I have nothing against psychiatry; certainly society needs you, Courtney. But, there's just no money in it."

"And," he added, "managed care is beginning to really beat up your chosen specialty. Frankly, I want to make as much money as I can as fast as I can, and then I might move on and do something else. I like medicine a lot, but I'm not sure I can stay passionate about it my whole working life." This was not a view often shared by many of Courtney's more traditional and professionally-conscious classmates, mostly from the northeast, who saw being a doctor as integral not just to their occupational future but also to their very identity in society.

While Lara had always imagined herself living and socializing in Hollywood circles amid the entertainment crowd, Jason had convinced her that their destiny lay in Orange County, where he would hook up with a progressive hospital after a residency at one of the Southern California medical schools, join a thriving practice, and support her in developing a large and devoted following at her own yoga studio that they would operate together as equal partners. After that, the sky was the limit. He had already done research on the financial management strategies of franchising, and he foresaw a future in which the two of them would run a chain of fitness studios that would leverage the Lara King brand. They would begin in Orange County, expand into L.A. and San Diego, and then start to think more nationally.

In Courtney's view, Lara's dynamism, drive, talents and allure to both men and women, along with her presence in a market with a seemingly unending demand for products and services that cater to physical beauty and spiritual fulfillment, made this plan appear to be anything but a pipedream. Actually, it seemed eminently pragmatic. While Courtney could not base this view on any formal business training or knowledge, her common sense told her that their fitness studio franchising idea was a very logical way to deploy and utilize the assets they both possessed. With his intelligence and entrepreneurship, and her alluring and highly marketable beauty, charm and show business aspirations, their success seemed inevitable. Though not formally engaged, Lara and Jason had bound themselves to this vision. They were devoted both to each other and to making this future come true in due time, much as Jason had outlined it.

"I really like Lara," Courtney once told Jason after they had dropped his girlfriend off at the airport following a visit to Philadelphia. "I think I hate to see her leave as much as you do."

Jason had looked at her with a lascivious grin, shaking his head slowly and dramatically.

"I doubt that very much," he had replied simply, leaving much about his private moments with Lara to Courtney's imagination.

As Jason announced himself at Courtney's apartment door, which she had left slightly ajar once she spotted him from the window approaching her building from the sidewalk below, he made it clear that he was anxious to get the moving process started. Courtney asked him if he wanted any coffee. She had one cupful remaining after brewing a pot earlier in the morning, in a coffee maker that now needed to be unplugged, washed out and carried down to the truck.

"No thanks," he replied from a distance, already starting to load smaller boxes in his arms. "Let's start getting things out of here, what do you say?"

As Jason began toting items out to the U-Haul parked on the street in front of the apartment building, he chatted amiably with Courtney, poking fun at her about some piece of furniture that he thought should be trashed instead of carried out, or whatever else came to his mind that might provoke a reaction from her. "You're not exactly a pack rat, are you?" he asked at one point, surveying the rather limited amount of boxes and furniture sitting by the door, ready to be moved.

"No, you know, three years ago I brought the bare minimum here, and I didn't add much at all," Courtney explained. "Whenever I bought something I liked for an apartment, I stored it at my folks' place. I guess I was waiting for the day when I could be on my own, somewhere I really wanted to be for awhile, you know?"

Jason said he understood fully. Their lives were purposefully transient, owing in part to the mere stopover for the both of them on this hostile planet called Philadelphia, and to an abiding need to focus exclusively on getting through the requirements of medical school. In many ways, their academically-oriented lifestyle was highly artificial and unreal. If one was very serious about optimizing a medical school education, it was difficult to have a life as well. Being surrounded by nice furniture was just about the last thing that either one of them considered important at this stage in their lives.

Since Courtney's apartment was on the second floor of a four-story building, Jason could have used the elevator. But he preferred simply to climb up and down the one flight of stairs, arms full of boxes or pieces of Courtney's limited furniture collection, heading right from the apartment building stairs to the stoop in front, then down another five steps to street level and up the metal ramp at the back of the U-Haul. When returning for his next load, he hopped up the apartment steps, taking them two at a time. His boundless energy hastened the completion of the moving project. To Courtney's surprise, the entire operation took just less than an hour, including moving the heavier items, which they handled as a team. After the last piece was safely secured inside the truck, Jason climbed down the access ramp, picked it up and slid it back into its proper slot, closed and locked the two back doors, patting them twice to indicate that the rig was secure and the hard work was done.

"Courtney, you're ready to roll, babe," Jason shouted up to the open window on the second floor where Courtney was making a final sweep of the bedroom that faced the street. She was checking one last time for any neglected items that were hiding out in the dark recesses of some closet or cabinet.

Soon, Courtney joined Jason down on the street, holding onto some possessions she had collected from this last go-through. She took these items and a few others she had separated from the rest of her belongings to the passenger side of the truck's cab, placing them either on the seat or on the floor in front of it. She did not trust leaving these items in the back with the rest of her belongings, either because they were fragile or too valuable to lose sight of during the haul up to New York.

"Let's lock this thing up and go over to the hospital for one last coffee, what do you say?" suggested Courtney. "I need a little more of a buzz in my system to handle the drive ahead." Actually, this suggestion was primarily a delaying tactic. Courtney was beginning to recognize the sadness growing within her that she had been warding off for the past few weeks. She was now only minutes away from beginning an important new phase in her life, which, for the most part, she was excited about and itching to get started. But the close bond she had built with Jason would be hard to leave behind. She was going to miss him terribly. It suddenly occurred to her that there was no real assurance that their paths would ever cross again, what with her vow to stay away from Philadelphia and his plan to return to California once he graduated at about this same time the following year.

They walked the two blocks to the hospital, continuing the type of customary banter that caused them to enjoy each other's company so much. They headed straight for the cafeteria—the same one they had met in nearly two years before. Courtney treated her friend to coffee and a bagel, a minor payback for his hour of heavy manual labor, and they looked for and found an empty table near the rear of the room.

Once seated, Courtney began speaking. For several minutes, she rambled on and on. She talked about how funny it was that she was going to be driving a U-Haul, what her snobby mother would think if she were to see her daughter pulling into the driveway in Scarsdale behind the wheel of a truck, about the best way to navigate her way to 95 north and then over to the Turnpike, what the traffic would be like once she hit the George Washington Bridge, how she was afraid of the skinny, curving lanes at the end of the Bridge that took her out onto the Cross Bronx Expressway just before the exit to the Deegan, how being in the far right lane at that spot just beyond the Bridge always panicked her because it was so elevated and caused her a slight case of acrophobia, how she would like to use her new mobile phone to talk to her father on the way since he had some advice for her about her interviews tomorrow. Throughout this one-sided exchange, Courtney avoided Jason's eyes, for fear of the emotional reaction it would cause. Jason's eyes, on the other hand, never left hers throughout Courtney's entire anxious monologue. He did not interrupt, choosing just to nod understandingly as she vented.

Ultimately, Courtney's uncharacteristic verbosity culminated in an audible sigh, a sign of exhaustion from the enervating effects of her long-winded chatter. When she reached down for more coffee, Jason slid his hand over the cup. "Whoa-ho, girl," he said, kidding her, "I think it's time for some decaf." They laughed together, knowing that her evident anxiety was induced less by caffeine overload than by her feelings about the as-yet unspoken terms of their separation, which was now just a few minutes away. Jason broached the subject first.

"Courtney, I'm heading out to L.A. on the red-eye tonight, and I won't be back here until after the Fourth of July, but I'll call you tomorrow to hear how your interviews went, okay?" During the graduation reception, he had asked her for her home number, as well as for the number of her new mobile phone, a graduation gift from her parents that he had witnessed them present to her the previous evening.

"That'd be great," Courtney murmured softly, still avoiding eye contact with him.

"Aren't you going to invite me up to New York on some weekend that I have off during the summer?" Jason asked. She knew he was trying to draw her back into a better frame of mind. And it worked, at least momentarily.

"Will you come up? Promise?" Her eyes darted up from her coffee and met Jason's for a brief moment, showing excitement by this offer to get together in the coming months. Then her glance changed slowly, betraying a return of sadness, reverting back to the downward stare toward the floor. A few moments of silence ensued between them. While Courtney avoided his gaze, Jason showed his support by leaning forward, never taking his eyes off hers.

"Oh, come on," Courtney finally added, "if you have time off, you should go to the shore and hang out there for awhile. I'm sure that's what you'll really want to do."

Jason gave no hint that he felt pushed away. His body language showed understanding, a willingness to allow the moment to run its course, to provide Courtney with the psychological space to work through her separation from him.

With a soft voice that trailed away at the end, Courtney finally continued on. "If I can, maybe I'll come down to Stone Harbor for that surfing competition you always enter at the end of the summer. I really love it there."

Another silence, more awkward that before. Each continued the body language demonstrated through the early part of this conversation—Courtney, hands on the table in front of her, fidgeting with her coffee mug, eyes downcast; Jason's manner remained alert and attentive, signaling a desire to process what was going on between them. Finally, he reached across the table, taking one of her hands, patting the back of it fondly. "You know, this doesn't have to be a good-bye between us, Courtney. We'll see each other again soon." She nodded, still looking away. But the message hit its emotional mark. A stray tear slipped out from her eyes, a single stream running down each of her cheeks, the flow creating large symmetrical drops that hung stubbornly near the bottom of each side of her jaw, defying gravity. Instinctively, Courtney moved each shoulder in succession to absorb them into her cotton blouse.

Evidently moved by this, Jason came around to sit next to her, bringing his face in front of her evasive eyes, demanding their attention.

"Our friendship isn't going to just end, because we are a few hours away from each other. No way." Typically, Jason would follow this kind of serious comment in a tense interaction with a light, witty aside, or a humble, self-critical comment. But, Courtney noted appreciatively, he stayed in the moment, maintaining an emotional presence for her. "You know one thing that I'm very convinced about?" he asked with a smile, reclaiming a grasp on one of her hands to gain her full attention.

"What's that?" Courtney replied, sniffing, and finally raising her eyes towards his.

"Lara and I will have kids…and our kids…they will know your kids. I don't know how it will all go down, and we have to find you a husband first, of course," he said, drawing a smile from Courtney, "but I'm sure they will know each other."

Jason had selected the right thing to say, as usual. Courtney looked up, responding with a broad, relieved smile, appreciating the tone, simplicity and message that lay behind this prediction. Whether it would come true or not, it was a wonderful framework from which to begin their imminent separation. To Courtney, it meant that this was not the end; they would stay bonded, as good friends do, despite any physical distance that lay between them. Brushing at the tears she had shed with the back of her hand, Courtney nodded vigorously, affirming her part of the deal. The understanding they had reached was consummated by a brief but heartfelt embrace, which she initiated and he welcomed.

"Yeah, I really hope that happens," she said softly as they released each other. She took a deep breath, gratified with the closure they had reached.

"Hey, good luck this year," she added, finally brightening, while pulling a tissue from her handbag to wipe away any residual moisture from her cheeks and from around her eyes. Her composure was returning. "It's not nearly as bad as the first two," she added.

"Ah, I'm not worried about it," Jason replied, with a tone that implied that his final year of medical school was nearly irrelevant at that point.

Courtney made up her mind that she did not want this conversation to end without a direct statement about how valuable their friendship had been for her, especially after the Colin fiasco. He had restored her faith in the male sex, and allowed her to appreciate the value of having someone close to her upon whom she could depend.

She sought his attention by grabbing one of his hands and placing it between the two of hers. "I'll miss you, Jason," she began, a bit self-consciously at first. "I am so glad you said what you did. I couldn't bear to think this is it, that you'd head out to west next year and…well, that we'd slowly go our separate ways. I just want to say that…it was so nice having you as a friend these last two years, you have no idea." He knew about Colin, and no doubt understood the unspoken meaning. After another moment, she began nodding, with a warm smile now, and affirmed her belief in his statement. "Yes, my kids will know your kids. How great will that be?"

She released his hand, made one last dab of her eyes with the tissue she had laid on the table, sniffed dramatically one final time, and straightened herself up. Courtney was feeling somewhat self-conscious about being part of any more theatrics right there in the hospital cafeteria. She signaled an ending to their conversation by pushing back her chair and grabbing her coffee mug. "Let's go over to the Clinic before I head out," she suggested brightly. "I want to say good-bye to some people who didn't make it to the graduation. You mind?"

Jason readily consented to this suggestion. For the two of them, it was time to move on.

The Public Health Outpatient Clinic at Temple University Hospital was where Courtney had performed the capstone clinical rotation of her medical school studies. It was the final course she had taken before graduating, and it had allowed her to integrate much from the textbook learning she had gained and lessons she had absorbed from the care planning discussions held in classrooms or during faculty-led teaching rounds around the hospital. At the Clinic, instead of considering patients as case studies, or reviewing someone else's treatment decisions, Courtney was able to take a primary role in direct patient care. During this assignment, she had been entitled to recommend treatment she and the nursing team thought best. Then she needed to document these recommendations fully in the patients' medical charts. Most of all, she learned *in vivo* what it was really like to be a physician. It was true that various credentialed faculty doctors from the Medical College were the physicians of record for her cases, and they had to review her plans thoroughly and go through the legal formality of signing her orders and co-signing her progress notes, since she was not yet a degreed physician. But, in effect, she was practicing medicine, albeit with supervision, including that of the very capable nursing staff that supported her training. As a result of this empowerment and the sense of professional identity she acquired during this rotation, the Clinic is where she had made the strongest ties to hospital staff during her entire medical school experience. She felt she could not leave without saying a final good-bye to them.

As Courtney reached the nursing station in the Clinic, her favorite nurse emerged out of a back room. Rolanda James let out a shriek of joy, recognizing that Courtney had gone out of her way to make sure a proper and intimate farewell occurred before she headed out of town. Their subsequent embrace was long, strong and sincere. Then Rolanda pushed Courtney's shoulders back with a light, playful push, turning around to the characteristically serious Unit Clerk, Charlene Barton, while shaking her head in mock disgust. "I thought this girl was goin' to fly out of Philly the first chance she got, you remember that Charlene?"

"Uh huh, I do," Charlene said, nodding dramatically, playing along with a grave voice intended to reinforce how Courtney was now exposed as a fraud. "First chance she got."

"That's right. Now what does she do? She comes to the Clinic 'cause she wants to stay here and really learn how to be a doctor. I bet if she stayed around, she'd never leave. Marry Dr. Burke here and settle on the Main Line, or over in Chestnut Hill. Send their kids to Germantown Academy and everything. Can't you see it, Charlene?" Rolanda did her best to maintain a serious tone and affect, enjoying an opportunity to get in a final dig at Courtney. For Rolanda, this type of banter was reserved only for those whom she admired and respected most. She tended to ignore, or subtly demean, the legions of medical students who rotated through the Clinic, due to an acquired distaste she had developed for many of these students' pretentious, "know-it-all" attitudes. Once every few years, though, a medical student came along that got to her, one Rolanda considered special, worthy of her effort to help the student along, to develop a mentoring relationship. Courtney was one of those rare students she liked, admired and, most of all, trusted.

"I can do more that see it," Charlene added dryly about Rolanda's vision for Courtney, adroitly maintaining an indifferent sense of detachment. "I kind of expects it."

This drew a roar of laughter from everyone—Rolanda, Jason and those within earshot who had been witness to Courtney's anti-Philadelphia ravings over the past six months. Even Courtney had to laugh in spite of herself.

But she could not leave without some type of comeback. Courtney had dear Rolanda to thank for developing this skill, because of the daily practice she got in during her six-month training alongside her at the Clinic. If medical school in an urban setting had taught Courtney anything, it had been that respect comes from standing up for yourself; not giving an inch, especially around nurses whose toughness was essential to their professional effectiveness. City patients were a needy and demanding group. Limits needed to be set early and often. She had not learned this lesson in textbooks or lectures; it had come from these types of interactions with Rolanda and observing her in action with the Clinic's clientele.

It was time for some dramatic flair. Pointing her nose high in the air and sounding very doctorly and officious, Courtney shot back, "The soon-to-be Dr. Burke will attest that my belongings are in a U-Haul truck as we speak, parked right over there," as she pointed out the window toward the general vicinity of her ex-apartment, "and that I am minutes from leaving this dreadful city, just like I promised. I just came by to check up on you, and make sure things hadn't completely fallen apart, now that I'm not around to make sure you guys are doing your jobs correctly." This provocation drew loud guffaws and a resounding series of competing retorts from the staff listening in, to the effect that Courtney better leave now or she would hear about how many times they had covered her behind after mistakes she had made, or how they had been here running the Clinic since she was soiling a diaper in her precious Scarsdale. The gibes continued as Courtney made her way around to everyone, with each hug bringing Courtney's already moist eyes again to the overflowing point.

Finally, Courtney gathered herself and asked for everyone's attention. "Okay, listen to me," she announced, using the thin counter that separated the Clinic's restricted nursing station area from the hallway that led up to it as a dais for a short proclamation to those around her. "Here's an open invitation to you all. I want you to visit me in New York whenever you want. I can't promise to come back here any time soon, but if you come up to New York, I guarantee I will show you a good time, just like I've been saying I would ever since you knew me."

Rolanda chirped in first. "Oh you'll be back, Dr. Brentwood," she said. "You're going to see ol' Rolanda again, and it won't be in no New York neither." The rest of the Clinic staff all agreed.

It was their way of saying, *"You made an impression, and that doesn't happen very often. Maybe it tells you something. Maybe you belong right here, with us."*

The first half of Courtney's trip back to New York was surprisingly easy—she encountered no real traffic getting out of Philadelphia, and even less on the southern end of the New Jersey Turnpike. From Exit 4 all the way up to just north of Exit 14, she was on auto-pilot while driving the U-Haul truck, lost in thought about separating from Jason, from medical school and her Temple colleagues, and about the warm messages of support she had received at the Clinic.

But as glimpses of the Manhattan skyline appeared to the east, she began to break out of this reverie. It was time to tune more into what lay ahead instead of what she had left behind.

Yet, even as she started to focus in on her immediate future, and her return to New York, she was having difficulty shaking off Rolanda's prediction at the Clinic earlier that morning.

Come back to Philadelphia? Love ya' babe…but not in this lifetime!

Chapter 2

▼

Inching forward in bumper-to-bumper traffic about a half mile short of the George Washington Bridge, Courtney decided to make use of this idle time by trying out her new toy. Although she would be seeing her father later, at home, Courtney yielded to an impulse to speak to him briefly right then. She and her father had an understanding that the best time to reach him was in the mid-to-late afternoon. Dr. Aaron Brentwood was an incredibly busy man, always booked back-to-back, hour-to-hour throughout the day and sometimes into the early evening. An Associate Dean at the Cornell Medical College in New York, he dealt with a daily onslaught of administrative and teaching duties, while still leaving time for a short panel of patients whom he saw right at his office at The New York Hospital. Aaron had always instructed her that the best time to call was between fifty minutes after the hour and the start of the new hour, because he typically scheduled ten minutes of open time between afternoon meetings, appointments or sessions with his patients. He always seemed to find a way to take her call, even though their conversations were usually limited to short exchanges that involved establishing a time for a more substantive discussion later.

While the plan was to mount the mobile phone she had just received from her parents inside her Camry as a hands-free car phone, her father had found one she could use right away, anywhere she went in the greater New York and mid-Atlantic area. She just needed to plug it into the cigarette lighter, to keep the battery charged, and pull up the antennae to create better reception. Aaron had liked the idea that Courtney would now have the ability to call him at any time, even when she was driving. Ready access to emergency assistance was another benefit of mobile phone service. These devices would become more and more prevalent, Aaron predicted. He foresaw a time in the not-too distant future when the beepers that most doctors carried everywhere would give way to these portable phones, since they would serve as an invaluable communication tool, facilitating immediate connection between physicians and their office staff, rather than depending on audio prompts from a pager, which required finding a nearby phone with which to respond. In any event, the mobile phone was a treat to Courtney. She felt very pampered, considering the gift an exciting, futuristic indulgence.

In addition to wanting to try out the phone, Courtney acknowledged an anxiety gathering in her mind about the interviews planned for the following day. Courtney was looking for the inside scoop on the three faculty psychiatrists, all men, who would be meeting with her. Her father knew *everyone* in the mental health field, it seemed, and she was sure he had a few "heads-up" recommendations prepared about these guys. He had never disappointed her yet, when sharing the wealth of information, insights and wisdom he possessed. And who better to know what went through these men's minds during an interview of a prospective resident physician than the eminent Dr. Brentwood, who had performed more of these interviews himself than he would care to count?

Courtney pulled up the antennae on the phone, dialed her father's number, located the "SEND" button, pushed it, and brought the phone up to her ear, waiting to see if this new contraption actually worked. The sound of the call going through thrilled her. Rachel Crispin, her father's faithful administrative assistant for the past fifteen years, answered her virgin mobile phone call.

"Dr. Brentwood's office."

These three words, uttered slowly and with more than a shade of indifference, amused Courtney. Every time Courtney called her father, which had occurred less in the past three years but still often enough to consider Rachel one of her closest allies and friends, the voice that picked up at the other end of the phone had this effect on her. Rachel's voice was classic New York. She sounded like an actor hired to play—even overplay, for comedic effect—a jaded Manhattan secretary who hailed from Staten Island, who couldn't be bothered. Rachel's accent and sense of detachment were so stereotypical, that an outsider must have thought it false or put on. But it was not. Her voice indicated she had little time for the caller's inquiry, and that she had seen and heard it all before—which she had. Interestingly, though, this manner did not correlate to the type of lazy, disrespectful or inefficient behavior one might associate with it. It did, however, cause many to feel more than a little intimidated by her, which probably created the desired end result of fewer unnecessary calls to the Dean's office.

Courtney had spent time observing Rachel at work, and had become amazed at how well she performed on the job. Rachel was a wonder of professional organization, interpersonal negotiation and time management skills. She certainly had to be, to last this long in her position with the reasonable but demanding Aaron Brentwood. Anyone who could maintain the senior Dr. Brentwood's administrative schedule, while fitting in a group of needy and often entitled psychotherapy patients, was deserving of the highest plaudits.

"It's me," Courtney began, knowing that Rachel would recognize her voice instantly. "Does he have a minute to talk?"

Courtney was in luck. The urge to call had come at an opportune time. "Hold on sweetie, I'll see if I can catch him," Rachel said, with far more informality and warmth than was evident in her initial token greeting. She lowered her voice, "Oh, good, his door is opening up. I'll let him know it's you."

Rachel put Courtney on hold, followed just a moment later by her father's robust voice coming on the line. "Well, Dr. Brentwood, long time no talk." The humorous effect he was shooting for lay in the fact that he had attended her graduation the day before, so they had been apart for all of about eighteen hours—although they had not seen each other for several months before that. Aaron, along with Courtney's mother Sheila, had taken time off from work, just long enough to drive down to Philadelphia in mid-afternoon, watch Courtney receive her degree, take some pictures, converse with a few of the senior faculty and Deans at Temple who cornered the three of them at the post-graduation reception, then flee back to Scarsdale. This return trip had been performed in separate cars, since Courtney had requested that one of them drive her Camry back home (her father had done the honors). Aaron's schedule, as usual, was very tight, and he had insisted that he leave Philadelphia in time to allow him to get in sufficient sleep, so that he could be fresh for the full workday he had scheduled. Her mother had pleaded the same case. An earlier-than-usual start to her morning loomed, due to a significant meeting she was required to attend. It was a meeting she could not miss, medical school graduating daughter or not.

Courtney's spirits rose upon hearing her father's voice. "Hi, Dad," Courtney said. "I'm almost home. I'm just short of 'the George,' talking on the new phone you gave me, driving a U-Haul truck. Can you believe it?"

"Don't let your mother see you behind the wheel of that thing, it will cause her untold grief," Aaron replied. "I also think it would have been wiser to ship your stuff up, rather than driving a truck home all by yourself."

"Yeah, Mother gave me an earful about that last night. But it would have been far more of a nuisance and much more expensive to do it that way. And it's surprisingly easy to drive this thing. My friend Jason helped me load it up, and I called Billy Andrews a few days ago and he said he would help me move all the stuff from the truck into the garage this afternoon." The Andrews lived next door to the Brentwoods, and their families had socialized together for years. Billy, heading into his senior year at high school, was the starting middle linebacker on the Scarsdale High football team, and was getting to be as strong as an ox. Courtney would give him a little playing-around money in return for his manual labor.

"That's nice of him," Aaron said, noting to himself that he would have to thank Billy's father, Jack Andrews, a principal at Cohen, Bartholomew and Shein, the top labor law firm in the City, and a close friend, for his son's generosity when he had a chance.

"Besides, it's kind of a mini-adventure. Hauling a load up the Turnpike, working the open road." Courtney transformed her voice for these last few words into a southern drawl, to reinforce the truck driver role she was now playing.

"You know, I've treated many truck drivers and none of them had a southern accent," Aaron replied, gently chiding her for the stereotype she was invoking. But then he joined in, just the same. "Lots of dysfunctional families among those drivers, by the way," he added, "so I am going to formally recommend to you that this be your last run. Okay, there, Bubba?"

Courtney laughed out loud. "I don't know, I read on a matchbook cover once that there's a good driver training program over in Elmsford, where I could 'earn while I learn.' It occurs to me that doctors don't earn too much while *we* learn, do we?"

"No, doctors don't, this is true. Truck driving does have that advantage," Aaron admitted, chuckling.

Courtney knew her conversation time with her father was limited, so she cut to the chase. "I want to talk to you tonight about my interviews tomorrow. When will you be home?" she asked.

"About eight. Is that okay?"

"Fine with me, I'm not going anywhere," Courtney replied. "You know these guys Blakeley and Fencik, whom I am meeting with, right? And, of course, I *know* you know Harold Hunt. I was told by the residency training office's secretary that he will definitely be there for my interview tomorrow. I've heard he's a really strange bird." Courtney was fishing, trying to coax just a little bit of information out of her father even though she knew she was up against his stringent ten minute inter-meeting limit.

"I'll be home about eight, like I said," Aaron responded warmly, aiming to put her off without putting her off. "We'll talk then, okay, honey? See you soon. And be careful about talking on the phone while you're driving. You need to concentrate."

"I'm not even moving right now. But I know what you mean. So, I'll see you later then. Hey, Dad, could you put Rachel back on, just for a moment?" With the bridge tolls still not in sight, and the traffic at a standstill, Courtney figured catching up with her father's secretary would be a way to amuse herself for a few more minutes.

"Okay. But be careful, honey," Aaron warned again, before putting her on hold.

Rachel picked up the line. "So, Courtney," Rachel began, "are you ever going to see your California medical student friend anymore, or what?" Courtney knew she was talking about Jason. Having been fully apprised about Courtney's friendship with him, Rachel was anxious to learn how the separation had gone.

"You know what he said when we said our goodbyes? He said, 'My kids will know your kids.'" Courtney felt warm thinking again about their earlier conversation.

"What does that mean, 'My kids will know your kids?'" Rachel asked, taunting Courtney in her cynical Staten Island manner. "What kind of statement is that? What, is he telling you he wants to move in next to you once you get married, or what?" As far as Rachel was concerned, Jason, about whom she had heard so much from Courtney, was a prize worth pursuing, distant girlfriend or not. Courtney had just kept telling her she had never met or seen Lara King. Otherwise, she would understand. *Victoria Secret models want this woman's face and body, understand?*

"Rachel, come on, quit being so literal. It was his way of saying, in a short and very sweet way, that we will always stay in touch, we'll visit each other, maybe vacation together or something. I don't know exactly how it will happen, but he was saying we're not going to just go our separate ways. It was a nice temporary ending," she concluded, saying this to herself as much as to Rachel.

"Sweetie, listen to me. Take the lead if you have to, but give him a call soon, like tomorrow, just to make the bridge from the old to the new. Know what I mean?" Courtney did know what she meant. But Jason had promised to call her, so there was already a plan for the "bridge" she was speaking about. She just let Rachel continue.

"I've seen it so many times," Rachel went on, explaining more about seeing students go their separate ways, after pledging to stay bonded forever. "These medical students get so wrapped up in their precious residency placements, they get there and get all tied up and before you know it, months have gone by. Old ties are lost and forgotten. Graduates call here for this or that reason, and they may ask, 'Hey, have you heard from so and so?' And I'll say 'yes' or 'no,' and then I ask them, 'Why, haven't you guys stayed in touch?' And they'll be, like, 'no I haven't heard a word from him, or her.' So I tell them, 'Well, do you want the number, because I have it,' and they take it from me but when they call again and I ask if they got in touch with their old friend, they rarely tell me that they have. So anyway, what I'm saying is, reach out to this Jason, make the effort, stay in touch with him."

She paused at this point, seeming to sense that Courtney was not too concerned about her warnings, at least with respect to her special friend from California. "Well, at the very least you'll always have a place to stay when you visit L.A.," Rachel said, to lighten the moment, in conclusion.

Courtney was sure Jason would call her tomorrow. He had promised. She was not going to worry about it.

"Okay, so what about you, Rachel? What's with you and Eddie?" Courtney had grown up learning about and trying to understand Rachel's love life, from her husbands—there had been two, so far—fiancés and boyfriends, none of whom Courtney sensed treated her all that well. Eddie Gomez was a fireman, and about a year ago he had just made it out of a warehouse that had collapsed around him, killing two of his closest friends and co-workers. He really had not been the same since. He drank more than he used to, was prone to stretches of severe depression, and Rachel had told Courtney that her supportive course of amateur post traumatic stress and survivor guilt-reducing counseling with Eddie was about to come to a close. She was ready to move on unless he snapped out of it. But she was feeling guilty about actually making the move.

"Eddie says that he really wants me—no, he needs me—to be around, like it's all about him, you know? I'm all mixed up about it," Rachel admitted. "Part of me wants to see if the old Eddie is still in there. And part of me wants to go out and hook up with someone who is just a normal guy, has a regular job, with no major psychological baggage. Dr. Brentwood said I'm allowing my ambivalence to rule my life, and that it's getting me into a rut."

"What, are you telling him about your personal life now?" Courtney had never heard any mention of her father having an opinion about Rachel's personal life before.

Rachel lowered her voice to make sure her boss could not hear her. "No, it was just that, a month or so ago, he took me out to lunch for Secretary's Day and we got to talking about Eddie, and then he told me that. Your father's so smart, I listen to whatever he says."

Aaron had that way with people. All psychiatrists are trained to synthesize problems and suggest courses of action, but Aaron's aptitude in this area bordered on genius. He preferred psychodynamic psychotherapy, which meant that he used Freudian concepts, spending much of the time with patients in therapy speaking about their "transference" reactions—feelings these patients had about others that they transferred onto him. But Aaron also was a generalist in technique and a humanist by nature. He understood day-to-day problems, and he was not averse to doling out gentle pushes in the right direction when the situation warranted it. Actually, Aaron's noteworthy expertise lay in his understanding of treatment selection for the mentally ill. His fame, notoriety, financial success and elevated position at Cornell all stemmed primarily from renown associated with the medical textbook—*Contemporary Psychiatric Practice*—that he had authored earlier in his career and since updated three times. It was required reading, widely acknowledged as a superior reference work, planted on just about every practicing psychiatrist's bookshelf in the country, if not the world. Rachel was right to listen to him. Courtney always had, too.

Courtney was nearing the toll plaza, on the upper level, and the majesty of the Bridge lay before her. She now saw the cause for the delay in getting through the tolls: a stalled car was idled just beyond the toll plaza, gumming things up at the point where there was already mass congestion, due to the sheer volume of vehicles trying to merge from ten or more toll booths into just three bridge lanes. Every car was jockeying for an advantageous position to get to the Promised Land, out beyond this funneling spot, and onto the Bridge itself. Courtney told Rachel she needed to put the phone down and concentrate on her driving. She promised to let Rachel know how the interviews went at the hospital the next day, and if Jason had followed through on his promise to call. Pushing the END button, she heard the call terminate. Since she was not moving at all at that point, she pulled a slip of paper out of her purse, upon which she had scribbled Billy Andrews' number at his home in Scarsdale. She dialed the number and pushed SEND once more. She wanted to prepare her neighbor that she was probably only about a half hour away. Billy was home and answered the call. He told her he would look for her truck, and would come over when he saw it. Courtney ended this call, and put away the phone, relieved that she had managed to make it and the others before it without crashing headlong into someone else while doing so.

When Courtney and her rented U-Haul finally earned access to the Bridge itself, the pace of traffic quickened. Once on and across the upper deck of the Bridge, and through the tunnel under the apartments on the other side of the Hudson River, Courtney carefully maneuvered the truck onto the curving exit ramp for the Major Deegan Expressway, heading north. Unable to drive the truck on the parkways she typically used to get home from the city, she was forced to stay on 87 until it met with 287, the Cross-Westchester Expressway. Then she steered the truck east toward White Plains, off at the Bloomingdale Road exit, then up Maple Avenue to the Post Road toward Scarsdale. Near the High School, she veered left up a hill onto Morningside Lane. Soon she was nearing her driveway only one half mile off the Post Road.

The Brentwood home, like many in the neighborhood, was surrounded by an abundance of shade trees—majestic maples and giant oak trees, in full summertime bloom, blocking out a clear view of the house and shielding almost the entire property from the day's sunlight. Even on cloudless days, the Brentwood home sat mostly in shade, like a pampered, umbrella-toting socialite trying to avoid the danger of sunburn on pale, rarely exposed skin. Only a solitary spot in the middle of the Brentwood's backyard attracted bright sunlight, and the grass looked a little browner there than it was on the more protected front lawn.

The home's exterior showed the traditional wide, brown wooden decorative lines characteristic of the Tudor architectural style. Parallel and angular pieces connected to each other, their darker color contrasting with the home's otherwise off-white stucco exterior, creating stark angles and formal geometric shapes that conveyed Old World decorative charm, along with the associated sense that this was a very exclusive spot, reserved for the rich, landed gentry.

Well-manicured hedges or broad, airy bushes separated one property from the next. Courtney could not help noticing, once she rolled down the truck's driver side window, how extremely quiet and serene this setting was. *A lazy mid-afternoon of early summer in bourgeois suburbia. But you have to wonder what is really going on inside those homes*, she found herself thinking.

When Courtney was younger, the Brentwood driveway was composed primarily of stones, with two parallel ruts directing the way onto the property and toward the entrance to the house and garage. Since then, the driveway had been paved over, with a stylish stamped concrete finish, to which Courtney was still unaccustomed even though it had been in place for well over seven years now. Courtney noticed that the Andrews and several other neighbors had followed suit, going either for the similar stamped concrete or the sleek, darkly paved driveway look, which owners would rejuvenate annually. In Scarsdale, neighborhoods upgraded en masse, with owners cognizant of the importance of maintaining parity in these types of property-enhancing improvements.

Courtney considered the idea of backing the truck into the driveway, to make the moving job a little easier, but then decided otherwise. *Let's not press our luck here.*

After waving a trailing car to pass her, Courtney made a slow, wide and successful sweep into the driveway. She headed straight toward the garage, careful to avoid her Camry that Aaron had parked thoughtfully out of harm's way. As she reached the garage, situated behind the home and slightly below ground level, she inched the truck forward as close as she could to the nearest garage door, and finally came to a complete stop. She turned off the truck's ignition, and sat back for a moment. *Well, I'm home,* she thought, emitting a deep sigh of relief that she was safe and this part of the move was over. *That wasn't so bad.*

Bounding down from the truck's cab and walking over to the garage doors, Courtney entered the four-digit code on the keypad mounted just outside the doors to gain entrance. The code was 2199, or C-A-S-S, for Courtney-Aaron-Sheila-Sigmund, the latter being the name of the Brentwood's eleven year-old cat. When the door opened, Courtney immediately noted the garage's characteristic dampness, and an odor of dusty concrete. She considered the prospect of turning on a dehumidifier in the garage as quickly as she could, so that her things would stay as dry and moisture-free as possible during their brief period of storage. Aaron had cleared out a section of the garage where his car would normally park, ceding this space temporarily to accommodate Courtney's immediate storage needs.

During a private moment with the Educational Department secretary during her interview the next day, she would have to discuss final arrangements about the cottage to which she had been assigned. Courtney's plan was to rent one of the furnished lodgings that the Fisher-Hunt Hospital offered at well-below market rates to their resident physicians. These cottages were situated right on the grounds—or "on campus," as the more traditional faculty leaders liked to call the environment at the hospital. It was a term they preferred, her father had told her once, because it reinforced their attraction to the academic mission of the institution.

Hopefully, she would be able to take a quick look at her new home. Aaron had said that she would be very impressed, both with the size of these cottages—they are bigger than her parents' first home, Aaron had said jokingly—and with the convenience factor of living just a short walk from the hospital. Compared to the apartment building near Temple where she had lived for the past three years, a non-descript and shabbily built box of low-grade brick, small windows, and not much else but flimsy doors, metal studs and drywall, the cottages on the hospital grounds would provide a welcome familiarity to the type of country home setting to which she had grown accustomed, as a result of her Westchester upbringing. The difference between the sheltered environment at the Hunt-Fisher Hospital and the crime-ridden location from which she was coming was going to be very comforting.

According to Aaron, Hunt-Fisher's well-maintained buildings and grounds helped reinforce the therapeutic nature of the setting, one that fostered serenity and peacefulness. It harkened back, he explained, to the days when patients literally lived at the hospital, often for years at a time, gaining a lengthy respite from the stressors of life outside the hospital's secure and protective care. Aaron spoke of being comforted that, instead of his daughter dreading to walk out of Temple University Hospital at night once off-duty—a trip fraught with such peril that she would often enlist an escort from a College-supplied security guard—she would now have to concern herself only with avoiding a scampering squirrel who dared to cross the slim hospital access road in front of her approaching car, or the occasional nocturnal skunk who might be on the prowl for unsecured garbage in cans out behind the residents' row of cottages.

A sound of footsteps approached. "Oh my, you startled me, Billy," Courtney said, more as a pleasantry than because she had been taken by surprise by her neighbor.

"Sorry, Dr. Brentwood," Billy Andrews said, rather sheepishly.

"Billy, for God's sake, don't start with the Dr. Brentwood stuff," she insisted warmly, understanding that Billy was probably following parental orders to call her by her newly-earned title. "It's Courtney, and it always will be, okay?"

Billy Andrews was the obedient, serious adolescent type, oriented to doing what was right and what was expected of him. His demeanor was quiet and polite, even shy, but Courtney sensed he was someone you would want on your side in a pinch. She had always been impressed with how well-grounded he was. In an area ripe with spoiled brats and rebellious kids dedicated to undoing years of devotion from their doting and wealthy parents, Billy Andrews was the kind of boy that received labels like "super-straight" from his peers, but "a great kid" from teachers and adults who admired his manners and respectful attitude.

Unlike the unimposing stature of his father and mother, Billy had size. Courtney noticed that he had grown even taller than when she had seen him last, during Christmas get-togethers in the neighborhood. He had a good eight inches on her, which meant that he must be nearly six foot three inches tall, or even more.

He was filling out amply in his chest and shoulders, and his arms showed the definition of someone who had been religiously performing curls, presses and other weightlifting exercises.

Aaron had recently told Courtney that he had gone with Jack Andrews to see Billy play football the previous fall at the high school stadium on the Post Road, and that on the playing field, any traces of Billy's timidity or passivity vanished. Apparently, donning football pads and engaging in fiery competition transformed the sweet, polite Billy into a snarling tough guy that no local opponent could handle. According to Aaron's report, Billy ran around the field hitting everything in sight, really standing out. Aaron had been very, very impressed.

"How long have I known you, Billy…since you were three and I babysat for you and Sally?" Courtney asked, attempting to re-vitalize the familiarity that had waned a bit during her medical school stint in Pennsylvania. Sally was Billy's older sister who now lived in Scottsdale. She had attended the University of Arizona and chose to remain in the Phoenix area, becoming averse to temperatures that ever fell far below seventy degrees Fahrenheit.

"Yeah, I guess," Billy responded distantly, adding a shoulder shrug, as adolescents do when they choose not to engage with someone they deem an authority figure.

"Well, I haven't changed that much, have I?" Courtney asked, looking to redevelop some rapport with him, and short-circuit the too-deferential attitude she perceived from her neighbor.

"No, not really."

Okay, I guess we are not going to get too far with the small talk. "So, what do you say? Are you ready to get started?" Courtney asked, hoping that getting to work would do a lot to help her neighbor feel more at ease.

Courtney opened the doors in the back of the truck, noting to her volunteer that the moving chore should not take very long. "Loading it took less than an hour," Courtney insisted, trying to rationalize the extent of the imposition on Billy, or at least to minimize it in her own mind.

"I'm ready," Billy declared. Given permission to start working, he immediately took the lead. He grabbed the end of the truck's metal ramp, pulling it out of its housing near the truck's rear edge, walking backwards and dropping it lightly to the ground. After jogging up the ramp, he brought together two shadeless floor lamps, grasping them in their middle section, two rods in one hand, while leaning down to pick up a small bookcase, placing his forearm under the top shelf then lifting it up with ease and carrying the entire load out of the truck.

"So, I guess I'm just putting these things in the open space there in the garage?" Billy asked, spotting the section evidently prepared for her things.

"You've got it," affirmed Courtney.

Billy warmed to the labor. Although Courtney still felt slightly guilty about asking Billy to come over to help her with this moving chore, she saw that he was rather enjoying the opportunity to put on display his physical attributes and his youthful athletic build.

"You've gotten so strong, Billy," she said, more in a matter-of-fact than flirtatious tone. She was playing to his vanity, though, and he responded to the praise with a slightly self-conscious, pleased smile. "Yeah, I'm working out a lot for football," was his reply, but saying nothing beyond that. Rather, he just picked up his pace a degree or two, appearing to be energized by the compliment, moving rapidly and steadily up and down the ramp, from truck to garage and back, arms piled high with furniture and boxes and as many loose items as he could manage to carry in one load.

The day was warm and muggy, and soon Billy's grey tee shirt showed dark splotches from his accumulating sweat. Courtney, sporting the dressed-down suburban outfit of khaki shorts and white, sleeveless Polo shirt, was also dripping with perspiration. She needed to wipe her brow occasionally, using a hand towel she retrieved from one of the boxes she had unpacked. It was especially hot and stuffy inside the back of the truck, the result of it having no ventilation during the nearly three hour trip from Philadelphia. But she and Billy plowed ahead, never malingering or disembarking from the truck empty-handed. Courtney more or less matched her eager neighbor trip-for-trip from truck to the garage, grabbing smaller items and light boxes, while he gravitated to the weightier and more cumbersome items. For the bulkier chest of drawers, mattress and box spring, they shared the load, working in tandem. Soon, the empty space in the garage was piled high with her belongings, occasionally requiring a re-assortment of items to maximize the available space.

Within the hour, the U-Haul was fully unloaded, just as Courtney had predicted.

"How long will you be keeping your stuff here?" Billy asked politely, setting down the last load from the truck in the only remaining open spot on the garage floor.

"I don't exactly know, Billy," she answered. "I'll know better tomorrow, when I go to the hospital where I'll be training for some interviews."

"Well," he said, declaring his offer of assistance more directly, "if you need some more help…"

Courtney had thought that she would probably just use the trunk and back seat of her Camry to move any belongings she needed to bring to her new temporary home, and lug them in herself, or enlist the help of her father if he was able to come along when she moved her stuff. But the offer of help was very sweet of her neighbor, she recognized. "Oh, thanks, Billy," she responded, appreciatively. "Thanks a lot. I have to wait and see what kind of layout and room these places at the hospital have." She explained that they might be quite fully furnished, and that she would only be able to bring some clothes and a few knick-knacks. "I'll know more tomorrow," she assured him. "But thanks again. You are a real sweetheart for offering."

"No problem, no problem," Billy replied, purposefully avoiding her name again, so as not to have to address the issue of either disobeying his father or acceding to Courtney's insistence on informality.

"Want something to drink?" Courtney asked, making her way inside to the Brentwood kitchen. Not hearing as Billy replied, "No, that's all right," Courtney soon reappeared with two large summer plastic cups filled with ice water. "Here," Courtney said as she handed him one of the cups. He took it from her appreciatively, and drank the entire refreshing contents in one long gulp.

"Thanks," Billy said, returning the plastic cup to Courtney, and showing signs through restless body language that he sought to be relieved of his duties.

"You know, you could do one more thing for me," Courtney said, a sheepish look on her face displaying regret for not informing him before about the request she was about to make. "I need to return the truck to Eastchester. Could you follow me there in my car, so I'll have a ride back?"

"Sure, no problem," Billy agreed. Courtney could tell he was proud that she trusted him with driving her car, that she was treating him more like an equal than like a little kid for whom she used to baby sit. "Want to go now?" Billy asked.

"Let's get it over with," Courtney decided, anxious to finish the moving chore and have a chance to relax at home by herself before her parents returned.

Ever the chivalrous one, Billy inquired if he should drive the truck.

"No, but only because I signed off on an insurance form that said I'd be the only one doing the driving," Courtney replied. "But I tell you what. I'll let you turn the truck around, if you want to, so I don't have to back it out onto the street. Think you can do that?" Courtney dreaded the prospect of re-entering Morningside Lane backwards and blindly.

"Sure, I can do that," Billy said, jumping at the chance both to drive a truck for the first time and to be of further value to Courtney.

The u-turn in the driveway was accomplished in a handful of back-and-forth transitions from forward to reverse gears, and soon the mini-caravan of truck and Camry was on its way to Eastchester, the suburban town just south of Scarsdale on the Post Road. A drop-off at the appointed garage was managed quickly and efficiently. In only a matter of minutes after entering the garage's office, Courtney returned to the car where Billy remained behind the wheel.

Courtney let herself into the passenger side, granting unspoken permission for Billy to chauffeur her home, a role he clearly relished. On the ride, she asked him about how his football team looked for the upcoming season, where he was thinking about going to college and how Susan was doing in Arizona. Billy was being recruited by Brown, Dartmouth and Lehigh to play football, and he intended to make a formal visit to each college after football season. His SATs had been just good enough to inspire interest from these prestigious schools. Courtney praised him for his academic and athletic accomplishments.

"I'm still going to root for Cornell, though, even if you're playing against us, you know that," she told him playfully.

"Cornell has a good team, from what I hear," Billy said. He told her he had been following Ivy League football since being contacted in his junior year by the Brown and Dartmouth coaches.

"Yeah, I went to the Cornell-Penn game last year in Philadelphia," Courtney said. "They were both undefeated in the league coming into the game. It was a great game, although Penn won." Courtney could talk sports with guys easily. She had played field hockey and some lacrosse at Scarsdale High, and she had continued with field hockey into the first couple of years at Cornell. She retained a former athlete's enjoyment of watching competition, just as she had enjoyed competing herself years ago.

Soon, Billy was pulling the Camry into the Brentwood's driveway, leaving it where it had been parked earlier. "Thanks again so much, Billy," Courtney said, reaching into the back seat to retrieve a card she had bought for him, and into which she had slipped a twenty dollar bill. "You were a lifesaver," she added, approaching him for a gentle hug, and handing him the envelope. "Here's a little 'thank you' for your help," she added, not telling him explicitly about the money she had placed inside.

Billy's adolescence showed in his slight awkwardness returning the demonstration of affection shown him, but he seemed warmed by the intimacy of the moment.

"Any time, any time," Billy responded, taking the envelope and backing away toward his home next door. He appeared sad, in a way, that their time together was coming to an end. "Let me know when you need help moving stuff to your new place," he reminded her before disappearing through an opening in the bushes that separated their respective properties. Through their entire time together, he had still managed to avoid addressing her directly by name.

Moving inside the garage again, Courtney located the suitcase full of light summer clothes she had chosen to knock around in over the next few days. She also grabbed a bag of toiletries gathered together earlier that morning from her apartment's bathroom. Rolling the suitcase with one hand and carrying the toiletry bag with the other, she moved inside to the foot of her home's front stairs, where she stooped over and dropped them both to the floor, deciding she wanted a moment to relax before starting to unpack. Then Courtney remembered that she wanted to make sure that a garment bag she had packed—the one that held the outfit she would wear to her interviews the next day—was fully under her control. She retrieved it quickly from the top of a pile in the garage, brought it in to the front hallway and flung it over the banister.

She eased into the living room, removed her sneakers and plunged onto the sofa, propping her stocking feet up on the shiny coffee table in front of it. *I'm bushed*, she admitted to herself, leaning back to relax on the sofa's embracing cushions. Nothing much had changed in the room since her last visit, she noticed. The art on the walls, much of it original works collected by her mother and father in SoHo galleries during her childhood, were the same as they had always been, for as long as she could remember. In fact, she could not recall the last time any major changes had been made in how her parents decorated this room of their home. The exterior looked different; it had been re-painted at least once recently. And the new driveway still made the whole outside area appear quite different to Courtney—much fancier than it looked when she was younger. But inside the home, decorative changes were rare. Her parents were both very busy physicians, and interior home improvements were never high on their priority list.

The maid who came in three times a week kept the place fully dusted and spotless, and the living room where Courtney now sat had an almost sterile cleanliness, as if no one really lived there. Her mother would not have it any other way. Actually, her parents spent very little time in this living room. Her father usually retreated quickly to his study in the evening, preferring the room adjoining the living room area that held his computer and the wall-to-wall shelves full of books. Her mother often relaxed upstairs, in a sitting area off the bedroom suite where she maintained a desk and comfortable chaise lounge for reading.

The living room had an enormously high ceiling, adorned with a thick joist, painted white, which carried from one side of the room to the other. The fireplace was never used, but it nonetheless served as a focal point of the room, due both to its central location and to the colorful house plants sitting on the brickwork and mantle, attracting the eye. The windows facing the front yard were both broad and tall, promoting an ample and wide view of the Brentwood property, along with part of the side yard of the Brentwood's other neighbors to the east, the Edwards.

Leaning her head far back, Courtney looked up at the ceiling, savoring the peacefulness and ambience of her parents' home, as well as the opportunity to be alone there for a time. Sigmund drifted in, tail high, curious about the unusual mid-afternoon visitor intruding on his domain. "Siggy, come here," she called, patting the sofa to encourage the cat to jump up and join her. Sigmund obliged. Stroking his soft brown coat, Courtney reflected back to Jason and their farewell. Rachel had sewn a slight seed of doubt in her, that medical school relationships like theirs are somehow fleeting and unsubstantial. The assurance he had given her had been heartening, but stuff happens. Was he out of her life now? Who would she call to see a movie with, to go out with for a light dinner, or to sit around with to watch something on the television? She had counted on Jason a great deal over the past two years, for friendship and camaraderie and emotional support.

From the standpoint of training to be a doctor, it felt like she was making a smooth enough transition to her residency years. Socially, though, it felt like she was completely starting over. Jason and many of her medical school chums were still in Philadelphia. Others were scattered around at medical schools and hospitals throughout the big northeastern and middle Atlantic cities—Boston, Hartford, New Haven, New York, Philadelphia, Baltimore and Washington, DC. She had made plans to meet up with some who would be doing their residency locally, at NYU, Cornell, Columbia or out on the Island, but she knew that none of them would constitute a solid social network for her. She had only a handful of friends remaining in Scarsdale, high school buddies with whom she had come to recognize that she had less and less in common. Many had begun working in Manhattan right after graduation, shunning the suburbs as boring and static. Others remained with their parents, ostensibly to cut costs, but in doing so, they betrayed either insecurity about becoming independent, or an inclination never to stray too far from the comfortable trappings that accompany living in wealth. She still communicated occasionally with college friends, but less and less so. And none of those to whom she felt the closest lived around New York at that point.

Courtney had to admit she was developing a little of her parents' tendency to gravitate toward socializing with other physicians. It was an in-bred clique, this field of medicine. At this stage of her training, she just felt like other physicians understood her life and issues better than others. She was anxious to meet her fellow residents at Hunt-Fisher. Maybe there would be another Jason Burke in the group. Or maybe someone she would be attracted to, and take a chance on in a relationship. She would need a Jason-type: smart and supportive. Someone as attractive as Jason would be nice, too. But obviously without the girlfriend back home. *Jason will be home with Lara tonight. I'm not going to think about that.*

She began succumbing to the gravitational forces of fatigue. Closing her eyes, she dropped down, laying herself out horizontally, melting into the comfortable sofa. Reaching for the soft, loose pillows lying nearby, she pulled two of them toward her, one into position under her head, one lain over it. She covered the top pillow with her free arm, wrapping the top pillow tightly around her ears. Sigmund, now relegated to the other end of the sofa, draped himself over Courtney's feet, continuing to re-bond with his former companion. So much was going on in her life, she felt almost guilty, lying there, doing what she had not done in what seemed like forever: preparing to take a lazy, mid-afternoon nap.

She was asleep in matter of moments, the emotional and physical toll of the past twenty-four hours finally catching up with her.

Chapter 3

Courtney awoke with a sense of foreboding, of imminent danger. Her intuition, only slightly dulled by her drowsy state, was on target. She sat up, seeing through the front window that her mother's dark blue Mercedes was pulling into the driveway. It was time to pull herself together. The battle would soon be waged.

She glanced at the clock on the mantle. *Six-thirty already.* Courtney was surprised that she had napped for a good couple of hours. She sat up on the sofa, rubbed her eyes and stretched her arms, hearing the garage door opening. It was a sound that she had always associated with some dread. It meant that there was a possibility that her mother was arriving home, and that soon Courtney would be hearing about some kind of irritation her mother was experiencing at the time—which had always tended to involve something Courtney did or did not do.

The point of contention this evening would be the same as it was the previous evening, at her graduation reception: Courtney's ridiculous decision to drive a rental truck by herself all the way from Philadelphia, how doing so was thoroughly unsafe, but more importantly totally unnecessary. Her mother would have been more than happy to pay to ship the items she had in her apartment by UPS. Courtney knew her mother's concern was less for the physical exertion or time she might be saving Courtney through the offer to ship her belongings. Her mother's focus was the ghastly prospect of a loud, sputtering truck, with her only child at the wheel, pulling up Morningside Drive and bringing their neighbors to their windows in disbelief.

But Courtney had experience in allowing her mother to pay a sum of money for the sake of her convenience, only to hear derisive comments about it later. *I hope you realize how much it cost me to pay for so-and-so*, she'll harp to me, again and *again.* So Courtney was disinclined to accept her mother's offer. Plus, how would UPS move her mattress, box spring, love seat and chair combination and other bulkier items? It seemed absurd to Courtney not to just rent a truck and get the move done. It had not been a big deal. Her mother, on the other hand, would never agree to this assessment.

Courtney heard a door open, the one from the garage into the nook area next to the kitchen.

"Courtney, are you here?" her mother's voice called in towards the living room.

"Hi, Mother. I'm in here," Courtney replied. *Okay...here it comes!*

"Oh, Courtney Brentwood, can't you do something with all that stuff in the garage? And why in heaven's name did you move your things yourself, all that way? I asked you not to, didn't I?"

"Mother, I told you last night, it wouldn't be that difficult. And it wasn't. Stop fussing about it," she snapped back, hoping the edge in her voice would make her mother back off a bit. Now Sheila was in sight, moving from the kitchen into the foyer next to the living room.

"I'm not fussing," Sheila replied, slowing her words to demonstrate her ability to remain calm. "I'm just unhappy you didn't take my advice. You shouldn't be driving rental trucks up the New Jersey Turnpike by yourself, and that's all there is to it." *I know Mother—there is a right way and a wrong way to do things, and I chose the wrong way. But let's move on.*

Sheila Brentwood was an elegant, tall woman—taller than Courtney by a full two inches, at least—and she retained a mature WASPy beauty that only now, as she reached her late-fifties, was beginning to fade behind the wrinkles and inevitable sagging flesh brought on by advancing age. Her hair, artificially frosted white against a backdrop of deep black she had used for years as its base color, was perfectly manicured. In fact, it had the look of a fresh shaping and cut, perhaps just accomplished in the hours before she arrived home.

"Did you just get your hair done?" asked Courtney, only slightly hurt that she would go for a hairstyling appointment the day after her medical school graduation instead of the day before it. "It looks a little different than last night?"

"Yes, dear, thanks for noticing. I'm afraid I have to work this evening. I'm going out to dinner with a couple from Edgewood named the Pentcheckis, James and Sylvia. They have given us signals that they might become a major donor, and tonight I get to explore if that is so, and what 'major' could mean," she explained, raising her eyebrows in excitement.

Sheila was a physician, but her professional practice no longer involved treating patients' physical ills. Instead, she devoted herself to the process of finding future cures, by leading the research Foundation at Montefiore Medical Center in the Bronx. Sheila's job was to keep the Foundation's till full, or at least full enough to keep the research continuing without significant budget cuts. Part of what she raised also went directly to offsetting some of the financial challenges at the hospital, where the institution appeared to be treading water in a slowly played out battle against Government cutbacks in Medicare and Medicaid reimbursements and academic hospital subsidies.

Sheila developed proposals to hit up the feds, the state, even local sources for a fair share of the money earmarked for the type of research Montefiore was performing. But much of the Foundation's new revenues came from her success in persuading private, high-net-worth individuals and families—like the Pentcheckis and many more like them throughout New York City and Westchester County—to choose her research Foundation for their charitable giving. Adept at the social aspect of the hunt for donations, Sheila made things happen. She had a salesperson's knack for knowing how and when to close deals. Evidently, this evening reeked with the scent of exposed money, and Sheila was preparing to move in for the kill.

Her days and evenings were often dedicated to power lunches and elegant dinners with a wide range of potential donors. Many weekends were spent at receptions and art auctions and other fundraising events of all types. Then there was the grand annual event she personally planned and executed each fall, The Montefiore Foundation Ball, which raised up to half of all the money the Foundation took in for the entire year. It was an event that often resulted in Sheila appearing in the society pages of the Sunday New York Times, posing with her benefactors—tuxedoed philanthropists or major captains of industry who loved more than she did to have their names shown in bold print below their picture in the only newspaper that mattered, documenting their eleemosynary proclivities.

"Where are you taking them to put on the big squeeze?"

"Courtney, I don't *squeeze* anyone," Sheila retorted, feigning insult at the notion that she did anything more than ask for other people's kind generosity toward a worthy cause. "Oh, there's a nice new restaurant in Armonk, right off 684, that I have heard great things about. I've got a reservation for eight o'clock. This is big, Courtney. The Pentchekis are very, very wealthy. I see a seven figure endowment coming, maybe a renaming of a wing at the hospital for them. The Pentcheckis are on that level, if we play our cards right."

"Who's we?" Courtney asked. "Do you mean the hospital or is someone else going to dinner?"

"Yes, Dr. Saunders and Rick are joining me." Sheila was referring to Robert Saunders, the hospital's VP of Medical Affairs, and Rick Walters, the hospital's President and CEO.

"Bringing in the heavy artillery for this one, huh?"

"It's very exciting, really. It's why we absolutely needed to come home early last night, so I could be fresh and 'on' tonight. You're not angry that we left so early, are you, dear?"

Courtney had actually enjoyed herself more the previous night, *sans* parents to entertain. She had hooked up with Jason and a dozen or so of other graduating students and they had partied well into the night—helping to explain the need for her cat nap this afternoon.

But she saw an opening to create some guilt in her mother, and she could not resist.

"Well, it was a bit awkward for awhile, I must say, being left alone like that, while everyone else had parents or family with them."

"Oh, dear, I'm sure you had lots of company, and many personal good-byes to say. But I'll make it up to you. Let's go to the City this weekend, just the three of us, for a celebration dinner. I can get us in at La Fourchette. It's a fabulous new place in the east 60's. And maybe a show. Have you seen Les Mis? I can get us tickets. Our treat. What do you say?"

"That will be fine," Courtney replied, half-heartedly, already earning points from the calculated reply to her mother's ostensible remorse.

Sheila wanted to head upstairs to freshen up, but her path was blocked by Sheila's suitcase and bag. "Courtney, please, have some consideration," she said with exasperation in her voice, pointing to the obstructions she needed to tip-toe her way around.

"Sorry, Mother," Courtney said, meaning it. *That wasn't very nice of me, leaving my stuff in her way like that.*

Her remorse was not powerful enough to get her off the sofa, though. Courtney had not really revived yet from her nap. She returned to her prone position on the sofa, thinking back to the previous evening. It had been a fun day and night, even with her parents' rapid exit. Many of her favorite faculty had hung around throughout the reception, drinking and getting looser than she had ever seen many of them. The congratulations and admiration flowed all around, warming her as profoundly as the abundant alcohol. She ended up dancing with many of her classmates whose advances she had rejected earlier in medical school, doing her part to make their graduation party a socially successful capstone event. And she saved the last few dances for Jason, who was Lara-less since he was not to graduate for another year, and was on his way to see her the next day anyway.

After about twenty minutes of continued lounging and reminiscing, Courtney stood up and went to the stairs to realign the placement of her belongings, so that her mother would not trip over or run into them on her way back down the stairs. Then she went on to the kitchen, in search of a caffeinated soda in the refrigerator. She had developed more than a slight dependency on caffeine in medical school. It went with the territory. When she was groggy like this, her brain sent out powerful messages, yearning for the drug. She found a Diet Coke in the refrigerator, opened it, poured it into a glassful of ice and garnished it with one chunk of lemon, from a pile of evenly sliced pieces she had produced on the cutting board. Taking a long sip, she noted a calming return to chemical balance within her brain's neurotransmitter system, owing to the ingestion of the soda's stimulant. *Ah, I needed this,* she thought. She wanted to be as alert as she could be when her father came home, so that she could get the most out of him about what to expect from her interviews the next day.

Sheila returned downstairs, freshly perfumed, donning a different and thoroughly gorgeous dinner dress. The image she conveyed was positively elegant. "You look great, Mother," Courtney said, admiring how this 50-something woman had managed to stay in such trim condition, given all the sumptuous meals she attended in performing her job.

Sheila brushed aside Courtney's compliment. She was running a little late, and her focus was on the Pentcheckis' millions. She picked up the car keys she had left on the kitchen table and moved toward the door. Then she caught herself for failure to provide a proper reunion greeting to her only daughter, who was now temporarily back in the nest. Returning toward Courtney, arms outstretched, Sheila offered herself to her daughter for a perfunctory hug.

"Good to have you home, dear," Sheila said lightly into Courtney ear, before breaking away quickly from this brief embrace. "I called your father earlier, but remind him that I'll be home around 10-ish, okay?" She turned to leave for good this time, giving a backward wave good-bye, and was almost out the door when she spun back toward Courtney, pointing her finger, mocking the role of the stern, disapproving parent. "And no more driving trucks! You hear?"

Courtney smiled and waved her away, shaking her head in amusement as her mother finally disappeared into the garage. *What a piece of work, my mother is.* Soon, she heard the familiar sound of the garage door opening, the Mercedes starting up, a brief interlude, then the sound of the motorized garage door again, and silence.

Courtney was relieved that Sheila had plans for the evening, not just because she would avoid the possibility of having to defend herself for hours about her trucking excursion, or about clothes she had not yet put away, or whatever else came to her mother's obsessive mind, but mostly because it offered Courtney a chance to have some quality time alone with Aaron. She looked up at the clock on the wall. He had promised to be home in about a half hour.

She leaned back against the kitchen counter top, finished her soda, and began plotting out how to best interrogate her father about what the next day's interviewers might ask her. She wanted to know what these guys had in their evaluation bag of tricks, what their agenda was when they met with first year residents who had already been accepted for a new class. She had heard from other medical students entering psychiatry that preliminary meetings like these with the senior faculty were crucial. They helped forge impressions that were instrumental in subsequent assignments of clinical supervisors. If one had aspirations to become Chief Resident in the fourth year, this was the interview that helped set the course toward that prestigious appointment. The residents that were deemed to hold the most potential would be steered toward more senior faculty supervisors, the ones who year after year were the winners or candidates for the resident-elected Teacher of the Year award. For the less impressive residents, an assignment to junior staff psychiatrists was likely, which meant they would be mentored by physicians who were only a year or two out of residency training themselves.

I might as well go for it, and get the best training I can, she told herself, betraying a nagging sense that she might have made an incorrect choice about which medical specialty to pursue. The Clinic experience was the culprit for her holding on to this uncertainty. Rolanda had raised doubts in her, saying she should have elected to become an internist, because Rolanda saw some real ability in her approach to treatment and her manner with physically ill patients. But Courtney had always felt destined to enter her father's specialty. She had wavered a bit, though, when exposed to different specialties and practices throughout medical school. *It's such a crapshoot, this decision about what residency to pursue,* she thought to herself. *How do, say, prospective ob-gyns really know if they are suited for coaching women through pregnancy, conveying over and over that the expected child was somehow the one for whom they had been saving up all their obstetrical expertise to deliver? And then delivering the baby at any hour of the day or night? Or how do future surgeons know if they have the poise and dexterity to cut out an appendix smoothly, time and time again? Or how ER physicians might react to seeing a rash of bloodied injury victims, or the emotional toll it would take on them to evaluate people dead-on-arrival, or when they fail in an attempt to revive someone after a traumatic accident, regularly watching people die right before their eyes?*

The medical school rotation Courtney had taken through psychiatry had been trying. Instead of caring for patients with fevers, aches and pains, or a malfunctioning heart or kidney, for which most of her classroom training had prepared her, she witnessed treatment planning for delusional thinking, and different types of debilitating depression and anxiety. Psychiatry, in her view, was a strong test not just of her knowledge of medicine, but of her character as well. She had witnessed patients battling with or belittling their therapists, resisting help rather than acceding to prescriptive care plans. And other patients would idolize and form an unhealthy dependence on their therapists, rather than developing the inner resources to overcome problems in their lives. Would she be sucked in by these battles and manipulations? The doctor-patient relationship in psychiatry seemed nothing like it was at the Clinic.

We're about to find out, she thought. *The die is cast. I'm starting this training whether I like it or not. So I better get it off on the right foot.*

Before leaving Temple, Courtney had done some research at the medical library to learn a little more about her interviewers. She wanted to find out what she could about their backgrounds and primary research interests, so that she might have a rapport-building strategy prepared. Robert Blakeley, the Medical Director at Hunt-Fisher, was a Yalie, and a noted authority and worldwide lecturer on psychosomatic behavior, which involved feigning non-existent physical ailments or focusing on physical symptoms to mask or somehow obfuscate one's primary psychiatric illness. The other important interviewer, John Fencik, was Director of Resident Education. Courtney learned that he had done his residency at Harvard, was a child and adolescent specialist, and had made a name for himself in the study of causes of teenage suicide. Reading this about Dr. Fencik, she recalled seeing him on television once or twice, serving as a guest expert on a news show, commenting on some tragic, high profile case in the suburbs when one or more young people had taken their own lives.

Then there was the eminent Dr. Harold Hunt, the son of the hospital co-founder Carl Hunt. He was eighty years old and still a factor in all hospital and resident education decisions. In his day, Dr. Hunt was *the* therapist of the stars—many depressed actors and actresses, alcoholic wives of politicians, cocaine-abusing athletes, schizophrenic sons of Fortune 500 CEOs had gravitated toward him for their mental health care. For decades, he had run a blue chip private practice on Park Avenue in Manhattan, while maintaining his leadership position at the hospital concurrently. In many ways, he was a deity in the field of psychiatry, a figure known worldwide because of the legacy of his father and the prominent clientele who requested his services. She had heard through the grapevine that his mental faculties were slipping a bit. But, according to everything Courtney heard, he still very much ran the show at Hunt-Fisher.

Courtney's anxiety lay in a concern that her interviewers made a living sizing people up quickly. How do you impress them? What general themes do they like to talk about? What topics should she shy away from altogether? It was not as if she had a glaring weakness that needed to be masked. She just did not want to walk into any traps that were better off avoided.

Suddenly aware of an overwhelming need for some food, Courtney opened the refrigerator to find something convenient upon which to nibble. Behind her, she heard footsteps approaching the door from the garage. Her father had arrived, a little before the appointed hour that he had predicted earlier in the day. She felt none of the anxiety now that attended the entrance of her mother earlier that evening. Quite the opposite in fact. Her father was such a loving, genial presence in her life, she welcomed every opportunity for time alone with him. Their separation during her medical school training and his growing duties running the same type of training at Cornell had diminished substantially the quality time they had been able to spend together. Once in awhile over the past few years she had driven home from Philadelphia impulsively, just to have an hour or so with him, in order to discuss some challenge she was facing or a decision that would benefit greatly from his input. And he never disappointed her. Aaron listened so well, Courtney always felt he was getting her, no matter what the problem or issue was. While many of her Scarsdale friends had complained about their aloof or out-of-touch parents, Courtney had been fortunate always to maintain an intimate, trusting relationship with her father. *Now, Mother—that's a little different story.*

Aaron spoke first. "Dr. Brentwood, you're home, I see," he said, moving toward her with arms extended for a long, affectionate hug that they had been too occupied and busy to manage during their brief time together the evening before. After the embrace, Aaron backed up, raising a hand to his mouth as if to shield his voice from an invisible adversary lurking nearby.

"So, where'd you ditch the truck?" he whispered hoarsely, for effect.

"I took it to a place in Eastchester where they rent U-Hauls," Courtney informed him, smiling. "Billy drove me back. It's long gone."

Aaron breathed an audible sigh of relief. "Whew. That's good," he said. Even though they were alone, his wife's presence could always be felt at the Brentwood home.

"Mother is still none too happy about my trucking through the neighborhood. I'm sure she's convinced I was seen behind the wheel by half of Scarsdale, and that she'll have to explain it to all her friends for weeks."

Aaron looked at her with a straight face. "Well…?"

"Well, what?" Courtney asked.

"Were you seen?"

"Dad!"

"I'm just kidding with you," Aaron replied, smiling, knowing how easy it was to get Courtney to respond to kidding aimed at reactions to her mother's attitudes or snobbish behavior.

"So," he continued, "Mother is out to dinner, I hear. What shall we do about eating? I'm really famished."

"Yeah, me too," Courtney said. "I started eating this pear because I realized I had gone all day without food."

"Oh my God, let's get something delivered right away then," he insisted, moving toward the kitchen phone, pulling out a drawer below it that held an array of miscellaneous papers.

"Chinese suit you?" he asked, knowing he had a take-out menu from a local restaurant somewhere in the pile.

"How about we order two salads and split a large calzone from Romanello's?" Courtney suggested, suddenly hankering for something Italian, and remembering that Romanello's, in the heavily Italian north end section of Eastchester, had the very best calzones in the universe.

"Done. And they deliver, I'm certain of that," Aaron said, already dialing the phone. He ordered the food.

"Thirty minutes?" he said into the phone, evidently repeating what he had just heard. "Is that okay, Courtney?" he asked turning to her.

"Sure," Courtney said. It would give them a chance to talk for awhile.

Having negotiated what they would eat and how they would get food in their respective bellies as expeditiously as possible, father and daughter made their way into the living room. Courtney returned to the site of her earlier nap, while Aaron nestled into the broad lounge chair next to her. They chatted some more about her moving adventure, about Billy Andrews, his football prowess and his college prospects, and how they would have to go see him play some time this fall.

"I suppose tomorrow you will get a chance to see where they are going to put you up on grounds," Aaron said, steering the conversation toward Courtney's agenda.

"Yeah, I think so," Courtney responded. "I'll make a point of speaking to the secretary who handles those arrangements. You said that you think the cottages are furnished, right?"

"Yes, I believe so, but you'll still need lots of the stuff I saw in that pile I just passed in the garage. I'm pretty sure of that. The cottages have nice large rooms, but I think the hospital only puts the bare minimum in them."

Courtney thanked him for opening up some room in the garage for her things and for driving the Camry up from Philadelphia the night before.

"Thank your mother, not me," he suggested, laughing, noting that he would have driven back either way, even if Courtney had not needed his assistance. It had been Sheila who had been inconvenienced, taking the wheel and driving solo. Her strong preference would have been to sit, relax, perhaps even sleep, for the nearly three hour ride home, allowing Aaron to serve as her chauffeur for the trip back to Scarsdale.

Maybe that's part of why she is being so pissy about this whole thing, Courtney recognized.

"I guess you're right," Courtney admitted, making a mental note to go out of her way to express her thanks to her mother, which she had not done earlier.

"So," he began, before pausing and sitting back in his chair, to create the effect of a conversational transition toward Courtney's interview concerns, "what do you want to learn from me that you think will help you tomorrow? I'm not sure there's a lot I can tell you. I know Hunt of course. He and I have worked together on some projects over the years. I know Blakeley a little better than John Fencik. Blakeley and I have done some APA committee work together." The American Psychiatric Association was the professional advocacy and self-policing group for psychiatrists, an entity that held its annual convention every year on Mother's Day weekend, a fact that Courtney and Sheila had always found odd and perhaps worthy in itself of psychological interpretation.

Courtney began with a few of the questions she had prepared in her mind. "Dad, when you interview new PGY1s, what do want to learn when you first meet them? Be honest with me." PGY1 meant Post Graduate Year 1, a classification used to separate the four years of residency.

"Well, learning why they chose psychiatry is always a good thing to find out right away," he answered without hesitation.

"Because we're crazy ourselves, that's why," Courtney remarked glibly, betraying some of the anxiety she felt about the choice of medical specialty she had made for her residency training. Her father appeared to take no offense.

"There is a small percentage of medical students who select psychiatry who are very troubled and might be better off on the other side of Quiet Room door, for sure," Aaron said, with a wry smile that betrayed experience with psychiatric residents who had fallen off the deep end themselves.

"Quiet Room?"

"You know, the famous padded room you hear about in popular culture. You'll see, it's just a room, with nothing in it but a small mattress, so patients don't have anything to hurt themselves with. No straight jackets are used or anything like that." Aaron became pensive for a moment, the scientist in him internally reviewing the literature. "But back to your joke's premise that the more unstable medical school graduates choose psychiatry, I don't know if the research bears that out. Frankly, from my experience, the most unstable group is the emergency physicians. Something about needing the excitement, the rush of saving a life with some quick thinking and action, just the frenetic pace of the ER is enough to make you think that some of the doctors who gravitate to it are very manicky by nature."

"My friend Jason at Temple, whom you met again last night…remember him?"

"The fellow with the sunglasses on indoors?"

"Right, that's him."

"I remember. Nice young man."

"Anyway, Jason says that psychiatry is a valuable clinical practice and intellectually very stimulating, but that it is very hard to earn a decent living at it, and that it will only get harder with managed care taking hold."

Aaron sighed, nodding his head. "There's some truth…no, there's a lot of truth in what he says," he pointed out. "Did you know—I don't think medical schools teach students the finances of health care as much as we should—did you know that if you went to a hospital with a serious heart disease, most private and public insurance plans will cover just about every cost, three hundred sixty-five days a year? Yet, if you go in with a serious brain disease—the brain being at least as important an organ as your heart, wouldn't you say?"

"Sure," Courtney affirmed.

"If you go in with a serious brain disease, like schizophrenia or bipolar disease or acute depression, diseases that science has amply demonstrated are firmly rooted in brain chemistry, you know what you are told by your insurance company?"

"That you're malingering and need to pull yourself together?"

"Well, it's not quite that sinister or simplistic, to be fair. But, they say, okay, for the heart problem, stay as long as you want. But for the brain, out in thirty days. And you're not allowed back this year. Some even say you're not allowed back ever. I saw a study by a group hired by the private psychiatric hospital association that found that thirty days coverage is the limit in many plans for someone's whole entire lifetime!"

"Why did insurance plans do that?" Courtney asked.

"I'm afraid we—the psychiatric hospital industry, that is—we brought it on ourselves, to a certain extent. Hospitals got greedy: some charged exorbitant daily rates, piled up all kinds of ancillary charges, kept patients in the hospital far too long, with no urgency to move them out, as long as their insurance held up. Then, there were those recent scandals in Texas, hospitals being accused of committing people to hospitals against their will if they had good insurance. Inevitably, the big corporations, especially the self-insured ones who essentially pay their employees' health insurance claims themselves, saw their costs for providing mental health care going through the roof. They said, 'enough is enough.' They needed to find a way to control the big cost increases they were experiencing, so they started to cut back the maximum dollars they would pay out for each policy, or they capped the number of days they would cover, or both. Insurance companies call it 'stop loss.' Stop the losses. Corporations and insurance companies saw mental health care expenses as one big albatross, growing larger and larger, strangling them. Then they brought in the managed care industry to squeeze even more costs out."

"So, now I bet you have to discharge patients early, to save the days available on the patients' insurance plan, in case you need them later."

"You're right. Very good. That's perceptive of you. It's exactly what happens."

Courtney found the financial perspective of her chosen profession interesting, but less so than she would toward the end of her training. For now, she wanted to steer the discussion back to preparing her for any trick questions or hidden agendas that senior psychiatrists might have in store for her.

"What else do you think I should expect them to ask me?" Courtney asked.

Aaron thought for a moment. "I often ask new residents about their goals, of course. Particularly whether they have a penchant to remain in academia, with the university-affiliated hospitals, conducting research and all that. It is good if you can smoke out a budding research superstar, someone who years from now might be heading NIMH or the state's Division of Mental Hygiene."

"I don't know if that is the way I want to go," Courtney admitted. "I think my future is in direct clinical work. I like working with patients. And their families."

"That won't cost you at Hunt-Fisher. In fact, the academic affiliation with UConn is nothing like the Westchester Division and Payne Whitney have with Cornell. Hunt-Fisher stays in the academic game partly because it needs residents as cheap labor, and partly for the prestige of being a training center. There isn't a big push to conduct and publish research at Hunt-Fisher. You can if you want to, but it is not like it is at Cornell, where, if you want to stay around for a faculty appointment after residency, you'll need to abide by the traditional 'publish or perish' mandate."

"Okay," Courtney summarized, "so they might want to know why I chose psychiatry and what goals I have. What else?"

"There's a lot of sub-specialties in psychiatry, and they may ask you about your interest in focusing on one of them. Fencik will want to know if you might be interested in children and adolescents, since he is prominent in that field. Or geriatrics; the overall population is aging, and that's a hot area. Or eating disorders or addiction medicine. So you might give some thought to a sub-specialty that you have in mind—not as a commitment, necessarily, but it would be good to express curiosity about one to which you might gravitate."

"Thanks. That's helpful," Courtney said, nodding because it made sense to her.

"Do you?"

"Do I what?"

"Have a sub-specialty in mind?" Surprisingly, Aaron had never asked her this before.

"Public or community health maybe. I like the outpatient or clinic setting a lot."

"Yes, there's a lot of interest in outpatient care, because it lends itself to learning how to develop a private practice, which is what many trainees dream about. But creating a real public mental health model, trying to raise the overall mental health of a population, that's exciting stuff. Doing prevention work, like going into schools or colleges, reaching out to adolescent girls about symptoms of eating disorders, or making deinstitutionalization of the chronically mentally ill work, by setting up programs with intensive case management and supportive housing. Or improving the detection of depression in the workplace. Yeah, there is a lot of need for a much better public mental health model than we practice now."

Courtney found her father's enthusiasm infectious. That is the feeling she needed to convey. She had to show that she was excited about learning and finding a niche for herself, one for which she could demonstrate a passion.

The doorbell rang. A teenage boy was at the door, sooner than expected, holding a square cardboard box with a white bag sitting on top of it, within which were their salads and enormous calzone. Aaron leapt up to complete the transaction, tipping the youngster handsomely for the prompt delivery.

They moved back into the kitchen and Aaron put the food on the small kitchen table used for these kinds of light meals. Courtney retrieved some silverware, plates and napkins.

"What are you drinking, Dad?" she asked, filling a glass of water for herself.

"Whatever you have is good for me, too," he told her.

Courtney set them both up with utensils and ice water, and soon they were digging into their salads heartily. Courtney felt very content. She looked lovingly at her father as he chomped away at the salad. She felt an appreciation back from him to her, as well. She sensed she was providing him with rare company at dinner. He often told her that since she left home seven years ago, the house could get awfully quiet. He pointed out the irony that he now missed times that he used to complain about, when she and her friends noisily buzzed around the place during her teenage years, disrupting his routine.

It was funny, but Aaron looked like a psychiatrist. He was balding—it seemed like so many in his profession were, like it was an occupational requirement or hazard or something—and slightly overweight. He sported a short-cropped, salt-and-pepper shaded beard, as many men grow who carry this larger body type around.

Unlike his wife, Aaron dressed conservatively: gray suit, button-down Oxford shirts, conservative ties, cordovan wing-tipped shoes. The suit coat came off the instant he had an opportunity, and it lay on the back of his chair as they ate. His tie was loosened but still around his collar. *My Dad is not flashy, but he's got such a professional look*, Courtney thought, looking at him. *He exudes confidence and intelligence, even when he's plowing through a salad and calzone.*

"So," Aaron said between mouthfuls of food, "what else can I tell you?"

Courtney thought back to what she had intended to learn from their conversation. "Dr. Blakeley," she said. "What's he like?"

"Blakeley's a good guy. Fencik's kind of...let's say...formal...," Aaron began, forming a sly smile, before adding, "which is a nice of saying he is a stiff, a tad pretentious and impressed with his own intelligence. I say that kindly, though, not in a vindictive or overly mean-spirited way. I like them both, actually."

"And Dr. Hunt?"

"He's a barking puppy dog. He's benign."

"What do you mean, benign?" Courtney asked, trying to get the gist of this description.

"He is a nice man. He can growl at you, but underneath he is an inordinately sweet guy. I'm just afraid he is getting a tad organic these days. Nowhere near full-blown senility, but he's, let's just say, a few bubbles off plumb." Courtney smiled at this apt metaphor.

"It's too bad," Aaron noted, somewhat sadly. "Years ago, there was no better thinker about an important issue or a better psychiatrist in the business."

"So, what does that mean in terms of what might impress them in an interview?" Courtney asked.

Aaron thought for a moment. "I suppose you can ask them about opportunities you might have to present cases to them in case conferences. They probably would feel very flattered by that."

"Ah, the suck-up approach."

"A reasonable one for an incoming PGY1," Aaron advised, wryly.

"Alright," Courtney said, finishing her half of the splendid calzone she had wanted so badly, "I guess that's it. Anything else you want to tell me?"

"No, you'll do fine. This is not much more than a courtesy interview, remember. You're in already."

"I know, but people tell me they like to meet everyone before making supervision assignments, so it has to mean something."

"It does, you're right," Aaron agreed. "But while you shouldn't take the interview too lightly, you might be more uptight about it than you need to be."

Courtney acknowledged this comment by nodding slowly and silently.

After getting up to take his now-empty plate to the sink, Aaron came around behind his daughter, crossing his arms affectionately in front of her, grasping one of his wrists with the other hand below her neck. "Just be yourself," he added, leaning his chin on her shoulder.

"Hey, that's all I can do," Courtney replied, tilting her head affectionately to touch his.

"You'll do fine," he whispered in her ear, before gently kissing her cheek just below it.

Chapter 4

▼

Driving through a residential area in Norwalk, Connecticut, in search of her new home and temporary employer, Courtney was incredulous that a major acute care psychiatric hospital was somewhere in the vicinity. The area appeared to her to be just a series of long, tree-lined country roads, surrounded by elegant homes and vast suburban properties. But Courtney had followed her father's directions to the letter, and this was where he had placed her. *Either I am horribly lost or this place is really in the sticks.* Perhaps she had missed a turn somewhere. But just as she reached for her newly-installed car phone to give Aaron a call to learn where she had gone wrong, far off in the distance a gated entranceway could be seen, one that looked different than the others she was passing. Sure enough, a wooden sign came into view more clearly, secured between two wooden posts like a piece of fencing, easily blending into the surrounding trees and bushes. Both the background and lettering were painted in discrete earthen colors, reinforcing the purposeful camouflaging strategy. The sign read simply:
Hunt-Fisher Psychiatric Hospital: Main Entrance.

I made it, she told herself, relieved that she could spend some time preparing mentally for the interviews rather than winding through the Connecticut woods in search of her destination. Courtney drove past the sign and then a vacant Guard House just beyond it, hoping for additional signage inside the grounds to direct her to Wilson Cottage, where she had been told to report for her interview. With no option but to proceed ahead, she made her way up the long, thin, winding access road. Tall, mature oak trees, symmetrically situated on both sides and spaced evenly apart from each other, seemed to stand watch over her oncoming car, their branches forming a protective cover high overhead, like stoic Marines crossing swords to commemorate a wedding of one of their own. A bit further up the hill, tennis courts appeared, with a fenced-in paddle ball court next to it. The outer buildings along the main access road were Victorian in style, some with tall conic spires on one or both sides. Almost all the buildings, Courtney noted, had covered wrap-around porches, designed to welcome entrants to their doors, while shielding them from the elements when need be.

Looking ahead to where the road ended in a large circular driveway, Courtney saw the Hunt-Fisher Hospital for the first time. It resembled the enormous, Colonial-era brick administration buildings she had seen at older colleges during her campus visits years ago. The setting did, indeed, remind her of a college campus, one situated "up on the hill," steeped in academic tradition and intentionally removed from the bustle of everyday life in the town or city below.

Closer now to the main hospital building, near the Doric-columned threshold that she assumed was the central point where visitors were supposed to enter the institution, Courtney was struck by another very significant distinction about this setting in which she now found herself, as opposed to the one where she had lived for the past three years: there were so many parking spots! And all of them evidently free of charge! She spotted a group of open places, each marked with its own small sign, declaring "*Visitor's Parking.*" She darted into one quickly, unable to cast aside the conditioned urban impulse to grab any available parking spot whenever possible, before a likely competitor could claim it.

She turned off the ignition, and sat back in her seat. Drawing in a deep breath, then closing her eyes, she made an effort to exhale with deliberate slowness, trying to promote optimum relaxation. She opened her eyes and gazed around the hospital grounds. It was all very impressive: the stately buildings, the beautifully-maintained grounds, the sheer openness and size of the area that contrasted so starkly with the compacted and space-deficient setting in which she had been immersed for three years. She rolled down her car windows, drawn to listening to the silence around her. Another car had followed soon after hers up the access road, but it had disappeared from Courtney's sight, moving either into some separate parking area she did not see, or turning off toward a set of buildings behind the tennis and paddle ball courts. Between buildings, she spotted an old pickup truck pulling an open trailer filled with lawn mowers, parked at a slight tilt since one of its sides had been driven up and over a curb, while the other side remained on the access road. Two maintenance men in green outfits were busily filling the mowers' tanks with gasoline, in preparation for an afternoon of outdoor labor. Finally, some additional signs of life: two women appeared through the Main Entrance, talking quietly. They walked down the six steps in front of the entrance, moving very deliberately, heading toward a pair of Adirondack chairs on a grassy spot just below her car. After taking seats in these chairs, they resumed their chatter, while closing their eyes and tilting their heads upwards to gain the full effect of the sun's warmth on their faces. It was a hot, lazy early afternoon in summer, and they evidently were staff on a lunch break who had decided to use their time off for some brief sunbathing.

Courtney could sense the environment at Hunt-Fisher Hospital operated at a far slower pace than the one from which she had just left. Here she was, about to interview with a group of prominent senior faculty, an event about which she had been fretting for the past twenty-four hours or so, and yet she felt strangely happy and serene. It had been such a long time since she had felt this much at ease—certainly not since before medical school began. *This is nice,* she thought to herself. *I really feel like I belong here.*

She glanced at the clock over the dashboard. *12:40.* She was twenty minutes early for the interview. Time enough to gather herself for a few more minutes, then find someone inside who could direct her to the Wilson Cottage administrative building. She pulled down the car's windshield visor and flipped open the vanity mirror placed there for just this type of moment: self-assessment on the run, a rapid tune-up of hair, makeup and overall appearance. Checking to make sure the slightly longer-than-expected ride from Scarsdale had not undermined her earlier grooming efforts, Courtney was relieved that only minor adjustments needed to be made. Her hair, straight and brown, just below shoulder length, looked fine, warranting just two or three quick strokes of a brush taken from her handbag, to engender an even fresher look. The makeup she had previously applied was still largely intact. Still, she decided to dab her cheeks with more powder that she pulled out from a makeup pouch she kept in her purse, and then refresh her glossy lipstick. The reflection she saw in her tiny mirror was satisfying. Courtney had little reason to be disappointed in the way she looked. She had been blessed with an attractive face, a trim stature maintained through sensible eating, along with plenty of appetite-suppressing caffeine. She had appealing legs, covered that day to mid-calf by a beige skirt, chosen, Courtney thought, as a perfect accompaniment to a conservative cream-colored short sleeve blouse, both purchased only a week before at the Bloomingdale's out in the Philadelphia suburb of Ambler.

After making final adjustments to this in-car touch-up effort, Courtney closed the windows, grabbed her bag, and moved out of her car. She actually hesitated for a brief moment as she extended her car key toward the door, thinking how safe she felt where she was. But she locked it anyway, a New Yorker's instinct for safety prevailing. *I may be in the woods, but I'm not stupid.*

She headed toward the Main Entrance just behind her. Inside the entrance door, she made her way into a wide reception area with a desk that evidently was intended as an initial source of information and directions for visitors. However, the seat behind the desk was empty. Courtney moved further ahead, toward an intersection of two prominent hallways, where there appeared to be a Directory on the wall. Many of the listings on the Directory meant little to her. She assumed the esoteric names there—*Unit 4 West, Unit 6 South, Unit 5 North*—were designations for treatment floors. A little further down in the alphabetically-arranged listings, she read *Medical Administration—Wilson Cottage*. Directions to the Cottage were provided; *straight ahead*. Courtney complied, heading down the hallway and then through a door that led outside. She proceeded down a few wooden steps of a makeshift deck, and then strolled across a short sidewalk covered by a semi-circular awning. The sidewalk ended in an entrance to another building. Above this door, a sign for *Wilson Cottage* provided final confirmation that she was in the right place.

Moving inside, Courtney was greeted immediately by a woman sitting at a desk behind a countertop that separated the office staff from the entrance area. Courtney returned the greeting, introduced herself and confirmed that she was there for an appointment with Drs. Blakeley, Fencik and Hunt, at one o'clock.

"I'll notify Dr. Blakeley's secretary that you are here," the woman responded courteously. "Please have a seat, and I'm sure she will be right with you."

From the available options in this waiting area, Courtney chose to sit in an elegant armchair, forsaking the antique, cushioned armless bench next to it, as well as the sleek mauve-colored sofa on the opposite side of the waiting area. The room was adorned with pastoral paintings of fox hunts over English countryside, in keeping with a cottage theme. A single, nonconforming framed piece was hung near the doorway, which Courtney faced. She read the inscription: "Certification of Compliance provided to the Hunt-Fisher Psychiatric Hospital by the Joint Commission on Accreditation of Hospitals." Courtney knew about this accreditation agency, having observed Temple University Hospital toil to meet its standards. *Well, at least the place will be in business for awhile longer.* Courtney noticed that the door that led to the Cottage's offices and conference room was open, a gesture of openness and trust: a welcoming attitude. Courtney waited, thinking to herself once again how amazing it was that she felt far less stress at that moment than she had felt talking about what it would be like for her, in the discussions with her father the previous evening.

A tall, matronly woman soon appeared at the door and introduced herself to Courtney.

"Dr. Brentwood, hello. My name is Brenda Washburn. I am Dr. Blakeley's Executive Assistant," she said, with some emotional reserve, but with her right hand extended courteously. Courtney greeted her with a smile, standing up, shaking the hand Brenda offered to her.

"Could you follow me, please?" Brenda asked.

Brenda led the way through the open door and into a conference room located at the end of the hall, accessible through two different sets of broad, oak doors. The room was dominated by a broad, highly varnished wooden table, around which were eight leather high-back chairs, arranged neatly and symmetrically. More pastoral artwork hung on the wall. *Very elegant and formal,* Courtney thought to herself.

"Please make yourself comfortable. Dr. Blakeley and Dr. Fencik are finishing up with a conference call with Farmington. It is scheduled to finish in about a minute."

"Farmington?" Courtney asked, wondering what she meant.

"The UConn medical school and hospital are located there. The people on the call are part of the credentialing staff who support our people here."

"It must be busy for you this time of year, with new resident staff coming aboard," Courtney offered, anticipating that academic administrivia peaked as the new semester began.

"Yes, it is. The busiest time of year for us, in many respects. There is paperwork we need to process for the resident class that just graduated, and then we need to make sure your group is all set up with their supervisors and clinical assignments. Every year it is the same. Lots of forms to complete and schedules to arrange. I haven't had a calm Fourth of July since I began working here seven years ago," she shared, more warmly than before. Courtney's impression was that while Brenda Washburn may complain about facing unmanageable administrative woes and work overloads, she was quite adept at keeping all the details very well under control.

"Well, I appreciate what you are doing for us," Courtney told her, showing her support.

"I have help, but thank you. Would you like any coffee, water or soda, Dr. Brentwood?"

"I'd love some coffee, black, if it is not too much trouble," Courtney replied, still nowhere near detoxified from the hypercaffeinism of her medical college years.

Brenda returned soon afterwards with Courtney's beverage request. After assuring her guest interviewee that Drs. Blakeley, Fencik and Hunt would be in shortly, she left Courtney alone in the meeting room and returned to her office at the end of the hall. Courtney, still standing at this point, thought it would be best to sit in the middle seat on one side of the table, figuring the end of the table was a spot more appropriate for Dr. Hunt or for her other two interviewers. She waited, alone in the utter silence of the large formal conference room. Occasionally, she peered out to the hall for signs of movement, for any type of signal that her interviewers were on their way to join her. She was eager for the interviews to get underway, and ultimately to be behind her. Some time off was beckoning, but not before finishing the inquisition she was about to undergo. *C'mon, let's get this show on the road*, she thought to herself.

Finally, after what seemed to Courtney like an eternity but was probably in reality less than ten minutes, a door opened out into the hall. Two men emerged through it. They were roughly the same height, both balding, one having sparse dark hair raked over the immense bald spot on top of his head from a part just a fraction over his left ear. The other maintained his sparse growth in a U-shaped pattern circling the lower portion of his head, but the gray hair that existed was short, neatly groomed and unabashedly ceding the top of the skull to bare cranial skin. They wore nearly identically-styled summer cotton suits, except one was gray and the other a dark olive. Stopping just short of the doorway to the conference room, they took a moment to speak privately to each other. Courtney caught them both turning their heads to glance at her again, in unison, before returning to a few final whispered comments to each other. Finally they entered the room. Dr. Blakeley, the one without the raked-over hairstyle, came over to her first, smiling, with his hand extended.

"Dr. Brentwood, sorry to keep you waiting," he apologized. "I am Robert Blakeley. I'm pleased to meet you."

"Hello, Dr. Blakeley. I am pleased to meet you, too," Courtney reciprocated politely.

"And this is John Fencik," Blakeley continued, introducing his partner. "He is our Director of Resident Education."

Fencik, appearing far more reserved as he addressed Courtney, greeted her only with a curt "Hello," while shaking her hand and scanning her from head to toe. He took the seat across the table opposite her.

"Dr. Hunt will be joining us at any moment, I'm sure," Blakeley continued. "I just checked with his secretary to make certain he was reminded of this meeting," he added, perhaps hinting, Courtney thought, about Hunt's rumored eroding cognitive capacities.

"I look forward to meeting him," Courtney said, a polite response that drew what she observed was a slight wry facial expression from Fencik to Blakeley, which she interpreted to mean something like, "I don't know if you will say that after you have actually met and interacted with the demented old guy."

"But let's begin, shall we?" Blakeley began, turning first to close the conference room door from which he had entered, before sitting, as Courtney had expected, in the chair at the head of the conference table. The other conference room door was left open, presumably to promote access for Dr. Hunt if and when he chose to grace the meeting with his presence.

"So, you are Aaron Brentwood's girl, I understand," Blakeley began, warmly. "What a wonderful fellow your father is," he added with sincerity. Courtney liked Blakeley right away. He was friendly and appeared to be a genuine, outgoing character. On the other hand, Fencik seemed, as her father had predicted, very stiff and distant. He made Courtney slightly uncomfortable, with his staring eyes and elusive manner.

"Yes, I am," she confirmed, smiling, not surprised that her famous father would serve as the initial focus of the interview. "And yes, I think he is wonderful, too."

"I am sure you do," Blakeley continued, pleasantly. He turned to look at Fencik. "Have you met Aaron Brentwood, John? He heads up the Department at Cornell. Good man."

"Certainly," was the extent of Fencik's response, presented as indifferently as ever. *This guy works with kids?* Courtney asked herself, jokingly. *What does he practice, sleep therapy?*

Blakeley took the lead, moving forward with the interview. He explained to Courtney that Hunt-Fisher takes what it thinks is a unique and progressive approach to the training of residents. First of all, he told her, the size of the incoming class of PGY1s is always limited to no more than eight. This is intended to achieve several objectives. First, it offers a far more intensive and intimate residency experience, since the group works together in various seminars and group supervision with the faculty. There is no chance that residents at Hunt-Fisher will find themselves unattended to. At this hospital, he noted, residents enter an environment that is much like that of an extended family. Fellow residents become, in many ways, like siblings, finding ways to support each other through their training. The faculty take on a role of mentoring aunts and uncles; they guide, teach, cajole, spark curiosity.

"I suppose John and I both play the father figure at times," Blakeley concluded. "It's an executive parenting role, though, much like we advocate with the mothers and fathers of patients on the units that John leads."

No response from Fencik, except for more staring, without emotion, and silent assessment of the future resident before him.

The sound of rapid, heavy footsteps in the hallway diverted Blakeley's attention. He turned his head toward the open conference room door, and Fencik and Courtney did the same. Before them all, in the doorway, stood a man Courtney immediately assumed was Dr. Harold Hunt. He was a smaller man than Blakeley and Fencik. He wore eyeglasses that remained near the tip of his nose, which appeared to cause him to raise his head slightly and squint at Courtney and then at the two men he employed. He, too, had no follicle activity on top of his head, but the hair he did have was white, bushy and slightly unkempt, as if he had just gotten out of bed minutes before.

"Is this where I'm supposed to be?" he practically shouted, looking directly at Courtney. Courtney did not think it was her place to reply, so she turned back towards Blakeley, expecting him to respond.

"Harold, come in, please," Blakeley said calmly, but in a way that seemed to Courtney like a slightly patronizing invitation a family doctor might give to one of his elderly patients. "Yes, this is our one o'clock meeting with one of the new incoming PGY1s, Dr. Courtney Brentwood."

"Dr. Corey what?" Hunt asked, appearing confused.

"No, no, Harold, it's Courtney Brentwood. By the way, you know her father."

"I do?" Hunt asked, taken slightly aback.

"Yes, she is Aaron Brentwood's daughter. You know Aaron…from Cornell…writes textbooks…didn't he serve with you and Bill Myers from Columbia on the DSM-III Committee?" The DSM, Courtney knew, was an abbreviation for Diagnostic Statistical Manual, the official standardized coding of mental illnesses in all of their observable forms. A trace of recognition showed on Hunt's face. After turning to Blakeley, he looked again at Courtney.

"Doesn't look like him, I don't think," he said curtly, eliciting a polite but nervous laugh from the three others in the room, including Courtney.

Hunt sat down at the opposite end of the conference table, so that the foursome around the table were arranged in perfect symmetry: north, south, east and west. Blakeley waited for Hunt to situate himself and show signs that he was ready for the interview to continue. He opened his mouth to begin anew with his overview of the Hunt-Fisher approach to residency training, but Hunt broke in.

"Where did you go to medical school, Brentwood?" Hunt asked.

"Temple, Dr. Hunt,"

"Temple. You're coming from Philadelphia then," he stated as a fact, rather than a question.

"Not really, sir. I live…or I grew up in Westchester. Actually, I just returned home yesterday."

"Right," he responded, now looking over to Blakeley and Fencik. After a few moments of awkward silence, he waved his hand at Blakeley. "Carry on, carry on," he urged.

Blakeley continued. "I was just starting to explain to Dr. Brentwood about how our residents get trained here. I was describing the family environment that we try to create here with all levels of medical staff."

"Uh huh," Hunt mumbled, looking inquisitively at Blakeley, then Fencik, then finally back at Courtney, as if assessing the room's emotional temperature. "Brentwood," he blurted out, to get her attention, "why did you want to train here at Hunt-Fisher?"

Damn the torpedoes, full speed ahead. Okay, here come the questions my father anticipated. "Well, I did some research, Dr. Hunt. I asked some Department leaders at Temple…"

"And your father, I'm sure," noted Fencik curtly, finally pitching in.

"Yes, and with my father, who knows you all and thinks very highly of you, I should say," she added diplomatically.

"Who is your father?" Hunt asked.

This caused another awkward silence, as Hunt started to betray the memory deficits about which she had heard so much.

Blakeley chimed in quickly, "Aaron Brentwood, Harold. We were just speaking about him, and your committee work with him on the DSM…from Cornell?"

Hunt seemed to recognize he had been caught in a senior moment. He quickly turned back to Courtney, hoping to sidestep the obvious memory lapse, and resumed looking at her intently. "So go on, what have you heard about training here? I like to know what the gossip is," he added conspiratorially, leaning in closer to her as if she would be required to whisper the secrets she had uncovered.

She opted to lighten the mood with a humorous response. "Well, for one thing, I heard the residents' cottages are bigger than a lot of most newlyweds first homes."

Blakeley laughed out loud, Fencik managed a slight grin. But old Hunt wanted more. "Come on, what do they say in Philadelphia about our little asylum?"

"Really, Dr. Hunt, the place has a wonderful reputation, yours, Dr. Blakeley's and Dr. Fencik's," nodding to each of them as she mentioned their names. "Temple, as you may know, Dr. Blakeley, does a lot of research in psychosomatic behavior because of some pioneering work by Ronald French." Dr. Ronald French was another father figure in psychiatry, like Harold Hunt, and he had been a Department Chairman at Temple for over forty years, from the late 20's through the 60's. Dropping his name, she thought, would impress.

"Is that old coot still kicking?" Harold asked her. Dr. French was about his age, maybe even older.

"Yes, he is. And he still does a lecture or two a year around Temple."

Hunt wanted more dirt. "Do they think we're out of touch here? You know, old fashioned, too analytic, not contemporary?" he asked.

"I didn't hear that, sir," Courtney responded, honestly.

Hunt did not believe her, and let out a grunt of disapproval, as if he had heard enough niceties. He wanted to hear something provocative, something that reinforced his expectation that the field had strong opinions, both positive and negative, about his little facility in the woods. He preferred that the place with his name on it be a tad controversial, following the public relations adage that it is better when you are being talked about, even if it is in a derogatory way, than when you are being disregarded altogether.

He silently signaled Blakeley to resume.

Blakeley now seemed even more congenial to her, perhaps warmed by her compliments. He spent some time reviewing how the incoming PGY1 class was outstanding this year, having been drawn from prestigious medical schools all over the northeast. He spoke of how faculty members remain with Hunt-Fisher even when lured by other institutions, because of its collegiality and intimate, small college-type atmosphere.

When Blakeley stopped, Fencik joined in. He wanted to know what questions Courtney had about her training curriculum. She had several prepared, particularly about the type of units to which she would be assigned in her first year or residency. Fencik explained that all PGY1s start on one of three first-year required clinical rotations, to which they were randomly assigned: a six week stint on the hospital's drug and alcohol treatment unit, a six month period on an acute treatment unit and about four and a half months working on what Hunt-Fisher Hospital called an admitting unit. This was a treatment program that evaluated patients for a short period of time, then transferred them to a separate unit, once the evaluation established which program best suited their current problems.

Courtney then asked what she thought was a savvy question: "How do the insurance companies respond to the hospital spending five days evaluating patients and then transferring them to another unit to begin treatment? I have heard they are getting very aggressive about how long patients stay in the hospital."

Hunt sat up in his chair as if suddenly prodded from behind.

"You've got to fight those managed care bastards, do you hear me?" he said, angrily.

Oops. Insurance and managed care. Perhaps I shouldn't have gone there.

Blakeley tried to mitigate Hunt's overwrought response to her question. He preferred to address her question with more academic deportment.

"Harold speaks for all of us in acknowledging our low regard for this phenomenon called managed care, where the decisions our physicians make after years of training—the type of training you are about to spend four years of your life receiving, I must add—are challenged, second-guessed and often overridden by nurses or social workers, some of whom have never set foot inside a psychiatric facility. One doctor of ours told us recently that during his first concurrent review with one of these managed care companies, he asked the alleged doctor what his specialty was, and the guy had told him he was a chiropractor! Imagine that! However, having said that," he said, nodding in deference to Hunt, "I think your question is a good one. And one that we have begun talking more about at the senior clinical level here at Hunt-Fisher. We have to keep up with the national and regional reimbursement trends, or our institution will almost certainly pass into obscurity."

Fencik was quick to agree, and he spent several minutes explaining the insurance realities of child and adolescent treatment, including the backhanded benefit that could now open up, offering the hospital a chance to develop some after-school programs and other outpatient services on grounds, programs that the hospital could never initiate before because no insurance company would pay for any care except inpatient hospitalization and a few office visits to a therapist. Fencik's newfound verbosity seemed odd to Courtney at first, until she started to sense that he, and probably Blakeley too, were speaking more to Hunt than to her. They were working the old guy a little bit, presenting ideas and views that would probably come up again in subsequent hospital strategic planning discussions.

"I want this place to fight them, these insurance charlatans," Hunt responded, a scowl never leaving his face. He was making his position known. Like Blakeley and Fencik, he was not just responding to a question posed by a new PGY1. He was reinforcing the institution's mission to his two chief lieutenants.

"We can't be bullied. We won't be bullied. Or," Hunt went on, "the whole purpose of Hunt-Fisher goes down the toilet."

Courtney observed that she seemed to be entering her residency at a time of upheaval in the way hospital care was financed. But then she steered the conversation elsewhere. She asked how how the training program supervised new residents' work. By the time Blakeley and Fencik had responded at length to this question, Hunt was getting antsy. He rose to leave.

"Good luck, Brently," he said, merging her two names, as he moved over next to her to shake her hand. "Welcome to Hunt-Fisher. And don't forget what I said about those managed care types, okay? You listening?" he demanded to know, eyeing her intently but sounding less hostile.

"Yes, sir," Courtney responded, "I hear you loud and clear."

"Good. It's going to be war, so we need some fighters for the battles ahead." He turned toward Blakeley and Fencik. "I'm excused, I hope," he said.

"Thanks for joining us, Harold," Blakeley said, continuing to demonstrate a pleasant, diplomatic manner. Hunt disappeared out the open door.

Blakeley suggested a tour of the hospital. Fencik agreed, and they got up to leave. Courtney asked for a short break, requesting directions to the Ladies Room in the Cottage. The coffee had gone right through her, and she thought it prudent to break up the interview schedule a bit. Her ulterior motive was that she figured if Blakeley and Fencik got wrapped up in some other business for a time during her bathroom break, she would have to spend a bit less time with them. *That would be a good thing.*

This prediction proved accurate. It was a full fifteen minutes before they reconvened. Blakeley started the tour by giving her a little more background about the origins of the hospital. He reviewed the history of the founders, Dr. Carl Hunt and his partner Dr. Fred Fisher. The hospital used to be the classic country asylum, the property having been willed to Hunt and Fisher by a wealthy gentleman farmer, who had lost a son to madness and suicide. It was to become a world unto itself, where the mentally ill came, in essence, for a vacation from life. Blakeley laughed as he affirmed her father's premise that it was difficult now to get thirty days coverage in the hospital, much less many years.

They moved on through wide hallways, where Blakeley described works of art that hung on the walls, or antique furniture that added considerable elegance to the interior design. One print hanging on a nearby wall seemed particularly arresting to Fencik. He peered at the print closely, spending time studying the painting by a seventeenth century Italian artist, showing mother and child. Fencik drew Courtney to the picture and asked her what she thought of it.

"It's nice," she said, a simple response that obviously disappointed Fencik.

"Doesn't this mother and child seem emotionally disconnected from each other to you?"

It's a freaking painting from the 1600s, there, Leonardo. What do you expect?

"Isn't that just the way they would pose for a painting back then?" Courtney asked instead, maintaining her diplomacy.

"Never make those kind of assumptions in art…or with patients either, Dr. Brentwood," Fencik admonished her lightly. "You have to read things, go beneath the surface, think about the hidden meanings," he added.

Lara would like this guy, Courtney thought. Her mind drifted to Jason and her, the two of them together in California, probably making plans for how they would handle his last year in medical school. He would be calling her later, she reminded herself.

She wished Jason was there with her. Fencik's pompous attitude offered an easy target for their shared sense of humor. Jason would call him some new California beach slang term that denigrated his lack of charm or common sense, his condescending attitude, and ultimately, his very manhood. The terms themselves changed a lot, but the meanings were essentially the same. Thinking about Jason brought a smile to Courtney's face, which Fencik noticed.

"I see that you are understanding me," Fencik said, seemingly convinced he had elicited a grateful response from this new trainee, and proud that he was able to show Courtney how well he would fulfill his academic role.

"You're so right," Courtney replied, saying this with a subtle, sardonic edge that she knew Jason would have silently but knowingly appreciated.

Blakeley suggested they head outside, to give Courtney a sense of the entire campus. Courtney readily agreed to this offer; she could use some fresh air. The stuffiness around where she stood was starting to bother her.

Nathan and Cecelia

Chapter 5

Pulling his aging Jeep Cherokee into the staff lot at the Hunt-Fisher Psychiatric Hospital, Nathan Bigelow was able to find a spot easily about halfway down the line of cars parked closest to the hospital's East Entrance. He sat there, in no hurry to emerge from his vehicle and head in to work, listening to the New York radio sports talk show hosts dole out their opinions about the Mets' manager and decisions he had made about changing pitchers in the previous game. While it had all worked out, because the Mets had won, the fans were still giving the manager an earful, through the intermediary of the show's knowledgeable commentators. Nathan could have lingered longer, listening to his fellow fans' viewpoints, because his 3:00pm to 11:00pm shift did not begin for another twenty minutes, and he knew it took him no more than five minutes to get from his car to the unit's locked front door. But when the show broke for commercials, he decided to get moving. By relieving one of his fellow workers a little early, maybe they would reciprocate his courtesy some time in the future.

Walking toward the entrance ahead of him, he turned to check out a pretty young woman leaving the hospital whom he had never seen before. She was walking with Dr. Blakeley, the big-shot Medical Director, and some other doctor whose name Nathan did not know but about whom he already had formed an impression. The guy had led a case conference on the unit where Nathan worked, and he had come across to Nathan as a real pretentious ass.

Looks like we have some talent coming in with the new class of residents, he remarked to himself, staring at Courtney's appealing presence for several seconds. Finally turning to walk through the entrance door, Nathan headed toward Unit 3 East, an acute treatment where he had worked as a psychiatric technician for nearly four years. He reached for the set of keys in his pocket, which, once taken out, hung loosely on a long chain fastened to one of the belt loops on his trousers. Coming to the unit's locked front door, he stopped short to take a deep breath.

Another day with the loony tunes, he thought, exhaling the breath with effect. He was encouraged only by the fact that he would not have to work for the next five days. He had arranged his schedule to take his two allotted days off for this calendar week over the next two days, then he would follow these with his Fourth of July holiday, and then he would use the two days off he had coming for the following week after these three. So, once he made it through this day's shift, he would have Thursday through Monday completely off, and he would not have to return to work until Tuesday afternoon at three o'clock in the afternoon. A nice five day mini-vacation. He was a little burned out, and felt like he needed this extended break.

He also thought about how, as soon as he was recognized walking on the unit, he would be quickly accosted, and asked to respond to all types of questions and comments by any number of the unit's patients. Two, in particular, were likely to be lying in wait on the other side of the door. Joe Morse and Tim Harris had taken a particular liking to him. Over the past few days, as he came on duty to work the evening shift, they had been camped out down the hallway from about two-thirty on.

Joe Morse was a young black man from Bridgeport, twenty-four years old, who seemed to complain of delusions and hearing voices only when he was behind in his rent or when his girlfriend kicked him out of their apartment. He was the loudest and most boisterous patient on Unit 3 East, by far. This was his third admission to Hunt-Fisher in the past two years, and he was wearing out his welcome.

As Nathan opened the door, he saw Tim Harris further down the hallway, seated and reading. Tim was a local Norwalk resident, also in his mid-twenties. He lived with his wealthy, executive parents, struggling whenever he made an effort to separate from them. He had been rescued from taking an overdose of pills by an alert neighbor who, while walking his dog, saw Tim collapse on the yard in front of his suburban home. Tim had claimed he was going for help himself, after changing his mind about acting on his self-destructive impulses.

On 3 East, every staff member was assigned to focus on the behavior and complaints of a few designated patients. The strategy was that the core treatment team who worked during the day—psychiatrists, psychologists and social workers—needed to hear about how patients behaved when they were not around, from the nursing staff who were always there, 24/7/365.

Tim was one of the patients about whom Nathan was assigned to report. Joe was not.

"Yo, Nathan, man," Joe called out once he spotted Nathan entering the unit, "check it out. I put my notice in, man. And don't you try to talk me out of it."

Joe was referring to the legal method patients had at their disposal to submit a formal request to be discharged, after which the staff had seventy-two hours to decide if they should commit the patient to the hospital or agree to the request for discharge, basing this decision ostensibly on whether the patient posed a suicidal or other type of societal threat.

"Get down off the back of that chair, Joe," Nathan said with a serious tone, pointing down at the chair's seat cushion where Joe's derriere belonged. Joe was using the top of the chair's back as a seat, and the chair's arms as foot rests. "Would you do that at home?"

Nathan was the only staff member who consistently confronted Joe on his behavior, taking every opportunity he could to call Joe on the undisciplined way he conducted his life, never letting anything pass. It was Nathan's way of making sure the rules on the unit meant something, so that other patients could not claim that Joe got away with things that they did not. But Nathan also used the tough approach with Joe as a rapport-building strategy. He sensed Joe admired people who could see through his self-defeating street behavior, and show interest in what he was really like on the inside.

"Sorry, Nathan," Joe said with sincerity. "You're right, man. My mama or old lady would kick my ass."

"We'll talk about your notice later, Joe," Nathan told him, walking by, making sure Joe complied with the order to sit in the chair correctly. "Let me get report first."

Nathan wanted to hear from the nurses what might have precipitated Joe's submission of a seventy-two hour notice. He guessed it might have been a conversation Joe had with his girlfriend earlier that day about her acquiescing to his request to return home, with promises to straighten out whatever damage he had done. Nathan had doubts about Joe's complaints about "hearin' them voices, man," symptoms that had gotten him admitted to the hospital several days before. It was not unlikely, Nathan sensed, that these "voices" were much more than self-recriminations for behavior he knew better than to do, but did anyway.

Tim was sitting next to Joe, holding his book, but he was looking to make eye contact with Nathan from the moment Nathan appeared on the unit, before Joe had usurped Nathan's attention. Tim, Nathan thought, needed to have some of Joe's assertiveness rub off on him. Yet, Tim had been getting better at asking for what he wanted, which Nathan took as a sign of real progress. For someone who seemed to get easily stuck in an indecision mode, not being able to conclude which action to take at a given point in time, about his life, his career and educational choices, or about his family and interpersonal relationships, the simple behavior of asking his 1:1 staff member for time to talk could be about as difficult a thing to do as one could imagine. But Tim was trying to perform these assertive behaviors, as his care plan dictated. He rose out of his chair as Nathan neared their seating area, and asked if he could schedule some time to talk with Nathan later in the evening.

"I think so, Tim. Let me get oriented to what is going on first before we set a specific time, though. Is that, okay?"

"Sure," Tim said, pleased that the tone of Nathan's response was so affirmative. "I'll check with you later," he declared before moving away towards his room.

Nathan entered the nursing station and walked into the back room where the unit's nursing coordinator, Emily Barnes, was preparing to go over each patient, one by one, so that she could hand off the unit to the evening charge nurse, Cecelia Reade. Another psych tech, Joan Truss, who had just started working on the unit less than a month before, also was there to listen in. Joan, Nathan could see very easily, was still highly anxious about how to handle the patients on a locked psychiatric unit. She almost always came in early for nursing report each time she was scheduled for an evening shift.

"Hi, Nathan," Emily called out warmly, seeing him enter the back room where the meeting was about to begin. "You in early to get report, too?"

"No, I'm in early because I just can't stay away from this wonderful place. There is just no other place I'd rather be," he said dryly, the sarcasm he was shooting for very evident to his fellow staff members gathered in the room.

Cecelia smiled at this comment and at him, but offered no greeting. Joan hardly noticed he was there at all. She had been hired by the hospital fresh out of Bennington, a psychology major who had never been near real mental illness before in her life, except for perhaps observing a case or two of bulimia or anorexia in fellow students at college. Joan was poring over the assignment sheet for the evening, memorizing the tasks she was being asked to perform and trying to mentally plan her shift, hour by hour.

"Joe handed in his notice a little while ago, Nathan," Emily told him, not knowing that Nathan was already aware of this news, having heard it directly from the source himself.

"Yeah, I know," Nathan said. "Is his doctor going to let him go?"

"I doubt it," Emily said, offering an experienced opinion about how Joe's psychiatrist, Chief Resident James Short, was likely to err on the side of caution and keep Joe a little longer, by committing him to the hospital against his will. Nathan concurred. The nerdy and officious Dr. Short would be concerned about the legal liability of letting Joe go. Short, Nathan guessed, did not want to risk the possibility that Joe might leave and do something illegal or impulsive, thereby causing serious scrutiny about the decision to release him. Dr. Short was not going to let an inner city readmission ruin the growing reputation he was building at the prestigious Hunt-Fisher Hospital.

Nathan liked the way Emily thought. She cared, but saw things as they were.

"You're probably right," Nathan said, shaking his head.

"Emily, do you mind going over this in report, instead of in a side conversation?" Cecelia asked, evidently feeling a bit upstaged by Nathan and the rapport Emily had with him.

"Fine," Emily responded curtly. She began her report by reviewing Joe's case, since they were talking about him. Dr. Short would be meeting with Joe at three o'clock, and the discussion was probably going to be about advising Joe to rescind the notice so that the existing treatment plan could be implemented fully. If Joe refused to take back the notice letter, Emily was fairly certain that Dr. Short would commit him.

"He's not going to like that," Nathan offered, anticipating that he was in for a loud and contentious evening attempting to cool Joe off once this message was imparted to him.

Joan chipped in, volunteering to help out. "He is one of my one-to-ones. I'll look in his chart, and then sit down with him and explain to him why he is being committed."

Emily and Nathan just looked at her, then at each other, not saying what they were thinking.

What a mismatch that will be...street-wise Joe and the prissy Bennington grad...and she is going to "explain why he being committed?" That should be interesting.

Cecelia was equally negative about having Joan create a confrontation with Joe, but for fundamentally different reasons. In Cecelia's case, it was less about avoiding the oil-and-water mixture of Joe and Joan. Cecelia, Nathan sensed, was concerned more with the potentially explosive results of this interaction to the serenity of the unit, which she needed to manage over the next eight hours or so. Further, Cecelia always liked to confront Joan's holier-than-thou, "I'm going to be a Ph.D. psychologist some day and come back here to give you orders" type of attitude. Cecelia hated having these entitled recent college graduates get hired as psych techs. She preferred having the more obedient, less educated types who knew their place and followed orders.

"Make sure you do your scheduled assignments first, Joan," Cecelia reminded her, looking to reinforce Joan's low level status on the unit, as essentially unskilled labor.

"I think you should use your time with him to listen, Joan, and make sure he is not disruptive to the other patients," Emily advised. "Let his doctor handle the explaining part."

"I *will* listen," Joan insisted. "I'll try to meet with him right after the session, when he might be the most upset," Joan declared, appearing to ignore her more experienced superiors. Another awkward silence followed.

Nathan agreed with Emily. She should just sit there and listen. Or tell Joe that if he wants to talk about it to seek her out. But not force the issue. *Another shrink wannabe, out to solve all the patients' problems with her infinite pearls of wisdom and magical therapeutic touch.*

Emily shook her head about Joan's response, but chose to move forward with her report. When she got to Tim, Nathan listened more closely. Tim was more alert and interactive, Emily noted. He was also one of Dr. Short's patients. The anti-depressant Short had prescribed for him now seemed to be taking hold. He was taking the initiative to seek out staff more.

Nathan shared that Tim had done just that with him, a few minutes prior. "I think he is a good psychotherapy case. This guy has stuff inside him he has to get out."

Cecelia noted that Dr. Short planned to follow Tim as his therapist after he left hospital. This made Nathan angry. *Why should Short continue to see Tim? Short doesn't give a shit about him. He just sees Tim as the ideal white, well-insured, upper class long term private practice case all these doctors crave.*

"I'm sure," Cecelia added, with just the slightest hint of derision, "that he plans to engage Tim in psychotherapy." This was a dig from Cecelia, Nathan sensed, about leaving the therapy work to the highly trained doctors. He made a motion to leave the meeting.

"I've got to escort the patients to the gym at three-fifteen. Have to stay on top of my assignments, right, Cecelia?" he said to his shift supervisor, with a slight edge.

Walking out of the nursing station, Nathan saw that a group of patients were already assembling there in the hallway, waiting for Nathan to emerge and walk them over to the hospital's recreational activities department. Nathan was handed a list by the Unit Clerk of patients approved for the activity. He cross-checked the list with a status sheet, making sure that each of the patients he saw assembled in front of him had earned the right to participate in this off-unit excursion.

The list checked out, and he led the group off the unit, through the halls and on outside. Nathan chatted easily with the patients: *What would they be doing at the gym today? Can you believe how gorgeous it is? Has anyone heard what's on the supper menu?*

On the way, Nathan's group came upon and passed the trio of Courtney, Blakeley and Fencik, who were returning from a tour stopover in the buildings where Nathan's group was now headed. Nathan turned to check out Courtney, who was once again listening attentively to what Blakeley and Fencik were telling her. Tim, who was one of the group on the way to the gym, noticed Nathan's admiring glance.

"I'd like *her* for my doctor," Tim said to Nathan, grinning.

It was probably inappropriate to say it, but Nathan could not resist. "If I were you, Tim, so would I."

Nathan lingered a few minutes at the gym, chatting with the recreational activities staff. He liked Dominic Vierno the most. Falling into the "it's a small world" category, Dominic had known Nathan's high school baseball coach. The two of them had played ball together in the 60's at Pelham High School, in Westchester County. So Dominic and Nathan had hit it off quickly. The conversation moved from the Mets' pennant chances to Nathan's upcoming days off.

"Any plans to go away?" Dominic asked him.

"Yeah, me and an old buddy of mine are going to go camping up in the Berkshires. Beartown State Forest, in Great Barrington. Ever heard of it?"

"No, you know, I don't go for that camping shit," Dominic responded, lowering his voice to make sure the patients could not hear his profanity. "I'm a city boy. I'd rather go to Vegas or A.C., do a little gambling, hang out by the pool with a G and T in my hand, you know what I'm saying?"

"I can do that too," Nathan said, lying a little. The problem was not his aversion to the gambling environment. It was just that, on a psych tech salary, Nathan had absolutely no extra money to put at risk on a blackjack table. His upcoming trip was on budget. Camping fees at Beartown were $5.00 for the day. And he was splitting that cost with his friend.

Phyllis Cimo, another RT, or Recreational Therapist, came over to join the conversation. Dominic and Phyllis were dating. This type of intra-staff romantic relationship was prohibited on the treatment units, but for some reason—Nathan was not sure why—the RTs did not have to abide by the same rules. Maybe it was that the patients experienced the staff on the locked unit differently than those they only saw for a few hours every week, at most. It still did not seem fair to Nathan, though.

"Phyllis, you taking the patients outside today?" Nathan asked.

"No, it's too hot," she said. "The docs say the sun doesn't mix well with their medications, in some cases. Better safe than sorry."

"That's too bad. It's so nice out." The three of them chatted some more, but Nathan needed to return to the unit, and Dominic and Phyllis had a group of patients waiting for them.

"Have a good time up there with the bears," Dominic joked, bidding him well, imagining that in a park named Beartown, these animals were likely to be roaming around Nathan's camping spot indiscriminately. Nathan laughed, waving at him to show his mock disgust about Dominic's myopic urban perspective.

It was the kind of day that made Nathan want to amble very slowly back to the unit, extending his time outdoors. The unit was like another world, he thought, so cut off from the environment outside the locked door. *Just look how nice it is out here, so peaceful and calm.* Yet, his intuition told him that trouble lay ahead this evening. Joe was going to be pissed off about having his seventy-two hour notice rejected. Nathan would have to try to talk him down, keep him under wraps, at least until eleven o'clock. After that, Nathan was out of there for five days, and as far as he was concerned, the place could go to hell in a hand basket, at least until the following Tuesday.

Nathan's sense of foreboding turned out to be well-founded. When he arrived back on the unit, Joe was pacing up and down in the middle of the hall, clearly agitated.

"Yo, Nathan, man, they're making me stay. They say I'm dangerous. Do I look dangerous to you? What kind of bullshit is this?" Before Nathan could respond, Cecelia poked her head out of the nursing station door to assess what was going on in the hallway. She stepped just outside the door, and called down to him, "Joe, that kind of language is inappropriate. You need to get yourself under better control."

Joe was not listening. He wanted to plead his case to Nathan.

"Nathan, man, I gotta get out of here. My old lady needs help with our son. He's sick and she needs me around to help with him while she goes to work. Her mother is old, and can't stay awake to watch over the boy. Nathan, I'm serious, man, I gotta leave. Can't you do something?"

"Let's sit down," Nathan suggested, not telling him that the answer was a definite "no." He motioned to Joe to have a seat in the chair where he had been when Nathan first came on the unit. Nathan sat where Tim had been sitting earlier.

Joe was frustrated, but he seemed relieved that he finally had someone he trusted to whom he could lay out his case, someone who would listen without giving him the feeling his life did not matter. He began by insisting his motivations to leave the hospital right away were honorable. The way Joe saw it, his wanting to leave was a sign he was maturing, willing to show some responsibility, being a man. The voices he had complained about when he sought admission were not there anymore. He was trying to do the right thing. His girlfriend and their son needed him. This place did not understand what it is like to have no money and have to do what you can to survive. Joe, the fast-talking man from the street, the loudest patient on the unit, had grown somber. Nathan thought he actually saw Joe's eyes welling up with tears. Nathan believed him that his girlfriend required his parental assistance. And Nathan saw no evidence he was psychotic or delusional. Maybe Short was just teaching Joe a lesson, that he could not just admit himself to and then discharge himself from this hospital as he pleased. Maybe Short wanted him to hurt a little, to see that he could not just work the system, based on his personal preferences or circumstances. Maybe Short was affirming that once Joe applied for and was granted admission at Hunt-Fisher, there was a new Sheriff in town. Sheriff Short. He held the keys to the jailhouse, and he was dangling them in front of Joe, taunting the inmate sadistically. Joe would get out when the omnipotent Sheriff Short decided, not before.

Nathan did not really know if Joe was truly delusional or not. He suspected that the reality lay somewhere between Joe's denial and Short's insistence that he was still psychotic. But Nathan's gut feeling was that the guy could walk out of the hospital that evening and take good care of his boy, while his girlfriend worked. It did not happen often, because he had seen so much in three plus years working in this freak palace, but Nathan felt a surge of sincere pity for Joe at that moment. Joe was hurting for sure; this was no act.

Joan walked over to where they were talking. She wanted to follow up on her plan to meet with her 1:1, since it was her responsibility—clearly specified in the grid on a clipboard in the nursing station. She might be asked to report on his condition to Dr. Short and the rest of the senior staff she so admired—and whose professional stature she planned to emulate some day.

"Joe," she interrupted, standing in between Nathan and Joe, "I'd like to meet with you this evening to talk about your notice and Dr. Short's decision not to release you. Is now a good time?"

Nathan reached up with his right hand, trying to rub away the tension around his eyes that Joan had just caused. He knew what Joe's reaction would be, and it was not going to be pretty. He could not believe the poor timing of this stupid bitch. *Joan shit-for-brains Truss. Here it comes…Joe's going to verbally lay her out…*

"Can't you see Nathan and I are talking?" Joe retorted, angrily, but not much louder than he was when talking to Nathan. "What would I want to meet with you for?"

Joan, while clearly detesting the insolent reaction she had received, was determined to do her sworn duty. "Joe," she replied, an anxious edge to her voice, "I am your one-to-one nursing staff member and it is my responsibility…"

Before she could finish, Joe blew. "I don't give a shit about no one-to-fucking-one. Get out of my face, girl," he shouted, waving her away. He was still sitting, but moving more upright in his chair.

Cecelia was now out in the hall again. Nathan observed her anxiety, and predicted her reaction. She had asked Joe earlier to remain in control, and he had not been able to abide by her request. A limit needed to be set, or the whole milieu would collapse, in her opinion. And she did not want him causing the whole unit to be on edge for the entire shift, of which she was in charge.

"Joe, I am going to have to ask you to go to the Quiet Room, *now*. You are out of control. We'll keep the door open, but you need to de-escalate."

Nathan was torn. He had things under control, until idiot Joan had interrupted them for no reason. He asked to speak to Cecelia in the nursing station. She said no, he needed to help escort Joe to the Quiet Room. Nathan asked again, with more insistence. Cecelia showed impatience with him, for his unwillingness to simply follow her orders. The answer was still "no."

Nathan turned back at Joe, whom he sensed was ready to explode. "Joe, how about we move to the Quiet Room, and we continue to talk there."

Cecelia disagreed. "Joe, I don't think you should be talking to staff from the Quiet Room. The door will be open, but you should be by yourself for a time, to think about what you need to do to regain control."

"But I'm not out of control, you stupid bitch," Joe yelled. He tried to continue to explain how he and Nathan were having a nice quiet talk until Joan had jumped between them for no reason. But Cecelia's face was now red with anger. It was hammer time.

"I want him down, on the ground," she exclaimed, pointing to the floor. "I'll sound the buzzer."

Cecelia went in to the nursing station to push an alarm button that summoned muscular help to the unit from other units. Nathan was feeling the whole situation was totally absurd, like it was out of a Cuckoo's Nest-type movie or something. He went over to Joe and asked him to lie down, that he would stay with him. Joan knelt down, wrapped her arms around Joe's leg as he stood there. She was not trying to bring him to the floor; she just knelt there, with her head down self-protectively, hanging on like a five year old girl trying to keep a mother from deserting her on the first day of kindergarten. Nathan's guess was that this was her way of showing that she did her part in physical restraints of patients, and no one could tell her differently.

Joe looked down at Joan, clinging to one of his legs. He shook his head, and turned to look back at Nathan. His eyes conveyed a combination of fear, anger, bewilderment and slight amusement. "Why couldn't they just leave us the fuck alone, Nathan?" he asked in anguish.

"I'll stay with you, Joe. Let's go." Nathan tapped Joan on the shoulder, signaling her to release Joe's leg, then he started to walk him to the seclusion room.

"Wait for help, Nathan," Cecelia insisted sternly. "I want him carried. It is not safe to move him yet."

"I think it's all right. You'll be cool, right Joe?"

Cecelia was not buying it. "I SAID it's not safe to move him."

The unit's front door opened abruptly and several very large men piled in, winded from the run to the unit, there to save the day.

Joe had been arrested by the police before, and he knew when it was best just to surrender to much stronger forces. The gig was up. He lay himself down, head first toward the unit's carpeting, and mumbled something about the staff being crazier than any of the patients. As the men held him down, awaiting instructions from Cecelia, Joe turned his head to the side, a wry smile on his face, and said, "Hey, I heard a good one today. You know how you can tell the patients from the staff in this place? The patients get better!"

Joe was relocated to the seclusion room, the room's door closed and locked. Joan was assigned to observe him constantly through a small window in the door. The situation was now under control. As the men who had created the show of force left to return to their respective units, Cecelia asked Nathan to join her in the back of the nursing station, alone. After Nathan trailed her in, she closed the door behind him.

"Nathan, you were working against me out there," she scolded him. "Don't you understand that we can't give the patients mixed messages? You were close to being insubordinate."

"Why, because I asked to talk to you in the nursing station, to explain what happened? Fucking Joan escalated him, for no reason. She was rude, for God's sake. Joe and I were sitting there, talking, and she puts her butt in my face and tells Joe he has to meet with her. She's an idiot." Nathan's face was flushed, his voice raised an octave or two higher than usual.

"Nathan, I'm not talking about Joan. I'm taking about you, and what you said and did out there. I'm in charge, Nathan. This unit is my responsibility. I am a licensed professional and you are not. If something happens here, it's me that gets called down to Miss Herlihan's office, to explain what happened and what actions I took. Do you understand? I can't have you sabotaging my direct orders. Understood?"

Nathan just stood there silently, eyes averted toward the wall, his lips pursed together, smirking, in an effort to hold back the comments that were on her mind.

"Understood?" she asked again.

"I hear you, Cecelia," he replied, barely disguising his disgust, with her and everything that had just happened.

"Good," Cecelia said, oblivious to his emotional response. Nathan felt he had been dismissed. He turned to leave the room, reaching for the door.

"Oh, and Nathan...," she said before he could open the door, her voice now softer and intimate, reaching her hand over and putting it on his. "You're coming over, tonight, right?"

Chapter 6

After his eight hour shift was over, Nathan went to his Jeep and waited, listening to a wrap-up show on the radio about the Mets game that evening. Frankie Viola had won his 11th, 5-2 over the Cardinals in St. Louis, John Franco getting the save. The Mets had now won nine in a row. Nathan was getting really pumped up about how his favorite team had turned things around under new manager Bud Harrelson. The announcers were insisting there would be juice flowing out at Shea all summer, as the Mets battled the Pirates for first place in the National League East. Nathan loved when the Mets were in contention. He was even trying to arrange a trip for the staff to go out to Shea for a game as a group, maybe some time later in mid-summer, to do a little informal team-building away from the stressful halls of Hunt-Fisher.

Cecelia had pissed him off, jumping ugly with him for trying to talk her out of restraining Joe. What a tyrant she had been. *Oh well. At least I'm going to have sex with her tonight.* She was too cute to stay mad at. And what an ass she had, firm and round from years of skiing in her native Vermont. It was the single best trophy ass at the hospital, and Nathan felt flattered that she would risk her job to give it to him. Man, he was ready for her to come out those doors. A twenty minute ride home to her place, a few glasses of wine to wind down and free up their inhibitions a bit, and then it would be time to get naked. *Let's go, Cecelia...what the heck is keeping you?*

The Jeep faced the East Entrance directly, so Nathan was in a prime position to monitor the hospital's evening shift departees, at a safe, discreet distance. Sometimes a staff member he knew would see him in his car and wave, and he would have to act like he was busy arranging something in his glove compartment, or appear as if he was looking for something in his passenger seat before preparing for the trip home. A few times in the past few months he had actually driven off the hospital grounds, before Cecelia had come out, just to fool a fellow staff member who had spotted him, who might suspect that he was secretly waiting for a prohibited rendezvous with a female staff member. He would leave the grounds behind the potential spy, only to veer off once outside the hospital's gates, do a u-turn in a neighborhood resident's driveway, and return to his previous vantage point as inconspicuously as he could. What a joke, he thought, this whole charade that he and Cecelia were playing. Just because some shrink thought it was "inappropriate" for staff members to date each other, because it somehow sent unhealthy messages to the patients, or something. As he thought about it, Nathan considered what the male patients would think if they knew he and Cecelia were lovers. *Probably they would be jealous as hell. All the young men patients have a complete hard on for her. And a couple of the doctors, too.* He had even noticed Tim trying to flirt with her a little tonight. *I like Tim, he's such a good guy. I hope he finds a way to dump Dr. Short, that shithead. He's such a nerdy freakin' wimp. I'd like to smack that uppity little....* Nathan was revved up. It was partly from the excitement and emotional roller coaster of the evening shift he had just finished, and partly from the prospect of having Cecelia's gorgeous ass in his hands within a short period of time.

Just then, the door he was staking out opened, and Cecelia's pretty face appeared. He watched her walk towards her car, pull her keys out of the handbag she was carrying, and use them to open the door to her new Honda Accord. Just before she dropped down to enter the driver's seat, she turned her head toward his Jeep, gracing him with a conspiratorial smile. *Let's get moving, there Cece, the bed's waiting.*

Their lovemaking that night was urgent and one-sided. Nathan took command from the beginning, Cecelia willingly acceding to his aggression. It was a noisy session, with Cecelia below, vigorously urging Nathan on. At the act's end, they were both drenched in sweat, which created a slippery lubrication between them that only intensified the pleasure of skin rubbing and thrusting against skin. Nathan finally sank down beside her, kissing her breast and shoulder on the way, and waited until Cecelia, still panting, could regain her breath.

Once composed, Cecelia made her own assertive move, abruptly rolling on top of him, everything from her naked waist down covering their counterparts of his anatomy; her torso, highlighted by firm breasts that Nathan now eyed with desire, rose up above him, supported by arms in a push-up position, one hand on each side of his head.

"Nathan, baby," she said, her skin still beading up with perspiration, the satisfaction in her eyes telling him he had performed magnificently, "that was so…intense…" She smiled deviously at him. "I have to bawl you out more often." Then she dipped down to kiss him, the nipples of her breasts that Nathan had been admiring so ardently descending to brush against his moist chest.

He did not laugh, or even smile, at her attempted humor. He felt like she was putting him in his place, once again. But the sex had been far too gratifying to brood about any silly workplace confrontation. He returned the kiss, then re-exerted control of the encounter by reaching near his ears, grabbing her wrists and pulling her arms out from under her, so that she plopped down flat on him.

"You're not mad at me, are you?" she asked with transparent coyness, her smiling face now mere centimeters from his.

Cecelia instincts were to leverage this post-coital intimacy, to smooth things over between them, and move on. *Nathan does not understand my professional requirements and the rapid judgment calls I need to make to keep the unit secure,* Cecelia insisted to herself. *I was just acting professionally, and he had resisted my orders.* But for now, well after work and with some wine distancing her from the realities of 3 East, Cecelia had neither the interest nor the energy to process the whole episode with him.

When Nathan took the bait, and asked, rhetorically, "How could I stay mad at you?" Cecelia smiled to herself. She felt him reaching down, lightly spanking and then grabbing a hold on the part of her anatomy that she knew so provoked his desire.

Cecelia liked that Nathan touched and admired her butt so much. She knew that she drew leering downward glances whenever she walked by or away from men. It satisfied a need she had to draw their attention. Sometimes, she was compelled to turn and confirm the lusting gazes she was attracting. She agreed with Nathan that her butt was her best physical attribute. It made the thrice-weekly toning and step classes at the fitness center she attended so religiously well worth the effort.

They slept holding each other, naked and wet through the muggy night, choosing to keep the windows to her apartment bedroom open, allowing in a light, warm breeze. They used only a single bed sheet to cover themselves, preferring this arrangement to having a chilling air conditioner undo the body heat they had generated.

When they awoke in the early morning, Nathan was fully aroused, ready for round two. The morning sex was more even-handed, and lacking the fury of their after-work romp. But it was very satisfying to Nathan, who was about to leave town for the next four days, and took great pleasure in fully depleting his supply of libidinous energy.

He was going to enjoy himself in the woods. And he was not fretting too much about the prospect of not seeing Cecelia for a few days. It was a nice arrangement the two of them had, Nathan thought. Cecelia was very caught up with her job and profession, belonging to an inordinate amount of committees and task forces around the hospital, activities that reinforced a career strategy to maintain maximum visibility there, offering her constant networking with nurses and doctors who might recommend her for any future promotional opportunities that might arise. Between her investment in professional advancement and the *verboten* nature of their relationship, they spent little time together acting like a normal dating couple. They had snuck off together on weekend getaways to New York, Providence and even Quebec City, Canada when their off-duty schedules had synchronized. But they never went out anywhere near the hospital, to eat or see a movie, for fear of being observed together in public by fellow staff members or faculty physicians. He liked being with her, and he loved the noisy sex, but he knew that this was not a permanent pairing. He asked her often if she was getting skittish about breaching the hospital rules to be with him, offering to do the honorable thing and break off their post-work coupling. But she expressed no interest in discontinuing the arrangement. Nathan sensed Cecelia got a vicarious thrill out of pulling something over on the hospital officials to whom she sucked up so deferentially. *Hey, it's her call. I'll ride this as long as it feels right, and she is game.*

Or, he predicted, until she comes to her senses and puts a stop to it.

Dave Shoenfeld, who was joining Nathan on the trek to Beartown State Forest, had been a close friend of his since high school. Dave was a large, thick man. All of six foot four, Dave stood three inches taller than Nathan, and he outweighed Nathan by probably fifty pounds, tipping the scales at a good 240. Dave had a dark skin tone and a thick mane of black hair that made him look Italian, even though he was half Jewish and half eastern European. An all-Fairfield pitcher in high school, Dave built a name for himself in the area as a big left-hander who threw heat and a biting curve, pitches selected by Nathan, in most cases, as his battery mate. Dave's high school and junior legion pitching performances had attracted the interest of many big league scouts, but his parents, never really finding his professional baseball dreams credible, pushed him toward college. The college years at George Washington University in DC—or really, just one year of actual enrollment prior to his academic disqualification—had not gone well for Dave; lots of partying, little studying, missed classes, ducked exams, getting kicked off the baseball team for academic ineligibility, never throwing one pitch in competition despite his being the school's primary baseball recruit. Dave's underachievement in the classroom belied his intellectual gifts. He was probably the single smartest person Nathan had ever met, including the academic types at the hospital who liked to show off their intellect so overtly. Dave could speak about a wide range of topics, from politics to sports to popular culture. His opinions were strong and mostly reasonable, if occasionally under-informed, but presented with confident assurance and a natural propensity for the dialectic argument. He made connections with people very easily, as if the stranger he was meeting had been an intimate friend all his life. It was a gift Nathan admired because he shared this skill as well, perhaps to a slightly lesser degree. When the two of them were younger and went out on the town around the waterfront bars in South Norwalk, they invariably developed rapid camaraderie with new people, often including the best looking available women.

Nathan always thought of Dave as a real character, an interesting study in contrasts. The dichotomy extended beyond the "college dropout who was also an intellectual" example. He was a hip, contemporary guy who happened to like 50's doo-wop music—The Five Satins, The Belmonts, The Teenagers. Unlike anyone Nathan knew from his generation, Dave listened faithfully to WCBS-FM, New York's oldies station. He sang along to the radio when they drove together, knowing every one of the old songs' words by heart.

He was a chain smoker, but was one who liked to run and work out. He kept up with Nathan during their jogs together, somehow finding some reserves of oxygen usually to outsprint Nathan as they completed their workout.

Finally, he was known as a legendary partier, but, at least for now, he did not drink. Dave was in Alcoholics Anonymous, sticking with it now for two years, after years of immoderate drug and alcohol abuse. He had been arrested in 1988, for trespassing at a construction site in Norwalk, passed out sleeping on bags of concrete, with a blue synthetic tarpaulin pulled over him as a blanket. He had absolutely no idea how had gotten there, or why he chose to crash at a construction site instead of heading home. "God watches over drunks," he said, "and maybe that was the night I would have run off the road and killed myself or another person." His arrest spurred some court-ordered counseling and mandatory attendance at AA meetings. He had begun the program in order to wipe the arrest off his record, but now his attendance was more voluntary.

His sobriety was an intrinsic part of his life at this point. Dave went to the meetings in church basements, listened to the speakers, even telling his own story of addiction and recovery to the groups in open meetings, from time to time. He had a firm grasp on his personal powerlessness over alcohol. Down deep, he had long since given up the notion that there might still be a way for him to drink without getting into as much trouble as he had in the past. His sponsor in AA, a former professional boxer known as "Nasty Steve" Hirsch, focused on this fundamental issue with him, over and over again, in their telephone conversations. Hirsch, a man who was once one fight away from battling for the heavyweight boxing crown, losing to Ken Norton by knockout in the final round of their title-qualifying bout, had spent several years after the lost opportunity in self-imposed exile, drinking to cope with the remorse he felt behind his failure. Steve would always threaten, in a way Dave hoped was not serious, that he was ready to "throw him such a beating" if he missed any scheduled meetings. Now a dozen years sober, Nasty Steve had prodded Dave to keep his body coming to the "rooms," and, sure enough, his mind had followed.

Dave had more behavioral health problems than just his alcoholism. He was also prone to fits of depression, along with, he would quip to Nathan, "a double shot of anxiety on the side." These psychological problems dated back, he now recognized, to his adolescence, perhaps even to his childhood. He had always been antsy, practically jumping out of his skin during times when he was required to sit for a long stretch. This anxiety had contributed, no doubt, to his poor performance in school and college. His tendency to provoke his teachers did not help matters either, especially when these adversarial encounters were combined with erratic class attendance and non-compliance with required course assignments.

Nathan talked to Dave frequently, and when Nathan decided he had wanted to get away from Norwalk during his mini-vacation, and seizing on the idea of a trip to the Berkshires to douse his job-related burnout, his first thought was to invite Dave along. Dave would be able to roam around the park, exercise a little by paddling a kayak across the lake or hike through the State Forest, smoke at will, as long as he was careful to thoroughly extinguish his butts. They would eat junky food, tell stories, even howl at the moon if they wanted to. There would be no one else around to express any disapproval.

Once invited, Dave was all for it, even offering to drive. Nasty Steve approved, especially since Nathan, a social drinker, had no need to bring along alcohol on the trip. They conceived a plan that included loading a rented double kayak onto Dave's Isuzu, bringing a tent for cover but maybe sleeping under the stars if they could, getting up whenever they wanted, and, mainly, just relaxing. There was plenty to do just beyond the State Forest, in Lee and Lenox, if they wanted to reconnect with civilization. Nathan had been to Beartown twice when he was younger, and he considered it holy ground for stress reduction and short-term isolation from life's petty annoyances.

It was drizzling in Norwalk when they started their trip, in mid-afternoon, but the weather report was promising for the next day and the weekend. They took Route 7 all the way up to Massachusetts, then turned onto Route 132 and headed right into the park. The trip took less than two hours. Nathan had pre-reserved a camping spot by mail, so after finding the Ranger's Office just before it closed for the day, and paying the balance of the modest park fees beyond the initial deposit Nathan had sent in, they headed into the State Forest to set up camp.

Dave was in a good mood. He had arranged, like Nathan, for five days off. They would each have to work on the Fourth of July to compensate, but once away in the Berkshires, they both agreed it was well worth it. Dave worked at a fitness gym in South Norwalk, managing the various class schedules, wiping off the Nautilus machines, working at the front desk, laundering and folding towels to give out to members. He hated the tedium of the labor, but Nasty Steve thought it was good for his humility, at least for the time being. The wages were ridiculously low, but he had a tidy inheritance from being the beneficiary of his parents' life insurance policies, after their deaths in rapid succession in 1988. He worked enough hours to qualify for the gym's health insurance plan, which Dave found was reason enough to stay at it.

They hiked from the Izusu out to a clearing, toting the light double kayak above them, backpacks slung over their shoulders. The park's central feature, Benedict Pond, was straight ahead. They drew close, dropped the kayak in the water, threw their gear inside, and paddled along the shore to the farthest end of the pond, thinking it best to distance themselves as much as they could from the park entrance, where more human activity was likely to interfere with the isolation and serenity they were seeking. After setting up a tent at an allotted site, they brought out sandwiches, bags of chips and salsa, and bottled water they had purchased along Route 7. The rain that had followed them to about Danbury had remained stopped, but it was still muggy and damp—not the best conditions for the start of their camping journey. But, they both figured, it was far better to be wet and damp where they were, in the solitude of the Massachusetts woods, rather than being in Norwalk, working at menial jobs, taking orders from others, just getting by.

In these instances when Nathan began a few days off in a row, he usually needed a day or so to wind down from the events and melodramas of Unit 3 East. But that evening, being with his buddy in this setting, gazing out at the still, moonlit pond, away from civilization, Nathan felt his life in southern Connecticut was far, far away—physically and emotionally. He was focused on the moment. Cecelia, Joe, Tim, Dr. Short and the rest were out of his consciousness. He felt tired, but fully relaxed. He had needed to get away, and now he was where he wanted to be.

The four days at Beartown flew by far too quickly for Nathan. He and Dave rowed the kayak around the broad pond each day, exploring different shore points, sometimes just stopping their rowing to lean back, close their eyes and sunbathe for hours on end. Their chatting was constant, with subjects ranging from other friends' jobs and relationships, to how the Mets needed to hang on to Strawberry because they could never replace his power in the middle of the lineup, and to their own memories of games they had played together: the no-hitter Dave had thrown against Westport Legion despite a fierce teenage hangover; Nathan's game-winning double down the line with the bases loaded and two out in the ninth inning of a big tournament game on Long Island; ditsy managers they had played for, men who knew less about baseball than their own mothers did.

Dave spoke often about his own fragile emotional state. He enjoyed the control he had regained over his life since he had stopped drinking, but he was not like many others, who felt emotionally renewed once the sedating effects of ethanol were out of their systems. Dave's view was that drinking had made him feel normal, more like the rest of the world; he needed to replace it with something, but he did not know what that something was, at least not yet.

"I'm thinking I may need to see a shrink," Dave confided in Nathan at one point in these midday conversations, surprising his friend. "Do you know a good one over at the hospital?"

After four years of listening at staff meetings and case conferences on 3 East, Nathan had come to the conclusion that his close friend did indeed have psychiatric symptoms worthy of professional intervention. But he was still startled that Dave would come to this conclusion on his own.

"The hospital runs an Outpatient Clinic. You could start there. It will probably be cheaper for you. You have insurance, right?"

"Yeah," Dave responded, "but the coverage sucks. I looked into it at work. It's like the bare minimum an insurance plan can offer. But at least it is something."

"So you'll need the number of the Clinic," Nathan affirmed. "I can get it for you on Monday. Or you can just call the main number and ask for the Clinic, and they will connect you over there." He would write down the main Hunt-Fisher phone number for Dave on the ride back to Connecticut.

Dave explained that his inquiry about mental health care was instigated more by Nasty Steve than his own motivations and insights. His sponsor had needed to be hospitalized at one point in the depths of his alcoholic despair, and he had found talking to shrinks useful, as long as they understood alcoholism and the value of the AA program.

"Steve said he was going to 'tro me a beatin'' if I didn't make the call," Dave admitted, revealing to Nathan The Nasty One's coercive motivational methods.

"So make it, dude. Go for it," Nathan said, encouraging his friend to pursue the recommendation his sponsor had given him. It would probably help him.

The hardest part of the weekend was packing up to leave. Even Nathan felt almost clinically depressed that this excursion into the Massachusetts wilderness, so relaxing, pleasant and carefree, was coming to a close. He knew Dave was feeling it too. Their good natured chatter began winding down the moment the tent was folded up. By the time they reached the Isuzu late Sunday afternoon, the two of them were deep within themselves, doing reality checks about what lay ahead upon their return from the outside world. Nathan did not need to gear up to return to work the next day; he had had planned the fifth day off to re-acclimate to his Norwalk existence. He would call Cecelia to see what the scoop was from the unit. Early July was always a high stress period, since it was the beginning of the new academic year and a batch of fresh residents would be assigned to the unit, and some of the current doctors would rotate elsewhere. He had heard that Dr. Short was leaving, to become Assistant Unit Chief on the substance abuse treatment unit, since his residency was now complete. *Good fucking riddance.* That meant that Joe and Tim would have to be assigned to new doctors. If Joe was still there. He might have challenged the commitment and convinced a court judge who came to the hospital to let him out.

Once they reached Route 7 and started heading south, Nathan and Dave had made the mental adjustment back to reality, and their banter returned. Dave tuned in WCBS once the signal was clear enough, and sang along to *Duke of Earl, Teen Angel* and other 50's hits he knew so well. The trip had been a great time, they both agreed. Maybe they could find a way to come again later in the summer.

Somehow, Nathan's intuition told him that was unlikely.

A New Academic Year

Chapter 7

The tradition at Hunt-Fisher was for new residents to begin on July 1st, as long as this date fell within the work week. In 1990, the 1st fell on a Sunday, so Courtney was blessed with an extra day before she had to begin her training. She had spent the four days since the interview at Hunt-Fisher relaxing around her Scarsdale home, reading, talking to her parents when they were around, and sorting through her things in the garage to determine which items might best accompany her to Connecticut. She spent a day in the City, shopping and visiting the Met, where there was an exhibit she had been longing to see. After taking in the exhibit, she sat by herself up on the second floor balcony, finding a lovely spot where museum-goers could enjoy a bite to eat or a glass of wine, the latter being Courtney's preference that day. It was a splendid, peaceful oasis of culture, a site where Courtney could savor an opportunity to steal a few moments of serenity, in contrast to the fast-paced urban chaos she knew was out just beyond the surrounding Central Park tree line.

On Sunday, she had enjoyed a wonderful day and evening in New York at her parents' expense, a celebration of her medical school graduation. It started with her mother securing them great seats for the matinee performance of Les Miserables, a feat Sheila achieved as a result of the extensive network she always nurtured among New York's cultural elite. In this particular case, she had hit up a Broadway producer who owed her one, after she had arranged a meeting for him with a potential financial backer of a new play he wished to stage, whom she knew because he was a regular donor to her Foundation. A quick call from this connected insider and the Brentwoods were set up in the second row, center. The show was amazing. In fact, the three of them all agreed it was far and away the most enthralling play they had ever witnessed in their years attending Broadway performances. The music was sublime, both touching and uplifting; the story of Valjean's redemption expansive and moving. The role of Inspector Javert, Valjean's dogged nemesis, was played with superb devious reserve by Terrance Mann.

On the cab ride to dinner on the East Side afterwards, they all remained euphoric about this wondrous theatrical experience, talking about what they had loved most about it. Courtney joked about how ironic it was that, on the day before starting her residency training, she saw a play whose positive, affirming message, of life moving forward, was conveyed in lyrics that rang so true to her.

"How did it go?" she asked herself out loud, searching for the words of the song printed on the liner insert to the show's music cassette she had bought on the way out of the theater. "Oh, here it is. *Tomorrow we'll discover what our God in heaven has in store.* I guess that applies pretty closely to me, doesn't it?" she mused.

At this point, and much to Sheila and Courtney's utter dismay, Aaron began belting out the song at the end of the play, the lyrics still ringing in his ears.

"One more dawn. One more day."

"Aaron, must you?" Sheila asked, pleading with him to stop.

"One day more!" Aaron sang, with arms outstretched, creating his own finale. He was a terrible singer, but he seemed not to care. At that moment, it was clear that he could not have been happier and more gratified. He had his small but loving family together, and he had just witnessed high culture. And they were about to eat, which he noted to his loved ones appealed to the empty stomach now making noises at him.

Sheila appeared to be in a glorious mood as well. She reminded herself out loud to drop a note to the Broadway producer whose influence had made her family's close-up theater experience so memorable. This kind of follow-up was *de rigeur* in the quid pro quo, high-mannered world of New York society within which she lived, worked and socialized.

Whenever Courtney's emotions were moved by art, she tended to scan her own affective state. Sitting in the cab, peering vacantly out the window, she reflected about the range of strong, ambivalent feelings gripping her. She loved her parents, and this was a very special occasion, being with them, celebrating her graduation. But she held out hope that she would be able to connect with people at Hunt-Fisher, to rid herself of the emptiness she felt over the last few days since moving away from Jason and her Temple-based social circle. She also remained edgy about the choice she had made to train in the field of psychiatry, although the discussion she had with her father on the day she had arrived home had given her a more positive perspective on it all. She loved the new environment she would be in, but would miss the sheer volume of people she connected with on a day-to-day basis in Philadelphia. The eight new residents in her incoming PGY1 class were about one twentieth the size of her class at Temple.

"You know," Courtney said as she disembarked from the cab and entered the restaurant alongside her parents, "the play was really sad in spots, showing life's hardships, how the world can beat a person's spirit down, and be cold and cruel. But the hopeful message remained clear, that one needs to press on, that love and caring matter in the end, even amid turbulent times. Pretty relevant for helping professionals like us to understand, this theme of pressing on when the odds are against us, isn't it, Dad?"

Aaron loved this type of discussion, and Courtney knew it. When she was younger, she would roll her eyes at her father's persistent analysis of movies or art they experienced together. But, at that moment, still glowing from the emotional impact of the play, and about to join the ranks of future analysts, so to speak, she was into it. She wanted to listen to her father break it all down for her.

"It most certainly is," Aaron agreed, with emphasis. He waited until they were properly seated by the maitre d' before expanding further about his views to her question.

"You know," he began contemplatively, "that's what we do, or what we should do, in mental health treatment. We instill hope, or guide people in a hopeful direction. We beat back the spirit of Javert that sometimes lies within people, Courtney. We reality-test this cynical outlook, which in Javert's case was a moral absolutism run amok, that there is not only right or wrong behavior, but also either a pure or innately evil human nature, that people either do right or are doomed by a character flaw, one they can not rid themselves of. Albert Ellis, a psychologist whose theories I do not always agree with, I should say, has an interesting label for this behavior: he calls it 'musterbation.' 'I must do this,' 'I must be like that,' or 'you must be this way.' It is thinking that is self-defeating and cruel, just as Javert was."

The waiter approached to take their drink order, and Aaron asked to see the wine list. After a quick review, he made his selection. "Let's see. Oh, here. We'll take this one: dix-neuf cent quatre vingt-cinq, Chateau Gloria, s'il vous plait." The waiter nodded impassively, and went to retrieve the order.

Without missing a beat, Aaron continued. "Emotionally troubled people tend to say, 'I messed up, therefore it is foreordained that I will continue to mess up, I am a bad person. They have difficulty being resilient, because the pessimistic spirit shown by Javert sits inside them, saying 'a man—or woman—like me can never change.' And it is worse if the people around them confirm this self-doubt." Aaron looked at Courtney, his eyes sparkling. "If it were true, that people couldn't change, we would be out of business pretty quickly, wouldn't we Courtney?"

"You know what I felt during the play?" Sheila asked, inserting herself into this father-daughter discourse about mental health therapeutics and intrapsychic phenomenon, raised by the play's characters and plot. "It was the peril of showing intolerance, of stigmatizing someone, or labeling them, like Javert did in always calling Valjean '24601.' Labeling someone because of the way he or she talks, or their ethnicity, or some label due to the way one behaved in the past, is so inhumane. It made me consider: what do I really think about not just ex-felons like Valjean, but even, say, your patients," she said, pointing her hand first toward her husband, then her daughter. "The mentally ill, or drug addicts and alcoholics, for example. If I was hiring someone, or dealing professionally with someone, and they owned up to previous mental health care, or to being a recovering alcoholic, would I pre-judge them? Or would I give them a chance, focusing on the here and now, what I saw before me, rather then taking a—what did you call it, Aaron?—moral absolutism approach. The label 24601 is like branding someone a 'psycho' or a 'drunk,' even after he or she has shown the courage to get help or stop drinking. I mean, do we, society—or, do I, for that matter—make judgments, and never give quote-unquote 'sinners' a chance, because of a label placed on them based on the person's past mistakes, or failings, which—like Valjean stealing a lousy loaf of bread—might not have been that horrible, maybe even a cry for help?"

Aaron and Courtney nodded, agreeing with the point Sheila was making. Sheila was very perceptive, especially about people. But Courtney thought her mother had a ways to go to reverse her tendency to pre-judge others. At least she was aware of it, Courtney noted. That was a positive thing.

"It was very moving, from start to finish," Sheila concluded. "That play is going to be the longest running play in Broadway history, I predict."

Courtney chimed in about being struck by the theme of the unflagging spirit of the disadvantaged—of *Les Miserables*, so to speak. She too had witnessed people willing to fight for what they believed in: not against the French Army, but in a battle to get the only type of healthcare services to which they had access, at public hospital clinics like the one she had rotated through in her last semester at Temple. She had liked the line in the play that the Gavroche character had sung about humble piety.

"I saw a lot of people living on humble piety at Temple, believe me," Courtney noted. She had admired patients who lacked financial resources, but remained strong advocates for their own and their children's medical needs. Courtney remembered how they stood in line outside the Clinic, waiting for it to open, to make sure they, their feverish child or their frail mother got seen as quickly as possible. It was a spirit that made Courtney want to help them even more, to treat them with the same kind of dignity they conveyed to her.

Aaron and Sheila looked at her lovingly, and then at each other in the same way. Their expression said, "We somehow managed to raise our only child into a gem, a wonderful and compassionate person." Pride radiated around the table, from Aaron and Sheila to each other, for their parental accomplishment, then on to Courtney.

The wine had arrived during Sheila's self-examining monologue, and it had now breathed properly. Aaron signaled the waiter to fill their glasses, then he toasted the new Dr. Brentwood, the kind of daughter every parent would be proud to have.

Courtney found herself still thinking about the play on Monday morning, as she drove from Scarsdale to Hunt-Fisher. The break between medical school and beginning residency training had been too short, but it promised to be a light week: lots of administrative matters to cover with the Education Department and Brenda, the woman she had met briefly at her interview; introductions to her supervisor—she had earned the right to be assigned to a very senior faculty advisor, Dr. Sid Roth—and to the house faculty; considerable orientation to and information about policies and procedures that needed to be explained to the incoming resident class. Another reason the week would be lighter than usual was that the Fourth of July fell in the middle of it, on Wednesday, so Courtney would have only two days of this orientation before getting a day off. Compared to her intense medical school schedule, she considered this was a breeze, at least at the start.

Her new home was to be resident cottage #3. But she decided to commute to Hunt-Fisher until the Fourth, when she would be in a better and more relaxed mental state to begin moving her things. She could then use the following weekend to complete the overall chore.

The cottage was, as her father had described, quite spacious. It actually was a duplex: two single apartments, adjoined by a common living room wall, with separate entrances on opposite sides. It had two floors, although on the second floor Courtney needed to duck down in places to make her way around the bedroom and the room that she would use as a study. After surveying the existing furniture the hospital had provided, she made mental notes about which pieces she might need from the collection now sitting in her parents' garage.

Her initial rotation assignment, she was told on the morning of her first day of orientation, would be on an acute treatment unit, 3 East. She would not formally begin working on the unit, or have patients assigned to her, until after her class's full week of orientation. However, on Tuesday afternoon, in the unit's weekly staff meeting, she and two of her classmates would be introduced to their new colleagues.

She met the seven other PGY1s throughout the day, and, although it was far too early to tell, she felt positive about all of them. She had talked the most to Robin Wang, a male Tufts Medical School graduate of Asian descent—Chinese, Courtney was pretty sure. He had a ready smile and seemed very sweet, and he struck her right away as being extremely bright. Sandy Paul, one of the three women in the class, had asked Courtney to lunch. She was from Dartmouth Medical School, and she had also done her undergraduate years at the same institution. Courtney told Sandy about how her neighbor Billy was being recruited there, and asked her new acquaintance if she would mind talking to him about college life in Hanover, if he was interested. She readily agreed, although Courtney had doubts that Billy would follow through if Courtney extended the invitation.

At lunch, Sandy brought up Courtney's father right away. Sandy expressed her admiration for his writings and his reputation in the field of academic psychiatry. Courtney reasoned quickly that Sandy's lunch invitation had an ulterior motive. Their conversation was pleasant, and Sandy asked considerate questions. But there was a mildly pushy and aggressive side to her that could not be masked. For Sandy, training at the Hunt-Fisher Hospital was more than an opportunity to learn from the faculty there—it was a chance to find some area where more clinical research was needed, a unique niche that she could exploit. She explained her residency plans to Courtney: she would join a research project by the end of her PGY1 year, co-author an article for one of the major professional journals over the following year or two, perhaps give a Grand Rounds presentation in her PGY4, building her *curriculum vitae*, so that by the end of her four years of residency, she would be in an advantageous position to join a good medical school as a junior faculty member, preferably somewhere around New York—hence her interest in the likes of the powerful Dean, Dr. Aaron Brentwood. *Wow, she's got it all figured out,* Courtney thought. Courtney's objectives at that moment were just to move her things from Scarsdale to Norwalk, and get them in her place without breaking any plates or dropping the artwork she wanted to bring along.

They both had been assigned to the same unit, and they learned their rotations would overlap throughout the PGY1 year. So it was likely they would be seeing much of each other. Courtney thought to herself that this seemed okay, although she was going to reserve some judgment until she saw Sandy in action. It might be that Sandy would be the know-it-all type that her friend Rolanda in Philadelphia always complained about.

Aaron had told Courtney that he was eager to learn about her first day as soon as possible, so, on her way home at the end of the day, she called him on her recently-installed hands-free car phone, hoping to reach him within the ten minute window she was allotted. Rachel passed her through to him, and she briefed him about what had transpired during the day, including her sense that some classmates were going to be very nice to her because of the potential pull she might have with a certain prominent Dean at Cornell, who may be interested in assessing good candidates for future post-residency junior faculty positions. Aaron laughed, trying to imagine how first year residents could have their future mapped out that far into the future, before they had even treated their first patient. He had promised to be home as soon as he could, probably around eight o'clock, and they would talk some more then.

Courtney pushed END, and got an impulse to call Jason at Lara's home in Santa Monica, where he was staying until he returned to Philadelphia on Sunday. Jason had been faithful to his pledge to call her after her interviews the previous week, and toward the end of this conversation they had established a mutual promise to talk again after her first official day at Hunt-Fisher. Courtney was actually a bit surprised to reach him, in mid-afternoon California time. She expected that he might be out and about, enjoying the California beach scene he loved so much. But he had just returned from a bike ride to Venice and back when she called, in the midst of preparing a late lunch for himself.

He sounded thrilled that she had called him. As was his style, Jason sought first to understand: did she feel like she would fit in at Hunt-Fisher? What did her gut tell her about the quality of the training she was going to receive? How much of the orientation was valuable, and how much did she find infantile "do this, don't do that" type of guidance? What was her residency class like? Were there any guys worth looking at? Courtney filled him in, trying her best to convey how stark a contrast their respective living environments would be this year.

When Jason's turn came to update Courtney on what was happening with him and Lara on the left coast, his voice became very excited.

"Oh my God," he began, speaking more rapidly than before, "I haven't told you this yet. You'll never believe what happened over the weekend. A week or so ago, Lara auditioned—she and about a million others actresses here in L.A.—for a show Fox television was planning to pilot for the 'second season,' as a back-up to their lineup once they know which new shows were not going to make it from a ratings standpoint. It's a show that will be one of those evening soap opera-type stories set in some California bohemian setting, with all the cast a bunch of hot 20-somethings…anyway, the studio called Saturday to tell her she *got* a part. She will be just one of a pretty large ensemble cast, but she will have lots of lines in every episode, have her name and picture on the opening credits and all that. I think she is going to play a very hip back-stabbing bitch type—they thought her look was perfect. And they complimented her on her acting in the audition, too. Can you believe it? I am now, officially, a TV star's too-cool boyfriend."

"Wow!" Courtney shouted out loud, "that's *amazing*. Lara is so talented, she deserves it…good for her! Is she there so I can congratulate her?"

"No, she's at her agent's office right now, going over contracts. Can you believe this? She is going to make a ton of money. It's very hard work, lots of hours, but she thinks that's okay since I won't be around until next year."

"When does the filming, or taping or whatever they call it…when does it all start?" Courtney asked.

"Pretty soon, from what I understand," he told her. "She is really pumped. This is her shot at the whole Hollywood experience she has always dreamed of."

"What about the Lara King brand and the fitness chain?" Courtney suddenly considered how this might be throwing Jason's future vision off course.

"Court, we're just going to go with this, and we'll see where it takes us," he answered, without a trace of hesitancy or uncertainty. "Think about it. It could be the start of a nice run in acting, which will certainly help with her face and name recognition. In a strange way, this could make the fitness chain business plan all the more viable." His view was that there was only an upside to this surprise development.

Lara, a real actress on television…and I know her…know her pretty well, in fact…her boyfriend is one of my best friends…these studios are great judges of talent, and they saw what we all see…she's just too gorgeous and alluring to ignore.

Jason would begin his third year of medical school on the following Monday. He and Courtney agreed to talk to each other in a week's time, on the parallel first day of his final training year, so Courtney could learn about any new developments at Temple, and about Lara's exciting new TV acting career. It had only been less than a week since they had had their emotional farewell in Philadelphia, and they had spoken twice by phone, but Courtney still felt disoriented without Jason's physical presence around her. It had always been so comforting, so special, to know he was close by. Maybe she could entice him up to New York again this summer. She decided to bring up the suggestion the next time they talked.

Aaron arrived home from the City a little after eight o'clock. He was in an upbeat mood, as he planned to take the next day off to create what he called a "weekend within"—two days away from work in midweek. It was a perilous time for the Dean to be away from the medical college, with the new academic year beginning and innumerable administrative details and snafus to attend to, but he was determined to maximize the time he had left with his only child before she moved out. His plan was to drive her to and from Norwalk the next day, spending the time in between doing some networking with Blakeley at Hunt-Fisher and with some of his brethren at Yale over lunch in New Haven. He would then take his daughter and wife out to dinner locally around Scarsdale, get home at a reasonable hour, and give Courtney a hand packing some of her things into the Camry for a first run they would make together to Hunt-Fisher on the Fourth.

Aaron listened attentively to Courtney's take on her training program's early orientation schedule and offerings, always anxious to gain some insights about the best way to plan and execute the initial phase of new residents' training programs. They chatted until about ten o'clock, when Courtney begged off, requesting some time to herself to get organized for the next two days. Upon heading upstairs, however, Courtney dropped onto her bed in fatigue, and soon she decided that sleep was more her immediate priority. The organizing would have to wait until the following day.

The schedule for the second day of new resident orientation at Hunt-Fisher was highlighted by the plan for 3 East's new residents to be introduced to the full interdisciplinary treatment staff on units where they were being assigned. Part of the morning orientation class was spent addressing how these introductions would occur, on 3 East and the other PGY1 training units. The Chief Resident would accompany all the groups, whose meetings had been scheduled on different days, to make the proper introductions. It would be a chance for the PGY1s to meet their respective Unit Chiefs, staff psychiatrists and psychologists, social workers and nursing staff, with whom they would be conducting their treatment planning. Courtney was excited about the meeting, and about getting started with relationship-building with fellow staff. Given her last training experience at the Clinic at Temple, she knew how important it was to build these types of bonds with those around whom she would be training.

The resident introductions planned for the 3 East staff meeting were purposefully scheduled around change of shift time, at three o'clock, so that both the day and evening nursing staff could participate. Courtney, Sandy and Robin Wang would be escorted onto the unit by the new Chief Resident, named James Bobrow, Dr. Short's successor. Courtney's instant reaction to Bobrow, once he introduced himself to the resident class during an orientation meeting, was that he was a classic preppie. The brown glasses, monogrammed shirt and bow tie gave his Choate and Princeton background away, far before he confirmed it to Courtney with an air of braggadocio. At around two-thirty, the four of them headed out of the orientation class toward 3 East. Bobrow and Courtney walked together, with Sandy and Robin trailing close behind.

Sandy asked for a quick stop in the Ladies Room, and Robin agreed he would like to use the adjoining Men's Room as well. Once they were left alone, Dr. Bobrow moved a step closer to Courtney.

"So, Courtney, we are having a little get-together at my cottage tomorrow, to celebrate the Fourth and the start of the new academic year. It is kind of a tradition for the Chief Resident to get the socialization aspect of training underway. Would you like to come over? Around four-ish? We're going to barbecue some steak and chicken, drink some wine and beer, and all that. It will be a great way for you to meet some of the other medical staff. What do you say?"

"Sure," she replied, more in a compliant tone than with excitement. She sensed right away he was attracted to her, based on his pairing up with her and his decision to bring this invitation up to her once the other two residents were out of earshot. "Are all the PGY1s going to be invited?" she asked, confronting this exclusivity of the invitation.

"Yes, yes," he answered with evident guilt, caught in the act. Courtney had been hit on many times, and Bobrow's tone in extending the invitation made Courtney sense that he was laying the groundwork, and that he would try for more exclusive invitations to his cottage in the future. Courtney asked if she could bring anything, but Bobrow declined her offer. Actually, he told her, the hospital paid for and provided the food, and sent food service staff over to serve prepare and serve it, as well as clean up afterwards.

Once Sandy and Robin rejoined them, Bobrow brought up the party he would be holding to them, needing to be consistent with what he had told Courtney.

"That sounds great," Sandy and Robin had said, almost in unison, appreciative of the opportunity to network with the Post Graduate Year "2s," "3s" and "4s," who had already been through what they were about to experience. They walked on, both peering over to Courtney, concern showing on their faces that they had not heard Bobrow invite her to the party as well.

Nathan trudged onto unit 3 East at exactly three o'clock in the afternoon, maximizing every minute of his time off before beginning his shift. This would be the first of six straight days of work without a break, including working the next day, on the Fourth of July, a hospital holiday.

Tim walked briskly up to shake Nathan's hand, showing delight in his return to duty on 3 East.

"How was your time off, Nathan?" he asked, smiling broadly.

"Nice, Tim, very nice, thank you," Nathan replied warmly.

"Did you go away?"

Nathan was trained not to respond directly to these types of personal questions from patients. He had learned never to reveal anything about what he did on days off, where he lived, with whom he lived or any other information of this sort. The less he told patients about anything remotely attached to his life outside the hospital, the less they asked.

"I just enjoyed a little break," he told him.

Tim understood that Nathan was being evasive, but he did not press as other patients tended to, despite the fact that Nathan's responses never yielded any satisfaction.

"I'm getting a new doctor," Tim reminded Nathan. "She will be on the unit any minute, the other people here tell me." Somehow, the patients knew a lot about what was going on with unit staffing, more than they were probably meant to know. Evidently, there was a leak in the nursing staff, someone who shared news with them without permission. Nathan suspected it was Joan. *She's got the judgment of a freakin' slug, that idiot.*

"How do you feel about that?" Nathan asked.

"It's alright. Dr. Short says he intends to work with the new doctor and make a good transition. Then he wants to see me after I get discharged."

"Is that your plan, too?" It was a fair question from a clinical standpoint, Nathan thought, given Tim's problem in asserting himself. But it was also a bit like an attorney leading the witness. In Nathan's view, Tim should look for a doctor of his own choosing, not one thrust on him by the hospital, just because it was Dr. Short's turn for assignment to the next admission when Tim came on the unit.

"I guess so. What do you think, Nathan?"

Tell that Dr. Short to go hell, why don't you?

But, even though he was thinking differently, Nathan responded without hesitating. "You need to make that call, my man," he said.

Tim nodded, showing he understood that Nathan was not being evasive but pushing him into making his own decisions.

"Did Joe get out, Tim? I don't see him," Nathan asked, peering around the unit.

"He left yesterday," Tim said. "He convinced a judge who came on the unit that he did not need to stay."

Good for him. Sheriff Short left the keys too close the jail cell, and the prisoner had escaped.

"Let me check in with the nurses, and I'll talk to you later, okay? How about around nine-thirty?"

Tim extended his hand, smiling. "Great. And welcome back."

The nursing station was jammed. Staff from the two shifts congregated there, getting ready for the upcoming staff meeting, in which the three new residents, now standing in the middle of the room a bit uncomfortably, would be introduced. Emily saw Nathan first.

"Hey, Nathan's back from dancing with the bears," she kidded. He had told her about his getaway plans with a close male friend, which helped keep the heat off any suspicion about him and Cecelia. Cecelia was in the room too, and stole a furtive glance at him, betraying no outward emotion about his return. Joan walked by, without even noticing him at all, heading right for a doctor to ask his advice about how to conduct a conversation with a patient.

Some of the day nursing staff picked up on Emily's comment, and Nathan was forced to share tidbits about his trip to the Berkshires.

"I almost did not come back," he said at the end of relating his camping tales, keeping a straight face, speaking broadly now to the whole room. "I thought about becoming a forest ranger," he deadpanned. "You know, I've always wanted to wear those brown suits, make sure people don't feed the bears, arrest some violators."

Only one person in the room laughed at his dry wit. Courtney thought it was hilarious; not humorous like a stand up comedian's obvious joke, just a little twisted, and well delivered. To her, it was very "Jason-esque." Nathan smiled at her, sensing she "got it." Nathan also noticed Cecelia looking at Courtney during this exchange, seeming to make a mental note of her amused reaction.

Emily barked out to the whole group that the meeting needed to get started, and to please head to the conference room at the end of one hallway near the women's bathroom. The Unit Chief, Dr. Sid Roth, had just arrived on the hall, trailed by a coterie of other clinical staff.

Nathan checked the staff assignment list. It indicated that he was to remain on the unit, to provide some staff presence while the large group met for about an hour. Nathan did not really mind. He had been to many of these resident introduction events, and he had always just sat quietly, except for when everyone went around the room and introduced themselves. *Nathan Bigelow, pysch tech.* That was the extent of his participation in these meetings, never anything more.

He remembered that he and Tim had seen the new pretty resident, the one who had just laughed so easily at his sense of humor, only last week when Nathan had escorted the patients over to RT. *It is going to be nice to have some more fine young women to look at around here,* he thought. The other woman resident, Nathan noted about Sandy, was more like the kind the unit usually attracted: short, thick and aggressive-looking. She might be a good doctor, but her looks are thoroughly unappealing, he observed. *Well, one out of two ain't bad.*

Nathan had no assignments, other than to stay on the hall during the staff meeting, before he was scheduled for an early dinner at four-fifteen. Cecelia, in a rare departure from her tendency not to schedule them to go to dinner together, also had chosen the four-fifteen dinner time slot for herself. Nathan was surprised, but he sensed she was anxious for a little time alone with him after their five day separation, and thus was willing to use this particular day as the one where the random probability had hit that their dinner schedules coincidentally overlapped.

The staff meeting let out at exactly four o'clock, and Nathan wandered into the nursing station after most of the staff returned there. No one noticed or acknowledged him. He finally pulled Emily aside and asked what the new residents' names were. Drs. Brentwood, Paul and Wang were their names, he was told. Dr. Brentwood was the taller and pretty one, Emily whispered to Nathan, and Dr. Paul was the other woman. Emily did not even try to identify Dr. Wang, whose identity was self-evident by process of elimination, if not by cultural stereotype.

"They all seem very nice," Emily told him, still whispering.

"Where are they from?" he asked.

"Let's see, Dr. Brentwood's from Temple, Dr. Paul went to Dartmouth and Dr. Wang...I forget...I think one of the Boston schools." She looked at Nathan. "Why do you ask?"

"I like to rate schools in my mind by the quality of the doctors they send here," he said, explaining his curiosity.

"Which school had given us the best residents, do you think, since you've been here?" Emily asked, considering how she would answer that question too.

"Brown, probably," Nathan said. "Remember John Bortman? What a great guy. He was from Brown. And a great...and I mean great...psychiatrist." Bortman was an outgoing and easy-going resident who was on the unit both for the requisite PGY1 rotation, but also as a PGY4, for his final "course," serving in a clinical supervisory role with the staff. Nathan and Dr. Bortman had hit it off quickly, socializing after work at Nathan's place, going to Mets games together at times, or joining each other or a group of staff from the unit heading out to post-work Happy Hours at local pubs. Bortman had even scheduled a few of his supervisory classes at the pubs, thinking he would get more attendance at these meetings that way, and that he could generate a more informal discussion if lubricated by light intoxicants.

In his friend's view, Nathan was a special, albeit under-educated talent. A gifted psychotherapist, Bortman had a keen eye for those with a naturally helping style. Even after returning to Providence to establish a private psychotherapy practice, Bortman felt compelled to stay in contact Nathan, and encourage Nathan to get going, to make the most of life. In Bortman's opinion, this did not include Nathan biding his time as a lowly nurse's aide in some country hospital in Connecticut. He needed to return to school, get his degree and find a niche out in the world, either by going on to graduate school to prepare for licensure as a bona fide mental health professional, or to use his communication gifts in business somehow. But, Bortman had insisted, it was up to Nathan to get off his duff and do it. The world out there beyond the hospital gates would almost certainly reward his type of talents, but it was not going to chase him, either. Nathan needed to make it happen.

Nathan was officially a first term junior at Southern Connecticut State College, majoring in counseling psychology, attending part time, using the hospital's tuition reimbursement plan to finance his undergraduate education. When he was motivated and had some money saved, Nathan worked on getting his degree. The previous fall, he had taken three classes in a single semester, while still working full time: a four-month ordeal that had burned him to a crisp. Since then, he had not enrolled in the spring or summer semester, the latter having already gotten underway. He had found a million different excuses not to return for more classes: financial difficulties, the unit was crazy, the classes did not challenge him. He had some money saved for the fall semester, but he was ambivalent about using it for fall tuition. He always needed money. In fact, he had frittered previous tuition reimbursement checks he had earned, rather than rolling them over to pay for tuition in the following semester. His car had needed a new valve job, and he used some on the weekend trips with Cecelia. The end he was seeking to reach, earning a college degree, still seemed so far away, and he was having trouble dedicating his meager savings to the effort, and re-motivating himself for the classroom.

Cecelia came into the nursing station, after walking down the hall talking quietly with Dr. Bobrow. She moved over to the clipboard where she had listed staff assignments, and looked it over.

"Oh, look Nathan, we're going to dinner together," she said, turning to him, hoping others would pick up on the surprise in her voice.

"Cool," Nathan said, nonchalantly. "Want to go to the cafeteria?"

"Let's take a walk outside first, would that be alright?" Cecelia suggested innocently. "It's so nice out, I'd like to get some fresh air. I'll meet you here in about ten minutes, okay?"

"You got it."

Nathan smiled inwardly at their playacting. *The two of them were good. Very good.*

Cecelia and Nathan walked along the sidewalks that led around the circumference of the hospital, careful to stay an acceptably safe distance away from each other, to reinforce their assumed roles of friendly co-workers. However, their conversation was intimate. Cecelia asked Nathan about his trip, and if he had missed her. Sure, he had missed her, he told her, knowing this was at least partially true. Walking beside her now, he wanted badly to be alone with her. But he knew that such a get-together was several days off. He was facing a "back-to-back," meaning that he was scheduled for the day shift on the following morning, only eight hours after getting off duty later this evening. And he knew that Cecelia had plans to drive up to Vermont early the next day. So they both needed to get to sleep right away if they could—something unlikely to occur if they met each other after work. Any reunion lovemaking session would have to be postponed. When Nathan pressed her about the plans she had for returning from Vermont, she informed him she expected to be home some time late on Saturday. Just like Nathan, Cecelia preferred having a full day back in Connecticut, to get recharged for the week ahead. And it promised to be a busy one, with the new residents starting, and some committees she was on reconvening after not meeting for about a month.

"I'm working for seven days straight; I won't be off until Tuesday," Nathan told her.

"I know," she replied. She typically knew his schedule, several weeks out.

"I can call on Saturday," he offered, hoping for an erotic rendezvous once she returned from Vermont.

"Yeah, do that. But I just don't know when I'll be home. It depends when I leave, and on the traffic. Plus, I'll be beat from the ride. But give me a call, anyway—say, no sooner than six. Okay?"

Nathan nodded silently. Looking down, he noticed part of a shiny coin lying in the grass just under the heel of the left sandal Cecelia was wearing. "Hold on, Cecelia," he said, grabbing her arm lightly to halt her in her tracks. He came over just behind where she stood, knelt down and lifted up the sandal to retrieve a ten cent piece upon which she was standing. He had now made a dime profit from their walk together, but more importantly, he had made physical contact with Cecelia's shapely appendages: first her arm, then her well-shaped calves, ankles and bare toes, in the retrieval process. *God, her feet are so sexy*, he thought. And the allure of her form did not stop there. Drawing himself up slowly after grabbing and then pocketing the coin, he stopped when his eyes were on an even level with the perfection of Cecelia's rounded posterior, so beautifully filling out the back of her light summer skirt, just inches from his face.

He fell victim to his lust, and asked her if she wanted to take a short ride off grounds. She turned, smiling, understanding how their touching had kindled his desire, and acknowledging that it had turned her on as well. She assented, showing an unspoken willingness to assume the risks involved. They scrambled back to her Honda hurriedly, looking around in a nonchalant manner that belied their evident haste, checking to see if any obvious onlookers might be around to sabotage the getaway. There did not appear to be. She drove them down the access road, with Nathan's hands immediately reaching for her. Cecelia slid down her seat slightly, leaned back, lifting herself up a bit, allowing his hands first to raise her dress up fully above her waist, then to slide her panties down her thighs, over her bent knees and down around her ankles. She separated her legs as far as they would go in the driver's seat, and he leaned over toward her and began probing and rubbing with his left hand, in exactly the way she had instructed him to when they first slept together. Once they were outside the hospital property, Cecelia steered aimlessly onto an empty residential street, driving slowly ahead, starting to moan out loud from the pleasure Nathan was arousing.

"Get unzipped," she urged softly, reaching for hand lotion she always kept in the storage area in front of the Honda's stick shift, ready to reciprocate the sexual favor. He complied, leaning back in the seat and pushing himself up with his legs so that he could draw his trousers' fly down with his right hand, while skillfully managing to maintain the steady stimulation he was performing on her with the other. Keeping her left hand on the wheel, she reached over with her free one, now freshly lubricated, and began vigorously massaging him.

The mutual arousal deflected Cecelia's attention from her driving. The Honda, though proceeding slowly, swerved erratically on the empty residential street, directionless. Cecelia closed her eyes for an instant, focusing on the pleasure Nathan was delivering below. As she opened her eyes, she let out a frightened scream. Her car was headed into a private driveway, a collision now unavoidable with plastic garbage cans filled to the brim with an assortment of refuse: pizza boxes half-filled with greasy remnants of a quick meal earlier that day; bags of dirt-filled weeds and sod from evening gardening; white plastic bags that collected what had been left in bathroom baskets around the house.

Cecelia braked hard, but too late to avoid the impact. When car fender smashed into garbage can, the result was a violent spray of items in many directions. The items that had been near the top of the unclosed receptacle flew into the air, and landed on the Honda's engine hood. The can itself, knocked in a whirling spin ten feet to the side, came to rest midway across the homeowner's lawn. The loud screech of brakes and subsequent thump disturbed the tranquility of the neighborhood, drawing a hard look from a woman walking her dog down the street. The onlooker began moving toward them, showing evident concern.

"Shit," Cecelia exclaimed, putting the car into park. At this point, panties needed to be yanked back up, skirts lowered, zippers re-zipped. Once decent, the two emerged from the car to assess the damage. The heat of the moment had now fully passed, and reality had set in. A rapid cleanup was required.

Cecelia retrieved the loose slices of pizza now spread on her car's hood and on the driveway beside it, returning them to the cardboard box. She tried to wipe the tomato sauce and pizza grease off her shiny new car's exterior. A blend of weeds, cotton swabs and soiled tissues had come to rest in the space between the engine hood and the windshield, which Nathan retrieved by the handful and re-inserted into the ripped plastic bag hanging precariously by its handles on the driver's side mirror. Then the two of them moved quickly to the lawn, set the can upright, returning spilt contents roughly to their original location, and rolled the can back toward the end of the driveway. The Honda remained covered with loose dirt and pizza grime, but the driveway and lawn had been restored to roughly the same condition it had been in before the hit. The offenders felt they could leave the scene at this point. They had exactly eight minutes to be back on the unit, and return to work.

The dog-walking neighbor stared at them, at a spot directly across the street from the accident scene, scowling, appearing to be mentally taking notes, of license plate numbers, car type and color, and descriptions of the two amoral culprits.

Cecelia took notice of the dog-walker's disapproval, and blushed with embarrassment. But her immediate concern was simply to drive away from the scene, and get back to the safety of the hospital grounds. *This is getting out of control,* Cecelia thought as she drove up the hospital's access road. She was angry with herself for agreeing to Nathan's suggestion, which had put both her car's pristine condition and her very reputation in danger. *It's just stupid, doing what I just did. And with a psych tech—from my unit, for God's sake.* She now would have to go home after work and make sure that acidic tomato sauce or anything else that could harm her new car's exterior paint was properly cleaned. In fact, she considered that it might be best just to clean the whole exterior, with a bucket of soap and wet sponge, even though it would be close to midnight before she arrived home.

The whole thing was extremely irritating.

She reminded herself that, after the staff meeting that had concluded just a little earlier, she had been approached in private by Dr. James Bobrow, the new Chief Resident, who had invited her to a party the next day, on the afternoon of the Fourth of July, at his Cottage.

Initially, although thrilled by the apparent exclusivity of the invitation, she had demurred, citing other plans. But as she drove hurriedly back onto the hospital grounds, Cecelia made the decision to go to Bobrow's party. She needed to take advantage of these opportunities that Dr. Bobrow and other doctors extended to her, to socialize with the hospital's medical staff, in a friendly, informal atmosphere. She belonged there. And she would not be the only nurse invited. Dr. Bobrow had mentioned a few others in her peer group who were planning to attend, evidently a short list of attractive single nurses he found also to his liking. A new plan for the next day evolved in her mind. After properly sanitizing the outside of her car later that night, she would call her mother in the morning, apologize for having to delay her trip by one day, but explain there had been an unforeseen staff illness for which she needed to cover. Cecelia detested the thought of lying to her mother, and she liked being home in Norwich for the fireworks display across the river in Hanover, but this was what she had to do: both for her career and to improve her social life.

Nathan observed that Cecelia seemed suddenly on edge, upset, as she drove them back to the hospital. A slight pang of remorse hit him, about what his request had led to. Here was a nurse, he started thinking, one who was hell bent on moving up the nursing ladder at the renowned Hunt-Fisher Hospital, engaging in impulsive and almost adolescent type of sexual play with him, during a short dinner break off the unit. She was risking her job, career and professional future, and what did she get out of it? Pizza goo besmirching her new car's paint job, and a guy with whom she could not even be seen in public. *The whole thing is very messy—in more ways than one.*

They did not speak a word to each other as Cecelia raced then re-parked the Accord in the same spot where it had been before their short, off-grounds excursion. They moved quickly together toward the East Entrance, Cecelia trying to conceal the handful of soiled tissues she had used to quickly wipe remaining smudges off her car's exterior. They had been fortunate; no one was circulating around the campus as they re-entered the hospital grounds and building. Without having a chance even to wash their hands, they returned to the unit, just at the five o'clock dinner break deadline.

At other times when they had entered the unit simultaneously after amorously spending previous time together, they would secretly revel in the subterfuge they were successfully carrying out. This time was different. There was no satisfying euphoria in which to bask. Instead, Cecelia's mood evidenced her annoyance and humiliation with what had transpired. For Nathan, the feeling was remorse, and sexual frustration. The odor of Cecelia's hand lotion remained with him, reminding him of what had been started, but not finished.

Later in the shift, when Nathan was alone in the nursing station, Cecelia entered but averted her eyes from his, still saying nothing to him, even in a supervisory capacity. *She's pissed,* he thought. *Gee, Cece, there's no use crying over a little spilt pizza, is there? It's done, over with. Let's move on.*

He spent a much longer time than he typically would in a 1:1 discussion with Tim that evening, part of a concerted strategy to avoid the awkwardness of crossing paths with Cecelia again, for the balance of the shift. At the tour's end, though, he took the initiative to bid her farewell, formally and at a distance, wishing her a nice trip home to Vermont. She was able to summon the effort to form a weak smile, thanking him in a formal, impersonal tone, before returning her attention to patient charting she needed to complete before taking her days off.

Chapter 8

▼

At three o'clock in the afternoon on the following day, America's official birth date and the nation's only mid-summer holiday, Nathan walked leisurely out towards his car parked in the nearly vacant lot just ahead of him. It had been an easy shift that he had just completed, with patients sleeping late, and a few, including Tim, getting permission to go out on a day pass to visit their families over the holiday. Nathan had thought about Cecelia a lot, wondering if her angry, avoidant behavior toward him the previous evening would last after a cooling off period in Vermont. *We'll see when she gets back on Saturday.*

He stepped back onto the curb because he saw a car slowly approaching, a Toyota Camry, that was loaded up in the front and rear seats with many boxes, a bookcase, a few lamps and other loose clothing on hangers. He quickly noticed who was driving. It was the attractive new resident who had been on the unit the day before, Courtney Brentwood he was sure her name was. An instinct struck him to lend his assistance with her evident move-in project. He waved the approaching car down, and it stopped next to him, in response to his signal. The driver's side window descended, giving Nathan a chance to bend down and extend his offer.

"Hi, you're Dr. Brentwood, one of the new residents on 3 East, right?" he asked, as non-threateningly as possible, once the window was at its lowest. "I saw you on the unit yesterday."

"Yes," she replied warmly. He imagined her thinking, *Hey, it's the forest ranger.*

"I'm Nathan Bigelow, one of the psych techs on the unit," he said, extending his hand to her, which she shook. "I saw you coming with all this stuff in your car, and I'm guessing you are moving into one of the residents' cottages. I was just wondering whether you could use a hand moving these things in?"

"Are you sure you wouldn't mind?" Courtney asked, but giving the impression that she welcomed the offer.

"Not at all. I'll walk over to the cottages and look for your car." Nathan decided to leave his Jeep where it was. Driving it such a short distance seemed like the type of comical behavior he had seen in a Steve Martin movie about the Los Angeles culture, where the Martin character got in his car, backed it out of his driveway, drove it to the driveway of the next house on the block, and parked it there. The "Nobody Walks in L.A." spirit did not translate well to the tranquil grounds of Hunt-Fisher Hospital, where ambulating from building to building was the norm.

"Great. See you soon," Courtney said appreciatively, before rolling up the window and driving away.

Nathan sauntered over to the area where the cottages were located, easily spotting Courtney as she opened the trunk of her Camry. There was something very nice and appealing about this resident, he was thinking, as he made his way toward her. Sure, she was easy to look at. But it was her pleasant manner that attracted him even more. And she obviously had a sense of humor—she had been the only person to laugh at his light sarcasm the other day in the nursing station. Nathan thought about how he liked that the unit upon which he worked served as one of the places where new residents trained. It lent itself to interacting with a variety of new people, at a job that otherwise could get extremely routine and tedious. This Dr. Bentwood, he noticed again, was the best looking resident he had ever seen in his four years at Hunt-Fisher, by far. Her physical attractiveness was now on broader display, since she was wearing only informal summer attire—simple but fashionable khaki shorts and a sleeveless polo shirt. Nathan admired what he had not been able to observe before, on the unit the day earlier, when she had on more business-oriented attire. *She is a babe, there is no doubt about it: gorgeous legs, slim figure, a knockout face.* Her rear profile was not nearly up to Cecelia's standards, but the overall package was far more appealing.

"So, Dr. Brentwood...," he began as they met up behind the open trunk of her Camry.

"Please, call me Courtney," she quickly insisted.

"Okay. So, Courtney, what goes where?"

"If you can grab those two boxes," she said, pointing to the two largest ones in the trunk, "I'll show you. Those are the ones I was concerned about carrying in by myself. They weigh a lot, don't they?"

Nathan tried loading up his arms with the two boxes, which he now assumed from their heavy weight were filled with books.

"Are you going to carry both of them?" she asked. "I was worried about carrying even one in by myself."

She was right, Nathan thought. *These things weigh a ton.*

"Yes, come to think of it, I think two trips are in order," he said, agreeing with her premise, and buying a little more time to be with this attractive woman, which, after all, was the point behind his offer to help in the first place.

Courtney moved to a rear door of her car and took out two lampshades and the clothes resting on the built-in hanger over the window. Carrying their respective loads, the pair walked over a slate sidewalk and into the cottage, Nathan trailing Courtney. She told him she needed the books upstairs, in her study. Nathan took the stairs easily, despite the weight he was toting, and dropped the boxes in a corner of the room opposite her bedroom, which was set up like a study. He returned downstairs and headed out to the car for the other box, then repeated his previous routine. After these two trips, he waited by her as she stood surveying the living room, considering various options for the room's layout. She noticed him there, smiled at him warmly, before starting to walk out toward the car again.

"Where did you have this stuff stored before bringing it here?" Nathan asked on the way to the car, making conversation.

"At my parents' place, in Westchester," she told him.

"So you grew up in this general vicinity, then?"

"Yes, I did. It's only about forty-five minutes away, with no traffic."

"I hear you went to Temple," he said, remembering what Emily had told him.

"Yes."

"Did you like Philadelphia?"

"No, not at all."

"I've never been around Temple, but I hear it's not the best area."

"The place really sucks, to be quite frank. Not the school, or the hospital. But everything around it, including the city. The place was the pits, in my opinion."

Nathan liked this informal manner she had, and her willingness to be that way with him. There was no sign of the social stiffness or subtle condescension he sometimes perceived from some residents who trained on the unit.

They reached the car and brought more items in, none of which required Nathan's strength. But he insisted on continuing to help.

"It means half the trips you'd have to make yourself, right?" he said, volunteering for further duty.

"Yes, but you just finished work. Don't you want to get home and away from this place now?"

"Ah, I don't mind. You never know, you may need to lend me a hand someday. Last year, my car battery died after an evening shift in the winter, and I needed to walk over here to the cottages and get this resident whom I knew from the unit, a guy named John Bortman, to give me a jump start. So what goes around comes around, you know what I'm saying?"

"I do," Courtney agreed. "I'll make sure I have some jumper cables on hand," she added, smiling again.

After a final trip left the Camry empty, Nathan asked her if she had anything to drink—a ploy to extend their time together just a little longer.

"How about a beer?" she asked, looking inside her refrigerator. "My father and I went out shopping this morning, and I picked up some at the grocery store. You can't buy beer in a grocery store in Pennsylvania, did you know that?"

"No, I didn't," he answered, welcoming the lager offered to him. "So, your father filled my role this morning, helping you out, huh? That was nice of him."

"Yes, it was."

"Is he a doctor too?" Nathan asked, without knowing exactly why he thought her father might be.

"Yes, he is. Want to sit for a minute?"

They moved into the living room, where Courtney dropped into a large cushioned chair, and Nathan edged onto the sofa. She had brought out a beer for herself as well.

"So, what did you think of your introduction at the unit staff meeting yesterday? How did that go?" Nathan asked.

"Oh, you weren't there?"

"No, someone had to keep an eye on the patients, and that someone, for that day anyway, was me." Nathan did not really expect that she would have noticed that he was not part of the staff meeting.

"It was fine," she said. "Lots of names to learn, and procedures to absorb. But it will be okay."

"3 East is a well-run unit, you will find. Emily, the Nursing Coordinator, she is great. The evening staff is very solid, too. And Dr. Roth is, from what I can see, a good teacher."

"I have heard that," Courtney affirmed. "How long have you worked here?" she asked.

"Almost four years," he responded, feeling slightly ashamed of the length of his tenure, since many psych techs lasted far less time, as they tended to move on to graduate school or other jobs.

"Wow, that's a pretty long time. Did you start here right after college?" she asked, assuming a level of education he had not yet earned, despite his age and evident maturity.

"I'm still going, if you can believe it," he responded, feeling a bit uncomfortable that she, like many others before her, had assumed he was well beyond his undergraduate years.

"Really? Where do you go?"

He told her about his on-and-off matriculating habits at Southern Connecticut State College.

"You should grind it out, Nathan," she advised, echoing John Bortman's encouragement. "That is the first and only career counseling I'll give to you. The fact is, I'm still trying to figure out my own career."

"What do you mean?" Nathan asked, not understanding. *She was here to get trained as a psychiatrist. What did she need to figure out?*

Courtney shared how she had had a nice experience doing internist-type medicine in a Clinic setting at Temple, liking that branch of medicine a lot. But she never changed her plans, which had always been to follow her father into psychiatry.

That made more sense to Nathan. He never really observed or sensed any uncertainty like this before, in the residents whom he had met on the unit.

"Well, this year you'll get a good crack at finding out if being a shrink is for you," he said. "Next week, you'll be thrown into the mix, really quickly." He wondered if she would be treating Tim. "Hey, do you know the names of any patients that you've been assigned to?"

"No, they will tell us their names late on Friday, I think," she told him.

"I hope you get assigned to a patient named Tim Harris. I work with him as a nursing 1:1. He is a great patient, the rare one who seems to be really trying, you know? I guess on some level most of the patients want to improve, but some fight you so hard, it can be frustrating. And let's just say I think he needs a fresh look at his overall treatment plan."

Courtney just nodded. Her reaction told Nathan that she was not really interested in any clinical discussions on this Fourth of July afternoon.

"We'll find out next week, I guess," Courtney said, distantly. Nathan sensed it was time for him to move on. He finished off the bottle of beer, stood up, and thanked her for it.

"Don't be silly, Nathan, it is me that needs to thank you. I was fretting about how I'd get those books in the house, unless I carried them in two or three at a time. You were a lifesaver."

Nathan checked his watch. It was a little after four-fifteen. He would be home in time to work out a little at Dave's gym, then watch a little baseball later that evening.

"Well, welcome to Hunt-Fisher, Courtney. I'll see you next week, I am sure."

"Thanks again, Nathan. Yes, I'll look for you on the unit."

Nathan ambled out of the cottage, starting to head in the direction of the hospital and his Jeep. As he walked toward the road where Courtney's Camry was parked, he noticed that many more cars had entered the area, parked on both sides of the street, centered around the cottage two doors down from Courtney's. *Someone's having a party,* he guessed. His eye was attracted to one vehicle, one that struck him as very familiar. *Isn't that Cecelia's car, there?* He changed directions, walking over to take a closer look. His eyes had seen correctly.

What is her car doing here? She is on her way to Vermont.

He walked to the side yard of the cottage between Courtney's and the one where the party was underway. Facing Bobrow's residence, shielded by a group of trees and random bushes, he heard music and voices, and saw perhaps twenty people milling around in the cottage's back yard. He felt a little sneaky doing it, but he found a spot behind a tree that offered him both cover and a relatively unobstructed view of the party going on in the backyard next to where he stood. He peered around the side of the tree, looking for his lover.

Cecelia was there all right. She was standing next to Drs. Bobrow and Short, a keg of beer at their side. She was drinking from a large yellow plastic cup, laughing at her companions' comments, her figure looking great even from a distance.

Son of a bitch, he thought. *She lied to me.* He watched her a little longer, but started to feel silly. Pulling his head back behind the tree, he hesitated for a moment, before peering around it just once more to satisfy his morbid curiosity about Cecelia's behavior and betrayal.

A voice to his side jolted him.

"Nathan, are you okay?"

Nearly jumping out of his skin, he turned and saw Courtney standing close by, evidently on her way to the party, looking at him with bewilderment on her face about why he was lurking behind a tree, sneaking a look at the resident cottage next door.

Nathan was horrified and thoroughly embarrassed.

"I'm…just…I…" He could not think of a reasonable explanation for what he was doing. "I'm…uh…hey, I'll see you later." He moved quickly away from the tree and then past her.

"Do you want to come to the party?" she asked as he passed her.

"No, no…sorry…I'll explain some time…see you later."

Nathan was jogging now, heading toward the hospital, thoroughly miffed with what he had just seen, but as importantly, mortified about what Courtney Brentwood, the nice, pretty resident with whom he would have to work for the next few months, must be thinking of him now.

She must think I'm a freakin' nut, a crazy person. She'll probably ask people if I am really a staff member, or just a patient posing as one. Shit!

Nathan's workout at the gym later was more strenuous than usual. He added ten pounds to his usual load on the Nautilus machines he was using, getting twelve reps easily despite the additional weight. He probably could have added twenty more, with the excess psychic energy he was generating. Dave was on duty at the gym, and he came over to where Nathan was engrossed in his shame-induced workout frenzy, responding to weights clanging together with far more ferocity than usual.

"Dude, what's up with you? You okay?" Dave asked.

Nathan did not answer him, and turned to set up on another machine beside the one he had been using.

"Dude, I asked you a question."

"Sorry, Dave," Nathan said, when confronted with his non-communicative behavior. "Let me finish this set, and I'll tell you. Meet me up there," he said, pointing toward the member's lounge on the second level.

Nathan was glad to have someone to talk to about Cecelia. Sharing his problem with Dave offered an opportunity for great insights. Dave was very perceptive about human behavior, and he had a knack for understanding people's motivations—especially behavior that had a touch of aberrance to it.

Nathan shared the whole story with his friend: what had occurred during the dinner time between him and Cecelia, the feelings he sensed from Cecelia in the car after their sexual play and on the unit all evening long, his helping the attractive new resident with her moving and the mortification he had felt when Courtney had caught him spying on the party.

"I couldn't think of anything to say…I was stammering, like Ralph Kramden on The Honeymooners. I was like—'a hom-ina, hom-ina…' What an asshole she must think I am."

Dave started laughing.

"That's a funny story, man," he said, beginning to laugh even harder. Nathan wanted to be put off at his friend for seemingly making so little of his emotional anguish. But Dave's laugh was so contagious, he found himself laughing out loud too.

"I'm sorry," Dave said, trying to compose himself. But he was unable to. He snuck a knowing sideways look at Nathan, which Nathan returned, and the two of them started roaring in laughter again. They were getting hysterical, rolling on the sofas where they were sitting, struck by the absurdity of the situation that resulted in his being caught behind a tree staring in at a party like a Peeping Tom. Tears of laughter streamed down both of their faces. It took several minutes for them to regain their composure.

"I'm glad my life is helping you out with any lingering depression you might be feeling," Nathan joked to his friend, in between more outbursts of laughter. Actually, this comment had a ring of truth. Nathan noted to himself that he had not seen Dave smile and laugh like this in a long time.

"Oh, man, that's a good one, one for the books," Dave said, winding down from his hysteria. He wiped off the tears around his eyes. Finally, he began thinking about Cecelia's behavior with some insight.

"Look, your relationship is steeped in deception, anyway, am I right?"

Nathan had to agree.

"I guess she got invited to this party and just didn't want to tell you, because it wasn't like she could take you with her, right? Maybe she just didn't want to hurt your feelings." Dave checked Nathan out to see if he was buying this. Nathan was not.

"But, more likely," he went on, "she wanted to be there alone. The truth may hurt, but that's probably what her motives were. She was invited, was probably thrilled about it." His voice changed into a falsetto, as he mimicked a flaky woman talking to her girlfriends. "'Hey, look at me, I'm hanging with the doctor crowd.'"

Nathan nodded in agreement, affirming Dave's assessment. It was the same one he had made himself, in his gut.

Dave did not trust Cecelia; he had shared this feeling with Nathan many times. He thought she was an opportunistic, self-important bitch. But he understood his friend's attraction to her sexual energy.

"I hate to say this, dude, because I know you like bedding her down and all, but my gut tells me it's over. It's time to move on. She is the kind who would like nothing better in this world than to hook up with a guy with an MD after his name. She's saying to herself, 'If I'm going to give this up,'" he said pointing down toward his crotch, "'it may as well be to someone I can put my claws into.' You can tell me to go fuck myself, Nathan, but I have to ask: am I on target, or not?"

"I've told her I'll get out of her life if she wants. And she has always said, 'no.' I guess the little tryst in the car put her over the edge, for whatever reason."

"Hey, look, it was heading in that direction anyway. If you two were a real item, really in love and all, you probably would have quit the hospital by now, to make the whole thing right. You were using each other. She was using you as much as you were using her, in my view."

Dave was right, Nathan realized. It's over. He wished the end had come by mutual consent, holding each other, pledging their respective willingness to be available to the other as a friend and confidant, with the door left open for some occasional lust-relieving sessions, during which no one got hurt. But that's Hollywood stuff. It is not how it really goes down. Intense physical relationships usually end abruptly, without the ongoing affection that builds up when the couple has an abiding respect and concern for the partner.

Nathan made a decision to leave the ball squarely in Cecelia's court. If she wanted their relationship to end, he was game. There were other women out there. He was tired of the deception and games-playing, anyway. It was fun for awhile, but it was getting old. Dave was right about it all.

Who am I kidding? I'm going to miss that ass and sex with her in the worst way. How will I be able to work around her, without getting anything from her, or knowing she is getting it elsewhere?

That was the part he had not yet internalized. Denial is a crazy and strangely powerful self-delusion, Nathan acknowledged to himself.

Nathan wanted to change the subject. He asked Dave about his success in getting help over at the Outpatient Clinic at Hunt-Fisher. Following through as he said he would, Dave had made the call on the Monday after his return with Nathan from the Massachusetts woods. Dave had not really wanted to get this whole mental health therapy ball rolling, but Nasty Steve was on him to take action. His first session would be later this week, with a Dr. Forbes, a fourth-year resident. Dave promised to keep Nathan informed about his impressions.

Nathan made a note to learn what he could about Dr. Forbes from his internal network at Hunt-Fisher. He wanted to make sure this Dr. Forbes was up to the task. Otherwise, it was likely that his friend Dave would eat him alive.

* * * *

Cecelia was having a wonderful time with Drs. Bobrow and Short and all the rest of the medical staff at the Fourth of July party at the new Chief Resident's cottage. This had been the right decision, Cecelia was sure, to stay around for the party. The networking she had been able to do had been fantastic. She and Dr. Short had spent hours together reminiscing about his time on 3 East. He is a smart man, Cecelia knew that from working with him for a year. But at the party she concluded that he was not bad to look at either. He was not the athletic type like Nathan, but he had an academic sexiness to him, and a wry sense of humor that had never come across in the more formal interactions she had with him on the unit. Cecelia's only regret was that they no longer worked side by side. What bad luck, she thought; getting to know him better only now, once he had left for duties on another unit. Her opportunities to leverage this time they had just spent together might be wasted. She had very little to do with the alcohol and drug unit, where he was now the Assistant Unit Chief. She might never cross his path at the hospital, except occasionally in the hallway or at the cafeteria.

Cecelia also spent time at the party with Drs. Paul, Wang and Brentwood, the new residents who would be starting on her unit the following Monday. Dr. Brentwood was very pretty, Cecelia noticed. She saw how Dr. Bobrow seemed interested in her. He kept meandering over to the four of them as they talked, squeezing himself onto the picnic table bench where they were sitting, always next to Dr. Brentwood, cracking jokes and acting like the consummate party host. Cecelia predicted they would start a relationship of some sort. She had keen radar for vibes people put out to each other, especially when there was a thinly disguised effort to try to hide it from others.

She and Nathan were through, Cecelia decided. It had been fun, and the sex had been fine, but the people at this party were the type of people with whom she belonged. Men found her attractive, and that allure could be used to gain entrance into this societal niche, the world inhabited by physicians. She could not wait to tell her mother about the people she was meeting, even if she had to lie to her a little about being at the party on that day, when she had promised to spend the holiday at her parents' home in Norwich.

Cecelia stayed at the party later than most of the nurses who had been invited. She just could not tear herself away. Then, just as she felt like it was time to make a graceful exit, Dr. Short resumed talking to her. He asked if she would like to go out to dinner with him some time. He told her he really liked talking to her, and wanted to learn more about her. They set a date for the following weekend, after she returned from Vermont.

Cecelia left the party in a state of near ecstasy. *Wow,* she thought, *I am now officially dating an Assistant Unit Chief at Hunt-Fisher Hospital. This is going to be a great summer.*

CHAPTER 9

▼

Courtney expected that she would feel very anxious about beginning her first day on 3 East, but the walk over to the hospital from her cottage calmed her down quite a bit. The weather was perfectly temperate, a bright sun was shining, the air was cool and dry, and Courtney's disposition started to mirror the morning's glorious weather. An optimistic outlook was gathering within her. *My training has to start sometime, so it might as well be today,* she told herself. The truth was that the Temple Clinic experience, with Rolanda, Charlene and the others building up her confidence, had prepared her well for serving as the lead caregiver on a multidisciplinary team. Psychiatry was different than the Clinic's care model in many ways, but Courtney resisted the premise that it was completely different. Medical care is medical care. There are diagnoses to make, goals to set and treatment strategies to implement. She was ready.

Once on the unit, Courtney made her way up the hall toward the nursing station. Patients sat quietly on both sides of the hallway, staring at her. They had been anxiously awaiting the appearance of the new doctors to whom their care had been assigned. And here was one of them, in the flesh. As she walked the gauntlet past these sets of staring eyes, Courtney made courteous, anonymous greetings to her left and right. When she was beyond the last chair, three patients got up to leave, their curiosity satisfied. Tim Harris was one of these three. He ceded his chair to another patient standing behind him, who was intent on waiting to get a bead on Dr. Paul, who was due any moment.

Courtney entered the nursing station, standing in the middle, awaiting her peers and further instructions from whomever might provide them. Emily approached her, extending a hand in welcome. "We're going to get Rounds started in about five minutes. Would you like some coffee, Dr. Brentwood?"

"Please, call me Courtney, Emily."

"I will do that, and thanks for saying so. Coffee, Courtney?"

"Absolutely." Courtney had two cups in her already, but a third would satiate her unremitting caffeine dependency.

Courtney was led to the staff coffeemaker.

"I better learn how to make the coffee here," Courtney told Emily. "I admit to being a slight addict."

"I'll show you where things are," Emily offered.

Emily opened the cabinets below the counter where the coffee machine sat, and pointed out the location of the necessary supplies: a large tin of grounds, paper filters, plastic spoons, stirring straws. The mini-refrigerator held a pint of half-and-half and milk.

"Does staff chip in for the coffee?" Courtney asked. That was the way it was done by the Clinic staff at Temple.

"We do, thanks again for asking. A dollar a week is the expected contribution for serious coffee drinkers. Sounds like you might fit into that category."

"Yes, I might have to give two dollars, to be honest."

Emily laughed. "Well, the Unit Clerk, Rosa, is in charge of the money and of buying the supplies. Let me introduce you to her."

Meeting Rosa was the first in a series of other introductions to the unit's staff: nurses, psych techs, social workers, even the unit's custodian. Sandy and Robin were now on the unit, surviving their own gauntlet run. A chime was sounded from the hallway, and the staff responded alertly. It signaled the start of the first official staff meeting on this day of doctor coverage transition on Unit 3 East, Morning Rounds. Because it was the new residents' first day, this meeting was scheduled for a full hour instead of the customary half hour.

Late on the Friday after the Fourth, Courtney had been given a list of three patients to whom she would be assigned when she began working on the unit the following week. Thus, she knew her patients' names, but she had yet to learn anything about them. The Morning Rounds would begin that process of gaining more familiarity with these individuals now under her care.

Roth was already there, talking amiably with the Assistant Unit Chief, Chet Sawyer. "*Velcommen*, welcome," Roth said forcefully, bounding out of his chair to shake hands with Courtney and her two colleagues, now joining his team. The additional German salutation was the remnant of his recent visit to Deutscheland, where he had presented a paper on borderline personality organization at a major psychotherapy conference. He had enjoyed the trip so much, he still felt compelled to greet people as he had in Frankfurt. A playful man, Roth was nonetheless serious about promoting the educational efforts of his unit's residents. Courtney had been fortunate to have him not just as the leader of her first rotation, but as the overall clinical supervisor with whom she would meet every week or so, throughout the year.

The meeting began with Roth confirming new patient assignments, now that the new residents were aboard. He read off the names of Tim Harris, Sam Bishop and Hattie Alford, assigning them to Courtney, just as she had been foretold. He also instructed Courtney that she would be "tailing" Dr. Sawyer later, when he went down to the Admitting Office to interview a prospective patient about which the unit had just learned. If the patient was admitted, Courtney would be this admission's doctor, thereby evening out her patient load with that of Drs. Paul and Wang, who had been assigned four patients.

"I know a lot of what we'll say here this morning about the patients who have been assigned to you won't make a lot of sense at all," Roth advised his novice threesome. "But don't worry about it. In a week or so, you'll be so familiar with what is happening with your patients, you'll make predictions about what Emily and her staff will say in their reports from the evening and night shift just passed…and you know what? You'll be right." The staff all laughed with recognition about the truth of his prediction. Roth then stood up and reached for a group of thick, blue plastic covered three ring binders that held the case histories and every last detail of a trio of patients on the unit.

"This, as you know from medical school," Roth began, holding up one patient chart, "is a legal document. It is evidence in a court of law, should something untoward occur. Treat it that way. Treat it like you will have to defend everything you write or consider in it, to a group of ten reasonable people from the surrounding community." He looked dramatically at each of the new residents, one by one. "I want these charts to be maintained so that I can come on the unit at any time, day or night—and, Emily will vouch for this, I have come on the unit at three in the morning to look over charts and make sure the night staff feels like they are part of our team—isn't that so, Emily?"

"Absolutely so," confirmed Emily.

"Okay? Now, I've got to tell you something," he added, still on stage. "I do come on the unit occasionally at three a.m., but I don't like it. When I do, I'm cranky and sleep-deprived. My wife has sent me off with an earful about how I wouldn't get out of bed to feed our infants when they were younger, but now I rise at two-thirty in the morning to go to look at some dumb medical charts."

More chuckling throughout the room. He looked again at Courtney, Sandy and Robin, then at the others, with as stern a demeanor as he could muster. "Okay? Got it? Don't make me grumpier than I already am, at three in the morning. I've been in court a few times, and believe me, it ain't fun. So now, I make sure that there isn't anything I should lose sleep about. I sleep well only when I am confident that you are keeping these medical records in perfect order. Kapish?" he finished, slipping into another Continental language, Italian, to confirm he was being understood.

The entire staff, including Courtney, was charmed by Roth. *Like he would have any trouble convincing a jury of anything,* she thought.

Emily began her review of all the patients, their outstanding issues, recent behavior, and any significant changes in treatment planning that the nurses were recommending, such as increasing, decreasing or modifying the medication regimen, changing their status with respect to being permitted off the hall, either with or without staff escort, or updating the doctors on family contacts that the nurses had fielded since the previous report.

After this summary, Dr. Roth asked Emily if it made sense to hold a special community meeting, to introduce the new resident physicians to all the patients. Emily had already scheduled one, since it was standard practice to give the patient group a sense of who the new, strange faces were that had joined the unit's staff, especially if these new faces were to be primary therapists for any of the patients.

Sandy asked when and where patients saw their doctors. Roth explained that the time for patient meetings needed to defer to other scheduled activities, such as occupational or recreational therapy. If patients had earned a status to leave the unit, they could meet their doctor in his or her office off the unit. A "closed hall" status meant doctors could escort patients to and from their office for individual therapy sessions. A "restricted to unit" status meant the session would have to occur somewhere on the unit.

"Then there is a special status," Roth added, "that a patient can earn that is one incremental level higher than the 'restricted to unit' status." This special status allowed a patient to be escorted to the doctor's office by both the doctor and a nursing staff member, just so there would be extra support in case the patient had any difficulty. Patients with this level of privileges were considered on "restricted to unit-session escort" status. It provided a way for staff to observe if patients were improving, gaining more responsibility for their behavior, and showing that they could handle the less restrictive "closed hall" status.

"Is that used for those whom you are afraid will run away?" Courtney asked.

"Yes. Running away, we call 'eloping,'" Roth noted. "The extra staff is there to give the message, 'if you try anything, like trying to run, there will be one staff trying to stop you, and your doctor will immediately be calling for help from Security, so you won't get far.' We don't use it a lot, but it is there as a way to allow our more restricted patients to see you, their therapists, off the unit, in your offices, which is preferable."

Roth's explanation elicited images in Courtney's head of wild-eyed maniacs running away from her, orderly-types trailing behind, lunging to grab at the disturbed person's ankle, general chaos and bedlam prevailing all around, the patient weaving in and out in main hospital hallways like a halfback caught in his own backfield, looking to reverse his course and avoid onrushing defenders.

She was going to try to avoid those types of scenes if she could.

Dr. Courtney Brentwood's first official admission to 3 East's acute treatment unit at Hunt-Fisher Psychiatric Hospital turned out to be her most memorable one.

She and Dr. Sawyer had little information about the admission until they received the call to come to the Admissions Office to interview a woman, named Georgeann Wagner. When they arrived at the Admissions area, they were greeted, to Courtney strong surprise, by Dr. Harold Hunt himself.

"You here to admit Mrs. Wagner?" he asked Sawyer intensely, in a demanding tone, ignoring Courtney for the time being.

Normally very self-assured, Sawyer became quickly subservient and solicitous. "Yes, sir, Dr. Hunt, we are." Sawyer nodded toward Courtney. "This is Dr. Courtney Brentwood, sir. Have you met yet?"

Hunt looked at Courtney. "Any relation to Aaron Brentwood?" he asked curtly.

Courtney was not going to chide him for not remembering their earlier meeting. "Yes, Dr. Hunt. He is my father."

"He is, huh?" He looked at Sawyer, then back at Courtney.

"You don't look like him."

We've established that already, sir.

Before Courtney could think of something more diplomatic to say out loud, a woman in the Waiting Room, who had been pacing anxiously nearby, moved over and tapped Dr. Hunt on the shoulder, and whispered something inaudible in his ear. Hunt introduced the woman to Sawyer and Courtney as Mrs. Georgeann Wagner, a private patient of his, who had agreed to be admitted to the hospital. Mrs. Wagner managed to nod her head in acknowledgement to the two strange doctors before her, but she was mostly interested in having a private conversation with Hunt, right away. Sawyer and Courtney deferred to this body language, leaving them alone for the time being, moving together into the next room where the Admissions Clerk sat.

"So that is our admission, I assume," Sawyer said to the clerk. She confirmed this with a silent nod.

"What is her name again? Georgeann Wagner, was it?" he asked.

"Yes, Mrs. Georgeann Wagner," the clerk reported. "She was referred by Dr. Hunt, as you probably just learned. She had an episode of some sort over the weekend, and Dr. Hunt felt she needed to be admitted, for her own safety. Here is her preliminary paperwork." Sawyer took the forms and began to read through them.

Courtney glanced over at Hunt in the next room, sitting beside his upset patient. They were huddling very close to each other, with Mrs. Wagner facing toward him, urgently whispering in his ear as he looked straight ahead, playing the seasoned confidant. He nodded occasionally, but said little back to her. Occasionally, during their hushed conversation, Georgeann glanced shyly over at Courtney, then returned her focus to her aging therapist, emotional pain evident in her countenance.

Once Sawyer finished reviewing the forms that had been handed to him by the clerk, he shared them with Courtney, to give her a chance to get updated about what he knew about the prospective admission. He was ready to begin the interview, and he led Courtney back into the Waiting Room where Hunt and his patient were sitting.

"Mrs. Wagner, could you please join us in the Interview Room?" he asked, interrupting her téte á téte with Hunt, in a tone that was overtly courteous but, at the same time, conveyed authority. He had work to do and a schedule to keep. It was time to get the admission started.

Georgeann grasped onto Hunt's upper arm harder, seeking protection. "Harold, do I have to go though with this? Can't Jerry just pick me up and take me home? Please, Harold," she begged.

Hunt was not wavering. "We agreed yesterday you would come in, Georgeann," he snapped, like a limit-setting parent. "Now I have to get back to work. I've got a hospital to run. I'll talk to you later, upstairs. You are in good hands, do you understand? Drs. Sawyer and Brently here are the very best physicians we've got here at the hospital." He turned and winked clandestinely at Courtney to reinforce his ruse, evidently intended to give the status-conscious Mrs. Wagner the sense that Hunt-Fisher had rolled in the heavy hitters for her.

Courtney's quick scan of the Admission Request Form revealed a few facts about the trembling woman in front of her. Georgeann Wagner had two residences, one in Manhattan and one in Westport. She was a widow, having lost her only husband, John Wagner, a wealthy financier and former Secretary of the Treasury in the Eisenhower Administration, roughly a year before. She had been seeing Dr. Hunt weekly since about a month after her husband's death, complaining of depression and anxiety. Prior to that, she had never sought or required mental health care. Over the previous weekend, she had called Dr. Hunt, weeping and almost incoherent, despairing over the big empty house she lived in mirroring the big empty void she felt all the time. She had shed ten pounds over the past three months, which she attributed to a loss of appetite. Dr. Hunt was prescribing an anti-depressant, Sidral, 10 milligrams twice a day, and, for the past two months, an anti-anxiety agent, Lorasis, at the same dosage.

As she sat beside Hunt in the Admissions Office of the hospital her therapist owned and operated, Georgeann Wagner looked like anything but the rich doyenne. Her hair, dyed jet black, was tousled about her head, like she had gotten out of bed just moments before, and had made only indifferent attempts to brush the unmanageable strands back into place. Her eyes had black smudges under them from the effects of weeping and wiping around hastily applied mascara. She was rake thin, and appeared very weak. Her hands and arms, which had been grasping onto her famous therapist's upper arm for protection, were still trembling slightly. But Courtney observed an aristocratic elegance in her, despite her disheveled state. She had been a beauty in her day, for sure. Now, though, she resembled an aging Judy Garland, toward the tragic end of the famous entertainer's life. At least for the moment, Georgeann Wagner was a fragile, despairing mess.

"Shall we?" Dr. Sawyer said, entreating Georgeann to join him and Courtney in the adjoining Interview Room.

Hunt helped elevate Georgeann to her feet, then guided her toward the room Sawyer was now entering. Trailing behind, Courtney observed the process, still holding the admission paperwork.

Sawyer took a seat at the desk in the Interview Room; Georgeann was led to a cushioned chair by Sawyer's side.

"I'm leaving now, Georgeann," Hunt told her. "I will see you in a few hours. Until then, please cooperate with these capable doctors. They are here to help get you back on your feet. Alright?"

Georgeann looked down at the carpet, nodding her compliance, showing less resistance to the process now, seemingly discouraged and defeated.

Hunt left, closing the door behind him. Courtney had taken a seat on the edge of the firm sofa in the room, readying herself to jot notes through the interview.

Sawyer began with a solid yet caring tone, seeking information from the prospective patient about a wide range of topics, most particularly why she was here, at the Hunt-Fisher Hospital, seeking admission. Georgeann was barely audible in her early responses to Sawyer's questions, sniffing often. She had "come a little unglued" over the weekend, she said, around the anniversary of her husband's death, crying hysterically for no reason, calling Dr. Hunt to ask him why she should go on, what was the point.

"So you had ideas of hurting yourself?" Sawyer asked, realizing this was no doubt the primary reason Hunt had recommended that Georgeann be admitted to the hospital.

"Vague ideas, nothing serious, I assure you," Georgeann responded.

"Did you have any kind of plan or method that you would use to hurt yourself?" Sawyer inquired, probing for how serious she was with her suicidal ideation.

"No, I didn't. I just felt miserable, and said out loud something like, you know, 'What's the point of living like this?'"

As the interview progressed, Georgeann became far more animated. She made better eye contact with her interrogators, smiling ruefully at herself and the behavior she had exhibited. She reluctantly admitted to her age, sixty-six, then jokingly added the qualifier, "and holding."

"Tell us about your husband's death," Sawyer urged. "How did it happen? Where were you?"

John Wagner's death had been sudden, and without prior medical warning. He had suffered what physicians like Sawyer and Courtney labeled an "MI," or myocardial infarction, commonly referred to as a sudden heart attack. It had occurred at night, while he was asleep, right next to her. Georgeann reviewed that horror-filled day, from trying to rouse him in the morning, to EMT staff arriving and doing everything they could, to watching his corpse leave their home for the final time. They had a son who lived far away in San Francisco, so she was alone, save for the four full-time staff she employed: a chauffeur, a cook, a maid and a gardener. The hardest part of life after his death was the need to make so many decisions while she was in such a state of disorienting grief. She had begun seeing Dr. Hunt soon thereafter, getting his name from her family doctor in Manhattan. They met about once a week, sometimes less. She took the medicine he prescribed.

"Are you going to keep me on the medicine?" she asked.

"We'll assess that," responded Sawyer. "What do you think? Has the medicine been helping you?"

"The Lorasis calms me down, and gets me through some panicky moments. I'm less sure about the other one, the anti-depressant."

Near the end of this admission interview, Sawyer performed a brief mental status exam, which included assessing her memory. He asked Georgeann who the current President was.

"Bush," she replied quickly.

"And before Bush?"

"Reagan. I liked him."

"And before him?" Sawyer continued.

"Carter. Yuck," she added, contorting her face in disgust.

Before Sawyer could ask, she blurted out Ford, Nixon—"double yuck," even though he was the Vice President in her husband's years around the White House—then Johnson and Kennedy.

"Jack Kennedy," she repeated, ruefully. "Surprisingly, I actually liked him, even though he and Jackie kicked us Republicans out of the White House in 1960." Courtney was not sure, but she suspected this was not just a political viewpoint, but perhaps more a personal opinion, based on direct social contact with the assassinated President.

Before being asked, Georgeann preemptively offered the next logical answer. "And Eisenhower was before him, but you know I know that, since my late husband was in that administration."

"Right," Sawyer noted, assured that Georgeann's memory faculties, at least for former Presidents, were firmly intact.

Sawyer spent some time explaining how she would be taken up to the unit, put on a status that required her to be observed closely for a short period of time. This, Sawyer explained, was customary, because it helped the treatment team get to know her. And it would help her too, by giving her a staff member to whom to talk and ask questions, if she had any. He assured her that the unit was a safe, therapeutic environment.

Sawyer concluded by framing the admission as a one-time circumstance intended to prevent any other psychiatric hospitalization in the future. "Let's try to understand what happened over the weekend, and what might have precipitated it, so that you never have to go through that again. Does that make sense?" Georgeann's gaze returned to the floor, but she nodded silently.

"Dr. Brentwood will be your primary physician and therapist while you are here," Sawyer said, a statement that drew a faint smile and look toward Courtney from Georgeann, seeming to show her approval and relief that she would not have to repeat everything she had just reported all over again, to someone new.

After notifying the Admissions Clerk of the formal decision to admit Mrs. Wagner, Sawyer and Courtney led Georgeann up to the unit. Georgeann became more anxious as she was led through the locked door. She despaired to Courtney how her life had come to this, that she was now confined to a mental institution. Courtney escorted her into the private bedroom to which Georgean had been assigned, and spent a long time with her, allaying her fears as best she could. They talked about her life with John Wagner, twenty-one years her senior: the politicians and banking elite with whom they mingled, the worldwide traveling they had done together, the time they had spent in Washington, when she was only in her late twenties, married to the man whose signature appeared on every U.S. paper currency printed from 1953 through 1960. The discussion had the desired effect; Georgeann said she was relieved that she felt like she could talk to her doctor, even though it was not Dr. Hunt, whom she trusted so much. Courtney seemed to understand her world and what she was going through. While aware that such compliments could simply be manipulations used to set up subsequent special requests, Courtney believed her new patient. *Time will tell if my instinct is right on that,* she thought to herself.

Eventually, Courtney resumed the more technical aspects of the admission evaluation. She wanted to learn more about her new patient's physical condition, given Georgeann's recent weight loss and rather rapid recent mental deterioration. Georgeann denied any physical problems, except for a slight bruise on the shoulder from a fall.

"How did that happen?" Courtney inquired.

"The fall? I felt dizzy and lost my balance."

"When did this happen?"

"The middle of last week."

Courtney examined the shoulder. Georgeann flinched slightly as Courtney examined around the minor bruise, evidently still tender to the touch.

"Had you ever lost your balance before?"

"No, not really."

"What had you eaten and had to drink before the fall?"

"Nothing to eat. I'm rarely hungry, and eat too little, I admit. And, I had had a few glasses of wine, to be honest."

"And you had taken the Lorasis that day?"

Georgeann nodded, a guilty look betraying her awareness that combining the sedative and alcohol was improper.

"I know, I know, I shouldn't drink while I'm on the medicine, I know that is something I'm not supposed to do. But I get lonely, and the wine helps me relax. It helps me get through the evenings alone."

"Had you taken the Lorasis exactly as prescribed? Twice a day, 10 milligrams?"

The guilty look reappeared. Georgeann had been caught. It was time to fess up.

"I'm going to be honest with you, Dr. Brentwood. There is no point in lying to my doctor, who is trying to help me, and I can tell you are trying to help me. I never want to have to come back here, and I want out as quickly as I can. So here is the honest truth. I've been taking a little more of the Lorasis than what was prescribed, for about a month. I just felt like I needed more. I loved the calm feeling it gave me. It was like a vacation from life."

"How much alcohol do you drink on a daily basis, Georgeann?" Courtney asked, non-judgmentally.

"Minimum two, sometimes three glasses of wine. This weekend, I just didn't care. I kept filling my glass until the whole bottle was gone, and then part of another one. That is not typical though, I promise you."

"You say you took more Lorasis than Dr. Hunt prescribed. What would happen when you ran out, sooner that expected? How did you get more?"

"I just called Dr. Hunt and said my Lorasis needed renewing, and he had it called in to the pharmacy."

"So this weekend, you both drank more than you normally do and you took double the number of pills you were supposed to. Is that right?"

"I'm afraid so," Georgeann admitted. "It's terrible, what I did, isn't it?"

"I'm not here to judge your behavior, Mrs. Wagner, I'm really not. I'm here to help you get back on track with your life. And it sounds like you are medicating yourself to ease the emotional pain you are still in."

"The Lorasis makes me feel better, yes. Are you going to take me off it, Dr. Brentwood?"

"It seems to me that you may be better off just with an anti-depressant, but I am going to talk it over with Dr. Hunt and the medical staff here first. It is not safe to simply take you off this medication, cold turkey. So we may start to taper you off, starting with the lunchtime medication."

"I see," Georgeann said, looking pensive.

"How would you feel about coming off Lorasis?" Courtney asked, echoing a question Dr. Sawyer had asked her before, to hear what her answer would be now.

"Honestly, I've never really taken pills before, and down deep, even though it made me feel calm and happy, I felt I was doing something wrong—not just about taking more than was prescribed, but just taking them period. So, strange as it may sound, I am a little relieved. I never saw myself as a drug addict, but maybe that was where I was headed if I did not stop."

"Do you drink more now than when you were married, that is before John's death?"

"Maybe a little more often, yes, because I now drink the wine every day, without fail. That was not always the case, when John was alive. But when John and I did go out, which frankly was a lot, I drank at least one glass of wine customarily. But never more than two. And once in a while we would drink a glass at home, together, before dinner."

"The problem with using alcohol along with most anti-anxiety agents," Courtney instructed Georgeann, "is that they can mask the depression symptoms. You even said it yourself. It gave you a vacation from your sad feelings. And it made you isolate yourself more, it seems. The combination also causes more intoxication than if the two drugs—alcohol is a drug, you know—are taken by themselves."

"So you want to find out how depressed I really am, without the Lorasis or alcohol affecting my mood, is that it?"

"More or less, that's right. Let's talk about your symptoms of depression. How have you been sleeping?"

"Lousy. I get a few hours, then I wake up. Then it takes me a few hours to get back to sleep. By morning, I am very drowsy."

"But alcohol can do that to you also, are you aware of that?"

"You mean interrupt my sleep?"

"Yes."

"I suppose I knew that. When I drank more wine than usual, I was almost sure to wake up in the middle of the night."

"And you have been feeling hopeless and helpless, you've told me that."

"Yes, I was really feeling that this weekend," Georgeann confirmed.

"Tell me, what has your social life been like since your late husband's death?" Courtney asked.

"What social life?" Georgeann answered quickly. The question was clearly a difficult one for Georgeann to consider. It actually elicited the first tears Georgeann had shed since she had pleaded with Hunt to allow her to go home. Georgeann told Courtney that she had rarely been out of her Westport home, isolating herself, for almost an entire year. She did not fit in anymore, without her husband. She could not bear to be out, say, at dinner, alone, with other couples patronizing her. Many old friends had called to ask her if she would join them at meals, parties or events she used to attend regularly, but now she always declined these invitations. She was homebound, a *de facto* shut-in, living for her next dose of Lorasis to ease the journey through her non-existence.

Courtney determined that, in addition to the routine blood work that all admissions have, she would order a drug screen on Georgeann, including a request for levels of Lorasis in her system. She needed to be careful with simply discontinuing the Lorasis, a drug in the benzodiazepine category, because of the potential that her first new patient might experience dangerous withdrawal symptoms. If what Georgeann was telling her was correct, and the abuse had been occurring for only about a month, the withdrawal would probably not be too severe. But Courtney had learned in medical school that it is best not to mess around with abrupt discontinuation of benzodiazepines. She would ask Roth and the rest of her medical team, but she thought it would be best to begin a slow taper off the Lorasis, take a conservative approach, and then monitor how well Georgeann was managing the taper regimen.

"Okay," Courtney said, looking to conclude this bedside evaluation, "we can talk more later and again tomorrow. But here's what I think we'll do. I'd like to get some blood work done, which is normal for every new admission. So the lab technician will be in some time soon to draw some blood, okay?"

"I hate needles, but, I guess I have no choice."

"Then we'll start to taper you off the Lorasis, if your doctor and our medical staff agree, and check how you are feeling over the next four or five days. If you have no withdrawal symptoms, if the taper goes easily for you, I expect we will get more aggressive and taper it faster. I'd like to see what you are like once the Lorasis and alcohol are not in your system. That should give us a good idea about treatment planning from there. I'll keep the anti-depressant at the same dosage you have been taking it. At least for now. Alright?"

"Okay. You're the doctor, and I have to believe what you tell me."

"If you need to get some rest, go ahead," Courtney added. "I'll check back with you in the mid-to-late afternoon."

Rising to leave, Courtney reassured the first new patient of her residency that everything was going to be fine. "I think you are in the right place, Mrs. Wagner," she said.

"Dr. Brentwood, could you do me a favor and call me Georgeann? It makes me feel younger."

Joan Truss had arrived at the room, to begin her assignment of 1:1 observation of Georgeann. Courtney needed to introduce herself to Joan, before introducing Georgeann to Joan.

Courtney turned back toward her new patient, smiling warmly and supportively. "I'll see you later, Georgeann."

What an interesting lady, Courtney thought, as she walked toward the nursing station. She is not pretentious or entitled, combative or disagreeable, like some of the types with her aristocratic background that Courtney had experienced in Scarsdale and on the Main Line in Philadelphia. She is friendly, motivated and cooperative; a lonely widow, who needs to get going with a new phase in her life. A little detox of the Lorasis would be the best way to start her treatment, then the harder part would come: starting to get her motivated to get out of her mansion, engage with the world again, resume life in her social milieu, perhaps even meet a new man with whom to share her life. *Maybe she can teach me a thing or two about how to do that.*

After documenting all the doctor's orders for the new admission, and completing all the required paperwork, Courtney called Dr. Hunt's office to give him a brief report on what had occurred. To her surprise, he insisted on speaking directly to her, leaving a meeting with Blakeley to do so.

"So, how's my patient handling things, Brentwood?"

He finally got my name right!

"Fine, Dr. Hunt. We had a long talk, and she is settling in."

"Good. Georgeann is a very nice and very classy lady, don't you think?"

"I do, sir." Courtney decided to broach the Lorasis abuse issue right away. "My sense of her, Dr. Hunt, is that she is depressed, but her erratic behavior over the weekend was primarily an anniversary-related intoxication event. It turns out she overdid it with wine and some extra self-dosage of the benzodiazepine you had her on, which, as you know, can get someone acting pretty strangely."

"I see," Dr. Hunt said. "So, how much Lorasis did she take? Was it an overdose?"

"No, no, not at all," Courtney responded quickly. "It turns out she had been ordering herself up some extra Lorasis for about a month, and drinking wine on top of that. Over the weekend, she drank much more than she usually does, which, combined with the extra ten milligrams of Lorasis, left her very sloppy and incoherent. I think that is what was causing the behavior which you were concerned about."

"So, let's get her off the Lorasis, don't you think, Brentwood?"

"I've started a taper already, sir. She should be off it entirely in a week, maybe less. Then we can see where she stands. Obviously, she was self-medicating a depression. The Lorasis was probably getting in the way of treatment, instead of calming her so she could focus on her issues."

"Good. Good work-up, Brentwood. I did not have a good enough handle on how much Lorasis she was taking."

"I think we caught a budding self-medication problem in its very early stages, Dr. Hunt. In that sense, she is lucky that what happened over the weekend happened. A year from now, if this type of behavior had continued, she would have been in far worse shape." Courtney had seen patients in medical school with long term benzodiazepine addiction, and the mental deterioration was typically very profound, especially when the patient was older.

"She must have gotten more Lorasis than I prescribed," Hunt realized.

"She said she asked you for a refill, and you phoned it in. I think it was a little manipulative of her, but, to give her the benefit of the doubt, she is a bit of a novice to the medication-taking thing, and it might have been that she just saw an emptying prescription bottle and thought, 'Gee, I'm almost out of my medicine, I need to call my doctor and get more.'"

"I still should have picked up on how it was too soon to give her more Lorasis," Dr. Hunt said, sounding irritated with himself. He hesitated, before indicating he was bringing the discussion to a close. "Thank you for the follow-up, Brentwood. Tell Georgeann I will be up to see her later." He hung up without waiting for Courtney to respond.

What a way to start. My first admission is the hospital owner's favorite private patient. Talk about hitting the ground running!

Chapter 10

▼

Any idea Nathan had that Cecelia would experience a change of heart over their weekend apart was quickly dispelled, the moment he made eye contact with her in the nursing station, as the evening shift started on the second Monday in July. He had held onto some vague hope that she would want to return to their previous secretive sexual arrangement, having had time to consider how much she would miss the chance to be with him, naked and in bed, opening herself to his adept methods of satisfying her. Would she come to him, tearfully apologizing for dissembling about leaving for Vermont on the morning of the Fourth, that she had made a big mistake, that she could not live without him in her life, that she had missed him every minute she was away from being in his arms? Her eyes told him otherwise. They conveyed distance and annoyance, Nathan sensed. The message he read was, "Why do I have to put myself through this? Won't you just go away?"

Cecelia had not returned the call he had made to her on Saturday. He had left an unemotional message, advocating that they have a frank, open, adult discussion about where they were in their relationship, that it seemed things were different between them, and asking to hear what she would like to see happen from this point forward. The message did not confront her directly on what he knew about her delayed departure to Vermont, about seeing her at Dr. Bobrow's. He had decided to leave the door open for a more dispassionate discussion, without accusatory statements to inflame the situation. But he received no return call. This did not surprise Nathan. *An avoidant behavior, to be sure.* For a psychiatric nurse, capable of confronting all kinds of evasive or disingenuous behavior by patients on the unit, Cecelia seemed remarkably superficial to Nathan—especially outside of work. She had difficulty talking about her feelings and about her attitudes within a relationship, at least to him. It was not like psychiatric nurses needed to be the picture of mental health to do their job well, but Cecelia seemed to lack basic emotional self-awareness skills. Nathan remembered the joke Joe Morse told as he was carried forcefully to the Seclusion Room, about distinguishing patients from staff by the fact that patients get better. In Cecelia's case, the joke rang very true.

Nathan gave a cursory "hello" to Cecelia, as he did with all the staff he encountered, one by one, as he made his way through the nursing station. He knew that it was not the time or place for any discussion about "them." And he was determined not to play the role of pursuer. He had done so in the past, with various women who had dumped him for this reason or that. And he had been on the other side of the equation, too, calling it quits with someone and then coping with her denial that he had meant it. He knew the distancing—pursuing relationship paradigm, and how it always left the two parties even further apart when one of them pursued the other. If Cecelia wanted to talk, the ball was in her court.

He worked through the shift, more sensitive than usual to Cecelia's presence whenever she was near him. Their level of communication slowly moved from formal to awkward to almost antagonistic. She barked a few orders at him, drew his attention to a duty to which he was assigned that needed to be accomplished. But, in general, she disregarded him.

Toward the end of the shift, he began to wrestle with the idea of waiting around her car for her after work, and having a talk with her there, or urging her to follow him to some spot in Norwalk where it would be unlikely they would be seen. But his gut told him to leave it alone, for now. He finally decided he would call her in the mid-morning the next day, and see if they could hammer out where things stood. *Which is probably nowhere.*

He spent time getting to know the new admission on the unit, Georgeann Wagner, who, he learned, was Dr. Brentwood's patient. He saw Courtney only in passing, and she greeted him warmly. *Well, at least she is not acting afraid of me, after the little Peeping Tom incident she witnessed the other day.*

Georgeann was feeling calmer. She expressed delight in the fact that she could have a long conversation with a nice young man like Nathan, who was such an easy person to talk to, someone who made her feel good about herself. They discussed her "little melt-down" over the weekend, and Dr. Brentwood's sense that she was a little out of it from the combination of the pills she had taken and the wine she had been drinking. She told Nathan all about it, leaving nothing out, unlike the minimizing responses he often received when he asked alcoholic patients over the years how much they drank. Not that he concluded Georgeann was an alcoholic. It was an interesting question, though. The more he thought about Georgeann, the more Nathan thought she might be one of those rare cases when more serious, compulsive drinking is prevented because it was identified early, before it became a more full-blown problem. Wouldn't it be great, he thought, if someone could have their problem identified at the very outset of their compulsive behavior, avoiding the more serious symptoms like blackouts and morning drinking and hiding bottles and all the other progressive behaviors that characterize the disease? Nathan made a mental note to ask Dave whether he thought a self-help type approach might help a woman with a drinking and pill-taking pattern like hers, someone who had shown a slight pattern of substance abuse, but hardly enough to be in the league with the many hard core alcoholics and addicts who populated AA. He would get Dave's take on it. His friend was usually right on about these things. And he wanted to do so quickly. Georgeann was open to suggestions at this point, recognizing that her drinking had been part of the episode that got her admitted to Hunt-Fisher. If something like AA would be helpful to her, the time to plant that seed was now.

After the shift was over, and remaining determined not to force a confrontation with Cecelia, Nathan returned home to the house he shared with a friend, Jim Scott, whom he had known since high school. He felt wound up by the anxiety of the evening—seeing Cecelia's evasiveness, running into Courtney, having lengthy talks with Georgeann and Tim. He found a beer in the refrigerator, and sat in the small living room, watching sports highlights on television, catching up on the baseball scores from the evening.

Midway through the beer, he decided to give Dave a call. Dave was a night owl, so the call was not likely to disturb him. In fact, Dave acted more put off when someone called him too early in the morning, like before ten o'clock. After a typical poor night's sleep, Dave's exhaustion was the strongest at that time. Nathan always wondered how his friend got through the day at work, without conking out from severe sleep deprivation that he put himself through.

In addition to the question he had for Dave about the new patient's fit in an AA-type program, Nathan was interested in learning how his friend fared talking to a shrink. The potential existed, Nathan knew, that Dave might manifest the type of behavior he exhibited in his short-lived tenure at college. He could be disputatious, enjoying a battle of wits, challenging statements made by others, especially if he sensed the statements were thrown out by self-important types impressed with themselves because they had two or three letters after their name.

He dialed Dave's number, and Dave picked up.

"Yo, Dave, it's Nathan. What's up?"

"Ah, not much. Trying to sleep without success, as usual."

"I figured it would be okay to call, even at this hour. So, how did your meeting go the other day at the Clinic?" Nathan began.

"Not so well," Dave replied, shortly.

Oh, shit.

"Why not so well?"

"He thinks I am pretty disturbed, that is my sense."

"He's right about that," joked Nathan.

"I know," Dave said, with a too-short chuckle, Nathan thought.

"But seriously, why do you say that?"

"Listen, Nathan, if I'm going to get involved in this therapy thing, I'm not going to hold back, play the nice, mildly disaffected, suburban angst-riddled young adult character, looking for spiritual guidance in a meek and subservient way. We got right into it. He asked me why I was there, seeking help and I told him. The fact is—I told Dr. Forbes this directly, and I will tell you too—the fact is I think about doing myself in all the time. And it doesn't faze me. It doesn't matter. Does that surprise you?"

"A little," Nathan acknowledged. Yet he knew his friend had a tendency to put on a bit of a show, perhaps reveling in a listener's grave concerns for him, even though Dave knew, down deep, that he could ultimately outthink any serious depressed thoughts and ultimately emerge victorious. But the victory would only be worthwhile if it started from a very low point. It was an alcoholic recovery paradigm, Nathan realized. The worse the story you tell in that program, the more heroic your recovery is, the more self-esteem that awaits you on the other side from where it all started. It was like a big pissing contest, to outdo another recovering person's ashes of despair from which the recovering addict Phoenix arises as a conqueror.

Dave's explained more about the blasé attitude he held toward ending his life, and toward his natural self-destructiveness in general, views he had shared with his new shrink. "I am one of those guys that a doctor is going to have a hard time figuring out, because I do what I'm supposed to, in many ways. I comply with what I am told to do in the program," he explained, referring to AA. "Yet, down deep there is a part of me that doesn't give a shit. It really doesn't. I am depressed, I can't sleep, and I struggle getting up in the morning. But once I am up and out, I enjoy people and mingling with them at the gym. So I'm not a total schizoid—isn't that the term for a kind of paranoid isolating personality? I am more like a dual personality, or something." Dave had obviously been reading up on psychiatry in advance of his treatment—ostensibly to learn more about mental illness so that he could confirm his doctor's impressions of him, but more likely to refute it if he felt the doctor was off base.

"You think so?" Nathan responded indirectly, as he did not want to reinforce too strongly his friend's self-diagnostic approach to treatment.

"So, anyway," Dave continued, "this guy said he was concerned about me, and about what I was telling him. He asked me all the evaluation questions, and he seemed really surprised that I had never had any type of counseling before, except through AA and that one meeting at GW just before I was kicked out, that the coach sent me to."

"Did you like the guy?" Nathan wanted to know, referring to Dr. Forbes. Dave had uncanny social radar, and he could sense if someone was genuine, concerned and likable, almost right away.

"Not really, to be honest," Dave replied.

"But you are going to keep going, aren't you? Give it more of a chance?"

"I am. The Nasty One told me he and his first counselor were miles apart at the start, but slowly it all came together. So I'll keep plugging away."

"Does your insurance cover the treatment?" Nathan asked.

"They'll pay fifty per cent up to a thousand bucks. We set a rate of ninety bucks per session. So I pay forty-five dollars, or about a day's take home pay for me. And I figure I have to get better in twenty-two sessions, because that is all the plan will cover, I think for my whole life. It sucks, this coverage."

"Wow. That is really bad."

"I know. But, anyway, I have another appointment next week, we'll see how it goes."

"Did he try to start you on any medication?"

"Not yet, but he is already talking about it. I don't know if I'm going to go for that."

"It might help. I'd listen to what he suggests. Hey, Dave, can I ask you something about AA? I need your opinion about the kind of people it helps. There is a new admission on our unit, a real nice lady, over sixty years old, but still looking good and, like I said, just really a nice lady. She had to be admitted because she was taking a little extra of a drug called Lorasis, which you've probably heard of."

"Sure," Dave confirmed. "Lots of people in the program abused it when they were out," meaning when they were still drinking and drugging.

"And she would drink a few glasses of wine every day, which along with the Lorasis made her very mellow, to say the least. She lost her husband about a year ago to a sudden heart attack, and she is lonely and depressed without him. Then this weekend, the anniversary of his death, she doubles up on the wine, finishes a whole bottle or more, and loses it. You know, slobbering around, out of her mind, talking shit. She calls her doctor in the midst of this, and the next thing she knows she's in the hospital explaining it all to me, as an inpatient."

"So, you want to know if AA could help her?"

"She had no problems before the old man's death, none whatsoever. And even when she overdid it this weekend, it was just like one bottle or so, like four or five glasses of wine. I mean, four or five fucking glasses of wine? What is that? It's nothing, really."

"Equal to what I used to have before I even went out for the evening, when I was drinking," Dave acknowledged.

"Exactly. I mean, would she get laughed out of AA? To my way of thinking—and I don't know a lot about alcoholism—but to my way of thinking, the base issue is that for the past few months, she was no longer a quote-unquote social drinker, you know what I'm saying?"

"I do know what you are saying. She may have caught herself early. Lots of the older women in AA talk about drinking socially for years. Then they gradually increase their intake until it gets out of control. So, the answer is, no, she would not get laughed out of AA. In fact, if I take her to a meeting, I'll make sure she is warmly received."

"Would you do that?" Nathan asked.

"Sure. It's all a part of the process of recovery, being of service, giving it back. Have her give me a call when she gets out."

"Well, I'm not in charge of her planning or anything, but I may slip her your name. I'll tell the doctor, a new resident, the one I helped move in that day when I was peeking in at Cecelia."

Dave laughed again, remembering Nathan's antics. "Tell her you can hook her up with a friend in AA, to at least try it out," Dave suggested. "What's her first name so I know who you are talking about?"

"It's Georgeann."

"Got it," Dave confirmed. "So," he continued, coyly, "what transpired with Cecelia tonight?" Nathan related the occasional hot tongue and general cold shoulder he had received.

"Hey, I'm facing up to shit, so you should too. It's over, my friend."

Dave was right. Dave was almost always right.

Courtney called Jason late, after midnight. When she had called him earlier in the afternoon, he told her he was exhausted from taking a red-eye in from the coast. He had delayed his return to Philadelphia until the very last flight he could take and still start medical school on time, hoping to wring every last minute of his time off between semesters. Starting his courses only a few hours after getting off the plane early on the morning, he desperately needed some rest. To accommodate her friend's request, Courtney had caught an after-work nap herself, so that she would show some energy and alertness for the conversation ahead—one she had been looking forward to for days. She recognized that these interactions might diminish in frequency, as the more unique, landmark moments—like their respective first days of training for the year—faded into more normal routines.

Jason answered on the first ring.

"Hi, Court," he said, answering instantly because he was expecting her call.

"Are you in better shape now?" she asked. "Did you get some sleep? I guess your body still thinks it is only nine o'clock, not midnight, doesn't it?"

"Yeah. I was out from five o'clock to nearly eleven," Jason noted. "It was probably stupid to come back so late, but I couldn't help myself."

"I don't blame you for avoiding Philadelphia until the last possible moment. You got to spend one more evening in California, right? So, what did you have to do today?" Courtney asked.

Jason walked her through the clinical rotation to which he was assigned, and seminars he had begun. He explained that he was having a hard time getting motivated for the final year.

"And," he continued, "I missed having you around."

"Oh, I miss you, too, Jason. I really do," Courtney reciprocated, meaning the words more deeply than she cared to admit to her friend. She knew that the void she felt in her life was due in part to the transition she was making, but it was also a response to missing Jason's daily presence around her. She told him she was trying to connect with her new peers at the hospital, including at the recent Fourth of July party at the Chief Resident's cottage. It just was not the same without him around.

"I think the Chief Resident has the hots for me," she added, looking to lighten the exchange a bit.

"Really? What's he like?"

"He such a preppie, it's scary. I'm not interested," she said. She might be forced to do the politically correct thing, and socialize with him casually around the cottages, but not to the extent she thought he was expecting.

Courtney asked about Lara's plans to start shooting her television show.

"The contracts are all finalized, and she began with some meetings today. I'm calling her after we talk, so I'll know more after that."

"She must be so excited. Who else is acting on the show?"

Jason listed some names, none of which Courtney recognized.

"I can't wait to see her on TV. Won't that be a rush?"

"It will be. So, when are you inviting me up to see your asylum in the sticks? Should we plan something?"

Courtney was thrilled he mentioned it first. Otherwise, she most certainly would have.

"Let's," she agreed. "When? How about three weeks from now? Say, last weekend in July? Is that too soon?" Courtney squinted her eyes, hoping not to hear that he was thinking of a much later time to come up to visit her.

"I think I could swing that," he replied. "I'll confirm my schedule tomorrow, and let you know. Put together a plan for us to have some excitement in the Big Apple, alright? I'll need it, after being here for three weeks in this hell hole. And I'm definitely coming out to see your new setup in Connecticut. I need to have a visual about where you are, so I can relate when we talk about it. Okay?"

Courtney tried to stay subdued as she confirmed that she would put a great weekend together. Inside, she was exhilarated. *Something to look forward to! It's only been two weeks, but I can't wait to see him again.*

Nathan did not sleep well that night, despite the fact that he was going to have the following day off. He could not get Cecelia off his mind. Intellectually, he had always understood that theirs was a transitory coupling. But the end was upon him, and he was having trouble just shaking it off. For Nathan, the hardest part of the apparent end of his relationship with Cecelia lay in the reality that he was no longer desired. His formulation about their relationship had always been that he was just too damn good, in bed and as a playmate—the career danger notwithstanding. *Not so, I guess.*

He summoned up the will to call around ten in the morning. When she picked up on the other end, he was actually slightly surprised to hear her voice.

"Hi, Cecelia. It's Nathan."

"Hello, Nathan," she replied, in a voice that conveyed an attitude not dissimilar to the one he had experienced from her the night before.

"Listen, Cecelia, since last week, since our little dinner break together, I'm sensing you are distancing yourself from me. I'm right about that, aren't I?"

"Nathan," she sighed, belittling him with her irritated tone, "you and I never, you know, pledged ourselves to the other. We had a few dates, and it was fun. I've just been doing a lot of thinking, and I'm finding myself interested in exploring other avenues in my life. You always said you saw a day coming when we would need to stop seeing each other."

"And that time is now?" he asked, hurt most by the glibness with which she was delivering the final blow.

"That time is now," she declared, forthrightly. There was silence as Nathan absorbed this statement, which verified what he understood already, even through moments of denial. But it was still difficult to hear the final confirmation.

"So that's it," he said, finally. "Just like that?"

"How else do you want me to say it, Nathan?" she demanded, her voice edgy with emotion. "I like you, and we have to work together, so this isn't good-bye," she added.

"I kind of expected a little more in terms of an explanation," Nathan responded. "You changed your feelings for me that fast?"

"Nathan, I don't think I need to explain anything to you," Cecelia insisted, appearing to want this conversation to end as quickly as possible. "We had fun, but like I said, I am keeping my options wide open right now. So let's leave it at that, okay?"

Nathan wanted to confront her about the "options" he saw her exploring at Bobrow's Fourth of July party. He hesitated. *Fuck it. It's not worth it.*

"I guess we will have to leave it at that. Alright, good-bye then, Cecelia. I'll see you tomorrow, I guess," his voice trailing off. He was feeling miserable, and not hiding it very well.

"And so we have an understanding, right, Nathan? My job is very stressful, and I need to focus when I'm in charge. So, well, I just don't want to deal with anything from you."

"Like what?" Nathan snapped back, angrily. "What might you have to deal with from me?"

Cecelia hesitated, then changed course.

"Nothing. Never mind. I don't know what I meant. I just want to go to work and do my job, that's all."

"And I'll go to work and do my job, that's all, too," Nathan said, still angry.

"Fine."

"Fine."

"Good bye, Nathan. I have to get going. I'll see you next time we are on together."

Nathan did not respond. He just hung up the phone, a little more forcefully than usual.

It's not easy getting chucked.

Chapter 11

By the third week in July, and after six weeks in the hospital, Tim Harris was nearly ready for discharge from Hunt-Fisher Hospital. His plan was to join a day treatment program offered by the hospital, using it as a transitional step between the twenty-four hour care at the hospital and returning to life at home. He would spend a few weeks in this program, while continuing to see Dr. Short as an outpatient.

Short's instructions to Courtney as she took over Tim's care planning were clear: he did not want Courtney playing much more than a relatively disengaged caretaker role with Tim; he wanted her to keep Tim on the medication regimen Short had initiated; and, he wanted her to focus only on encouraging Tim to comply with the aftercare plan Short had set up already. She was to briefly answer questions Tim had about the day program and why it was a useful follow-up plan after the hospitalization, reporting any behavioral changes to Short so that he could decide if a medication change was in order. Otherwise, the message to Courtney was "stay out of the way." Short discouraged Courtney, in very direct terms during their case handoff meeting, from engaging Tim in any psychotherapeutic interactions. It would be very unwise for an interim therapist to foster a bond with Tim, Short explained, especially at a time when he was in the midst of the process of establishing such a bond himself with his patient. It was best for Tim and for Courtney to keep their meetings brief and highly task-oriented. Her role was to be a short-term administrator of his care, not his therapist.

In the first few meetings Courtney held with Tim, she followed Short's orders to the letter. Their initial meetings rarely lasted longer than even ten minutes. Tim tried to talk about his fears about returning home to what he describes as his "dysfunctional" family, which included parents whom he described as career-focused and emotionally distant. He spoke of an adolescent brother who menaced the household with his behavior: partying with drug-addled friends who cavorted around their upscale Norwalk home throughout the day, loud music blaring, while the parents were at work. Tim wanted Courtney's advice about how he should cope with the frequent fighting he witnessed between Tim's brother and parents when they returned in the evening to find the home a mess and Tim's brother in various states of inebriation or disorientation. But Courtney told Tim that it was best that he convey these fears to his therapist, Dr. Short, once he completed the hospital stay. Tim could not understand why she would not at least talk to him, give him her perspective, as Nathan, his favorite staff member, did all the time. Nathan, Tim noted, always encouraged him to get his feelings out, to develop an awareness of his emotions so that he could better manage them. That was the main thing he had learned in the hospitalization, Tim explained to Courtney. The best way to work through a problem was to talk it out, trying to learn from others and confirm or dispel your own take on situations. He complained that his meetings with Short were usually curtailed, for this reason or that. According to Tim, Short seemed mainly interested in getting him on the correct medication rather than getting to really know what troubled him on the inside.

About a week before Tim's scheduled discharge, Courtney relented to Tim's request for a little more time to talk about his fears of returning home. They used the full hour that was the normal time devoted to therapy sessions with patients. Courtney rationalized the lengthier session to herself by framing it as an extended discussion of Tim's discharge plan. Yet, she knew that Short would have frowned on the way she acceded to Tim's request for more time together. Courtney's first reaction to Short was that he was an arrogant man, not one to solicit input from others. He knew what was best, period. That kind of attitude irritated her. Perhaps she was responding to his manner when she stayed with Tim longer than Short would have liked. *What's the harm, really?* she asked herself.

Two days later, only forty-eight hours before Tim's scheduled discharge, they met again in the late afternoon, and the session lasted for another fifty minutes. Courtney had begun with her customary exploratory questions: did Tim understand his discharge plans, did he have any questions about what these plans entailed, did he understand what was expected of him? But Tim wanted to go beyond the "yes" and "no" responses to these closed-ended questions. He spoke of running out of time to talk about how to work on his coping skills, his ability to react to his family in a healthy way, rather than isolating and building an internal case for self-harm. Courtney listened attentively, and posed questions about managing different situations as they arose. At one point, one of her statements drew a wide smile from Tim, and she asked him what caused it. He said Nathan had said the same thing to him the previous evening.

"If one person you trust tells you something, it is input to think about. When two or more people you trust give you the same input, it becomes feedback that you need to take a hard look at," he said, philosophically.

"I'm glad you trust me, Tim," Courtney responded. "It is important that you develop and maintain that kind of trust with Dr. Short, as well."

Tim became pensive, seeming to perform an inner assessment of his trust level in Dr. Short. "Basically, I do trust Dr. Short. He is smart and has always been straightforward with me. But," he added after hesitating slightly, "I have never gotten the impression that he gets me. Do you know what I mean? I don't get the feeling he *really* knows what my unique circumstances are."

"You have a role in creating that understanding, though, don't you?" Courtney asked.

"I know, part of it is up to me. But, I just don't feel as understood by Dr. Short as I do by Nathan, or even by you in these last two sessions."

This comment from Tim forced Courtney to consider that Short might have been right, that having two doctors with different styles might be confusing Tim. She did not want Tim comparing her against Short; that was not her job, especially since she would be his doctor for only a few days more. But what if he were right, that the doctor Tim just happened to be assigned to did not practice the way Tim most needed a therapist to practice? Did Tim really have a choice of therapists? What if Tim was showing healthy insight, and beginning to stick up for himself, exercising his rights as a patient to choose the best caregiver for himself? At that point, Courtney realized she had a lot to learn. She really did not know the answer to these questions. Her skills and insights were too raw, as yet. She needed to cut Tim off, and refocus him on the value of his overall discharge plan and working with Dr. Short.

"You know Tim," she replied quickly, "it really does you no good to compare me to Dr. Short. Maybe it is just your way of expressing your ambivalence about leaving the hospital. It is a little frightening for you, isn't it?"

Tim nodded.

"And it may be easier to spend time thinking about comparisons between two doctors you have met than focusing on what it is going to be like for you once you leave. So let's get refocused on what we have to do to prepare you for your next phase of treatment, with your doctor, Dr. Short. Does that make sense to you?" She looked for a verbal confirmation from him, in order to cement in her own mind that she had performed her duties correctly in Tim's case, per Short's orders.

"I guess so," Tim said, unenthusiastically.

"Alright, then, let's stop for now. Next time we talk, let's really drill down to specifics about your schedule, day by day, right after your discharge. Okay, Tim?"

"Okay." Tim's spirits appeared low at the end of the session. Courtney sensed he was chiding himself for trying to open up to her. That had not been her intention, but she needed to comply with Short's plan.

Courtney was surprised to get a call from Short the next day.

"Dr. Brentwood, this is Dr. Short. I am calling because, well, I'm a little concerned about what I am hearing from the unit, 3 East, about how you have been spending longer with Tim Harris in your sessions than we agreed you would. Is that the case, Dr. Brentwood?"

Courtney felt her face warming in anger, frustration, a small dose of guilt and a feeling of being betrayed. She had just started, and already a staff doctor was upset with something she had done. And someone from the unit had taken it to Short, to create this confrontation.

"The session might have lasted a bit longer than you and I talked about, Dr. Short, but he had some questions, which I tried to answer. We were focused on his immediate discharge plans. I didn't think it was the time of the session that mattered as much as the nature of the interaction. And that stayed right on target with the goals you established, I can assure you of that." She said this feeling it was the truth.

"I thought we had an understanding about how important it was that Tim stay away from any psychotherapeutic interactions with you. You understood why that was recommended, didn't you?"

"I did. I think this is a misunderstanding. Tim has been told, by me and others, that it is best that he work with you in therapy."

"Then I still don't see why your sessions lasted as long as they did," Short repeated.

What is wrong with this asshole? And how did he learn about the sessions going that long?

"I was just answering his questions, like I said," Courtney responded. "Is that all, Dr. Short? I have some charting to do." *I have had enough of this inane conversation.*

"Don't take this the wrong way, Dr. Brentwood, please," Short added, in conclusion, in a patronizing voice. "I am just very meticulous in the way I take care of my patients. Therapist switches in midstream are very hard for patients. And you are so…well, let's say you are just learning. I'm making sure that the plan we all agreed to is being followed, that's all."

"I understand. Very commendable of you," Courtney said. The sarcasm did not escape Short.

"It might help if Dr. Roth and I discuss this. He is your supervisor, isn't that right?"

Courtney was astounded that Short had gone to the effort of learning who her supervisor was. All because she spent a little extra time with a patient? This, she thought, was absurd.

"He is," Courtney confirmed. Short told her he would call him tomorrow. Courtney barely heard this, as she was already hanging up.

I can not believe this, she thought. *I have to talk to my Dad about this.*

Short had been tipped off to Courtney's extended sessions by Cecelia, who was thrilled to find any reason to call and make contact with the man she had just dated, to talk. Courtney and Tim's extended session had offered the perfect opportunity for her to reach out to her new boyfriend, or at least so she hoped. The call was a professional courtesy, she figured. The doctor covering for him, the pretty one that drew all the stares away from her, was not following the plan that Cecelia had read about in Tim's chart. Ten to fifteen minute sessions to review a few discharge-related items, that was all Tim was supposed to receive from his interim doctor. But they had been gone off the unit for a full hour, if you include the time it took to get to Dr. Brentwood's office and back. Dr. Short would want to know this. And their talking would give him a chance to broach the subject of seeing each other again.

Cecelia and Short had gone out on their date the previous weekend, just as they had planned at Bobrow's party. She considered it a great night. They had a nice dinner at a chop house in Westport, he had managed all the food and wine orders, and done so with such a confident and polished demeanor. Then they had stayed at the restaurant for a few more drinks, and had returned to her place. She decided she would not sleep with him on this first date. Her instincts told her that would start things off between them too fast, and he might think less of her. He had taken the initiative to kiss her good night, and she had responded. The kiss had been long and intense, certainly giving him the message that there was more where that came from. Yet, he had not called her the next day, which was not necessarily a bad thing—he had not promised to, or anything. But Cecelia had wanted him to in the worst way. She wanted him to be infatuated with her, she hoped he would feel an overpowering need to talk to her, a need to be with her again, as soon as possible. Maybe she should have slept with him after all. Give him a taste of what it was like to climb on top of her and love her. She would have responded to him, made him feel so special, like he was such a natural at lovemaking, no matter how she really responded. But he would have to ask her out again before that could happen. So, her job was to give him all the chances he needed, by staying in touch with him as often as she could. He had thanked her for the information, and promised to speak with her again soon, but he was late for a meeting. She had hung up convinced that it had been very shrewd of her to make the call, in many ways. She made up her mind to keep looking for these types of incidents where their respective professional practices intersected, to make sure she stayed in his awareness as much as possible.

Nathan acted very distant towards Cecelia on 3 East, even more so than she did towards him, once they were no longer a couple in any sense of the word. When they worked together, he rarely initiated even so much as a courtesy greeting, only nodding in superficial, silent response if she made any attempt to recognize his presence. His distancing was not a ploy to draw Cecelia closer. If anything, it was an exercise in purposeful restraint, a way for him to detach from the situation and gain a sense of the bigger picture, more with respect to his own behavior than hers. He was beginning to realize that as hurt as he was by the suddenness of their break-up, he was also relieved to begin feeling more in touch with his values somehow, with what was really going on, inside and around him, than he had during the period of his illicit romance with Cecelia. When he was involved with her, he recognized that he had slipped into a more devious mindset, becoming more beholden to his impulses, and exercising far less judgment about how to conduct himself. The relationship had devolved into a submissive hunt for pleasure, into an illusion of superiority over a system the two of them were a part of, and yet were sabotaging in their own way. Cecelia had been like a recreational drug that turned addictive for him, offering steady, palliative relief from facing up to his aimless life, his financial impoverishment, his status as unskilled labor in a workplace that rewarded only licensure and academically-earned letters after your name, letters like BA or MS or PhD or MD—none of which he had, nor had real prospects of gaining any time soon.

His self-critical assessments were coupled with more discerning observations about Cecelia's act, as well. He felt like he was finally seeing Cecelia as she really was, now that he no longer focused only on her sublime gluteal curvature and unique sexual appeal. It was all so much clearer now. He described to Dave that his perspective had morphed from lusting after her to being put off by her immaturity and arrogance. Dave synthesized this change in his friend's viewpoint simply and succinctly: Nathan had stopped seeing Cecelia as a piece of ass, and now saw her just as an asshole. And this assessment, Dave reminded Nathan, just corroborated what Dave had been telling him all along.

Behavior Nathan had excused before as evidence of Cecelia's managerial toughness he now perceived as an unkind, bossy manner with subordinates that wore employees out, at least spiritually. Actually, what was clearer to him now was that she was uneven in the way she comported herself professionally. As demanding and difficult as she was with nursing staff under her command, she was obsequious and fawningly sweet to the doctors on the unit, especially the male ones. It was clear there was a sexist nature to her interactions with the doctors. It was pretty obvious that Cecelia had no use for Courtney. Courtney had encroached on her space. Nathan often observed how Cecelia would respond to the sight of Drs. Roth, Sawyer, Wang and nearly everyone else perking up around Courtney, looking for ways to engage her in conversation and then trailing her with their eyes, admiringly, at the conversation's end. Cecelia's eyes would narrow in rage, and Nathan knew what she was thinking. Prior to Courtney's appearance on 3 East, Cecelia had forged a virtual monopoly on the titillation of male staff. But her apparent reign as the sole source of men's admiration on the unit was over—or at least until Courtney rotated to her next training assignment.

Nathan secretly took delight in finding ways to converse casually with Courtney in front of or around Cecelia. He asked Courtney often about how he could support her work with Tim, what to do to prepare Tim for discharge. He also asked her for suggestions about how to talk to Georgeann. He made a point of inserting flippant, derogatory remarks about Philadelphia whenever he had cause to make them, because he remembered how she had told him at her cottage about her distaste for the city where she had attended medical school. He even engineered it so the staff outing to Shea Stadium that he was planning and promoting would take place when the Phillies were in town, so that Courtney would be more likely to come along. He sensed she would love to watch a New York team beat up on the hapless team in red from the Vet.

When Cecelia was in the rear of the nursing station as these exchanges between Nathan and Courtney took place, Nathan could sense her attentiveness to their interaction. He did not turn to confirm her reaction—that would be too obvious. But he could tell she was annoyed, the way men can sense the vibes of women with whom they have been intimate.

Courtney called her father the evening after Short had challenged her clinical decision-making and case management behavior in the Tim Harris case. She would remain open to her father's experienced viewpoints, and she wanted to learn what she could from this incident. But about one thing she was adamant: Short was a jerk, a pretentious and arrogant man from whom she did not think she could learn much of anything. In fact, her intuition told her that if Short took one side of a reasonable clinical argument, she would be almost certain that the other side was correct. She wanted no part of him.

Aaron took the call from his daughter in his study.

"Hi, honey, how are you doing?" he began.

"Okay, Dad. But not so great about something that happened earlier today. Mind if I get an expert third party perspective on it?"

"Talk to me," Aaron encouraged her.

Courtney laid out the situation that led up to Short's challenging phone call: taking over Tim's case for just a few weeks, the plan to take a more administrative role on the case, and to avoid any semblance of engaging in psychotherapy. She recounted the case hand-off discussions she had had with Short, and his recommendation of a time limit to her sessions with Tim. A brief review of the way she had conducted the sessions followed, then the words and final threatening remark Short had made.

"What do you think, Dad? If you were in Dr. Short's place, what would you have done?"

Aaron paused for several seconds. Courtney waited patiently, being accustomed to this tendency of his to take some time in thought, synthesizing the information with which he had been presented before sharing his reaction.

"Well, I have a couple of thoughts. Let's consider the more supportive angle first. The reason Hunt-Fisher has a residency program is that it wishes to be a teaching institution, correct?"

"Right," Courtney affirmed.

"So, when faculty members have interactions with residents, especially PGY1s just getting started, they have a duty to approach a clinical discussion from an educational perspective. From what you told me, this Dr. Short failed miserably in this respect."

Courtney nodded, reviewing the call in her head. Her father was right. Short had taken a blaming rather than an instructive approach.

"Plus," Aaron continued, "there are human relations conventions that Dr. Short either ignored or chose to ignore. Doctors are notoriously bad about presenting criticism artfully. They feel pressed for time. Many suffer human errors poorly, and they go right for the jugular, with no concern for the short and long term effects of their criticism. The conversation should have started with Short asking you how things were going, drawing you out on how you were acclimating to Hunt-Fisher, then finding a way to present his concern in a way that would make you less defensive, and actually want to explore your decision—or let's say, your behavior—in treating his patient."

"You're right. I'm here to learn, and if he had presented it as something to look at and learn from, I actually might have been grateful for his willingness to care enough to want to encourage me to learn from the case."

"Exactly. I mean, he treated you like an attending would treat a house physician at a general hospital. If I was arbitrating this conflict, as Roth might be asked to do, from what you told me, that is the first thing I would focus on." Courtney nodded silently, wondering if Roth would have the same perspective as her father. Her sense was that he would.

"Now, let's look at the clinical issue itself, rather than the manner in which the issue was discussed and handled, which, again, I think this Dr. Short butchered. The concern about this young man getting psychotherapy from you when Short was in the midst of developing a therapeutic relationship with him is a sound one. Framing your work with the patient as more administrative and case management-oriented is very reasonable, especially given the plan for Short to continue with the patient after discharge. And your responses to him in the sessions sounded very appropriate and consistent with this arms-length role. Essentially, the length of the session is of far less importance than the maintenance of the administrative role you were taking. It is reasonable to ask, though, why would any session last very long if you were taking this role? One answer might be the patient's confusion about his plan, or his need for more understanding about what was expected of him in, say, this day treatment program he will be discharged to." Aaron paused to allow Courtney to think about whether this was the case.

She acknowledged the difficulty of separating the two roles. "The kid is frightened to leave the hospital, that's for sure, and I did my best to avoid much more than an acknowledgement that this was what he was feeling. But I have to say, he was trying desperately to engage me in a therapeutic-type of exchange. It was hard to play the stone-walled position, 'I'm sorry, we can not talk about that, you must bring this up with your therapist when you leave.'" She used a deep, affected monotone for this final hypothetical statement, to make her point.

"And that is what you are in a residency program to learn, dear," Aaron replied quickly. "You must be flexible, yet disciplined. Tough but caring. Confrontational without engendering unhealthy defensiveness. You have a lot to learn, but so did I and every other psychiatrist who is worth his or her salt when they were at your stage of training."

They processed the conversation and the Harris case a little longer, but Courtney got the gist of her father's perspective: Short was not a natural teacher, he was controlling and prone to demeaning criticism rather than collaborative learning, but she needed to look at why she had ventured slightly outside the plan that was established, and what that might indicate about areas in her training upon which to continue focusing. She could live with that.

The next day, Courtney had a scheduled clinical supervision with Dr. Roth. He had heard from Short, but his reaction to him had been much the same as Aaron's.

"I said to him, 'You just finished working here as Chief Resident, and you know what the story is. We're a team, and he fell short—if you pardon the pun—on his responsibility to provide you with academic leadership, in the team context. I told him to discuss any such issues that he had with you or with any of our residents with me first. And I added that he should not expect any patient referrals from us to his practice if he maintained his controlling attitude. I think he was properly humbled. So let's not fret about him. Let's see what there is to learn from this little incident."

The supervision sessions with Roth were proving to be the highlight of her residency training. Courtney admired Roth a great deal. If her afternoon of sucking up to Blakeley and Fencik in late June had had anything to do with her getting him as a supervisor, it had been well worth it.

Chapter 12

▼

Courtney parked her car in the garage at the South Norwalk station, and caught the 5:48 train for Grand Central Station to meet Jason. She had just made the train in time. A few last-minute tasks had kept her at the hospital until just after five o'clock, as she could not leave for the weekend until all her charting and doctor's orders were completed. But the train-catching instincts she had developed over the years were still intact. Just as she had done many times in taking a train into the city from Scarsdale, Courtney left just enough time to arrive at the platform as the train rolled into the station.

It had been a long and emotionally-draining day, filled with many sessions with patients and their families. Many had requested weekend passes, and Courtney was required to approve or deny these requests, and to set the therapeutic terms for the off-grounds visits she granted. This often included the need to negotiate the specific goals that these passes would hope to achieve. Everything needed to be fully in place before Courtney could escape for the weekend. In one instance, she had to deny such a pass request made by an impulsive and still self-destructive patient, out of Courtney's concern, shared widely by the nursing staff, that the patient posed an elopement risk. The patient had reacted bitterly to the news of the decision to deny her a pass, and this confrontation was still on Courtney's mind as she found a seat on the train. She sighed in relief that the work week was over. Between the excitement she felt all day about seeing Jason and the emotionally taxing work with the patients and families, Courtney was spent. She needed an extended train ride to decompress, and to catch her second wind.

Arriving in Grand Central about an hour later, Courtney felt sufficiently distant from her issues at work to begin focusing on how excited she was to start the weekend with her medical school companion. But she was pressed for time. She had agreed to meet Jason at seven o'clock in front of Penn Station, and that deadline was now less than fifteen minutes away. While she might normally enjoy a midsummer evening stroll between the two rail stations in Manhattan, the tight deadline forced her hand; she would need to take a cab. After a short but nettlesome wait in line in front of Grand Central, she was granted access to a waiting taxi, from which she directed the driver to her destination, asking him to hurry. The traffic cooperated on the Avenues—the driver chose 5th Avenue for the first leg of the trip—but the cross town leg of the voyage on 37th Street over to 7th Avenue was frustratingly slow.

As seven o'clock came and went, and with the cab still several blocks from Penn Station, Courtney began fretting about her tardiness. She had wanted to be at the top of the escalator at 32nd Street and 7th Avenue, to welcome Jason to New York, smiling and with arms outstretched, eager to get their weekend started properly on her turf. It was only right that she be there to demonstrate how appreciative she was of his effort to come up to see her, to prove that their friendship had, indeed, stood the test of a temporary separation, just as they had said to each other that it would.

Perhaps, she hoped against hope, his train had been delayed. Many trains she had taken to New York from Philadelphia over the past three years had arrived late. Who knows, she might actually beat him to their rendezvous spot, she thought. It was possible she was worrying needlessly. But if his train had arrived as scheduled, he would wait for her, right where they had planned to meet, she was sure of that. Sitting forward on the edge of the cab's back seat, Courtney mentally urged the traffic forward, but to little avail. The intersections were clogged, and the cab made little progress when the light turned green. "Come on," Courtney pleaded out loud in anguish, more to herself than the cab driver, when the cab was held up by the same light a second time, after making no more than a car length or two of forward progress. Finally, the cab turned onto 7th Avenue. As it edged close enough to her ultimate destination, she was able to scan the mass of humanity assembled along the broad sidewalk in front of Penn Towers and Madison Square Garden, looking for some sign of Jason.

Just east of the taxi stand where they were to meet, she spotted him. He was standing alongside the curb, wearing a blue floral Hawaiian shirt and khakis, holding a small black duffel bag, eyes concealed by his trademark wraparound sunglasses. Courtney's heart raced. *There he is!* She felt such a warmth and happiness looking at him, she could not contain a broad, affectionate smile. As she continued to stare longingly at him, the cab inched forward. Her impulse was to burst out of the vehicle and rush across the street, but the cab needed to get to a spot closer to the crowded curb, where it could safely drop her off and allow the driver to transact the fare payment. As the driver began his move to terminate the ride, Courtney was reluctant to lose sight of Jason even for a second. If he made any kind of move, she needed to know he was doing so, and adjust accordingly. Before the cab had even come to a complete stop, Courtney had the appropriate amount of cash already drawn from her wallet, tip included, ready to extend to the driver through the clear plastic separator between the front and rear seats, to hasten the payment process along as quickly as possible. Her eyes returned to Jason as she opened the door to leave the cab. She felt an almost breathless excitement about their reunion, an impatience to greet him instantly. Yet, once out of the taxi and standing on the sidewalk in front of the Hotel Pennsylvania, she briefly remained motionless, compelled to reflect on what was going on inside her. She admired this man so very much, the one upon whom she had focused her attention over the past few minutes, the one who now stood across from her on the west side of 7th Avenue. He had come up from Philadelphia just to see her. He meant more to her, she realized at this moment, than she had ever been able to admit. She was too aroused, too eager, the warming within her too profound and authentic to accept the premise that this was a simple reunion of two ex-medical student friends.

Damn. I think I am in love with this man.

She allowed herself a brief instant of self-indulgent fantasy. She wanted Jason Burke to herself. She wanted to be with him, to spend the type of special intimate time with him that lovers spend with each other. She wanted to hold him, to kiss him and touch him without constraints. Most of all, she wanted him to feel the same way about her.

Pull yourself together, Courtney, she told herself, trying to rid these fantasies from her mind, now fearing that she might betray these inner thoughts to him in some way. She needed to get back to reality. She chided herself for being so selfish. After all, she had gotten what she wanted: he had followed through on his promise to visit her, and this was to be a brief, cordial reunion with a close medical school friend, and nothing more. She tried to rationalize the emotions that had surfaced so surprisingly within her over just these past few moments. Perhaps she was just overreacting to being with someone she trusted and with whom she felt a special bond, especially after a month of lacking this type of relationship. Maybe she was just emotionally vulnerable right now, feeling lonely and a little disoriented as she faced new challenges in her professional training. This fantasy of a loving, intimate relationship with Jason was irrational, a result of coping with transition. She theorized that she had simply fallen victim to temporary, fleeting self-pity—a feeling that would evaporate once she got fully settled at Hunt-Fisher.

The fact was, he was taken. *And by a friggin' Hollywood TV star, for God's sake.*

She was trying her best to talk herself into these rationalizations, seeking to regain the better judgment she had always shown, and hoping to dispel quickly the notion that she could really harbor such out-of-bounds ardor for her classmate.

But it did not work. Courtney trusted her feelings. Her love for him was real, all right. *Shit! I can't deny it. Not to myself, anyway. I am wildly in love with this man, and probably always have been.*

She even recognized how these feelings had developed within her over time. No one understood her better than the man standing across the street did; no one looked after her and cared for her like he did; no one could see what was going on inside her and read her mind and soul like he did. No one attracted her physically like he did. If this was not love, she did not know what love was. She ached for what could be, even though she recognized it was an exercise in futility.

So, for the time being, it was necessary to regain her composure, to act "as if," at least for the weekend. She needed to accommodate the current situation, that Jason loved Lara, not her. She would maintain the pretense of having a sisterly affection for him, because she would never want him to feel awkward around her. She needed him in her life, she knew that for sure. The one outcome she absolutely could not tolerate was pushing him away or alienating him somehow.

Courtney stood frozen on the sidewalk, still looking at Jason, contemplating her new awareness, and trying to find a way to gather herself emotionally for the reunion that would commence the moment she made her first move toward him and called out his name in greeting. Jason was still peering uptown, searching for her familiar face along the same sidewalk he was on, fully unaware that the two of them were now apart only by the width of 7th Avenue.

She took a deep breath, and finally initiated the reunion. Jason spotted her coming once she was halfway across the street. He reciprocated the broad, genial smile Courtney had now affixed to her face. "There's my Court," he shouted to her, stretching out his arms for a hug once she was within reach. With the feelings she had just recognized still raw within her, Courtney felt a surge of response to his touch on the skin of her exposed arms. It revived a sexuality that had been latent in her, pushed to the side for over three years through immersion in schoolwork and a preference for his romantically neutral company, over that of more available men who declared their attraction for her. She found herself a bit flushed by her physical response to Jason, caused merely by this mild physical contact between them. But she gave herself permission to return his embrace passionately, taking advantage of the opportunity that reunion hugs provide to clinch a little harder than usual.

"I'm so sorry I'm late, Jason," she apologized, as she broke off her grip around him. "I didn't think it would take me as long as it did to get over here from Grand Central. The traffic was ridiculous."

"Not a problem, Court, not a problem," he reassured her. "I'm just glad you're here, and I'm here, and we're here together. This is fun, isn't it? Hanging out in New York, near Madison Square Garden, away from Philly for a couple of days?" It was clear to Courtney that Jason meant it. He was glowing at the sight of Courtney and, she guessed, at the chance to forget about Temple and Philadelphia and rotations and case studies and all the rest of the trappings of his medical school training for a couple of days.

"Well, what should we do? Are you hungry?" Courtney asked, knowing it was likely he was.

"Famished. And you?"

"Absolutely starving. Let's go for it. Italian in Little Italy is what we decided, right?"

"If that suits you, I would love it." Jason shared Courtney's preference for any kind of Italian food, so the decision about where to eat was simplified. Another cab ride beckoned, but Courtney suggested that they make their way over to Broadway to catch one. As they began walking in that direction, she clamped both her arms around his free one—the one not toting a small, black duffel-type bag which held the belongings he needed for the weekend. She leaned into him playfully and affectionately.

"It is *so* good to see you, Jason," she said, smiling up at him broadly. "Thanks for coming up. It really means a lot to me."

"Hey, what could be better than this? Dinner in New York City, then a weekend in the country. I feel relaxed already," he said, smiling down to her, freeing the arm she had grabbed so that he could wrap it around her shoulders.

"I can't wait to hear about Lara and her show," Courtney said quickly, appeasing the guilt she still felt about the feelings she had acknowledged just a bit earlier to herself. "You'll tell me everything, won't you?"

"We have all weekend, Courtney, so there shouldn't be much you won't know by Sunday, I suspect." He added that he and Lara had made an arrangement to speak with each other later, so he would try to call Lara from Courtney's place, if that was all right.

"Of course," Courtney insisted with as much enthusiasm as she could muster. She wondered if Jason picked up anything in her voice that would betray her true feelings, about him and about her reaction to speaking to her rival in California. He was such an empath, this Jason, and so good at sensing everything she felt, so easily. This "we're just friends" charade might be harder to pull off over the weekend than she thought.

They hailed a cab without difficulty, and headed to Mulberry Street. They chose Rico's, primarily because it was quieter than some of the other spots Courtney had been to before. She wanted a dining environment that suited her interest in being able to have an easy conversation, with some privacy. They needed to catch up on so much, from what was going on at Temple with their common friends, to his fall schedule, to the challenges she was facing in her residency. She did not want to have them battling to hear each other all night.

They ordered a carafe of Chianti to share, and it was almost empty by the time they had even begun their appetizers. They ordered another carafe, with Courtney too revved up in excitement to even feel much of a sedating effect from the alcohol.

The conversation flowed easily, going from one subject to another. They each felt a need to satisfy their respective curiosity about how the other one was faring. Jason's humor was always greater with a few drinks in him, and Courtney felt the muscles in her face begin to ache from laughing so often at his witty remarks and unusual take on things. As they left Rico's, they both agreed that the dinner was a perfect start to the weekend.

The alcohol and fatigue hit Courtney hard on the Metro North train ride back to South Norwalk later that evening. She felt a little dizzy from the wine, all the excitement of the day and the emotions about Jason that she had uncovered in herself. As the train pulled out of Grand Central, she could not resist leaning her head over onto his arm, a comfortable position that Jason made even better by bringing her closer to him, so they both could relax in a semi-prone position, with Jason's arm around her and head resting against the train window by their seat. Once again, Courtney responded secretly to his touch, warmed by his gentle, affectionate embrace. It had been a very long time since Courtney was as happy as she was then, with nearly two days ahead of her offering continued private time with the man she loved.

Jason thought her cottage was fantastic. He had never seen anything quite like it before. And, even though it was too dark to absorb the full extent of the hospital grounds, it was clear enough to him that there was an amazing amount of wide open space in her new environment. She planned to give him more of a tour on Sunday.

They were both spent, so Courtney's preparation the previous evening in making up the pull-out couch for him turned out to be well worth the effort. She set out towels and soap for her visitor on a table beside the sofa, and made sure he was comfortable, before starting to head off to bed. He asked if he could use her phone to call collect out to California, and once they had haggled back and forth about not wasting the money on a collect call, Jason acceded to Courtney's insistence about dialing her directly and made the call. Lara was not home, which surprised Jason a bit, since they had made plans earlier to speak to each other at about that time.

"Probably another late night at the set," he figured out loud, after leaving his girlfriend a message to call him at Courtney's when she got in. "Maybe it's just as well. I'm pretty beat, and wouldn't be much a conversationalist tonight. It's okay that I left this number, for her to call me here, isn't it Court?"

"Absolutely," Courtney said, with extra emphasis. She felt for him, noting his evident disappointment, but she shared his relief that she would not have to put forth the effort to talk to Lara, at least not in the state she was in, completely out of mental and physical energy. She started to wonder how well she would handle future conversations with Lara at all, feeling as she did now, desperately wanting Jason to herself. Duplicity was not her strong point. Her feelings were too transparent, especially to Jason, and perhaps also to Lara as well. As an actress, she might be easily prone to pick up on any playacting on Courtney's part.

Courtney wished her visitor a good night's sleep, and watched from the stairs as, almost immediately, he drifted off to unconsciousness. She spent some time looking at him, much as she had done earlier that evening in New York, from a safe, anonymous distance. She would love to join him in the sofa bed, snuggle in next to him, and sleep wrapped in his arms, then wake up in the morning and make love to him. But that was not happening. Not tonight. Not tomorrow. Not ever. But, for this night at least, she was not too dispirited about this fact. She was happy to have him there, in her new home, focusing on her, and their friendship. Courtney headed off to bed sensing that the two days ahead, spent alone with Jason, needed to be savored. It was possible that it might never happen again.

After Courtney was asleep about an hour, she was startled to hear the phone ring. Looking at the digital clock, which read 1:30, she sat up with a jolt. Was it the hospital? Had something happened? Had she forgotten to do something in her haste to leave for the weekend? But as she got up to walk downstairs to answer the call, she heard Jason beginning to speak in a familiar tone. *Oh, it's Lara. Calling at ten-thirty, L.A. time.* Courtney eavesdropped for a moment at the top of the stairs.

"Hi, honey," Courtney heard Jason say, groggily. He then reassured Lara that it was fine that she had called back, even at this hour.

"Where were you tonight?" he asked.

A long silence followed, as Jason listened to Lara's explanation. Courtney heard Jason mumble a few words to show that he was listening, like, "sounds great," or "wow, that's awesome."

Courtney retreated to bed, not needing to hear Jason coo and pledge his love from across the continent to Lara. This was not easy, being in love with a man fully devoted to someone else. But she would have to make do.

In the morning, just before seven, Courtney awoke and looked down to the first floor from the top of the stairs, finding Jason alert, showered, dressed and, surprisingly, very much raring to go. "Let's get this show on the road," he called out to her as she made her way down the stairs. The slight hangover and interrupted sleep was not going to deter him, he insisted. He was very excited about their impending road trip.

After Courtney cleaned up as rapidly as she could, and prepared a Thermos full of coffee to take with them, they headed out toward the Camry, with Jason taking the lead. "I'll drive, and you navigate, how's that?" he suggested, adding that he wanted her to be comfortable so that she could tell him more about life at Hunt-Fisher.

As they opened the doors to the car, Bobrow appeared nearby, finishing a morning jog. His face betrayed a strong curiosity about Courtney's visitor—quite evidently, an overnight visitor—who was now letting himself into the driver's side of Courtney's car, early on a Saturday morning. Courtney waved nonchalantly at the Chief Resident, before ducking into the car.

That was just too perfect; it was like I planned it, or something, she thought, covering her face with her hands to hide the broad smile that she was unable to contain.

Courtney directed Jason off the hospital grounds and out of the surrounding neighborhoods, then on toward Route 95. As they approached the Interstate, she pointed to the ramp he needed to access, which would get them heading east toward New Haven. Once safely on the highway, they were able to redirect their focus to each other. Courtney skirted any discussion of the late phone call from

Lara. In part, she was respecting their privacy, and leaving it up to Jason to be the one to initiate such an exchange. And he chose not to bring it up, which was fine with Courtney. The fact was that her focus was on Jason, not his girlfriend in California. Courtney now acknowledged that her feelings for Lara had changed. Courtney felt a little ashamed about it, but it was a feeling she could not disown. Lara was a competitor, a foe in the race for the affections of Jason. And it was a race that really had just one contestant, the gorgeous Lara King, soon to be seen weekly in living rooms across America. At this point, Courtney's role was like that of a pace-setter in a long distance track event, an enabler rather than a real competitor, one who may hold fantasies of going to the lead and then never getting caught from behind. But, in the end, she always ended up disappearing from view, once her supportive work was done. But not for this weekend; the Olympic champion runner had skipped the race, and the enabler had a rare chance to be the featured contestant, to be the one solely in the spotlight.

Courtney felt especially grateful for this opportunity for in-person, one-on-one conversation with Jason—the type of exchanges they had had on almost a daily basis in Philadelphia. She told him more about the aging psychiatrist owner she had been forced to encounter in her very first new admission; her charismatic supervisor, Dr. Roth; the other residents, including the preppie Chief Resident whom they had seen jogging earlier, and whose romantic advances she was warding off, and, of course, her apparent nemesis, Dr. Short.

Jason listened intently. But he quickly steered her into talking about how well she was absorbing all the requirements of the role she had been thrust into, as the primary doctor of a set of patients, who depended on her to lead them to mental health, or at least to symptom amelioration. It was the next major step in his training, and he sounded intrigued by what it felt like—handling the executive role of performing as a physician, with real patients' lives at stake—from Courtney's perspective.

Jason told Courtney about a family practice rotation he had started. He had grown close to one of the faculty, Dr. James Sheridan, who would be supervising him extensively through this rotation. Sheridan also hailed from Southern California, so their bond developed quickly and very naturally. Sheridan had chosen to stay on in the east coast after doing his residency at Penn. Jason told Courtney that Sheridan, much like the two of them, was not that crazy about living in Philadelphia. But he had accepted it as a trade-off for being able to accept a faculty appointment at Temple.

"He and I have just clicked, you know what I mean?" Jason said. "He treats me like a peer; like a friend, even. We eat lunch together a lot. It makes some of the other students jealous as hell probably, because they all want a piece of him, too. He is such a great teacher, and very charismatic. But at this point I don't care that much about accommodating their envy, to be honest. I am going to ride this relationship for all it is worth." Courtney asked if he was reconsidering the type of residency he planned to enter once he graduated, now that he had a stronger interest in family practice and had a mentor whose influence he respected. "No, I don't think I'll change my mind. It is all too settled, the way the next few years will roll out. But, you're right, he is pushing me in that direction, that's for sure."

"Well, don't close your mind to it totally, just yet," Courtney suggested. "Maybe you need a little more time to make your final commitment."

"I must admit, I do like the challenge of working with kids, and doing primary care with all different types of people and ages," he confided to her. "With managed care going the way it is, primary care is really where the action is, I think. They want problems fixed without specialists involved, to save money. Let's face it: specialists see all problems from their particular specialty's perspective. How does the saying go? 'When you're holding a hammer, everything looks like a nail.' Or something like that. Anyway, you know what I mean."

Courtney sensed that Jason seemed much more engaged and enthusiastic about his medical training now—far more than ever before. He was not just going through the motions, which Courtney thought had been the case at times over the past two years. Jason had the intellectual talent to get by, even to achieve superior grades, with far less time investment in book studying than his peers. But he never gave Courtney the impression that he really cared deeply about his medical studies. He had always seemed to her to be holding back on the profession for which he was preparing, tiptoeing around the edge of a fuller commitment, afraid to dive in. But it was obvious now that he was far more enthusiastic about his academic program than he had been in his first two years.

Courtney knew that one thing she had in her favor over Lara was an ability to talk comfortably about the nuances of academic life. Lara probably felt a little intimidated by the topic, a bit insecure about her ability to really understand what post-graduate medical school training entailed. Courtney sensed that Jason recognized this, and chose not to focus on areas that were not in the area of common ground between them. Plus, the dynamics of their relationship, Courtney observed again to herself, worked better when the focus was on the aspiring actress, not the aspiring doctor.

Courtney was surprised how quickly they reached Mystic, where she planned for the two of them to stop, stretch and have some breakfast. After parking and strolling around the relatively empty streets in the business section of town, they found a restaurant, a place named Abigail's, which had an inviting appearance, and which looked like the type of informal eatery that would give them a less touristy taste of the quaint seacoast town. The choice turned out to be very fortuitous. Abigail Combs herself—owner, hostess, short order cook, waitress and cashier all rolled into one—greeted them from behind the front counter, across from where Courtney and Jason chose to sit, on traditional, red vinyl-topped rotating stools. Abigail was, as Jason quipped later when thinking back to their lively breakfast experience, a "recovering hippie:" now in her fifties, with graying auburn hair flowing down over her shoulders as she had no doubt worn it ever since the late sixties and early seventies when alternative lifestyles were the rave, Abigail came across as extremely friendly, affable and credible in expressing her left-of-center viewpoints about everything from politics to current events to art. She easily struck up a lively conversation with her guests, whom she assumed right away were tourists. After hearing where Jason and Courtney were from and where they were headed, Abigail shared how she too had lived in Philadelphia for a time, years ago, also when she was in graduate school, studying architecture at Penn. She had known and been taught by the famous Lawrence Kohn, about whom both Courtney and Jason were well aware, due to his towering architectural and artistic legacy in Philadelphia. Abigail hinted that the Professor had shown a little more interest in his somewhat naïve student than he should have—meaning, of course, that he had hit on her, and, probably had been successful in doing so, though she did not confirm this outright. This type of enticing gossip, and the ease at which she made her guests feel, facilitated a steady and compelling back-and-forth dialogue that all three of them clearly enjoyed. After the omelets and toast and extra coffee on the house that Abigail served them amid the storytelling had been consumed, the time came for Courtney and Jason to hit the road again. They almost hated to leave at the end of their meal, because the proprietor had been so interesting and entertaining. But Newport awaited, and Courtney wanted to stay reasonably on schedule. Their departing promise, to return whenever they were in the area again, was genuine and heartfelt. Courtney certainly hoped that would happen: it would mean that, at some future point in time, she and Jason would be traveling together again. And nothing would make her happier than that.

Courtney had visited Newport, Rhode Island as a teenager, with her parents, but she had not been back since. Her recollection of the resort town was that it was a strange mixture of the old and the new. As the most prominent summer retreat of the fabulously wealthy earlier in the century, Newport provided visitors like Courtney and Jason a rather intimate look into the past, showing the mansions of the Vanderbilts and others whose properties had abutted the ocean. Yet it also had the kind of familiar modern retail outlets one sees in far less appealing places like Reading, Pennsylvania or Flemington, New Jersey. Courtney yearned to browse through the outlets, but she did not suggest it, knowing that there just was too little time during this tightly-scheduled day trip to submit to such a shopping indulgence.

Like many visitors who take these mansion tours in Newport, Courtney and Jason were at once amazed and slightly repelled by the ostentation displayed within these expansive homes-turned-museums. The Marble House mansion was definitely over the top, in their view. Courtney was repulsed by the opulent attitude it conveyed, but she found herself admiring the unique work of the artisans who had built the home, and the workmanship shown in specific interior decorations and many pieces of furniture on display. Jason loved the way the mansions, particularly the largest of them all, the Breakers, had considered how to best leverage the coastal views throughout the home, for both its occupants and visitors.

After these two mansion tours, they hiked a portion of the Cliff Walk, a boardwalk-type trail with a panoramic view of the glorious ocean below, which that day sparkled in seeming celebration of their visit. By late afternoon, they were on their way to Point Judith, Rhode Island, a spot along the state's coastline that Courtney had always admired. She liked the idea that Jason would be able to see, compare and contrast this kind of oceanfront life in New England to that of coastal Southern California. She sensed that, to Jason, the ocean had always been primarily a surfing, swimming and boating playground. In spots like Point Judith, the ocean was more like a prominent community neighbor, a source at once of commerce, of aesthetic delight, and occasionally of fear, when its fury was on display during coastal storms. Jason considered the little town awesome, and he appreciated Courtney's thoughtfulness in showing him this slice of Americana—a special corner of the country located in the smallest state in the Union. It certainly was easy to see, he said, how different life was there than in Santa Monica, Venice Beach or Hermosa Beach, where he had grown up or lived most of his life.

A seafood dinner of fresh scallops and lobster at a local restaurant was inevitable, accompanied by one glass each of a delightful Sauvignon Blanc from New Zealand that Jason ordered. Climbing back in the Camry for the two-plus hour trip back to Norwalk, with Jason still at the wheel, they thanked each other for the wonderful day. Jason noted how the trip had been a real eye-opener for him—the scenes he had witnessed were now pleasantly etched in his brain. For Courtney, it had been a perfectly-timed mid-summer weekend escape, one that could never have occurred without the catalyst of Jason's visit. She thanked him for making the effort to come see her, a gratitude she had probably emphasized too often since he had arrived.

Jason liked New England more than he thought he would, he told Courtney. He spent the first part of the return drive chatting about the allure of the region. Californians can get very snobby about the ideal environment in which they live, Jason acknowledged. But he could envision a good life in this area, even with it being so different than his hometown in "la-la land." For almost the entire last hour of the ride, he spoke some more about what his third year of medical school looked like, the things he hoped to do before he graduated. Courtney listened attentively, prodding him with an occasional question about what he was telling her, forcing him reflect about his feeling or attitude he was expressing. He was actually quite adept at self-exploration, Courtney noted, despite his tendency to be more comfortable in a listening role or when probing others.

It surprised them when they pulled into the hospital grounds in what seemed like just a short time later. They had been able to remain alert and active in conversation all the way back to Hunt-Fisher.

After leading her guest into the cottage, Courtney noticed that Jason made no effort to call Lara. In fact, he was asleep on the sofa bed in just a matter of minutes. The fatigue of driving all day had finally taken its toll. Courtney hardly made it up to her second floor bedroom herself. She was out from the moment her head hit the pillow.

Sunday morning started much later than Saturday morning had. It was almost eight o'clock when Courtney started to rouse, still groggy, but knowing that the clock was ticking away the final hours of Jason's visit. Jason had told her he would need to leave on a train from South Norwalk at about three o'clock, to make it on a four forty-five train that he wanted to catch at Penn Station. So they had just six hours or so more before they would head out to drop him off. She lay in her bed, feeling both depressed about this, but also exhilarated by how wonderful a time she had had with him over the last day and a half. If what she felt for Jason as she left the cab on Friday evening was a sudden surge of loving feelings, she had that same feeling in double doses now. *What a predicament, being in love with a guy who seems to enjoy being with me, but is in a romance with a gorgeous Hollywood star. You couldn't make this situation up if you tried.*

She showered and dressed, then made her way downstairs, where Jason lay on the sofa-bed, awake but resting, still in his shorts and tee shirt. He smiled at her warmly.

"I guess we needed to sleep in a bit, huh, Court," he said.

"Yeah, we might have overdid it a little yesterday," Courtney replied.

"I don't think so. I wouldn't have done anything different. It was really fun, the whole thing. A great escape from the doldrums of North Philly."

Courtney understood what he was saying. She had almost forgotten how sad she used to feel on Sunday mornings over the past three years, when she was somewhere other than Philadelphia, knowing she had to return there later that day, and resume her schooling and life amid the perils around Ontario Street.

Courtney offered to make a big breakfast, but Jason only wanted granola cereal and orange juice, which sounded good to her, as well. After this light meal, they lounged for awhile, before deciding to take a walk out toward the hospital. Courtney explained what type of service or function different buildings provided, as they passed each of them. They entered the hospital in the East Entrance, and walked toward the hallway just short of 3 East, which, Courtney told Jason, looked no different from the outside than other unit entrances, but she still wanted to give him an authentic sense about where she was now working. Then they returned outdoors, ambling over to a couple of Adirondack chairs, where they sat for an hour or so, chatting softly and absorbing the sun's soothing glow on their faces, before returning to her cottage for a leisurely lunch. Soon, it was less than an hour until Jason had to leave for the train station. Courtney sadness began to grow stronger, far outweighing the gratitude she had felt earlier in his visit. She hated to see him leave, not just because she loved him so much, but because he was someone to whom she could easily talk, someone with whom to share a meal or a drink. She would have to face up to the loneliness of another late Sunday in summer at Hunt-Fisher.

But she was not going to cry, like she had in the Temple cafeteria when they had parted over a month before. If she needed to, she would do so later, once he left, if the tears came. But not in front of him. She needed to be strong.

Jason had grown quiet, too. Like in their cafeteria farewell in late June, he felt compelled to address the sadness he sensed in her, but acknowledged in himself as well.

"Court, this was too short a visit. We need to do this again, don't you think?" he asked.

"How about next weekend?" she asked quickly, only partially kidding. Jason laughed. "I guess you won't come to Philly to see me, huh?"

"Oh, Jason, I would, to hang with you, but the question is, if neither of us want to be there, why visit in Philadelphia? Let's meet in the City again, or go to the shore."

"You're right. When you're right, you're right."

"When, then?" Courtney asked, trying to keep from seeming too aggressive in prodding him to confirm another get-together.

"Actually, I don't know. You said you might come down for the surfing competition the weekend after Labor Day in Stone Harbor. Do you know if you have off for that weekend?" he asked.

"I bet with a month's notice I could work it out," she told him. "It might cost me if I am unlucky enough to be scheduled to cover the hospital that weekend, because I will have to give up a holiday or some other high-demand time off. But what the hell, life is short, right?"

They left it at that. A possible meeting in Stone Harbor was on the table, at the Jersey Shore, the weekend after Labor Day. Jason volunteered to be in charge of finding them accommodations.

They were both uncharacteristically quiet on the ride to the station to drop him off for his return trip to Philadelphia. Courtney walked Jason all the way to the platform, clinging to every last second of their time together. She knew she was close to tears, waiting for the train by his side, acknowledging the emotional impact of his departure already. But she put on a brave front, trying to focus on the prospect of seeing Jason again relatively soon. And she wanted to reinforce to him that the weekend had been wonderfully reinvigorating for her—tears might detract from their shared positive memories of the weekend together. The message she wanted to convey was how appreciative she was that he had come up to see her, and how much fun it had been. When she verbalized this—for what must have been the umpteenth time in their two days together—he concurred. The visit had been just what the proverbial doctor ordered for him, too. But once the train arrived, exactly on time, and Jason boarded it after giving her a rushed departing hug, Courtney knew the void within her would be returning shortly. The automatic twin doors to the train closed between them, forcing a physical separation, and officially ending their weekend together. Jason stayed by the doors as the train slowly pulled away, waving to her, and then he put a thumb near his ear and pointed his index finger out in front of his mouth, to mime instructions to call him later. Courtney smiled, nodding to confirm she had understood the message, and blew him a kiss good-bye.

It was only minutes later, as she pulled the Camry out of the station parking lot, that she gave herself permission to let out the sadness that she had been restraining for about an hour. It started with tears leaking down her cheeks, managed with tissues from her pocketbook, but by the time she was nearing the hospital grounds, Courtney was sobbing, an intense paroxysm of emotional pain released, elicited by the bareness of life without Jason around her. He was gone, and with him left her sense of feeling normal, of being herself again. During their forty-four hours together, she had felt so relaxed and comfortable. But more importantly, she had sensed her natural optimism and spontaneity returning, a result of feeling connected again to someone about whom she really cared. It was an amazing revelation, which had somehow eluded her consciousness before: *I just haven't been myself since the moment I left his side in Philadelphia.* She had moped around her parents' house and stayed pretty much to herself for the first month of her residency, because she was separated from someone with whom she was desperately in love. It would be five weeks until she saw him again, and it would probably be that long until she felt like herself again. And after that? There was no telling. They were both so busy with their medical training, it was impossible to foretell what the rest of the fall would be like. *Why can't I feel like I just did, all the time?* she asked herself, self-indulgently. *I know I sound like a spoiled, Scarsdale brat, and it is childish to feel this way, but it's not fair. It's really just not fair.*

Chapter 13

Taking it upon herself, Cecelia asked Short if he would like to go along on the outing to Shea Stadium, with his previous colleagues from 3 East. She positioned it not as a date but as a natural offer to someone in the extended Hunt-Fisher family, someone who had been a part of the 3 East team until very recently. Short had been starting to call Ceeclia on his own, without her prompting him to do so with some specious rationale. Her staying in touch with him over the past few weeks seemed to be paying dividends now. They were planning to go out on their second date, to dinner and a movie on the weekend following the outing.

Cecelia did not care much about team sports or baseball in general, even though she had been a champion skier in high school—she had actually participated in the U.S. Olympic Trials in the Giant Slalom in 1984. But the outing seemed like a great opportunity for her to get some quality time in, not just with Short but with other doctors on the unit. After all, Roth, Sawyer, Bobrow, Brentwood, Paul, Wang and now Short had all agreed to come along. Cecelia appreciated her previous lover's enthusiasm and determination in putting the outing together, and promoting it whenever possible. She just hoped he stayed far away from her at the game. *God forbid Dr. Short or anyone else suspects that anything went on between us.*

Courtney was looking forward to the outing. She liked going to live sporting events. The psych tech who had put the outing all together, Nathan Bigelow, the same one who had helped her move some things into her cottage the first week of her residency, impressed her with his tenacity in getting everyone, including the Unit Chief, Dr. Roth, to come along. Nathan had told her he picked a Phillies game just to make sure she came along, knowing that she would not want to miss an opportunity to root the Mets to victory over the hated team from Philadelphia. She enjoyed talking to him in the nursing station. Early in her rotation the subject had been Tim Harris, the patient with whom she had gotten into trouble with Dr. Short. But now it was mostly about Georgeann Wagner, who was almost ready to leave the hospital. Nathan had gone so far as to suggest that Georgeann connect with a friend of his to be escorted to AA meetings in the Westport area, an idea that seemed logical to Courtney. While abstinence from mood-altering chemicals would certainly prove to be a useful outcome, Courtney was more impressed with the opportunity that something like AA would provide for Georgeann to get out and interact with people, rather than staying holed up in her home as she had for the past year, prior to her hospitalization.

The Lorasis was now well out of Georgeann's system. And Georgeann had thrived without it. She had become almost an extension of the clinical staff on the unit, acting in a parental role to younger patients who needed guidance from her, or in a supportive role to other women who had suffered losses of their own. It was Georgeann's self-appointed duty to keep everyone's spirits high, and the other patients responded to her by getting more involved in the activities she arranged.

Courtney's tie to Georgeann was so strong, Courtney sometimes wondered if it was almost unhealthy. Courtney felt so blessed that she had been able to care for this impressive woman, as the very first admission she had processed after starting her residency. Their sessions were the most engaging of any she held with her patients. The truth was Courtney really looked forward to them. Georgeann taught her a lot, in fact, particularly about facing fears head on, about resiliency and about building an ability to learn from mistakes.

After several weeks of therapy with Courtney, Georgeann started to show determination to move forward with her life. She had come to appreciate that her deceased husband John, her "Rock of Gibralter," would have wanted her enjoying life, developing rewarding relationships with others, taking advantage of her well-established role in New York's social elite. She was enormously wealthy, since he had amassed an impressive fortune through carefully transacted equity plays over the years. Therefore, she had the wherewithal and financial leverage to seize on a cause, and make a difference. John would want her to remember him, but not by wasting her life, sedated by pills and alcohol, focused only on her grief. She needed to reenter life, to take advantage of what it offered, while she still was blessed with good health of her own. This awareness had come slowly; self pity, Georgeann had come to realize, can be as addicting and hard to give up as the euphoria-inducing substances she used to take. But, with Courtney and Nathan's help, and Dr. Hunt's ongoing support, she confirmed to all those treating her that it was time to move forward.

Nathan had been quite successful in generating strong interest in having a large group form to represent Hunt-Fisher Hospital for the outing to Shea Stadium in mid-August. Nathan worked it hard, convinced that the success of the outing he was championing depended on his aptitude for persuasion, his ability to sell the idea that the staff needed this team-bonding opportunity. By mid-July, he was bringing up the outing in the nursing station every chance he got, corralling staff members who had yet to confirm their attendance, pointing to the sign-up sheet to urge them to participate, and bird-dogging them until they acquiesced to his entreaties. He had the Unit Clerk collect all the money—people needed just $25.00, which entitled them to a seat with the group in the back of the lower loge, just beyond third base, along with a free program that Nathan had personally negotiated with the Mets' sales staff. On the evening before the game, the number who had agreed to attend the game came to eighteen, including the unit custodian, Hector Torres, who was more of a Yankees fan but loved baseball with all of his Latino heart.

For all those going to the 3 East Mets outing, the meeting spot was the parking lot by the East Entrance to the hospital. Nathan was there early to hand out tickets and a program voucher to everyone. As attendees began to gather, he asked for volunteers to drive others to the game. He figured that five people would need to drive, and he made a suggestion that the passengers agree to do their part by splitting the parking fee and tolls.

Nathan volunteered to chauffeur a group, and asked Emily and Courtney if they would come with him. Hearing this, Bobrow promptly invited himself along in Nathan's Jeep. This was the first time Nathan had noticed how Bobrow was making the move on his favorite doctor on 3 East. He felt somewhat awkward with the preppie Chief Resident along, since he hardly knew the guy, but this was not a time to be causing any friction.

Once the group arrived at the Stadium, and it was clear which bloc of seats was theirs, individual members of the party made their own seating assignments. It was an interesting process, Nathan observed. He saw Cecelia practically push her way into position between Short and Roth, which he assumed was her typical way of sucking up to the doctors. Nathan was not sure who had invited the asshole Short along, but he liked the fact that the outing was so attractive that a doctor who had already left the unit would want to come along. Bobrow had clung to Courtney's side, to make sure he sat beside her. Nathan felt like the host of the evening, so he deferred to all other requests or maneuverings, taking the last available seat, which happened to be right in back of Courtney, Sawyer and Bobrow. Thankfully, Emily made sure she stayed beside Nathan. *Emily is the best*, Nathan noted. He recognized how Emily did not want him left on the outskirts of the party, after having put the whole event together.

Bobrow bought beers for his mini-threesome, ignoring others around them. Cecelia seemed clueless about the game, asking questions about why the player did what he did, like turning to bunt instead of just swinging at the ball like every other batter was, or why the ball was thrown to second base instead of first base, when it was obvious the batter that the fielder was trying to get out was running toward first base. *It's a good thing for her that Cecelia has a gorgeous ass and good looks, or people would just write her off as a self-aggrandizing airhead, and ignore her altogether*, Nathan observed to himself.

Courtney occasionally turned to slap Nathan's outstretched hand in mutual congratulation, when the Mets scored a run or performed a special feat in the field. Nathan saw that Courtney was that special kind of doctor, like John Bortman had been, who was genuine and real. No pretenses or self-important attitude. She was the real deal. *And such a babe. I wonder if Bobrow will succeed in his obvious efforts to get in her pants.*

The Mets won the game, so the group was in high spirits leaving the stadium. Nathan announced a plan for everyone to meet back at the hospital, and then each person could decide whether to join in the final event of the evening, a trip to a bar named Johnnie's in South Norwalk. Back at the hospital, Courtney bowed out, as did Bobrow, who volunteered to walk her home. Short was game for a quick drink at the bar, as was Cecelia, Emily and most of the evening staff since they would not need to get up in the morning to work.

The sub-group reassembled at Johnnie's, a loud smoky bar along Washington Street. A band called Wild Oats was playing there, sharing a loud medley of classic southern rock tunes from the Allman Brothers, Lynyrd Skynyrd, the Eagles and others. Nathan danced with Emily. She seemed to be reveling in the free time she had to be with Nathan and the rest of the staff in a social context. Their work was so difficult, Emily told Nathan, it was important to do this kind of thing that he had arranged, a team outing, to engage with each other as people, off the stressful unit. During their subsequent game of eight-ball at the bar's pool table, she thanked him again for his organizing efforts.

After the initial round of drinks was consumed, the 3 East group started to disband. One of the first to show intent to leave was Cecelia, and Short quickly echoed her sentiments, noting to all around him that it had been a great night but he needed to be at work in the morning.

Nathan picked up on their body language. *Holy shit, they are leaving together. He is going home with her, I'm sure of it.* Nathan had thought he was completely over Cecelia, but seeing this happening in front of him upset his mental equilibrium.

He's going to go bang her, I can't believe it.

Nathan submitted to a compulsive need to confirm his hypothesis. Just after Cecelia and Short left, he said a hurried round of goodbyes to everyone still remaining, and nearly sprinted out of the bar. He made his way quickly to the parking lot, and observed from a distance what he expected to see. Cecelia and Short were standing close to each other, in a way that resembled how he and Cecelia used to act together months ago, huddled in seeming conspiracy. He watched as they broke off the discussion, and headed for their respective cars. Short got into a Saab, and backed it out of the spot. Cecelia's Honda backed out at about the same time, and the two cars left the lot, Short's car following closely behind Cecelia's, the two vehicles turning onto Washington St. in the same direction. Nathan ran to his Jeep and peeled out of his spot. His plan was to beat Cecelia to her apartment, and park inconspicuously, to confirm or disprove his suspicions about what might be happening in Cecelia's apartment later—the same apartment he used to visit so regularly, the one he still associated with pleasure and well-consummated desire.

He knew a way to her apartment that might be faster than the one he predicted she was taking. The streetlights would have to cooperate, but if all went well, he would have an opportunity to pull into a parking spot near Cecelia's assigned spot, and witness the drama unfold—or simply watch Cecelia return home, alone—an outcome for which he yearned but sensed was just an attempt to dupe himself.

He sped away, sometimes driving dangerously through lights that had just turned red, knowing that his margin for error was very thin, if he was to succeed in the espionage plot he hoped to carry out. Upon reaching Cecelia's apartment complex, he was pleased to find her spot still vacant. He pulled into a space behind a garbage shed, which hid his Jeep effectively from view. Getting out of his vehicle with alacrity, he scurried to a corner of the apartment building, where he could lurk clandestinely in the darkness. He leaned against the bricks of the building, and waited.

Just a few minutes after Nathan's surreptitious arrival at Cecelia's apartment complex and subsequent dash for opportune cover, the Honda appeared, pulling easily into the assigned spot that Nathan knew so well. The Saab was right behind it. Nathan watched in dismay as it parked in a Visitor's spot—the same one he had always used. Short got out and met Cecelia by her car, where she stood waiting for him. They moved up the sidewalk toward her front door together, talking and laughing, and disappeared inside.

I can't fucking believe it. Cecelia and Short.

As he stood there, once again playing the role of furtive spy to Cecelia's behavior, he shook his head, considering why he was so upset by this. Was it just because Cecelia was sleeping with someone else? Why would that upset him so much? They were over, he and Cecelia, and had been for some time. Perhaps it was that the one she was doing it with was Short, the one doctor at Hunt-Fisher he thoroughly despised. Or maybe it was a little of both. Or maybe he was just horny, and had never really detached from Cecelia's sexual magnetism, her unusually passionate behavior in bed, the best fuck he had ever had.

He felt a surge in his loins, thinking about Cecelia naked, moaning, prodding Short on, as she had prodded Nathan on, demanding that he make her come, sweating, her ass cushioning the thrusts...

Fuck this, I gotta get out of here.

He returned to his car, sped off to his rented house across town, and masturbated. He was still so stimulated by the image, stuck in his mind, of Cecelia engaged in rollicking, noisy lovemaking. Short played no part in his mental imaginings. No, in the masturbatory fantasy, it was Nathan with Cecelia, enjoying her flesh, her curves and her indulgent, wanton attitude in bed.

When he was finished, he felt ashamed of himself, because he knew there were women who would sleep with him, women at the hospital with whom he flirted when he answered an emergency buzzer on their unit, or who crossed paths with him when dropping patients off at RT, or who even invited him for a late drink at Johnnie's or other bars in town after the evening shift was over. He could think of a host of his former lovers who would be thrilled by a call from him, who would readily accede to his request to join him for dinner or drinks or whatever else might follow. All he really had to do was make the effort. Instead, he was stuck, unable to get into gear. *The story of my recent fucking life.*

To Aid and Abet

Chapter 14

▼

Courtney received a surprise phone call at her office the following morning, from the hospital's owner and most prominent executive physician, Dr. Harold Hunt. Courtney answered the phone sleepily, having stayed up a little later the previous evening than she usually would have. Bobrow had asked himself in for a nightcap, and, while he did not make any overt moves on her, he had malingered until well after midnight. Courtney was fine with having an occasional beer or glass of wine with Bobrow. Actually, he was a wealth of information about the hospital and its eccentric personalities, and she learned a lot about the academic politics of the place from him. But she felt absolutely no physical attraction to him at all. Even though her weekend with Jason had reactivated her moribund sexuality a bit, Bobrow was not going to be invited to any sexual coming-out-again party she might be holding. *Tough luck, there, doc, but you're not the one.*

Hunt's voice, which she recognized right away, caused her to spring up in her chair, and focus.

"Brentwood, we need to talk," Hunt began, curtly as ever. The legendary psychiatrist did not introduce himself, but there was no mistaking Harold Hunt for anyone else. Courtney knew his call was about Georgeann, and the patient's upcoming discharge, but she could not help feeling somewhat defensive in responding to this opening.

"Yes, sir, Dr. Hunt, what can I do for you?" she asked, trying to hide the trepidation in her voice.

"I hear good things about what you are doing with Georgeann Wagner, both from her and from Dr. Roth," he said matter-of-factly, not warmly or with a generous tone. He might as well have been telling Courtney that he heard there was new carpet on the floor in her office, she noted. But it still thrilled her to hear such positive reinforcement, especially coming from someone of his stature.

"Thank you, Dr. Hunt. That is nice of you to say."

"Listen, Brentwood, I have a favor to ask of you. And of a certain other member of your family whom I admire."

"I'm going to take a wild guess and assume you mean my father," she quipped. This drew a short chuckle from the old guy.

"I'm sure your mother is very admirable herself, but, yes, I meant your father," he confirmed. "Listen, Brentwood, I've been giving it a lot of thought, and I think I'd like to refer Georgeann to someone else after she leaves the hospital. I'm thinking of pleading with your father to see her as long as she needs to be seen. I'm slowing down my practice, not taking any new patients at all, and Georgeann, well, she just means a lot to me, and I'd like her hooked up with the best. I'm calling you first to see if you will aid and abet this special request. I wonder if a call from a daughter, along with one from an old colleague, more or less in unison, might sway him to do it. What do you think?"

"Wow, Dr. Hunt, I had not thought about it," she answered, thinking on the fly. Georgeann had a home on Park Avenue, so seeing Aaron in New York, the only place he practiced, would not be a problem. No, the problem was that an opening in Dean Brentwood's panel of patients occurred about as often as U.S. presidential elections—maybe even less than that, Courtney thought. "So, you are saying we should double-team him, so to speak?"

"That's right, Brentwood, the old double-team. I don't really have any chits to call in with Aaron, or at Cornell, although I may have forgotten something," he acknowledged, citing, in part, the very reason for his request in the first place.

"I'm for giving it a try, Dr. Hunt. But I think you might be selling yourself short. My Dad will probably do anything you would ask him to, knowing that you wouldn't ask if it weren't important." Courtney knew her father, and that this was likely to be his response, before he considered the commitment it might entail.

Courtney asked Hunt about the sequence: who should call first?

"Come to think of it, why don't you come down to my office and we'll just call together?" Hunt suggested.

Courtney told him about how her father often took her calls at ten minutes before the hour, in mid-afternoons. She would make a preliminary call to his secretary after she hung up with Hunt, to get the scoop on what her father's schedule looked like for the day. She told Hunt that she always seemed to get through, even if it was for a very brief chat.

"Good. Let me know when we should call and we'll do it," Hunt proclaimed.

"Can I ask you…do you mind if I ask you to tell me more about why you are giving Georgeann up as a patient?" Courtney asked.

"Like I said, Brentwood, I think I'm done seeing patients. I care too much to shortchange anyone. And my mind is not what it was, even a year ago. Georgeann's case reinforced that. I needed to be more on top of the Lorasis problem she had. But there are lots of different reasons. My energy is diminishing, for one. I've been running back and forth from Norwalk to Manhattan for over forty years, can you imagine? And leading a 125 bed hospital at the same time. I'm done, finished, at least with private practice. And as for Georgeann, well, I knew her husband, John Wagner, and I feel particularly responsible for making sure she is well taken care of. Plus, the coincidence that you were here, treating her, doing such a good job, it seemed to be written in the stars, don't you think?"

Courtney flushed again with pride at the compliments she was receiving from him. The fact was, Georgeann had been a delightful patient. If all patients were like her, every doctor would want to be a psychiatrist, Courtney thought. Georgeann was a gem, so motivated and honest and genuine. A real class act. It had been Courtney's pleasure to be her doctor, and she told Hunt that.

"Let me know when we are going to call, Brentwood," Hunt said, cutting her off. "I need to go now. But whatever time you want to do it, that is when we will do it. I'll change whatever I have planned." And with that, he hung up: no good-byes or closure.

Courtney immediately dialed Rachel's line at her father's office.

As expected, she heard Rachel's voice intone, "Dr. Brentwood's office." Courtney smiled.

"Hey, it's me," Courtney said.

"I'm sorry, I have no idea who I'm talking to," Rachel responded sarcastically, maintaining her off-putting tone, a way to chide Courtney for neglecting her. Rachel knew her boss's daughter had been back in the area since late June, but had made no real effort to stay in touch to her.

"I'm sorry, Rach. You're right, I've been bad," Courtney admitted. "So tell me, what is going on with you, Rach?"

"Don't try that make-up-with-Rachel-so-I-can-get-a-favor-from-her stuff with me, Courtney Brentwood," Rachel said, trying her best to show irritation. Rachel easily saw through Courtney's intentions, knowing that an early morning call from her was not initiated purely for socialization purposes. But she loved Courtney like a sister. Her boss's daughter would get what she wanted, but not before absorbing a little more grief.

It took ten minutes of contrition and several reassurances that her calls would be far more frequent before Courtney was able to get down to the business at hand. She finally elicited her father's schedule for the afternoon from Rachel, learning that the time slot just before 4:00pm would probably get Courtney and Hunt the audience with Aaron they were seeking. *Rachel's right, I need to be a better friend, and call her more often.* She made a mental note to slot a time in every week for this.

"Tell my Dad I need to speak with him, and that I'll call at three-fifty sharp, okay Rach?"

"If you're lucky, I will. It depends on my mood," Rachel said indifferently, still tweaking Courtney, in a last-ditch effort to leverage the power she held at that moment.

Courtney thought about telling Rachel what she needed to talk to Aaron about, but she was overdue for Rounds on 3 East. Plus, her intuition told her that Aaron should be the first to hear about the cabal she and Hunt had formed to try to persuade her father to do as they would ask.

She hung up, then called Hunt's office quickly, and left an important message with his secretary, that a 3:50pm call to Dr. Aaron Brentwood's office had been arranged. Hunt's secretary affirmed that she would move things around to make sure he was there, at his office, by 3:45.

Heading out of her office for the unit, she thought about what Georgeann would think about this switch. It might throw her at first, and then she would meet Aaron, which, of course, would end her concerns. But only if he was willing, which he might not be. Despite this uncertainty, Courtney sensed that, one way or another, things would work out.

The call to Aaron from Courtney and Hunt went far better than either of the callers expected. As luck would have it, one of Aaron's business executive patients was going to be traveling in Asia for an extended period of time. Aaron was the one who felt this was especially fortuitous, he told his daughter and Hunt during their call, since he would not have turned them down anyway.

"It just would have meant that I would be getting home at nine instead of eight one night a week," Aaron explained.

"Let's arrange a time to brief you on her problems and therapy, okay, Aaron?" Hunt suggested. But then he changed the course of the conversation. "But before we do, Aaron, I want to tell you that your daughter is doing an excellent job here, she really is." Courtney imagined Aaron, in his office, beaming with pride upon hearing this. Old Hunt was such a sweet man, down deep, even in a slight state of pre-senile dementia.

"We, her mother and I, are very proud of her, Harold, so we expected she would do well for you—you know, I begged her to come to Cornell, to the Westchester Division or Payne Whitney, but she really wanted your program," Aaron said, adeptly returning the compliment. He omitted the part about her reluctance to be in the training program he led.

But Hunt seemed extremely pleased to hear this. He actually laughed out loud, a broad smile overcoming his typical ornery visage. Courtney read this reaction easily, even though Hunt kept his thoughts to himself.

He's thinking, "Hunt-Fisher had stolen one from Cornell!" The old guy loves hearing that. His little hospital had gone one-up on the Ivy League.

Jason called Courtney at her hospital office, leaving bad news in a recorded message. He could not make it to Stone Harbor the weekend after Labor Day, after all. Lara had time off from shooting her show that weekend, and had booked a flight to Philadelphia without telling him. He might be able to arrange something a few weeks later, he said in the message, if he could swing a schedule change at the hospital. He expressed his apologies, said he owed her one, but he hoped she would understand.

She understood, but it did not make it easier to accept. Their weekend together in late July had been so wonderful in many respects, because Lara had intruded only minimally into it. True, Lara was always present in spirit, and her late call the first night had reinforced her ability to interfere with Courtney's otherwise exclusive, one-on-one time with Jason. But Courtney had allowed herself to enter into a state of euphoric denial for much of that weekend, largely ignoring the reality of the girlfriend Jason had back home. For those two days they had spent together, Courtney focused only on Jason and her together, as a twosome that fit together perfectly. They were both in the field of medicine, had many mutual acquaintances, they read each other like a book, and they had reached an incredible level of comfort with each other—so much so that she could nod off leaning against him in a train, and he would respond by wrapping his arm around her.

But now, reality was striking back. While Lara had vanished from Courtney's consciousness for a short time, she had not gone away in fact. Jason's canceling their plans to go to Stone Harbor was a rude awakening about that reality. It did not make her hate Jason. She clearly loved this man—as much as she thought she could love any man. But how much longer could she spend witnessing Lara monopolize his affections? Love is a possessive, sapping emotion, one that draws energy and attentiveness away from other opportunities. For every day she spent devoted to him, she thought to herself, she was unable to get to an emotional space that freed her mind to entertain the prospect of seriously dating other men. It had probably been this way since she had first met him, over two years before. Maybe there was someone in her sphere, perhaps someone like Jason, whom she would fall for, who would restore her romantic side, and most importantly, who was not bound to someone else. It occurred to her that her only real relationship, with Colin at Cornell, had failed miserably. And she had shown little resiliency recovering from that failed coupling. She had taken cover under the sheltering protection of her ostensibly platonic friendship with Jason. And for the month since his visit to Connecticut, she had felt mired in self-pitying questions about why he could not be hers, about why two people who obviously cared for each other as much as they did were not able to find happiness with each other. It was getting old, already. She needed to move on.

She knew this intellectually. Now, it was a matter of her head persuading and overpowering her heart. Courtney recalled learning in an American history course at Cornell about how Thomas Jefferson had written a piece to himself about the same emotional dilemma, a clash within himself of reason and emotion, of "the head and the heart." The dialogue was elicited by the great Virginian's unconsummated love affair with a married Countess, Maria Cosway, while he was in Paris in the early post-Revolutionary War period, serving as an Ambassador to France. Over time, Jefferson was able to slowly distance himself from Maria, to the point where they essentially became only infrequent writing correspondents—that era's equivalent of the occasional phone call from an old friend, on a birthday or anniversary of some kind. Maybe Courtney could taper herself off the love she felt for Jason, as Jefferson had been able to do with Maria Cosway, ultimately cleansing him out of her system.

But Courtney's ardor for Jason was not something she could discard or flush out quite that easily. He was not like a previously favorite outfit she felt like trashing, after it had lost its appeal, or the Lorasis she had weaned out of Georgeann in the hospital. He was within her, still a part of her. But as their planned weekend in Stone Harbor evaporated, a change seemed imperative. Reason might need to usurp passion. Perhaps, Courtney thought, it was time for a Jason-ectomy.

But for such a meta-surgical procedure to take place, she would need to grant her permission, without reservation. And down deep, she was not ready to do that. Plus, she sensed that if she did go forward with it, she would want what had been extracted kept alive somehow, by whatever means necessary, just in case she changed her mind and insisted on having the operation reversed.

Chapter 15

▼

Georgeann was discharged by Courtney two days later, into the care of Dr. Aaron Brentwood, with community linkages to self-help therapies, facilitated by Hunt-Fisher Hospital's newest community re-entry resource, Mr. Dave Shoenfeld. Leaving the unit with Jerry, her chauffeur, who was there to help carry a month's worth of belongings out to the limousine parked outside, Georgeann promised Nathan she would call Dave at work that afternoon. Georgeann liked what she had heard about Dave from Nathan. It was splendid, she said, to have someone who could serve as her escort to these strange meetings of fellowship about which she knew nothing. She would follow this Dave's lead, just as she had done in following the staff's directions while she was in the hospital.

Nathan called Dave to remind him to expect Georgeann's call. The truth, as Nathan perceived it from conversations with Dave as Georgeann's discharge date neared, was that his friend needed Georgeann needing him. In his weekly sessions with Dr. Forbes, Dave talked about feeling less and less like psychotherapy would be the answer to his inner turmoil. He was at his best with other people, rather than inside himself, exploring his inner demons. The reason his recovery, at least from his drinking problem, was still on track was that he thrived in a fellowship, where people depended on each other. In Georgeann he had a pigeon, one who was unsure how and where to fly. Dave would take her under his wing.

The next day, Nathan received confirmation from his friend that Georgeann had indeed followed up on her promise to connect with her new community aftercare resource the previous evening. They had gone to their first meeting together that very night. Dave had picked her up at her elegant home in Westport. "You should see this place, buddy," Dave said with amazement in his voice.

He described a large colonial home on a fashionable beachfront property on Long Island Sound. Dave was not easily intimidated or overly impressed by wealth, but the Wagner mansion had left him awestruck.

Georgeann had appeared, ready to attend the meeting, in a state of overdressed elegance, so Dave had sent her back upstairs to get into a more casual outfit. He was going to have a hard enough time getting her acclimated around some of the hard-boiled characters that populated these rooms. He did not want her to stick out too much, at least not at the very start.

Dave had coached her to tell the group that she was there to listen that night. And that is what she had said when her turn came to share, repeating Dave's recommendation word-for-word, just as she had been instructed. Her time to tell a little bit more about herself would come in due time, Dave had advised her.

Nearly daily updates from Dave continued—he was relishing his role nurturing his pigeon, and he also enjoyed sharing the progress Georgeann was making with Nathan. Two weeks after her discharge, in mid-August with five meetings under her belt, Georgeann was given the release by Dave to "share." She kept it short, telling the group that she had lost her husband over a year ago, and had coped with this loss through a growing reliance on the comforting effects of alcohol and sedatives. She did not tell the group, on Dave's advice, about the amount she used, only the reason she used what she used: to escape from emotional pain. She did allude to the "bottles and bottles" of wine she was going through, depleting her supply far more rapidly than she ever had when drinking in a more social manner during her husband's life, all of which was largely true. She was warmed by the heads she saw nodding to her story, giving her the sense that these AA members had themselves experienced the type of emotions she was sharing. It affirmed to her that she belonged there. When she finished sharing her story briefly, she smiled appreciatively at Dave, thanking him silently for coaching her so well.

At the coffee urn prior to one of the next meetings they attended together, Dave introduced Georgeann to Sara Fieldstone, another doyenne from Westport society, who had been coming to meetings in the area for over thirteen years. At Dave's urging, Georgeann summoned up the courage to ask Sara to be her temporary sponsor, at least until she could learn more about who might be the best person to help guide her through recovery. Sara was quick to comply, hearing a bit of herself in Georgeann's story, and very willing to help out someone who seemed so eager to learn what the program had to offer.

The pairing turned out to be a fortuitous connection—one Dave considered divinely inspired. Sara was also a widow, and she too had an apartment in New

York, although she did not spend much of the summer anywhere but Westport. Sara and Georgeann lunched together three or four days a week during their bonding period, acting like the oldest of friends. By late August, Dave's influence with Georgeann had started to wane, which gratified him in one sense, since his program integration role evidently had been performed quite successfully. But in some ways he missed being needed, like he had been when Georgeann first left the hospital.

The maturity of his pigeon was not the cause for Dave's worsening mental state, but it did not help matters. The primary cause of his unremitting depression, he told Nathan, appeared to be biochemical. At least that was the evaluation Dr. Forbes had made. Forbes had described Dave's depression as "endogenous," a term Forbes had said was used less often than it used to be by psychiatrists, but it still aptly conveyed the sense that the depressive symptoms were less a result of situational stressors or some loss he had experienced, and more to his brain's electronic activity misfiring somehow. Dave finally had surrendered to Forbes' recommendation to begin a trial of medication. The drug Forbes had recommended, Soldan, was fairly new on the market, and it was purported to alleviate both depression and anxiety concomitantly. The only reason Dave acceded to Forbes' suggestion was the threat embodied in the alternative: if Dave did not show some clinical improvement, Forbes told him, he might have to be hospitalized. "With that," Dave joked to his friend, "I said to Forbes, 'What did you say the name of that drug was again? Soldan?'" The prospect of being confined inside a hospital, behind a locked door, with crazy patients invading his space, was more than he could bear or even think about. He started the medication that evening.

The late August heat and humidity in Norwalk was nearly unbearable. Temperatures had soared into the mid-nineties, and the humidity made it feel even warmer. Nathan was perspiring heavily when he returned to his shared house after an evening shift on 3 East, eager for a cold beer and a chance to chill out. As he entered the dark house, though, the hot weather followed him in. There was no cooling relief, as he was anticipating.

He tried to turn a light on, but nothing happened. *What, did we forget to pay the bill?* He was irritated, with the heat and now the lack of light to guide him.

"Hey, Jim," he called upstairs to his roommate, whose car he had seen in the driveway, and whom he assumed was sleeping. But Nathan did not care about potentially waking Jim up; he needed to know what was happening. "Why isn't the AC on? And why aren't the lights working, dude?"

Jim appeared at the top of the stairs, wearing only gym shorts. "The electric is off, man, didn't you hear? There's a brown-out going on. We haven't had power since five or so."

"Oh, c'mon, man, you've got to be shitting me," Nathan said, reacting with frustration to this news. *No fucking AC, on a night when it's like 88 degrees outside, at midnight.* Nathan thought about what was in the refrigerator and freezer that was likely to have spoiled already, since the power had been off for about seven hours already.

He continued to curse to himself, as he threw out mayonnaise and milk and about half the contents of the refrigerator, bagged it all up in a green garbage bag, and took the bag out to the metal cans at the end of the garage. The beer he was craving was lukewarm. It was going to be a brutal night in the house, that was for sure. He opened more windows and tried to create some cross-ventilation. But there was little wind, only oppressing, searing, sauna-like heat. Nathan pulled off his shirt, revealing his thin, fit torso. He moved over to the sofa with his warm beer, and sat down, but he quickly grew uncomfortable with how his perspiring flesh was sticking to the sofa's fabric. He did not know what to do next. He was not sleepy, and the heat was going to make falling asleep a difficult proposition anyway. His beer was now beyond tepid, approaching warmth. He could not watch television, because the power was out. *Man, this sucks,* he thought, his irritation rising even more.

Nathan decided to take a cold shower and head off to his room, to try to find some way to fall asleep. But it was not until three o'clock in the morning that Nathan finally was able to drift off, with the heat still enveloping him, a wet heat from which there was no escape. He woke several times during the night due to his discomfort, and had difficulty reentering unconsciousness thereafter.

In the morning, about nine o'clock, the phone rang at Nathan's home. Nathan was still lying in his moist bed, awake but drowsy from starts and stops of overheated sleep, and still considerably shy of the eight hours of rest he liked to get. Jim knocked on his door and called in to him. "Yo, Nathan, it's Dave on the phone."

Nathan sat up in bed slowly, shook out the cobwebs a bit, and walked slowly downstairs to the phone in the living room. It seemed a bit strange that Dave would be calling at this hour, before late morning. Dave rarely was alert before noon. Something must be up, Nathan figured.

"Hey," Nathan said, announcing himself groggily to his friend once he reached the phone.

"Hey buddy, what's up?" Dave began.

"The fucking temperature, for starters," Nathan quipped. "Plus, my power is out. Is it at your place, too?"

"It just came back on. But it is going to be hours until the place cools off any. It sucks, man."

Nathan tried the switch on the lamp to test out if power had returned. No luck.

"We're still out here, I just tried turning on a lamp. Nothing."

"You'll probably have it on soon, if I have power now."

"Hope so. I can't take this. So why are you up? The heat?"

"No, buddy, actually I have some…some interesting news. I saw Dr. Forbes again yesterday…" Dave hesitated for a moment, long enough for Nathan to sense that something was different, something was amiss.

He was right. Dave began by telling Nathan that the drug he had begun taking was doing nothing for his depression and anxiety. If anything, it made him worse. Dave went through the days on Soldan agitated and in despair, practically jumping out of his skin. When he reported this to Forbes late in the last week of August, his doctor evidently had seen and heard enough.

"He says, 'Dave, I think it would help to do a full work-up of you in the hospital. We need to find out what is happening with you. We need to draw bloods and run some endocrine tests. It will be more of a medical evaluation than a psychiatric admission. You are what we call a diagnostic puzzle. The stay on this evaluation unit should only be five days. I'd really like you to agree to this, Dave,' he says."

Nathan was shocked, but he did not react immediately to what his friend was telling him. His mind was racing, though. *Dave, my good friend, needs to be admitted to a mental hospital? And to the one where I work?* Nathan was dubious that this recommendation was necessary. He felt like he knew Dave as well as anyone could, and he certainly knew the criteria for having to go the inpatient route. Dave did not need this, to go in the hospital, Nathan sensed. Dave just needed to stay with the AA program, keep in contact with his sponsor, maybe talk things over once in a while with a shrink. *Dave, locked behind the door of a closed unit? I don't think so. He will be climbing the walls about an hour after admission.*

The designation, being a "diagnostic puzzle," must appeal to Dave, Nathan surmised. It could be that Dave construes this label as a source of pride—being an anomaly, the unique one with symptoms that even the smartest diagnosticians have a hard time deciphering. Indeed, an anomaly is what he had always been: to his parents, his teachers, his doctors, even to himself.

"Maybe," Dave added out loud, "this hospital stay would provide the secret, hidden code that would unlock the cause of my enigmatic behavior. I told him that I needed time to think about it for a day or two. Forbes said that was okay, but he set a deadline to discuss it again today." If Dave agreed to be admitted, Forbes would arrange for it right away.

"Will your insurance cover it?" Nathan asked.

"Forbes is going to check into it. But I think so," Dave responded. "At least for the brief evaluation we are planning."

"I don't know, man. I have to say I'm not for it. I think it would drive you more nuts being locked up in a hospital unit at Hunt-Fisher."

Dave seemed to hesitate, absorbing his friend's input. "I went to an AA meeting last night, and I saw Georgeann there. She said she was sorry I felt so bad, but that the hospital worked for her. She told me it might be good for me, and that she would come and visit me." He added that he felt a bit awkward, seeing how their respective roles had reversed themselves over only the past few weeks. The former coach now needed her guidance, to learn what it would be like getting treatment in a mental hospital. Somehow, Georgeann had morphed into mentor and advisor, and Dave had become the insecure neophyte.

"But maybe Georgeann is right, that it might be okay. And by the way, Forbes is threatening—indirectly, but the threat is there—to commit my ass if I don't go in," Dave mentioned.

"Commit you? On what grounds?" Nathan asked, incredulous that Forbes could be inferring this from Dave's behavior.

"I told him I think of harming myself, remember? He had already charted it, in my record, to cover his butt if he needs to push the commitment thing."

"Shit, man, why did you have to tell him that? That is like the psychiatric kiss of death. It's the one statement that gives an M.D. control over your life. Judges are not going to rule against a doctor when the patient says that. They don't want to make a mistake that one time, letting out someone who was suicidal after all."

"I think about it, but I cannot say I'm really, really serious about it," Dave explained. "If push came to shove, I'd probably drink first, which actually is just a less direct way to kill myself. But at least I'd go out in glory!"

"You're leaning toward going in, I can tell," Nathan remarked. "But let me make a call first. I want to get an opinion on this from someone I trust. You remember John Bortman?"

"Yeah. A good guy."

"Hang tight. I'll get back to you." Nathan hung up the phone, and shook his head. He was already irritated, and at that moment the focus of his rising frustration was Forbes, Dave's therapist. *Why didn't he just try Dave out on another medication? Why wasn't he just seeing Dave a little more? How hard was Forbes really trying to get Dave straightened out, or at least to keep him out of the hospital?*

Nathan understood the premise of the short-term evaluation-based hospitalization, but distrusted the reality. In Nathan's view, this "evaluation unit" offered no more intense a work-up for new admissions than new patients received on his unit, 3 East. He had occasionally moonlighted on this evaluation unit, to make a few extra dollars, and while he thought the premise of a short-term evaluation unit was a good idea in theory, it was poorly executed by his hospital. *And what if they thought Dave needed to be kept longer? What would happen then?*

Bortman had met Dave once or twice during instances when Bortman was hanging out with Nathan around Norwalk. Nathan hoped Bortman would be able to lend some insight into this situation. As a physician who had been around hospitals, he knew what it took to manage a troubled patient on an outpatient basis, and when it was time to push inpatient care.

After finding Bortman's office number in his address book, Nathan punched it in on the phone keypad, and hoped against hope that Bortman would be there to speak to him. The phone rang once, and Bortman's pre-recorded voice immediately came on the line, asking the caller to leave a message. Nathan tried to be as upbeat as he could, requesting a call-back about a pretty urgent matter upon which he wanted Bortman's take.

Bortman's advice would sway him, one way or the other. That was how much he trusted and admired his friend and former teacher. If Bortman said it was a good idea, Dave should take the plunge. It was going to be interesting to learn what Bortman recommended.

About an hour later, Bortman returned Nathan's call. He had missed Nathan's call because he had been involved in discussions with owners of a new private hospital in Newport, scheduled to open in less than a month, about the possibility of him leading the clinical supervision and quality assurance services there. The hospital, Bortman explained, was situated right on the ocean, it was backed by some serious money, and, if he accepted the job, Bortman would have a great deal of latitude in developing the programs right from the inception.

"I'd take the job in a minute, except I still want to do psychotherapy, not just hospital-based work," he told Nathan. "I am already doing pretty well with the practice, so I just can't give it up."

"Too bad this place isn't open right now. I might have a patient for you."

"Who's that?" Bortman asked.

"Ready for this? My friend Dave. You remember him, right?"

"Sure. Why, is he drinking again?" Bortman knew Dave was in sobriety, right from the first time Dave refused his offer to buy him a drink at a restaurant where they were eating at the time.

"No. He is depressed, a little anxious, and not reacting well to the Soldan his doctor prescribed for him. They want to do an inpatient eval."

"Who's the doc? Do I know him?"

Nathan told him it was Forbes, a PGY4.

"Yeah, I know him. He could have gotten worse. Forbes is not bad…not great, but not bad."

"So, Forbes wants to put him on 5 North, the eval unit, for five days. He says they need to do a whole bunch of tests and psychological testing. I don't know, John, I've been on that unit and they don't seem like they do any more or anything really faster than we do them on 3 East."

"You're probably right. He would have to get lucky and get a good, committed doctor, one who really wanted to figure out what the hell was going on. Not just treat him like just any other admission."

"So what's your advice?"

"My advice is that I'd like to see him myself. Can you get him here, to Providence, later today?"

"Shit, I don't know. I'd have to call in sick, if I went along."

"Okay, you're right. It turns out today I've probably got the more flexible schedule. I tell you what…I'll come there."

"Wait, John, I didn't call to ask you to do that. Wow, you're unbelievable. No, man, I'm just asking for your advice, that's all."

"It's ten-thirty. I can be there by one-thirty. At your place. Have him there, okay?"

"John, wait, don't drive all the way here. We'll figure it out. Can't you just talk to him instead?"

"Not as good. Listen, you called because you were worried. You know the hospital is good, and you know your friend. Why would you call, unless you felt like you really needed a good second opinion? If it was a slam dunk, he would be in already, with your blessing. But you called me. That says you're not convinced about something. Besides, I wouldn't mind running this job offer by a couple people there, at Hunt-Fisher, to get their opinion."

"If that's the case, okay. You know, John, Dave's very antsy, he has a hard time being confined. He can hardly sit through dinner out at a restaurant. His sponsor is out of the country, which might be affecting him. I think he needs help, I just don't know if going into a hospital is what he needs right now."

"I'll be there, at your place, at one-thirty, no later. Have him there, okay? We'll chat for a bit before you have to head out to work. When is the latest you need to leave to get to work?

"Two-forty, I suppose."

"Call someone who is working who owes you one, or who you can pay back soon, and get them to stay an extra hour for you."

Nathan figured he could ask Emily to squeeze someone to stay on until four o'clock. He would pay the person back the first chance he got.

"Alright. We'll get it done. See you in a few hours."

Bortman was an amazing man, Nathan realized. Nathan would owe him, big time. He called the Unit Clerk on 3 East, and asked to speak to Emily. She was unavailable, he was told; she was involved in a special meeting in the conference room. Nathan asked the Unit Clerk if Pete Azumah, the psych tech whom he knew best and whom he was pretty sure was working the 7:00am to 3:00pm shift that day, was available to come to the phone. Moments later, Pete picked up the line, and Nathan made his request: could Pete stay a little late, hanging on until he got there? Nathan alluded to unusual and unforeseen personal things he had on his plate. Pete readily agreed.

"There's a lot going on here, too. You'll learn about it when you get here," Pete forewarned him.

"What is it?" Nathan asked.

"Take care of your stuff, Nathan. Whatever it is, that's what should be your focus. See you when you get here."

That's odd. I wonder what is going on. But he did not have time to dwell on the melodramas of unit 3 East. He had his own soap opera going on at the moment.

Nathan called Dave, to tell him about Bortman's impulsive decision to come meet with him. "That is awful nice of him," Dave mumbled, clearly a nervous wreck thinking about the whole idea of going into a locked unit of a psychiatric hospital. Nathan assured his friend that, one way or the other, Bortman would steer them in the right direction.

Just after noon, Dave arrived at Nathan's house. About ten minutes before Dave arrived, the power had returned to the house. It was still hot and steamy inside, but at least there was relief on the way. Nathan and Dave hung out on the deck in back of the house, a shady setting that enabled Dave to chain smoke and pace up and down. At one-twenty, a bit earlier than expected, Bortman's car pulled into Nathan's driveway. He entered with a smile, giving both Nathan and Dave a gentleman's hug. The three of them chatted for a few moments in the kitchen as Nathan fetched Bortman a soda, which was still on the lukewarm side but met Bortman's essential criteria: it was wet and caffeinated.

After taking a quick gulp of the drink, Bortman asked Nathan if he and Dave could talk alone for awhile, a request Nathan expected and readily accommodated.

Nathan spent the next forty minutes cleaning and vacuuming his house, compelled to devote some energy to making things tidy and neat, to removing soiling influences, to putting things in order. When Bortman and Nathan came back into the house, Nathan could not tell by their expressions what they had decided. So he waited for them to tell him. Bortman spoke first.

"I think it would be okay for him to go in, and Dave seems a lot more comfortable with the decision now, I think."

Dave nodded in agreement. "I need to get a handle on this depression. Let's see if a stay in the hospital will make it happen."

Bortman had some words of caution, however. "We need to keep those guys on this unit humping for Dave. We don't want to hear about needing a few extra days for the tests to come back. No prolonging the stay to have him seen in case conference with Blakeley or something. I've seen that type of stuff go down. Days turn into a week, a week turns into two weeks."

"No fucking way, man," Dave said, shaking his head. "That can't happen."

So it was decided. Dave was going in. He left to call Forbes and tell him the news, pack a bag, and, if Forbes pushed him, head right to the Hunt-Fisher Admitting Office.

After Dave left, Nathan and Bortman stayed inside, evading the heat outdoors. The topic turned from Dave's impending admission to Nathan's near and long term plans. This was a favorite topic of Bortman's. He liked to hammer away at Nathan, relentlessly, knowing Nathan was a procrastinator, prone to skating through life instead of attacking it. Bortman was not happy to hear that the rolls of matriculated students for the 1990 fall semester at Southern Connecticut State University did not include the name of junior Nathan Bigelow.

"Why aren't you taking any classes, Nathan?" Bortman asked, exasperation in his voice. "Do you realize that at the rate you are going, you won't finish your bachelor's until you're like thirty or something? Then you'll need more time for your masters, much less a Ph.D. You won't start doing what you should be doing for another decade. You're drifting, there, tough guy."

"I know, I know," Nathan acknowledged, apologetically, understanding that he was letting his friend down, the one person he knew who saw his full potential. Nathan spent a lot of time pushing people into making the correct decisions in their lives, but he rarely goaded himself into the same type of introspection. Bortman was the one person in Nathan's life who seemed to care enough to provoke him about identifying his goals, and then about doing something to reach them. "You've got to plan your work, then work your plan, my man," Bortman would often encourage Nathan. It was sound advice. The previous fall, this type of push had spurred Nathan to take three courses in a single semester. But his initiative had waned. Nathan considered the unconscious implications of his call to Bortman that day. Maybe his decision to reach out to Bortman for help in assessing Dave's illness was an effort to get unstuck himself, by engaging someone who was not afraid to kick him in the ass, at a point in his life when he needed it more than ever.

"I guess you won't buy it if I tell you I'm a little tapped out for the tuition money?" Nathan asked, displaying a diffidence that was not an integral part of his character.

"No," Bortman responded, quickly and curtly. The physician sat back in Nathan's sofa, raising his eyebrows, reaching both hands out in front of him, an invitation for Nathan to respond, as if to ask, "Now what?"

"Well, I guess I could find a way to beg them to take me in this semester."

"Oh yeah, you look like you're ready to go in and bust their door down right now, to do anything to get in," Bortman noted dryly. "Right." Bortman knew that Nathan responded more to this kind of sarcasm than to gentle supportive encouragement, which Nathan tended to feel like he could duck, bob and weave through, finding a way to get off the hook somehow.

Nathan fidgeted in his seat. He was smiling, though, knowing Bortman cared enough to try to get under his skin a little bit. "Don't you have to get back to Providence?" he finally retorted.

Bortman laughed. "Okay, I'll back off. But I'm not going away. I'm going to keep after you until I see you move off the dime."

"I need a push, I realize that. And a dime is about what my net worth will be, if I don't get into gear, I realize that, too." Nathan had been called on his behavior, just as he had confronted Joe and Tim and many patients from 3 East on their directionless behavior. In his gut, Nathan was grateful to Bortman for staying on him. Bortman was to him like Nasty Steve was to Dave, someone who pushed just the right buttons; except that the motivational jabs were figurative, intended for Nathan's ego, instead of the potentially literal punches Nasty Steve threatened to throw to get his point across.

Changing the subject, Bortman talked some more about the hospital opportunity he was considering. The facility he had visited earlier was planning some innovative programs, like a residential program to be located in a home-like setting on the grounds of the hospital, where the daily rate charged would be about one-fifth of what the hospital would charge. Patients would be able to move to that program rather quickly, once stabilized, and get a little more out of their insurance policy than they were getting now. Bortman said that the managed care firms were already agreeing to offer twice the number of days in this residential setting than they would in the hospital. "Forty per cent of the cost of a hospital day—twenty per cent times two—is still better than one hundred per cent, in the insurance companies' minds."

"How is the program set up? You know, what do patients do all day? How is it going to be different than what they do in the hospital?" Nathan asked.

"Less doctors and nurses, mainly. They are the ones who cost the most. It will be mostly social workers and counselors, some OT and RT. Lots of family counseling."

"No doctors or nurses at all?"

"Less, not none. One doctor will know what is going on with patients in the house, will drop by to write orders every day, and there will be one nurse covering at all times. A counselor will run the show at night."

"A place run by a covering nurse and lots of psych techs or counselor-types…you know, it just might work," Nathan said with a smile.

Bortman returned the smile, before pausing for a moment, in thought. Then he announced that he had to get going. "Keep me informed about Dave, Nathan. I'm going over to the hospital to see if I should talk myself out of taking this job, because right now I am inclined to go for it. We'll see."

"What you did, coming here, it meant a lot to Dave. And to me," Nathan said earnestly.

They shook hands, and Bortman left, returning to the searing heat outside. Nathan was going to be only about fifteen minutes late for work, if he got moving. He wondered if Dave was on his way to the hospital already. These next five days were going to be a challenge. *At least it better be just five days.*

Driving onto the grounds of Hunt-Fisher Hospital to begin his evening shift, Nathan was on edge. His car's air conditioner was working erratically, leaving him sweaty and clammy. And, of course, he was worried about Dave. Plus, there was this thing that Pete had mentioned, about something happening on the unit. *Just my luck, after the morning I've had.* Nathan figured a patient had upset the unit somehow, that he was in for some time on Quiet Room duty, constantly observing the agitated patient in question. He started to try to guess which patient it might be, but decided it was not worth the effort. He would find out soon enough.

Making it onto the unit only fifteen minutes after his scheduled reporting time of three o'clock, Nathan walked into a nearly empty nursing station, and looked over at the Quiet Room. No one was being secluded there. He asked the Unit Clerk where everyone was.

"They're meeting in the conference room. Something happened earlier today. I'll let them tell you."

Gee, what the hell is it?

Emily emerged from the hallway of the unit into the nursing station, a concerned and empathic look appearing in her eyes as she noticed Nathan standing there.

"Nathan, can we talk for a moment in back?"

"Sure, Emily. What's going on?"

She waved for him to follow her. When they were in the room, she closed the door behind her.

"Nathan," she began, blinking rapidly, "we received some bad news today. Tim Harris made another serious attempt this morning, an overdose of his meds and aspirin. He is in very bad shape at Norwalk Hospital. They say it is touch and go whether he makes it. I know you bonded real well with him, so I wanted to let you know."

Nathan looked vacantly at the wall, slowly shaking his head. He felt numb, drained, and at that moment, shut down, a victim of sensory overload. He had begun the day sleep deprived, spent the morning focusing on Dave's condition, heard the taunts from Bortman about his life's state of inertia, and now Tim Harris was near death, after giving up on his life again. Why, Nathan asked himself, is all this happening at once? *On the other hand, why am I focusing only on myself?* It was Dave who was behind a locked door this evening. It was Tim who was comatose in a hospital bed across town, desperate enough to end it all, throwing away all that he and Nathan had talked about during his stay in Hunt-Fisher. Thinking of this, Nathan's face flushed, from a combination of embarrassment about his selfish thoughts, the many frustrations he had already experienced this day, and simple anger—at too many things to even list.

He thought about his work with Tim. Had anything that he and Tim talked about really mattered? In fact, did *any* of his conversations with patients matter, period? When a patient does so well in the hospital and then collapses outside it, the first reaction is to question whether everything done to help was a fruitless, wasted effort.

Nathan's anger honed in on its favorite target, the attending physician in charge of Tim's inpatient care, the one who insisted on following him once he was discharged, the empathically-challenged Dr. Short. The man had never really given a shit about Tim, Nathan was sure of it.

Plus, he happened to be banging his ex-girlfriend, which made it even easier to detest the guy.

Nathan remained still and silent, staying inside himself, gazing at the wall vacantly. Finally, he moved his gaze from the wall to Emily. They looked at each other directly, gaining full eye contact for several long moments, saying nothing.

"What's going on with you right now, Nathan?" Emily finally asked.

"This could not have come at a worse time, Emily. I have had a rough day already, which I will tell you about later. And now Tim. Barely a month after leaving this place. Wow."

"He was going to the day program regularly, from what I hear," Emily mentioned. "But the staff over there said he expressed feelings that he did not fit in, that he was a little different from the population he was in with. It's true actually. Many of the patients over there tend to be pretty chronically mentally ill, to be fair."

"What was Dr. Short's reaction?" Nathan wanted to know what he had said about his patient giving him the not-too-subtle message that their precious therapeutic alliance, the one he had been so intent on maintaining with Tim, had never really meant diddly-squat, in the end.

"He is upset, of course. We all are."

Yeah, right.

There was a knock on the door. They turned their heads and saw Courtney duck her head into the room. Hearing from the Unit Clerk what was going on behind the closed door, Courtney evidently wanted to be a part of the conversation.

"Nathan, Emily, mind if I join you?" she asked softly.

"Please...," Nathan responded, waving her into the room. Courtney entered and closed the door behind her. Nathan saw right away that her heart was in the right place. *She's all right, this Dr. Brentwood,* appreciating her effort to talk with him about what had happened with Tim.

Courtney moved into the room and closed the door behind her. She looked at Nathan, who appeared appropriately subdued and mournful. "Nathan, I know Emily must have just told you about Tim," she began. "I'm really shook up about it."

Courtney had heard about Tim's overdose two hours before. She had felt in a daze since, canceling her scheduled sessions with other patients because she was having difficulty concentrating. Tim had been special to her in the sense that he was one of the first patients to whom she had been assigned, on her very first day of residency. First patients are always unique, because they are associated with the heightened excitement and anxiety of assuming a leadership role of a patient's care planning for the very first time. Plus, the whole conflict with Short made Tim's case stick out to Courtney even more. Short had not spoken to her yet, and Courtney doubted he would extend himself to do so.

The most difficult part for Courtney in coming to grips with Tim's suicide attempt was the nagging feeling that she could have been the type of therapist with whom Tim would have thrived. She was just starting her training and had much to learn, but her sense was that she was a better therapist match for Tim than the former Chief Resident. It was crazy for her to think this way, she understood: it sounded so arrogant, so self-important. But she could not help it—that was the way she felt. She was nowhere near being a Board-eligible physician or a full-fledged junior faculty member, like Short was, but she knew people. Probably better than Short ever would.

Courtney had observed how dedicated Nathan had been to Tim's effort to become more assertive, resilient and self-sufficient. As she looked at Nathan now, she saw he too was dazed by the news.

"We really have not heard what happened, you know, what might have precipitated the attempt," Courtney informed Nathan. "His family is with him at the hospital, but it is not the right time yet to ask those types of questions."

"Right," Nathan said. "No, the family shouldn't have to deal with that now."

"The day program nursing staff said he came to their program regularly," Emily reported again, "right up until two days ago. Apparently, he missed yesterday without an explanation. But they told me he had been very withdrawn for the past week. The chart said he was talking about his parents fighting, with his brother and each other, all the time."

The three of them stood in silence for several moments, looking at each other and the floor. Finally, Emily indicated she needed to take care of a few things, and made her way toward the door. "Nathan, take as long as you need before going out on the floor. Okay?" Emily moved over to him and touched him on the bicep, saying nothing but still looking in his eyes. Then she turned and smiled silently and supportively at Courtney, and left the room.

"Thanks for coming in to talk about this, Courtney," Nathan said after Emily left. "I have had a rough last sixteen hours."

"Really? Why? I mean, beyond the obvious reason we are talking about now?"

"If you can believe it, my best friend just got admitted to the eval unit, 5 North, like, within the last hour. He has been seeing a guy over at the Clinic who wanted to work him up in the hospital. Dave—that's my friend's name—he has a hyperactive thing going on, and has trouble being cooped up even in a room. I worry about him." Then it occurred to Nathan that Courtney had a connection to Dave, too, through the discharge planning for Georgeann. "Actually, you have heard about Dave," Nathan continued. "He is the one who took Georgeann Wagner to the AA meetings when she got out of the hospital."

"Oh, yeah, I know who you mean. Gee, that's too bad. Did he start drinking again?"

"No. He is depressed and has some anxiety mixed in. Dr. Forbes, his Clinic doctor, put him on Soldan but it made him worse, at least at first."

"That happens, especially with some of the newer drugs," Courtney explained.

"Yeah, I know," he said. Then he managed a weak smile. "Plus, the power at my house went out last night during a brownout, so I slept really poorly. Did it go out at your place?" He remembered helping her move in on the Fourth of July, and getting caught by her soon after spying on Cecelia.

"No, I never lost power. It did flicker once or twice, though."

"I was hot and cranky already this morning. Then Dave tells me about his hospitalization plans, and now this about Tim."

"Wow. Well, look, I know you have to get out there on the unit. But let's get together tomorrow, when things are a little more back to normal, and we have both had a little more time to absorb the shock of this thing with Tim, what do you say? Can we do that?"

"I'd like that a lot, too. I'll be in during the day tomorrow."

"Good. Maybe we can go to lunch together. I'll look for you." Courtney turned to leave, also touching Nathan around his shoulder before doing so, just as Emily had, showing her emotional support, before leaving the room.

Nathan stayed in the anterior room of the nursing station, alone. He leaned back against the wall and looked upwards toward the ceiling, and let out a huge, exhausted sigh. *This is going to be the longest and most difficult seven-plus hours of work ever.* He just wanted to go home and crash in his bed, and put his feelings and problems on hold for a few hours. But instead, he needed to head out to the unit and do his best to be available for other patients who would be looking for his guidance. In truth, he felt he had very little to give. The pessimism he had felt upon hearing the news about Tim, involving a sense that what he did with these patients amounted to very little, hung with him still. It impaired his readiness to return to the fray, out there on the treatment unit. Then Nathan thought of Dave, a patient on a unit elsewhere in the hospital, who would need someone to care about how he was doing, to give him support on his first day of admission. *C'mon, suck it up, Nathan*, he told himself. He would have to charge himself up for a few hours, and fight his way through the shift. Then he would race home and get as much sleep as he could. He did have something to look forward to—lunch with the appealing Dr. Brentwood tomorrow. Forty-five minutes with Courtney would make getting up in the morning and coming to work a lot easier to do.

Chapter 16

Courtney called Jason back later that day, to confirm she had received his message of cancellation of their Stone Harbor weekend. They did not talk long; Jason had to leave shortly for an evening seminar led by Dr. Sheridan. When Courtney, sounding disappointed, implied that she had had a rough day and was looking forward to chatting with him, Jason told Courtney that he and Sheridan might go out for a beer afterwards, so he would not be able to call her back that evening—he would try her the next day. *So much for my being able to unload on Jason, like I always could last year*, Courtney thought as she hung up the phone. The pattern was developing, Courtney sensed, in which she still depended on Jason for support, but he was less and less available to meet her needs. It was not purposeful on his part, she knew that. He was just doing his thing, with girlfriend and medical school. Which is what he should be doing, she acknowledged. But for Courtney, it felt like it was potentially the beginning of the end: perhaps their relationship's closeness could be graphed like a bell curve, and the current status was evidently now on the down slope of the curve's back side. If she held on to some unrealistic hope that the two of them could, somehow, end up together, it was a hope that was faring about as well as her former patient Tim Harris was: lying comatose, with those in charge able to easily pull the plug.

Courtney tried to read and watch television that evening, but her mind could not focus on anything except what had happened in the last twelve hours or so. She found herself looking forward to seeing Nathan for lunch the next day. He was the type of guy she had always liked: he was funny, but with a serious side; attractively slim and tall—she liked men being about six feet tall or so. He was great with people, she could see that. So, the lunch would be enjoyable—not just a meeting to process what had happened to Tim, but a pleasant conversation with a good guy.

She moved upstairs to get undressed and prepare for bed. After beginning to wash up, she decided to shower completely. She needed to rid herself of the days' impurities, both the literal type associated with the sticky weather, but also the work-related grime that Tim's suicide attempt had left on her soul. The shower, with the temperature of the water adjusted to a cooler-than-usual setting, worked to rejuvenate her spirits. After drying herself off, she slipped into some light cotton pajamas, grabbing a book before climbing into bed. The book was an Updike novel she had always wanted to read, The Witches of Eastwick, set in Rhode Island. It made her think once again of her day with Jason there. She got through only a few pages, and began to nod off.

Asleep for a just short time, Courtney was jolted awake when her telephone rang. She sat up with a start, disoriented, not sure if she was dreaming or awake. The phone rang again. She scurried downstairs quickly to answer it, fearing some difficulty at the hospital. She reached the phone just as the fourth ring ended.

"Hello," she answered, her voice tinged with anxiety.

"Hi, Court. It's Jason. Okay, tell me…what happened today?"

Once Courtney and Nathan went through the cafeteria line and chose their food, they purposely selected a spot far in the corner to sit down with their trays. They would be talking about Tim and did not want other staff joining them, at least at this meal. Plus, they hoped it would be evident to others that their disassociation from the spots where most of the other staff typically ate would indicate to anyone who wished to join them that they were meeting about unit business, and wanted some privacy.

"Have you heard anything about how your friend Dave is doing?" Courtney asked.

"No, not yet," Nathan told her. He had not had time to check in with his friend.

"Let me know if I can do anything, okay?" Courtney added, more as a courtesy than because she thought she could really add value to Dave's care in any way, as a PGY1, just two months into her training.

"I will. Thanks. So, Courtney, did Dr. Short ever contact you yesterday?"

"No, he didn't. But that doesn't surprise me."

"Why is that?" Nathan asked.

"He and I crossed wires a bit during Tim's stay, when I was acting as Tim's doctor for those couple of weeks before he was discharged."

"Oh, yeah, I remember now. Something about you seeing Tim for too long a time in your sessions. Like that's something that is worth getting real upset about," Nathan said, sarcastically.

"Exactly," Courtney replied. "You know, I've wondered often, who was it that told Dr. Short that was happening? He evaded the question when I asked."

"I know who it was," Nathan said coyly.

"You do? Who was it?"

Nathan hesitated for a moment, a grin spreading across his face. "Maybe I shouldn't tell you," he finally said.

"Why? Tell me," Courtney insisted, smiling a little at him because he was obviously provoking her, knowing he had aroused her curiosity about the spy network that existed on unit 3 East.

"You'll owe me one, if I tell you."

"Okay, I owe you one. Who was it?"

"Cecelia. Cecelia Reade, the evening charge nurse."

"What? Cecelia? Why?" Courtney tried to think of something she might have done to make Cecelia an enemy.

"Well, there are probably lots of reasons," Nathan answered. He seemed to be reveling in his knowledge of the secret intrigues on their unit, and the leverage he held in knowing what Courtney did not.

"Like what?" Courtney asked, shaking her head in continued disbelief.

Nathan hesitated again. Finally, he shared what he knew was true, but could not prove.

"She is probably threatened by you," he suggested. "Let's just say she used to get most of the men's attention on the unit, and you've displaced her a bit in that regard."

Courtney blushed at the compliment about her looks. She had never picked up any jealousy from Cecelia, and she honestly was not aware of attracting men away from Cecelia on the unit. The truth was that, having drawn glances of admiration from the opposite sex throughout most of her life, Courtney honestly did not really notice it that much anymore, especially at work.

"I doubt that," she responded. "Come on, tell me for real. Why would she do that?"

"I am telling you the truth. She strikes me as the type who would try to diminish you somehow. I know it is soap opera stuff, a back-stabbing type of behavior, but she probably rationalized it that she was just doing her job."

"I don't believe it."

"Believe it," Nathan said with a low-voiced directness that made it clear to Courtney that he knew something else, but he was not telling her.

"Even though you don't believe it, you still owe me," Nathan went on, smiling. "Plus, I think I have a chit left over from the furniture move-in help I gave you, when you first started, remember that? Alright! I have you over a barrel if I ever need a favor."

"Okay, you do," Courtney acknowledged. "Let me know when the debt must be paid off."

The rest of the lunch was spent talking about Tim Harris and their respective feelings about his suicidal behavior. Nathan added another surprise to their conversation.

"I'm going to tell you something now, Courtney, and it is confidential. I am not going to swear you to secrecy though, because I trust you will understand why I am doing what I plan to do, so that binding you to secrecy is not really necessary."

"What is it?" Courtney asked, intrigued by this preface.

"I'm going to go see Tim in the hospital. I don't give a shit if somehow the hospital finds out and fires me. I'm going over there. That's it. I've made up my mind. If he comes to and sees me, I think it will help. Fuck the rules here. Sorry about my crude language, but like I said, that's what I'm doing." Nathan paused, checking out Courtney's reaction. "What do you think of that?"

Courtney knew about the strict prohibition on fraternizing with patients after their discharge. The basic premise made sense: patients need to understand that the staff members were not their friends, but instead were fulfilling a role only as caregivers, as treatment professionals. If that boundary was fuzzy, some very bad things could happen. It was better that everyone knew up front that the relationships built in the hospital were not social, but only therapeutic. Therapists can not date their patients, or go on vacations with them, or meet them at a bar for drinks. The same principle applied to hospital staff. No matter how much you like the patient on a human level, a proper boundary must be maintained, for the viability of the treatment structure to remain intact.

But some rules were made to be broken, or at least bent, when it was the right thing to do. Courtney could not overtly condone what Nathan planned to do, but she felt no compunction to try to stop him, either.

"Go for it," she said simply, without judgment. She also added a signal, with her thumb and forefinger pinched together and then moved from one side of her mouth to the other, that her lips were sealed.

Nathan heard from Dave later that day. Dave was in the hospital, but he was not a happy camper. Unit 5 North was not big enough to handle his anxiety. He paced the unit constantly, even when the nursing staff asked him if he could try to remain calm, by either sitting or lying in his bed for a period of time. But he could not accede to their request; he needed to keep moving. The tests that were supposed to be underway were not happening with any kind of intensity. When he asked nursing staff about this, they asked that he be patient, that the people from the lab were on their way, or delayed, or backed up by other units' requests. Eventually, he had his blood drawn, but when he asked what type of analysis the staff would be performing of his blood, he got back very nebulous answers. This inpatient stay was not working out anything like he had been expecting.

"What is wrong with this hospital, man? These people are idiots," Dave declared in the phone to Nathan, loudly enough that Nathan imagined he was drawing concerned looks from any unit staff on duty who might be overhearing his angry remarks. Among those who were watching him at that very moment, Dave told Nathan, was the therapist to whom Dave had finally been assigned, a PGY1 named Dr. Arnold Fish. Fish, Dave described, was a tall man, from Wyoming, whose bonding techniques with both patients and fellow staff was to spout off some country truisms that many considered quaint and funny. Dave did not. His reaction was that he wanted to smack the guy in the mouth.

"Have you heard from Forbes yet?" Nathan asked. Dave had tried to reach Dr. Forbes to give them his "thumbs down so far" appraisal of his institutionalized care, but Forbes could not be reached. He had a long weekend planned over Labor Day, and had left a little early.

"Nice of that fuck to tell me, huh?" Dave said. "I feel like a customer at an auto dealership who's been taken by a classic bait-and-switch technique." Nathan was stunned that Forbes had admitted Dave and then just went away for the weekend. He understood that Forbes probably had longstanding plans, but he was dropping the ball.

"So what are you up to? How are you spending your time?" Nathan asked.

"I pace, I confront the staff about why their diagnostic work is lagging so slowly behind schedule, I make myself a pain in the ass to them."

See, we're off to a bad start. Nathan worried it could get worse before it got better.

Nathan drove to Norwalk Hospital to try to visit Tim Harris. Once inside the hospital, he found his way to the Intensive Care Unit, despite taking a few incorrect turns. The sign on the door to the ICU made it clear that only authorized personnel were allowed in, but that patients' families could reach the nursing station from the phone in the Family Waiting Room. Nathan moved into this room cautiously, less sure then that he had done the right thing in coming to check in on Tim. A few others were there, watching the television mounted high on the wall. But Nathan did not recognize any of them as Tim's parents, whom he knew from their numerous visits to 3 East during Tim's hospital stay. At this point, Nathan was not sure what to do. Should he call to the nursing station? They would ask him who he was, and probably not reveal anything to him since he was not a family member. He hesitated, and considered leaving, thinking he might call the parents to ask them about Tim's condition and when they might be at the hospital.

Then he heard his name. "Nathan, is that you?" It was John Harris, Tim's father, who had evidently been out to buy a newspaper and some coffee, since he was holding these items in his hands.

"Hello, Mr. Harris," Nathan responded, remaining somber, befitting the context of their meeting each other again. "I came over to see how Tim was doing. Can you tell me?"

Mr. Harris was a lanky man who looked like the Fairfield County business executive that he was. He carried himself impressively, with a serious but not mean-spirited demeanor. And he commanded attention, even in a Family Waiting Room of a community hospital. It was easy for Nathan to see how he also led his middle management minions at General Systems, the global corporate giant based in Stamford, where he held a position that earned him an office just down the hall from the company's CEO.

"I'm surprised to see you here, Nathan. No, actually, I'm delighted, but not surprised."

"I have to tell you, Mr. Harris, I am really not supposed to do this, interacting with a patient who has been discharged..."

"Say no more," Harris said, interrupting Nathan. Harris said he knew that Nathan was here because he cared, even if his actions broke a hospital rule. He admired Nathan's courage and willingness to act in a way that was consistent with his values. Then Harris invited Nathan to sit with him in the corner of the Waiting Room.

"Tim is still in a coma of sorts," Tim's father began. "His brain may have suffered some damage, but they are not exactly sure how bad it is yet."

"But he is going to make it? They think he will live, don't they?"

"It looks better today than it did yesterday, Nathan. The doctors think he will live, yes. And, if we get lucky, he might not have any damage…how do they describe it? Organic damage? Essentially, that means brain damage, right? Plus his stomach, the gastrointestinal tract or something, it may have suffered some serious damage. Looks like his ability to eat hot chili is over," Harris said, forcing a smile, but his lip was trembling, his eyes glassy. Nathan nodded, listening, sensing Harris needed to talk some more.

"Nathan, your hospital did him a world of good, especially the inpatient part. Don't ever doubt yourself about that. I've never seen Tim in such good shape, as when he left Hunt-Fisher. Wow, I mean he was talking to me with such maturity and poise, I was flabbergasted. Then he started to fight with my other son, who is a druggy. You know what I mean, right? He is a drug addict. He taunts Tim, and Tim won't fight back because Tim is too good a person, he knows his brother is sick and that it is useless to try to reason with him. So we—my wife and I—we play that role. We fight, we scream, we cajole, we do everything to get him to accept treatment. He is only sixteen, this boy, and we have not been able to summon the nerve to force him to go to a rehab or whatever treatment might help him. Tim got more and more withdrawn with every fight he observed, and then, yesterday, he did this."

"Tim will bounce back," Nathan said, supportively. "I have faith in him. Let's get him better and then see what can be done to turn this all around. I have to tell you, though, that it may be that he should not be living with you." Harris nodded his head silently in agreement.

Nathan was treading on shaky ground, acting like Tim's case manager, when he had no authority whatsoever to do so. But he felt confident in his recommendations, anyway. Tim had to get out of that noxious household, once he was back on his feet again. Otherwise the pattern was likely to repeat itself.

"Are you able to go in and see him?" Nathan asked.

"Just once. And there is not much to see or do. He is out of it, and surrounded by machines and tubes stuck in his mouth and up his nose. He does not know we are there. But I feel better being here than home."

"I understand," Nathan said.

After getting a bit more of an update, Nathan got up to leave. He felt better for coming over to the hospital, and for the chance to get the full story from Tim's father.

"Nathan, I appreciate you coming over," Harris said, putting his hand on Nathan's shoulder. "You are welcome back, any time. And no one will know you were here, at least I will not tell anyone." They shook hands. "You are a good man, Nathan. I can see why Tim thought so highly of you."

Nathan thanked him for saying so, and left. He felt encouraged by Tim's father's report of the likelihood of Tim surviving. His former patient would have one more chance at life. Tim would need to make changes, though. *And it is time for me to make some, too.*

Chapter 17

▼

Nathan heard from Dave on the fifth day of his admission to Hunt-Fisher. Dave had imagined when he signed himself in voluntarily to the hospital that by this time he would be preparing to leave, a new man in many respects, bright and cheerful, having cast aside his tormenting depression and anxiety. The reality of the situation, however, was quite different. Dave had spent three of his five days hardly seeing a psychiatrist at all, because it was Labor Day weekend and everyone was away. He continued to pace up and down the halls, smoking cigarettes, unintentionally intimidating all those around him. He prodded the nursing staff as often as he could. But these questions, he reported to Nathan, were answered by staff with vague, impersonal assurances that he would get his concerns addressed very soon.

Dave reported some relief from this misery on the Sunday of Labor Day weekend, when Georgeann came by to visit him. Dave said that she immediately saw how distressed he was, and sensed that his hospitalization was not working out nearly as well as hers had. They sat and talked for over two hours, which gave Dave's spirits a big lift. But the moment Georgeann left, Dave went on to tell Nathan, he was pacing and irritable again. Approximately twenty times a day, perhaps more, he asked the staff, "Why can't I get any answers from you people?" The fact was that Dave had been seen no more than two times by his psychiatrist, once by a psychologist and not much else had happened. He was off the Soldan altogether. The other patients on the unit continued to be completely terrified of him, which isolated him from interactions with any other fellow patients, except for one very delusional man who thought Dave was the resurrected Jesus Christ.

"I told this psycho that I'm part Jewish and sometimes my mother thought I was God, but that's about as close as I come to being JC," Dave quipped.

On the day after Labor Day, the fifth and assumedly final day of his stay, Dr. Fish met with Dave. Fish told Dave that he wanted Dave to talk to an alcoholism counselor from the substance abuse treatment unit, to review where he was in his sobriety. There would be more testing later in the day, Fish promised.

"I asked this guy, 'What time are you discharging me?'" Dave said, repeating the conversation he had had with Fish for Nathan. "I was still working under the assumption that this would be my last day. My bags were packed, I was ready to book."

But Fish apparently had other ideas.

"'No, Dave,' Fish told me," Dave said, "'we are not done with the evaluation.' Fish insisted that the hospital needed to do more of an assessment before it could let me go." Dave paused, emitting an audible sigh that conveyed his ongoing frustration. Nathan and Bortman's fears were coming true.

"I said, 'What? That was not the deal, here, Doc,'" Dave continued. "It was to be five days and then I would be out. That was the deal.' But he said, 'Well, I don't think I ever said that to you, Dave.'" Dave, who had a great ear for imitating people, was mocking Fish's western accent and manner. "He said, 'Dr. Forbes might have said that to you, but I didn't.' I told him that he and Forbes needed to get their act together, but he just put me off. He said that he would know more about the next steps by the end of tomorrow."

"Did you mention anything about signing out?" Nathan wanted to know if his friend had taken any legal moves to get discharged on time, as he had expected, after five days.

"Yeah. I said, 'Oh, this sucks, doc. This can't be happening.' Then I asked him, 'What is the point of keeping me? Can't all these tests and discussions get done while I'm an outpatient?'"

"What did he say to that?" Nathan asked.

"He said, 'No, Dave'"—the Fish accent reappearing—"'I really think it is best you stay here.' So, I said, 'Okay, then, I'll put my seventy-two hour notice in.'"

"He didn't like that, I bet." Nathan had found in his experience that psychiatrists were more than risk-averse; they just had a professional distaste for the challenge to their authority that the seventy-two hour notice implied.

"No, he did not like that idea, at all. Fish said, 'Dave, I'd like to keep this as a voluntary admission. For your sake and everyone's. Let's get these tests and discussions done and see where we are.' So, I confronted him. I said, 'What, are you saying that you would commit me? Why would you do that?'" Dave's anger was escalating now, as he retold the story of his exchange with Fish. And he whispered how he was very cognizant of staff near him, still observing his every move and words.

"Fish told me," he continued, in a softer voice, "'Dave, let's not go there. Let's keep this positive.' But then he goes into the nursing station, and I can tell that he was talking to the staff about me. Other staff in there started glancing over at me, to observe for themselves what Fish was reporting to everyone." Or so Dave perceived.

"This is hell. I'm in hell," Dave moaned.

Forbes, they both agreed, had duped them, to a certain extent. During one of their Labor Day weekend conversations, they came to the conclusion that Forbes, knowing he was going away for an extended weekend and worried about Dave's condition, had engineered the admission to feel more comfortable that nothing bad would happen while he was away. He had not really lied, but he had been very selective in what he told Dave about how available he would be over the weekend to check in on Dave and to assess what was happening with his testing.

"I'm firing his ass, Nathan. Forbes is through. I'm not seeing him anymore."

"I agree," Nathan said. "But my advice to you is to get out first, then do it. The docs will only make it harder on you if you fire him during your stay inside. They will judge that you are delusional or paranoid or highly impulsive, and they will want to keep you longer. And, Dave, whatever you do, do not put in your notice. They will commit your ass, I'm sure of it. If they commit you, you are in for weeks, maybe months. They may even send you to the State Hospital."

"What the fuck," Dave exclaimed, exasperated. Nathan felt his pain. All Dave had wanted was a few days to serve as a poster boy for the value of modern inpatient evaluation psychiatry, have his condition assessed in fine detail, and emerge from the hospital with a miraculous cure in hand. He would then get on with his life, prospering in the knowledge that he had gained about himself. Instead, he was stuck behind a locked door, living a nightmare.

Nathan predicted that Dave would be transferred to another unit within two days. The hospital liked to keep this evaluation unit's average length of stay of patients to less than a week, because that is the way the unit was described to the insurance companies. He suspected that the unit being considered for Dave's transfer was the alcohol and substance abuse unit, because a counselor from the unit was coming over to assess him later that day. The unit sometimes took patients who were still "dry," or not actively using alcohol or drugs, but who were having emotional problems nonetheless. This unit had developed a special program that treated patients with what was labeled a "dual diagnosis"—addiction and mental illness co-existing together. That meant that the unit offered both rehabilitation from alcohol and drug abuse, but it also could be a psychiatric unit for a small group of patients who both abused alcohol or drugs but also had major mental illness problems as well. The door was locked on this part of the unit where they provided the dual diagnosis track; the rest of the unit—the rehabilitation portion—was unlocked.

Nathan's prediction was right on target. Fish told Dave later in the day on the Tuesday after Labor Day, after the counselor's evaluation had occurred, that Dave would be transferred to the dual diagnosis program.

A team of three psych techs walked Dave over to the new unit, backed up by a high alert status at the hospital's Security Department, who monitored the transfer as well. The show of force, Nathan figured, was intended to prevent Dave from trying to run away once he was outside the door of the locked evaluation unit. And it worked; the fact was that Dave had been plotting his elopement throughout the night before the transfer. But once he saw all the bodies sent to escort him, and the security force as well, he decided this was not the place or time. "Too risky and too obvious," Dave told his friend, after sharing his covert plan to flee from the hospital.

"Don't worry," Nathan responded. "Your time will come."

"Yo, buddy, I just fired Forbes," Dave told Nathan the next time they spoke. "I know you told me to wait, but I couldn't help it. I hate the guy."

Nathan understood. He wished Dave had playacted a little, and did it after he got out of the hospital, but he understood.

Dave continued. "You aren't going to believe this next piece of news."

Oh, shit, what now?

"I just got assigned a doctor. It is your old friend, Dr. Short. They tell me he is the best doctor for me, because he knows medications so well."

That's it. I have got to get Dave out of there.

Nathan could not bear to think that Short was Dave's new therapist. This was the guy who did not help Tim, who did not really care, in Nathan's opinion. Nathan could see maybe using Short as a resource to do a fifteen minute medication consult, but that was it. But having him serve as Dave's doctor? No way. No, this was not going to work out. Short was not going to be allowed to screw around with his friend. He had done enough damage already, to people Nathan cared about.

And, of course, he was banging his ex-girlfriend.

Nathan concluded the call with a cryptic message. "Dave, I have an idea about how to handle this situation. Everything is going to work out. Let me do some legwork on my end. Call me tomorrow at this time, without fail. Okay?"

After work on the Wednesday after Labor Day, Courtney had just reached the sidewalk to her cottage's front door when she heard her name called. She turned to see Nathan coming towards her. Seeing him, she quickly assumed he was bearing news about Tim Harris, but wanted to tell her what he knew in confidence since he was not supposed to be investigating Tim's status, per hospital policy.

"Courtney, can I have a word with you?" Nathan asked as he got close enough for Courtney to hear him.

"Sure, Nathan. Come on in."

They went into her cottage and closed the door behind them—something Courtney did not always do in the warm weather, as she enjoyed creating some cross-ventilation between the screen door and the screened windows that were opposite the entranceway, off the living room area. But she felt a need for privacy, given the subject matter she assumed Nathan was there to share.

"So, Nathan, I bet you are here to give me some news about our friend over at Norwalk Hospital."

"I can give you a report, but that is not why I am here," Nathan responded, surprising her somewhat.

They sat in her living room area, and Nathan provided an update on his visit to Norwalk Hospital. "Tim is still in a coma, but his brain activity indicates he will come out of it shortly. The doctors are reasonably optimistic he will not have too severe brain damage. His stomach, though, is in rough shape. He has some internal bleeding, still."

Courtney winced when she heard this. Having bleeding ulcers is no way to go through life. But Tim was alive, and probably going to make it, that was the important thing.

Courtney asked if he wanted a beer, and Nathan responded that he would love one.

"How is your friend Dave doing? Is he still in the hospital?" Courtney asked as she retrieved two beers from the refrigerator, remembering what Nathan had told her the day they learned of Tim's suicide attempt.

"Well, it is funny you should ask. Courtney, I am here to ask for your help with Dave. It is going to sound crazy, what I am going to ask you to do, but I am as serious about this as I have ever been about anything."

"Okay," Courtney responded, saying the word slowly, with effect, as if to tell him, "You've got my attention." She handed him a beer and sat down. "Okay, ask away," she encouraged, prompting him to tell her what was on his mind.

"Alright, here goes," Nathan began. "Dave was told when he agreed to go in the hospital that he would be in for five days, tops. His outpatient therapist gets him in the hospital for an intensive work-up, then what does he do? This guy Forbes splits for an extended Labor Day weekend. Dave goes in the hospital, just like he was asked to do. But there is no real urgency to his evaluation. Forbes does not advocate for him, at all, because he is off in the Hamptons or something. So the unit performs a test here, an assessment there, but five days go by and it is clear that the alleged five day evaluation was not going to be the end of the inpatient part. The hospital tells him he needs to stay longer. At this point, Dave, who is very hyperactive and anxious—I think I mentioned that, right?"

Courtney nodded.

"Well, he is climbing the walls. He is getting ill-tempered and a little paranoid, even, but perhaps appropriately so. He meets with his doctor and the doc tells him he is going to be transferred to the alcohol and drug unit, on the dual diagnosis track. The stay is going to be longer, so that they can evaluate him on a new medication, which they have not even started yet. Part of the rationale for the transfer to this unit is to match him with a unit that knows about alcoholism and addiction, since Dave definitely is an alcoholic, even though he is not drinking and has a pretty good recovery going right now. The doc tells—or at least strongly implies—to Dave, before he transfers him, that Dave will be committed if he puts in his notice. And that if he is committed, with Dave's insurance plan running out, he might end up in the State Hospital. Getting the picture?" Nathan stopped at this point, looking to confirm Courtney's understanding. Courtney was following the story, but she had no idea why Nathan was there to talk to her. She was not on this unit where Dave had been admitted. It was not like she could do anything to help on the unit itself. But she was willing to hear him out. She remembered she owed him one—no, maybe two favors, confirmed in the lunch they had together a short time ago.

Nathan went back to work on her.

"So Dave is scared silly at this point. He has said that he will not, under any circumstances, go to the State Hospital. He will find a way to do himself in at Hunt-Fisher before it comes to that. And I believe him. He is just too proud. How did this happen—going in for a short diagnostic evaluation, almost like a medical evaluation he was told, and ending up being threatened with a State Hospital stay, probably for three months or so?"

"I don't know," was Courtney's simple and honest answer. She still wondered where this was leading.

Nathan went on. "So, Dave is a nervous wreck at the hospital, he wants to go home, and yet he is not able to. And he does not want to get committed. His insurance is going to be running out soon, making a transfer to State even more likely. He has his back up against the wall, he is between a rock and a hard place, use whatever expression you want to. If you pardon my French, he is fucked."

Courtney was not thrown by the profanity. In fact, she had said more or less the same expression to herself, "this guy is screwed" just before Nathan said it out loud. She still wondered, *why is he telling me all this?*

"Okay, so now comes the coup de grace, the final wrinkle that has led to me coming over to see you today." Nathan took a swig of his beer, partially for dramatic effect and partially to add a little inhibition-reducing ethanol into his nervous system.

"Dave is on the new unit for one day, and a nurse comes in to tell him his doctor has been assigned." Nathan stopped at this point to see if Courtney was guessing who that doctor was. She did not say anything, so he told her.

"Dave's life is now in the hands of our mutual friend, Dr. James Short."

Hearing Short's name elicited the most unsavory reaction, like one has after a swig of spoiled milk, or after smelling the foul air in a town dominated by a large paper mill. She could honestly say that Short was the only real blemish on her whole experience at Hunt-Fisher thus far. She had yet to build any real strong bonds with others in her class, but there was no friction with anyone either. That is, except for the run-in with the former Chief Resident and now Dave Shoenfeld's doctor, the arrogant Dr. Short.

Nathan finished his beer and dropped it on the table. Without prompting, Courtney stood and went to the refrigerator, grabbed another beer, opened it, and placed it in front of him on the table.

"Thanks," Nathan said, acknowledging her generosity. He took a long gulp, finishing a good third of the twelve ounces. "So, I've been doing a lot of thinking. I'm going to share a little about myself to you, Courtney. I have been acting a bit too passively lately. People I trust have pointed that out to me, and I acknowledge it. I am not taking life by the horns. I feel stuck a lot. But it is not me, you know, it is not my nature to be passive. I like taking action, and making things happen. But I've fallen into a role that offers very little opportunity to do much but take orders and just get by. It upsets me that I am this way, but I've floated along, ignoring my inner frustration. A resident I got to be friends with, who has now graduated and is practicing in Rhode Island, is always busting my chops to get moving with my life. So why am I telling you this?" He looked at Courtney to confirm she was still listening and attentive. She was. In fact, she related a bit to his personal sharing. She was stuck too. The engine inside her that needed someone in her life, a romantic interest with whom to form an intimate relationship, was revving in neutral. It had horsepower to spare, after Jason had replaced the broken parts. But she still had difficulty getting herself into gear.

"I am telling you this because I can not stand idly by and watch Short fuck up my friend. I wouldn't be able to live with that. I think our hospital has shortchanged Dave, Courtney. They have told him half-truths, and there has been a total lack of urgency to get him better, or at least to get him properly evaluated, and out the door. And with his lousy insurance, I have seen it happen, that patients run out of time and the only option is to ship them to State." He took another gulp of beer—it was now two thirds consumed.

"So here comes the shocker," he went on, grabbing Courtney's attention even more. "I really can't do anything to get Dave out. I guess I could sneak him a key, by putting one in a present like they do in prison movies," he said, smiling, and getting a laugh from Courtney in return. "But that would only lead back to me and I'd certainly lose my job, or even worse. I figure the better route is something that is, say, less high profile. So here's what I came up with. Ready?" Courtney raised her eyebrows to indicate she was.

"What I have decided is that Dave needs to elope. And I'd like you to help him."

"Me? How? Why?" Courtney was baffled, and very uncomfortable with the suggestion.

Nathan now leaned forward and looked directly at Courtney, speaking in a steady, confident tone. "Last night, I developed a plan, a plan to get Dave out of Hunt-Fisher without a lot of flak afterwards, a plan so intricate and so complicated, it should leave everyone unscarred. Everything will work out for the best, I am sure of it. But I need your help. And the help of a couple of others I will need to recruit."

"I'm still lost," Courtney admitted. She had no idea what Nathan was getting to. Certainly, he did not expect her just to march on the unit and walk away with Dave in tow. That would get her thrown out of the residency program and hospital so fast, it wouldn't be funny.

"I know you haven't a clue about what I am talking about, right?" Nathan asked.

"You are right about that," she concurred, suspiciously.

"Okay. Well, here is what I hatched last night, lying in bed, and thinking about the whole thing. The outcome we want is what? Dave is out of the hospital, and no one really gets hurt. Okay? And by 'no one gets hurt,' I mean hurt in terms of their jobs, reputations, training program status, future plans…all that. Except maybe Short, who deserves to get dinged a little. But he will survive anyway. Now, like any well-conceived heist, all the bases have to be covered, all contingencies planned for, all obstacles removed beforehand, to the extent possible."

Courtney was starting to think Nathan had lost his mind. But she listened, anyway, a bit intrigued by his thought process, if nothing else. And he had mentioned Short, and that there may be a chance in all this to screw him over somehow. That was reason enough to keep learning what he had in mind.

"As you know, I am sure, from watching television and movies, the key to subterfuge is an effective diversionary tactic. That, and planning, with good execution of the plan. Here is where you come in. I need you, Courtney, as a diversion for Short. I am going to get Dave to suck up like no patient has ever sucked up before, to get himself elevated in status to Closed Hall-Session Escort. You know what that is, right?"

Courtney had never had a patient on this status, but she remembered Dr. Roth explaining it the first day she began on 3 East.

"Yeah, it is when patients can't leave the unit except for a session with their doctor, but the patient needs to be doubly escorted, by the doctor and by someone else—usually a psych tech."

"Right. Now, sometimes I have seen it, that the doctor escorts the patient to the session in his or her office, but asks the tech to handle taking the patient back to the unit. The reason they do this is that they have another meeting or someone is in their office, and they can't be bothered with the escorting duties. But they may alert Security just in case. So, what I need you to do is to divert Short right after he finishes up with Dave. That's all. You'll need to give him a reason not to escort Dave back to the unit, or to call Security. Then we will create another diversion on the way back to the unit, and get Dave out. I will tell you more about the details later. But that is the basic plan."

"You are out of your mind, Nathan. There must be an easier way. Are you sure he will be committed if he puts in his seventy-two?"

"I am sure, plus I do not want to risk it. The heat rises when someone is committed. It looks bad for everyone, including the hospital, when an involuntary patient is allowed to escape. But voluntary patients elope a lot. And the after-effects are less messy, because the eloping patient, after all, is there on his or her own volition."

"But what if Short says, 'I'll be right back, I just need to get this patient back on the unit?' That is what I would do."

Nathan smiled. "That is where you have to turn on the charm, put an alluring smile on your pretty face, and con the shit out of him." Nathan's smile was devious and gleeful as he finished this sentence.

"I don't know," Courtney said, sidestepping another of Nathan's compliments about her looks. "It is too much. Plus, Nathan, for God's sake, I am a doctor at the hospital. Do you realize what you are asking me to do? You are asking me to purposefully sabotage another doctor, to aid and abet an escape of a patient. This is absurd. I can't do that."

Turning serious in response to this comment, one he seemed to expect, Nathan shared his response. "Listen, Courtney, this is my best friend we are talking about. He does not belong in the hospital. That is the key point. The hospital did not do its job well. It misled him. And I'll be damned if I am going to let Short get involved with my friend's care. I never liked Short, and I always thought he had a secondary agenda, to show patients he was the boss. He and Dave are not going to click, I guarantee it. Dave will piss him off, and the next thing we know Dave will be in deep shit. I am taking proactive action, for once. I want Dave out of there. And this is the best plan."

"What about after he gets out?"

"My friend from Providence, the one who busts my chops all the time, he will see him the day he gets out. He confirmed that to me yesterday, without knowing all the details. But I understand that Dave needs a good doctor to work with. But it is not Forbes, and it is definitely not Short."

"Nathan, I see you are doing what you think is the right thing," Courtney said, earnestly, touching his knee. "But I can't help you. I'd be going against my values and beliefs, I would be acting like some sort of double agent, or saboteur, or something. I can't do that."

"You would be saving a life, Courtney. I mean that. Don't you wish you could have had a better crack at Tim Harris? Let me ask you, do you think if you followed Tim as his therapist after his hospital stay that he would be lying in a coma at Norwalk Hospital right now? No, he wouldn't. You would have taken care of him. You would have responded when he told you he did not fit in at the day program. You would have seen the family more often to address all the chaos and craziness they have at their house. You would have cared enough to intervene. And he would have had hope, because you instill hope in people, Courtney. I have seen you in action. You are very good. You are still learning, but the underlying skills are already there. And every patient you care about like that, you are saving a life. And Dave is worth saving. He is a great guy. Help me save him, Courtney."

Courtney paused, but her mind was made up. "I can't Nathan. Sorry."

Angry and disappointed with the one doctor he thought he could convince to enact his plan, Nathan stood up to leave. Now he would have to think of another method. "Let me know if you change your mind, Courtney. Thanks, anyway. I am going to take off now."

"Sorry, Nathan," Courtney apologized again. "Your heart is in the right place. And if, somehow, I get wind that there has been a well-orchestrated elopement off the alcohol and drug unit, my lips remain sealed, I promise."

"Thanks," Nathan said, before heading out the door. He thought about saying something sarcastic about her having a nice week and that it was too bad Dave could not have one too, but he held himself in check. He would give her a little time to think about it. Maybe Short would do something to piss her off. Come to think of it, maybe there was some way he could make that happen, in fact. He nodded to himself. He would develop a plan.

The next day, Nathan sat outside Short's office, coming to the hospital on his day off to scope out the environment within which his plans for a Great Escape might be enacted. He sat by himself in an armchair in the broad hallway, imagining different plots and scenarios. It all came together for him, the perfect scheme, if only he could get Courtney to cooperate. He got up, and left to go home.

He needed to get Courtney pissed off at Short. But how? The opportunity, clearly, lay in their respective involvement with Tim Harris. Nathan figured Short would be touchy about responding to questions about how he had managed Tim after the hospital. If he hinted to Short that Courtney was hoping for a call from him, to be briefed on what happened to Tim, the rest might take care of itself. Short would get on his high horse, offended that a PGY1 wanted to talk to him about the way he handled his case. If they spoke, while he was in such a defensive and imperious mood, he would be bound to say something to make Courtney furious. Then she would remember that Nathan had offered her a chance to humiliate him further, by exposing him as derelict in his duty to escort a patient back to the unit, an action which then contributed to a suicidal patient's elopement. She would change her mind, and help him. *How perfect! That's it! That's the plan.* Now Nathan had to make it happen.

He needed to concoct a way to bump into Short coincidentally. The cafeteria was probably the best venue for such an innocent-looking meeting, Nathan figured. He returned to the hospital around lunchtime and staked out Short's office again. Luckily, Short was just getting done with a meeting, and appeared to be heading toward the cafeteria. This allowed Nathan to move in behind him, follow him there and trail him in the line to select food. Nathan grabbed a tray, and pushed it up against the edge of Short's.

"Sorry," Nathan quickly apologized, nonchalantly. Then he acted as if he had just recognized a doctor who used to work on his unit. "Oh, hello, Dr. Short. Sorry, I wasn't looking."

"What? I'm sorry, what did you say?" Short asked, acting unsure about why Nathan was talking to him.

"Oh, I just said, since my tray banged into yours, that I was sorry. So how are you doing, Dr. Short? New unit treating you okay?"

"Yes, fine, Nathan," Short replied, evidently trying to be cordial to the help at the hospital.

"That's good. So, that was bad news about Tim Harris, huh? I know Dr. Brentwood was very upset about it. Have you talked to her about it yet?"

"Uh, no…" Nathan could tell Short probably had not even thought about it, that calling Courtney was about the last thing he had on his mind, or wanted to do.

"Yeah, she was saying Tim was one of her favorite patients, since he was one of her first patients and all."

"She said that?" Short said.

"More or less. But she would love to learn more about your take on what happened, your assessment, I am sure of that."

Short said nothing, looking casual. But Nathan could tell he was burning inside. Tim was not her patient, Short was thinking, Nathan bet himself. Dr. Brentwood had been nothing but a temporary and very unskilled caretaker.

"So you'll give her a call?" Nathan was pushing it, getting off on his own manipulativeness.

"I don't know, Nathan. Can I ask, what is it to you if I do or I don't?" Nathan sensed Short felt like he was being played, at least a little bit. It was time to end this ruse.

"Just conveying a message, that's all. Hey, it was nice seeing you, Dr. Short. Have a nice day."

With that, he left the line for the salad bar across the aisle. All he could do was hope that he had nudged Short enough emotionally that he would call Courtney. If Short did, Nathan was almost one hundred per cent sure they would get into it: he would say something, she would react to it, he would react to her reaction, etcetera, etcetera.

Courtney passed Nathan the following days on 3 East, greeting him with a smile, showing no sign that Short had given her a call. Nathan already had conceived a Plan B, one that would up the ante and turn up the heat, if Short did not take his initial bait. The key was to create a situation that would get the two of them talking to each other, somehow. If they would happen to run into each other, somewhere around the hospital, perhaps a discussion would take place. He needed to set a trap for Short and Courtney to bump into each other, to get her exposed to Short's abrasive, condescending personality, to remind her about what an asshole he was.

Earlier, Nathan had reached Dave on the unit, and asked him to keep up his playacting, performing the role of the submissive, obedient patient for just a little longer: a week at the most. It was Dave's sole job to get Short to upgrade his status to Closed Hall-Session Escort. Nathan told Dave he had permission to rekindle the con man personality that had thrived during his drinking and drugging days. He would need to tap into it again, just this once. Then he had asked Dave to tell him when Short might be walking back toward the unit after a session later that day. Dave was sure he would be doing so at about three-fifty, since he had told Dave they would meet at four o'clock after he got back on the unit from having a session with another patient. Once Nathan knew this, he conceptualized the plan: he would ask Courtney if he could speak with her briefly, off the unit, after he got off duty, say around three forty-five. If she agreed, he would develop some ploy to guide her to the spot where they would cross paths with Short. A greeting would take place, and Nathan would find an excuse to beg off, leaving them to converse together, alone. Courtney would know Nathan had set it up, but he sensed she would be at least partially amused, and then let it play out. Her enmity for Short would be such that she would think, "Okay, as long as I'm here with this ass, let me be the judge of whether Short is worth sabotaging." She would be curious to know how Short would act if they got into a discussion about Tim. It would be almost like when an intrusive matchmaker creates an ostensibly impromptu meeting between two people at a party, with one of these two people in-the-know that it is a setup all along. While annoyed at the contrivance of the matchmaker, the in-the-know party might play along, just to find out what might happen as gently-nudged fate takes its course. Nathan had seen the gleam in Courtney's eye when he mentioned the chance to exact some vengeance on this sorry excuse for a therapist. And he had also sensed that part of her would love to participate in the scheme he was hatching. Nathan hoped he had read her correctly.

The plot worked perfectly. Nathan even asked a friend on the unit, without explaining why, to stroll by him at around ten minutes to four o'clock, near the alcohol and drug unit, and to call out to him, asking if he could ask Nathan a question. When Nathan heard his name and excused himself from the threesome that he had brought together in the hall outside the unit where Dave was being treated, leaving Courtney alone with Short, he pleaded with some righteous divinity to allow the interaction he was leaving to have its expected result. He walked toward his unknowing partner in crime, without looking back to check Courtney's facial expression, which he assumed would show some annoyance but perhaps some amusement as well. The actors were now in place for the drama Nathan had in mind. By six o'clock, when Courtney finished up at the hospital and headed back for her cottage, Nathan would know how the staged exchange had ended. He would wait around at the hospital to find out.

With nothing much to do for a couple of hours, he walked over to the gym, to see if Dominic was hanging out. Dominic made him laugh, and Nathan needed to be amused. As Nathan walked into the gym area, he saw that Dominic was involved with a group of patients, shooting baskets at the far end. Nathan greeted Dominic with a wave, and signaled that he was headed in the office just above the gym floor.

Once in the recreational therapists' office, Nathan had a thought that he would like to talk to Bortman in Providence, to confirm his willingness to see Dave next week if all went well. He walked back to the gym floor, and called out a request to his friend.

"Yo, Dominic, mind if I use your phone? Hospital business." It was true, to a certain extent; he and Bortman would be talking about Dave, who was now a paying customer at the hospital. Dominic gave him the thumbs up to go ahead.

Nathan had to call information to get Nathan's number, since he did not know it by heart. When he placed the call to Bortman's office, he got a break—Bortman was in the office, with an open hour caused by a patient who had canceled a session at the last minute.

"Nathan, I've been thinking just now about you and Dave. How is it going?"

"John, it is going okay. Hey, the last time we talked you said you would see Dave when he got out, if we got him to Providence, right? I just want to confirm that."

"Sure, Nathan, sure thing. Forbes lost my confidence when he blew out of town as Dave was going in the hospital. It is not that he went, but that he didn't seem to follow up closely over the weekend. It's not the attribute you want for the physician treating you, or treating your friend. I tell you what…I'll see him and then we will just play it by ear. I'll figure something out, in terms of what happens then. I might refer him, or see him myself for a while...we'll cross that bridge when we come to it. When do you think he will be discharged?"

Nathan was hesitant to tell Bortman of the elopement plan. It just added one more person to the conspiracy, Nathan figured, and one who could not really lend a hand in pulling it off. Bortman actually might try to talk him out of it. His gut told him to hold off on disclosing the plot, for now.

"It may be as soon as next week."

"Good. Hey, listen, Nathan, you have a minute to talk? It's about something serious, so I'll need some time and your attention. Can you give that to me, now? Some time and your attention?"

Nathan pulled back the curtain to the large window that looked out toward the gym floor from the RT staff office. Dominic looked occupied, with no evident end to his RT duties in sight.

"I have time and you have my attention. Shoot."

"Okay. Well, I told you I interviewed for that clinical leadership position in Newport at Oceanview Hospital, right? The new one that intends to open up in a few weeks? Well, as I sit here, talking to you, the contract for the position is right in front of me. They want me. I've been offered the job. Now it is just a matter of negotiating all the details."

"So you are going to take it?" Nathan asked. "You said you were worried about whether it would leave you time to maintain a practice."

"Not a big issue any more," Bortman said. "Actually, these private hospitals like their medical staff to have practices, since they expect that from these practice, they will get admissions steered toward them. And they are right. I admit my fair share of patients to hospitals, and now I'll admit them all to Oceanview."

"Congratulations, John. I assume they are making it worth your while."

"It is going to be a fair compensation package. That is what we are negotiating now. I have some leverage at this point, because they need someone aboard quickly, to get them ready for licensure inspections and the like. And the scope of these negotiations can be as wide as I want it to be."

"What do you mean?" Nathan asked.

"I mean that I can throw a lot of demands—reasonable ones, mind you—but demands that might fit both the hospital's and my needs. So, I've been thinking...Nathan, how would you like to join me there, at this new hospital, as the lead residential counselor, in charge of the first residence we start once the hospital opens? Before you say anything, I have to tell you that I would have some demands of you, too, if I put this requirement—to hire us as a team, a pair, where I don't come if they don't hire you, too—before the hospital."

Nathan was stunned by this offer, or at least by the prospect of this offer. He was anxious to learn the rest, the caveats, that appeared to be a part of any deal. And yet he was warmed by the bond he had with this fabulous human being, someone who would think of him for this opportunity.

"Okay, let me have it…What's the deal?"

"I am going to demand that they give you a sign-on bonus, but start you at a little lower salary than they would offer to someone else. That way, you have money right away to attend college here in Rhode Island. You'll need to transfer to Roger Williams in Bristol, or maybe URI, but I don't think that is a big deal. What *is* a big deal is that you study somewhere, for credit, this fall. That's not negotiable. No classes, no job. Kapish?"

Nathan considered what this all meant: a chance for a new job, more responsibility, probably more pay, getting going with school again, but also relocation, leaving a steady job as well as the area where he grew up, and where he had always called home. There were two major "x factors": on the plus side, there was the chance to work and be around Bortman again; on the negative side, there was the issue of Dave. It did not feel right to split with Dave right now. Dave was a big boy, and he had the fellowship to support him, but somehow the timing did not feel right. Nathan shared this concern with Bortman.

"Yeah," Bortman responded, "I've thought about that. So here is what I think we should do. Why don't we get him a job at the hospital too, as a counselor on the alcohol unit or the halfway house they have in mind? He would not be a true counselor or leader, like you will be, but he would be a great peer counselor, I think. From what you tell me, he is great around people and he had good sobriety going. They require at least two years for these peer counselor jobs, which he has." *Wow*, Nathan thought. *Dave will be in on this, and land on his feet, too.*

"So where would I live?"

"That's another thing we could negotiate with the hospital, to ease your relocation. It takes a while to get enough patients in the program to fill the house they have built for the program you will lead, so what I am going to ask them is to let you live in the residence until it starts to fill up. It will probably be the end of October before you would have to think about moving out, maybe even Thanksgiving. And it will be rent-free. It will give you a chance to save some money, and it will help the hospital because you can get everything set up correctly in the house, developing all the rules and regulations, procedures for the patients to follow, and all that. Nathan, you would own this program. It would be your baby, from the ground up. But the big picture here is you have got to get some letters after your name, so you can really start to lead treatment, as a professional. I told the hospital you were in school for psychology, with just a little left before getting your degree. So I am out on the limb her for you, big guy. I want you out of graduate school by 1995, no later. Then, maybe you can join my practice, and we'll go from there. But you would have to be a licensed mental health professional to make that happen. So we've got to get you in school, so you can get out of school and working with me."

At this point, Nathan felt light-headed from the combination of excitement, euphoria, a little dread about the potential changes he was facing and a deep affection for his friend Bortman, for thinking all this through and developing this plan.

"Wow. Wow. I am speechless, John. My knee-jerk reaction to the idea, though, is: I want to go for it. I will call Southern Connecticut and Roger Williams Monday, just to learn about credit transfer and application procedures, okay? This feels right to me. And I think my time has played out at Hunt-Fisher. The timing could not be better."

"So I can lay these demands out there to the hospital people I'm working with? Or should I wait for you to think about it?"

"I have no time, really, to think about it, do I? I'm sure school starts in a week or so. You have my blessing to throw what you just said on the table, and see if it flies. It is a little impulsive, but what the hell? I mean, what really do I have here that is not transferable to Rhode Island? I don't own anything but some clothes and an old Jeep. I have no girlfriend. My folks are in Florida. Let's do it." Nathan felt a vibrancy running through his soul, a new feeling of direction, of following a sensible course toward something, toward a goal that had real meaning. Bortman had popped the clutch in Nathan's life, accelerating him forward, with momentum already building. Nathan would be in his debt forever, if this all happened as planned.

Courtney smirked at Nathan as she approached him near her cottage, where he was leaning against his Jeep. "Why did I expect to see you here?" she mused, feigning irritation, and giving him an intentionally light but purposeful slug to his arm with her closed fist. She was reacting to the setup Nathan had arranged between her and Short, without prior warning, earlier that afternoon. The manipulation had irritated her, especially when he left her there with Short in the hallway. But once Nathan walked away, and knowing she was a pawn in his game to provoke a change of heart about her willingness to contribute to his scheme, she took Nathan's bait and played along.

Actually, she did want to hear from Short about his take on Tim's self-destructive act. A curiosity took over about what Short's reaction had been. Was he more sensitive and caring than she or Nathan gave him credit for? Was he as upset by Tim's behavior as they had been, and looking for an opportunity to process it with a colleague who also knew the patient? What was this guy like, really? Maybe she had misjudged him. So she went with the flow; maybe she would learn something.

The flow of their interaction, it had turned out, was choppy and contentious: another outcome for which she knew Nathan was hoping. When she saw Nathan near her home's entranceway, she decided she would need to be difficult at first with Nathan for conning her. And she still was not inclined to help him with the crazy plan for a Great Escape. But ultimately, in their distaste for Short, they were firm allies. Secretly, she was glad to see Nathan, if for no other reason than she had little else planned for the evening, given her aborted trip to the Jersey Shore.

"I know, I set you up," Nathan confessed, semi-apologetically, rubbing the spot where he had been assaulted, massaging it a little more than he needed to in order to augment his contrition. "I just wanted to open your eyes a bit, and have you see what Dave and I are dealing with."

Courtney let them into her cottage. Laying her briefcase on a chair by the door, she went to retrieve two beers from the refrigerator, without even asking her guest about his beverage preferences. Nathan took his spot on her sofa, as he had in his previous visits with Courtney.

"Before you tell me anything," Nathan said, "can I ask you, do you want to go down to Washington Street tonight, for a burger or whatever? My treat. It is the least I can do for my behavior today. And I am in a celebratory mood, which I will tell you about later."

"Really? A celebration? I'm intrigued. Okay, but I'll pay my own way. Remember, I owed you for a couple of things, too."

"I remember. But I was hoping those would go toward you helping me free Dave."

She dropped a beer on a coaster sitting on a side table beside the sofa. "Nathan, please, don't start with me about that." She sat on the chair, already taking off her sandals and propping her feet on the edge of the coffee table. "So, you want to hear about the interaction you so carefully orchestrated?"

"I wouldn't mind."

"He is an infuriating man. He said, 'Dr. Brentwood, there are psychiatrists who have had one of their patients attempt suicide, and there are those who *will* have one of their patients attempt suicide.' He said it so impersonally, so dryly, it was creepy."

"Did he say what he was working on with Tim? In therapy, I mean?"

"All he did was talk about adjusting his medications. He blamed Tim's attempt, in essence, on Tim's missing his evening dosages of medications, or whatever."

"The prosecution rests," Nathan said, provocatively.

Courtney was silent for a time, taking a few swigs of her beer, thinking back to her restrained fury at Short. She had not snapped back at him during their brief conversation, or challenged him; she had preferred to listen, acting in the role of the attentive student. And Short gladly assumed the professorial stance, as Dr. Roth had encouraged him to do after the first verbal run-in with Courtney. He seemed to take Courtney's nodding and asking polite questions, she sensed, as signs of deference to his experience and clinical wisdom. He did not read her thoughts, which, in truth, involved very unkind descriptions of him, with words that conjure up images of human orifices and male genitalia.

She found herself momentarily loosening her resistance to his pleas to free Dave and embarrass Short. Nathan obviously cared about his friend, and he had good judgment about people. What would she really have to do, but sit and wait for Short and entice him into a conversation that would cause him to be lax in his patient supervisory duties? It would be great to put him in a position to explain why he did not do what he was supposed to do. But she was not biting just yet. She saw her father's image in her mind's eye, and she knew he would disapprove of a plot to embarrass another physician. Her father was a smart and caring man, and he had correctly judged Short as a poor, self-centered teacher, but doctors just do not do to other doctors what Nathan was contemplating. And how did she know that Dave did not really belong where he was? Based on the opinion of a psych tech? She liked Nathan, but she could not be that irresponsible.

Courtney brought Nathan another beer and slipped upstairs to change out of her work clothes, and into something more casual to wear out to South Norwalk. It amused her that she had resisted Bobrow and a few other doctors' social advances, but she was so quick to agree to head out to town with Nathan. But she felt more at ease with him than she expected. He had Jason's easy manner, his subtle humor and his evident empathy for others. She thought of Jason, with Lara for the weekend, in Philadelphia. She would not be hearing from him until next week, she was sure of that.

They took the Camry to South Norwalk. Like she had done with Billy in Eastchester and with Jason during their road trip to Newport, she ceded the driving to the male companion. Nathan knew the area better than she did, anyway.

Nathan chose an informal restaurant he frequented, Nicky's Place, a spot with reasonable American fare and friendly service. They sat at a table by the window, looking out on Washington Street, to add some Friday night people-watching to their overall entertainment. Nathan agreed to have just one more drink, because he was driving. When the drinks came, he caught Courtney's attention, and proposed a toast.

"To Dave's freedom," he declared, hoping to engage Courtney in the excitement and spirit of this concept. Courtney smiled, and clicked his beer glass.

"So, Courtney," Nathan began, "tell me about yourself. Are you seeing anyone right now? Is there a man in your life?"

Courtney blushed slightly. Talking about men and intimacy was not her favorite dinner subject. But she trusted Nathan somehow, and took a chance to admit to someone, out loud for the first time, about her secret, unrequited affection for a certain fellow medical student in Philadelphia.

"I, um, in a bit of a unique situation with another man right now. Do you really want to hear about it?"

"Desperately," Nathan said, actually meaning it.

"I met a man a couple of years ago, at medical school, who was someone who had everything I wanted in a man and a relationship. One teensy-weensy little problem, though," Courtney said, holding her hand up with her thumb and forefinger a half inch apart.

"He's married," Nathan guessed.

"Almost. Not married, but totally devoted to someone else, in California. And to make the story more intriguing, this woman, who is absolutely gorgeous, and I mean jaw-dropping, stops-people-in-their-tracks beautiful..."

"Prettier than you?" Nathan asked, with genuine incredulity.

"Nathan, please. This woman makes me look like the homeliest girl on the block, believe me."

"I don't, but go ahead."

Courtney smiled self-consciously at Nathan. He was a nice looking man himself, an ex-athlete, no doubt. She never dug others for compliments, but Nathan's almost off-handed statements about her good looks came across less as flirtatious and more as simple, matter-of-fact observations. *Very smooth, this guy.*

"Well, I have never said this to a single soul, and certainly not to him, and I am obviously trusting your confidence here, but this summer, we spent some time together in a kind of a reunion context, you know, old medical school chums getting back together, and, from the moment I first saw him again, I just stopped kidding myself. I love him, Nathan. I would never tell him, because, you know, I don't want him acting different or awkward around me. Like I said, I've actually never told anyone what I am telling you right now. In fact, why am I telling you?"

"Because you can't keep it all inside and not tell anyone. It will drain you, or change you. Or it will make you bitter. So, you have no hope with this guy at all? Couldn't he drift apart from the girlfriend, what with the long distance relationship thing and all?"

"They seem as tight as ever, at least so it seems. And meanwhile I sit around thinking about him, like a girl on prom night who stays home because she turned down invitations from other guys, but the guy she wanted to go with invited someone else."

"Tell me about him. What's he like?"

"Jason Burke is his name. Jason is…" Courtney hesitated to find the right words to describe him. She loved thinking about him, and about his qualities. "Jason is kind, caring, very nice looking, smart, the best listener I've ever been around—although I must say you have that trait, Nathan, you really do."

"What? I'm sorry, I wasn't paying attention," Nathan deadpanned, causing Courtney to burst out laughing. "No, but that is nice of you to say, Courtney."

"It's true. Anyway, Jason is also a top-notch student and doctor. He is the antithesis of Short. That is a good way to conceptualize him. He is the un-Short."

Nathan returned the laugh. "He sounds like a great guy. I'd like to meet him."

"Oh, and there is one other thing. His girlfriend just started taping a television show for Fox. You'll be able to see her every week, and see for yourself what I am talking about."

"What's her name?"

"Lara King."

"And the show's name?"

"I think it's, like, Pacific Place, or something like that. They are together this weekend, in Philadelphia." Courtney explained how she had been blown off once the girlfriend decided to come for the weekend, which had included plans for her and Jason to re-assemble on the Jersey Shore.

They ordered dinner. Courtney realized she had yet to learn what Nathan's special news was, and asked him about it.

"Well, it looks like I am leaving Hunt-Fisher, after I get Dave out. It looks like I am going to be offered a job in Rhode Island, as a lead counselor in a new psych hospital. In Newport."

Courtney saw Nathan's pride in this job offer, and felt good for him. But she was also a bit sad that she would lose another person she had come to enjoy talking to and being around. But she showed only the congratulatory side.

"Wow! I guess that's great. Is it at all because of how you would feel strange at Hunt-Fisher if you succeed in getting Dave out?"

"Not really. It came out of the blue, this offer, just an hour ago, in fact, from this doctor I know who trained here, and who is going to see Dave when he gets out."

"Newport is where Jason and I went during his visit with me. I really like it there."

"I haven't been there in awhile, but I know I will love it."

"Let's buy some champagne on the way home, and toast your new opportunity."

After dinner, they stopped at a liquor store to make the purchase. They returned to her cottage, and Courtney popped the cork. Pouring the bubbly into some wine glasses—not exactly the right ones for champagne, but neither of them cared—Courtney toasted Nathan's future. After two glasses each, they were starting to feel the effects of their evening of celebratory drinking. Courtney felt dizzy, but happy. She liked being with someone this weekend. It would have been so much harder being alone, knowing what was happening in Philadelphia. Nathan had filled a void for her.

She looked at her guest, and, perhaps spurred by the alcohol's judgment-impairing effects, made the decision to change her mind, and help him with his scheme to get Dave out of Hunt-Fisher. She changed her mind because she felt for Nathan, and she hated Short. Nathan was leaving. It was the least she could do for him. She would just pick a case that she really could use some advice about, and ask him for guidance. She would have a solid cover for her actions.

"Nathan, I think you are going to like what I am about to say."

"What is that?" Nathan asked, not thinking at the moment about Dave and the elopement plan.

"I'll help you."

"What? With Dave you mean?"

"Yes. With Dave I mean."

"Seriously?"

"I'll help you."

Nathan stood up and went over to her, put his palms on her cheeks and kissed her lips in celebration. He drew his head back after the brief kiss, beaming, and told her she was the best.

Courtney responded by moving forward, wrapping her arms around him, then reaching up and placing her hands on the back of his shoulders to bring Nathan toward her, prompting another kiss. This kiss, the one Courtney initiated, lasted longer than either of them expected—far longer than the celebration peck Nathan started as a way to say "thank you."

For the first time in well over three years, Courtney was making out with a man.

Nathan was stirred by Courtney responsiveness, by the kiss's passion, and his desire for her. But he hesitated in making the next natural move, which would have been to begin rubbing her everywhere he could, under her blouse and summer skirt, and move his lips from hers and head south for her neck and below. And he knew he had a condom in his wallet. But he felt Courtney's passion for Jason, his presence in their kiss. She loved this man, Nathan had heard that clearly, and in her state of inebriation and loneliness she was thinking of taking on a substitute. As physically pleasant as that would be, it did not feel right to Nathan.

"Courtney," he whispered, after breaking off the kiss and moving his lips up her cheek to her ear, "I'm sorry, but…you know…I'm not Jason."

Courtney stopped, and regained her composure. Nathan was right. She still loved Jason, and she would have been sleeping with Nathan, by proxy, seeking to create equilibrium with what she assumed was probably happening at that instant in Jason's apartment in Philadelphia, with the voluptuous Ms. King. She was jealous, frustrated, a little drunk, and now a little angry and hurt by Nathan's rejection of her response to his kiss. Then she realized that he had said and done just what Jason would have.

The tears this insight caused came quickly, but they did not last long. With Nathan's arms around her, gently caressing her back, she felt protected and understood. Nathan was a very special guy, she acknowledged. Her decision to help him with his wacky scheme was the right thing to do. She pulled back from him, sniffing but smiling, and informed her visitor that he was welcome to stay the night, in her pull-out sofa bed. She did not think it wise for him to get behind the wheel after all the alcohol he had been drinking. But the truth was that she wanted him to stay. For this evening, he fit in with her perfectly.

This, Nathan thought, *is a memorable moment.* It was the closest he had ever felt to a woman, even those with whom he had been sexually intimate. An appealing woman's body was pressed up against his, her eyes buried in his shoulder, leaning on him for support. He felt immensely connected to her, and more importantly, in control of himself.

When they separated, Nathan moved to the sofa bed where he had been invited to crash, stripped down to his boxers, and lay across the bed Courtney quickly made up for him. After leaving him to go up to her room and change into light summer pajamas, Courtney returned downstairs, and, without announcing her intentions to do so, crawled in next to him. A sleepy Nathan enveloped her with his arms. They slept that way, with Nathan embracing her affectionately from behind, through the entire night.

When they awoke in the morning, Nathan shared the elopement plan in its entirety with Courtney. He did this prone on the sofa-bed, semi-naked and lying intimately next to her, even touching her and nuzzling his face into her neck occasionally as they shared a laugh, as lovers do. It had the feel to the both of them of pillow talk, but without the customary sex preceding it. But it felt right, especially after sleeping next to each other the previous night. Nathan found himself simply more focused on his short term plans and long term future than on manipulating his way into morning intercourse with Courtney. Not that he wasn't aware of an occasional rush of blood to his loins when he touched her, tempting him to give up the high road he had taken, and just bang her silly. The thought crosses your mind, he noted to himself, when a beautiful woman wearing only light cotton shorts and a shirt leaving much of her trim midriff exposed is reclining next to you, laughing with you, even touching your nearly naked body. But then he would recall the ardor with which Courtney described this Jason person in Philadelphia, with whom she was so evidently smitten, and then his focus would return. He wanted, above all, first and foremost, to get Dave out of Hunt-Fisher Hospital. Then we wanted to get to Rhode Island to enroll in college, and start a new job. And when he had sex again, it would not necessarily require that the woman he was with have the same passion for him that Courtney had for Jason; but at least she should not be thinking of another guy the whole time they were together, or be trying in a perverse way to get back at him for canceling a planned weekend getaway. It was all clearer now than it had ever been— he had choices, and he was in control. This was the way he would conduct his life going forward.

Courtney was having fun, laughing and joking with a man in an intimate bed scene, as she had not done for far too long. She would have made love with Nathan, if he had pressed the issue, because she felt sexual again, and she was interested in finding out how she would respond to him. But he was right—she had flashbacks of Jason in the same bed as they were in now, and her fantasies were about hours of lovemaking with him, not Nathan.

Now, she was in on Nathan's scheme; she had given him her commitment, and she could not back out. So she wanted details. What would the pretext be for her need to discuss something with Short? How would the psych tech that was assigned to the escort be eliminated from the picture? How would Dave avoid detection leaving the hospital, and how would he get by the Security Guard House at the bottom of the access road? She had many questions, and Nathan had all the answers. But not all the actors that were needed had been recruited as yet.

"What we'll need is another guy, the bigger the better, to be part of the group."

"The gang, you mean," Courtney joked, using the term that more appropriately described the outlaws that would be needed to pull this off.

"Okay, the gang," Nathan conceded, smiling.

"I have an idea," Courtney said. She jumped out the sofa-bed and went to the phone and dialed it, not telling Nathan what she was thinking. She brought the receiver up to her ear, and waited.

"Hi, Dad. It's Courtney," she began, looking at Nathan with a sly grin. "What are doing today? Nothing much? What do you say we go see Billy play some football?"

Chapter 18

▼

The annual pigskin clash between Scarsdale and Eastchester was being played in the early afternoon that Saturday, at Scarsdale High School's field just down the street from the Brentwoods' home, on the Post Road. It had just gotten underway when Courtney, Aaron and Jack Andrews, Billy's father, arrived and assumed their spectator positions in the bleachers. Jack told his neighbors that Billy wore number 36, and that he played fullback on offense and middle linebacker on defense. Courtney spotted him right away. He was defending at the time, leaning forward, directing his teammates to make adjustments as the Eastchester quarterback started calling out signals. The ball was snapped, and a handoff to the Eastchester running back set Billy laterally in motion. He pushed aside a burly lineman who attempted to block him, darted through a slight opening in the Eastchester line, and reached for the running back's jersey. With one hand, he grasped the jersey and yanked. The much smaller back was down on the ground in an instant. It was a marvelous athletic play, and an early sign about how Billy would dominate the game from that point forward. The score was 26-0 at halftime, the start of a 38-0 Scarsdale victory, with Billy running for two touchdowns of about thirty yards apiece, and making countless tackles and other outstanding defensive plays.

At halftime, Aaron summarized what he had been observing. "Jack," he remarked to his friend and neighbor, admiringly, "your son Billy is a star."

"He really is," Courtney said, marveling at Billy's strength and power, a notch or more above every other player's capabilities on the field.

"Well, Eastchester is a much smaller school, so Billy was not expecting them to give us much of a game," Jack Edwards explained. "It will be harder when we play White Plains and New Rochelle. Those are the tough games on the schedule."

"Has Eastchester ever beaten us?" Courtney asked. She did not remember losing to the school just down the Post Road from her alma mater, at least not during the time she followed her high school team's games.

"I think I read in the paper that it has been like eighteen years, not since 1971, that Eastchester has won."

Make that nineteen, Courtney said to herself, as she took in the rout. She would have left before the end of the lopsided game, but her primary purpose for being there was to accost Billy after the game and make a unique, secret request of him.

She told her father she wanted to walk on the field after the game and congratulate Billy. When the horn sounded to mercifully end the affair, Courtney made her way toward the game's most valuable player, who was walking off the field surrounded by a couple of his teammates and a few fellow students.

"Billy! Billy!" she shouted, raising her voice to get his attention, as she neared him. He turned, helmet in hand, and recognized her.

"Doc…"

Before he could finish calling her by her professional title, she overrode him.

"It's me, Courtney." She said her first name with such emphasis, he consented to her implied preference for a more familiar exchange.

"Hi, Courtney. Thanks for coming to the game."

"I enjoyed it. You played great, Billy."

"Thanks."

"Hey, Billy, do you mind if I ask you a special favor? Could you call me at home tonight?"

As Billy agreed to do so, his teammates, overhearing her request, gave Billy an admiring look and a few playful elbows. Billy blushed. Courtney observed this scene with amusement. She realized that her request would greatly upgrade Billy's overall social standing and reputation with his teammates. She surmised Billy was establishing himself not just as a great football player, but as a "chick magnet" as well. The locker room gossip was bound to be boisterous. *Look what I've done. Billy is definitely the man now!*

Nathan had been busy that Saturday, too. He decided to visit Dave at the hospital, to assess where his friend stood in his con game with Short. The stakes were rising, Nathan sensed, and Dave needed to get his status upgraded as soon as possible—on Monday, ideally. Dave's insurance would be elapsing soon, and

Nathan knew from experience that State Hospital transfers were usually planned in advance. It occurred to Nathan that some preliminary paperwork might have been initiated already, if Short was really thinking that such a transfer was likely. He would do a little espionage in the unit's nursing station, and see if he could find out just what kind of time frame he was dealing with.

Nathan walked onto the unit as anyone could, since the external entrance was not locked. He peered into the nursing station to assess who was on duty, hoping he would notice a staff member from whom he could extract some information. He was in luck; Betty Farmer, another psych tech whom he had once briefly dated, was sitting by the door, busy with some patient charting. He gently knocked, and waved at her.

"Nathan, what are you doing here?" she asked, smiling, as she opened the door.

"I'm off duty, Betty, here just as an ordinary citizen, visiting my friend Dave. How is he doing?"

"Pretty well. A bit antsy and anxious, but okay."

Nathan decided to take a stab at eliciting the information he needed. He leaned in close to her and asked in a confiding tone, "Betty, tell me straight. Is Short thinking of transferring him to State any time soon?"

Betty looked around to assess if anyone was within earshot, then whispered back, "I heard something about that last week. Do you want me to look in his chart, and see if anything is documented?"

"Would you? I'll leave now and come back, okay?" Nathan did not want Batty to be exposed to others in the nursing station giving out information freely to an outsider, even if the outsider was a Hunt-Fisher staff member. It was best to be as discreet as possible.

Betty came out the nursing station and unlocked the door to the secure unit where Dave was assigned, so Nathan could visit him. Dave was sitting on a sofa in the common area for the patients, watching a football game. They talked about his prospects for getting his status escalated.

"By the end of Monday morning rounds, I'll know," Dave assured Nathan. Short would need to hear that Dave had behaved himself all weekend, but Dave had been assured by his doctor that his status would be reviewed at the meeting. Short loved having this type of infantilizing leverage with his patients, Nathan told Dave quietly—but Dave would have the last laugh. If the new status was granted on Monday, Nathan said, the escape could happen as early as later that day. Dave could be free within forty-eight hours.

As Nathan was conferring with Dave, Georgeann appeared, a surprise visitor wanting to check in on Dave as well. The three of them sat and spoke together for more than an hour, conversing like old friends.

When visiting hours were over, Nathan checked in with Betty, to find out what she had uncovered from Dave's chart.

"The transfer application is in the chart, Nathan," Betty confirmed in a conspiring whisper, out in the hallway. "That doesn't mean he is definitely going, you know. The application is filled out for many who do not actually get transferred to State. But at least the application has been made. If his insurance runs out, you can be sure he will be transferred pretty quickly."

"When does his insurance run out, do you know?"

"I think he has about ten more days, that's it," Betty said.

"Thanks, Betty. And do me a favor—forget I asked you about this, okay?" Betty gave him a quizzical look that implied, "What are you up to?" But she nodded, and then turned to resume her duties on the unit.

The escape would need to occur next week, for sure, Nathan now understood. The closer Dave got to needing to be transferred to State, the closer they would watch him, and take more precautions than usual to make sure he was secured to the unit. The window of opportunity was very limited, and would close rapidly, probably near the end of the week, Nathan judged.

He left the unit with Georgeann, who waited for him during his exchange with Betty. He escorted Georgeann to the waiting chauffeured limo in the visitor's parking lot.

"I am so frustrated with this hospital, Nathan," Georgeann noted, with exasperation. "I know you work here, and my stay on 3 East could not have been better, but keeping Dave in the hospital just because he said something off the cuff about wanting to hurt himself, it is just not right. In fact, I called my former doctor, Dr. Hunt, about it."

"You did?" Nathan asked. "What did he say?"

"He was in a hurry. Actually, he asked if I would tell him more about it over dinner next Friday, since he was booked solid until then."

Nathan smiled. The hospital owner was going out to dinner with an ex-patient. *How ironic.*

"What if I suggested a slightly more aggressive strategy to helping Dave?" Nathan asked her, somewhat impulsively. Once again, he was breaking the hospital rule that prohibited fraternizing with this ex-patient. But his inner guidance system was in far more control that any external mandates that did not feel right to him anymore, especially ones that might impede attainment of the ultimate prize—he and Dave, moving to Rhode Island, starting fresh, empowered.

More importantly, Nathan just did not see Georgeann fitting the mold of the fragile ex-patient with whom a Berlin Wall-type boundary needed to be established, to make sure she did not form some type of unhealthy dependency on him as a former caregiver. *Let's be honest, this is a woman who just had a couple of extra cocktails and feel-good pills. Now that she has stopped with that, she is a more together person that any of the staff who were paid to treat her. She has more money than God, she has been to more State Dinners in Washington than anyone except former Presidents, for goodness sake. She is smart, pleasant and her heart is in the right place.* To be honest, Nathan thought, he would be honored to have Georgeann Wagner consider him a friend. The pleasant visit with Dave they had just ended confirmed this to him even more. The decision to ask her to help free Dave was impulsive, but it felt right. Georgeann belonged in their break-out gang.

Georgeann had no idea how she could help, but if it meant Dave would be in a better place, safe and happy, she was all for it. Nathan asked her if she knew where he could buy a blue sports coat, as similar as possible to those worn by the hospital's security staff. Georgeann immediately demanded that Nathan get in the limo, and away they went. When it came to finding and buying clothes, Georgeann assured her new partner, she could add real value.

They drove to the Lord & Taylor's and then to the Bloomingdale's in Stamford, and found what they were looking for at the latter store. Nathan thought a 42 Long would be the best size, since that was his size, and Jim Scott, his roommate who would be the one who would play the imposter role, had borrowed his coats from time to time. Georgeann took the coat they chose to the cashier and began to pay for it, waving away Nathan's protestations about her funding his scheme. But before signing for the transaction, she scurried back to the salesperson who helped her, grabbed an identical coat in size 44 Long, and paid for that too. She told Nathan it would be better to have two sizes, just in case the 42 Long did not fit.

"Now, Nathan," she began when they were back in the limo, "I have a tailor who could come over later, and do whatever we need, like adding the same kind of buttons the guards wear." Then she hesitated, smiling as she entertained another thought. "Should we go back to the hospital," she suggested, "and take a good luck at those security guards' coats, to make sure we get it right? What do you think?"

They decided it would be best to conduct this extra piece of research. Driving all the way back to Hunt-Fisher Hospital, they stopped at the Guard House just inside the hospital property to ask the guard on duty some bogus question, just to draw him out of the House and give them a chance to focus on the details of the coat he was wearing. Then they thanked the guard for the irrelevant information, turned around, and left the grounds for a second time that day.

"Did you notice the gold buttons on the sleeve?" Georgeann asked, excitedly. She was getting thoroughly immersed in the thrill of espionage. "And the matching gold thread in the lapel? And the shoulders looked padded to you, didn't they? But I think the color is a good match with the ones we bought. I'll call my tailor as soon as I get home."

The Brentwood home in Scarsdale was chosen as the central planning headquarters for the Sunday meeting of participants in the plot to free Dave. Courtney extended the invitation to Nathan when she learned that Aaron would be out playing golf Sunday morning at the country club he belonged to, and that he intended to stay around after golf with the other members of his foursome for drinks and dinner. Sheila had been invited to an art auction in Manhattan by one of her leading donors, and she intended to stay in the City for dinner as well. The Brentwood home would be free for the meeting by eleven o'clock in the morning or so.

The Free Dave gang membership now stood at five: Nathan, Courtney, Georgeann, Jim, and Billy. Georgeann was not inconvenienced by coming to Scarsdale, since she was on her way to the City for a Sunday evening in the City anyway, to see the Philharmonic. She told Courtney she had a date with an old friend, whom she refused to identify.

Courtney's initial reaction was negative to Nathan informing her that Georgeann had been invited to join the group. After all, the lady was a former patient of hers. But she relented because she realized that this action was focused on Dave's plight. And given Georgeann's relationship with her AA mentor, it was reasonable that she would want to help out any way she could. The whole thing was so crazy and convoluted already, that adding this new twist really made little difference, Courtney thought.

When Georgeann's limo pulled into the driveway at Courtney's house, their reunion felt to Courtney more like one she might have with a longstanding high society acquaintance of her mother's whom she had known for years, rather than with someone she had once treated as a patient in a mental hospital. *Either this is a very unique case,* Courtney thought to herself, *or I am a novice psychiatrist breaking all the boundary rules in the book.* She understood that she had set aside her common sense and professional responsibilities for the time being. But down deep, it felt right, somehow.

Another complication, of course, was that Georgeann was now a patient of her father's. Aaron would freak out, Courtney knew, if he discovered that a current patient of his was there in his home, plotting a carefully orchestrated elopement from a prestigious psychiatric hospital, in cahoots with his only daughter. But Courtney pushed aside her father's likely disapproval. She was on auto-pilot, tuning out thoughts of propriety and professional responsibility. Instead, she chose to focus on the fact that she had given her word—which is as important a value for any type of person or professional to uphold, or at least so she rationalized.

Billy arrived through the hedges separating the Andrews' property from the Brentwoods', just as he had when he helped Courtney move her things in late June. Courtney had convinced Billy the previous evening that he would be helping her and a friend of hers out a great deal if he would contribute to a little scheme. It involved getting another friend of theirs out of a bad situation. The situation, as Courtney explained it carefully to Billy, involved an unfair confinement in a hospital. As a doctor, she wanted to do what she could to help this individual out, but she could only do so much. She was not the doctor in charge, otherwise the person would never have been confined, or at least not as long as he had been or might be in the future, if he did not get her help. Could Billy lend a hand, she had asked him? The plan might require some muscle, or at least some physical size. It could be used for intimidation purposes, or actual coercion. Courtney did not know for sure how Nathan would want to use Billy, but she knew he was the kind of person who would be an asset, in some way or another. Then she begged Billy not to tell his parents, her parents or anyone else about her request.

Billy told Courtney he trusted her, so he was enlisting without a second thought. Courtney was more than a former babysitter; in many ways, she was his idol, someone he had looked up to his entire life. If she needed Billy's help, he was ready to comply with her request. It was about as simple and straightforward as that, he said. Courtney smiled affectionately at her neighbor. *What a sweet thing to say*, Courtney thought. Having Billy involved actually made Courtney feel safer and more confident that the escape plot would work out well.

During their private conversation the previous evening, Billy had told Courtney that schools in Scarsdale would be closed Monday for a religious holiday. And, as luck would have it, the football team would not have an official practice that day, because between the observance of the holiday and the team having no game scheduled the following weekend, the coach had given them the day off. It was clear to Courtney that Monday was the best day to enact the escape plot. Now it was a matter of getting all the pieces lined up, and gaining a full, mutual understanding about how it would happen.

Nathan came prepared to the meeting. He had purchased a flip chart and tripod easel from an office supply store on Saturday night, along with several magic markers for writing on the flip chart paper. He marched into the Brentwood house like a corporate trainer, setting down the easel on the living room floor in front of the fireplace, then hanging the large pad of flip chart paper on it. Nathan was clearly assuming his leadership role, and taking it all very seriously.

"Thank you all for coming, on such short notice," he began, standing by the easel, once the group had gathered around him. "And thank you to Courtney for having us here. This should not take long, but I wanted everyone to know how this plan I developed will work. Everyone will have a role. The plan is not foolproof, but if all the roles are performed right, we have a very good chance of pulling this off."

He moved around to the other side of the flip chart, and sketched the hallway outside Short's office: he showed where the sofas, chairs and end tables were situated, the location of exit doors and, of course, Short's office itself.

"Okay, this is a rough layout of the area where we are going to make this all happen. The basic plan, my friends, is to create two diversions. One will happen here," he said pointing to his representation of Short's office doorway. "Courtney's role is absolutely crucial to this plan. When Dave comes out of Short's office at the end of his session, Courtney will be here, in this chair next to the office door. Courtney will stand up quickly, and get right in Short's face. She will tell him she desperately needs to talk to him about a case with a medication issue, and she only has a small window of time before she is due somewhere else. She will beg Short to give her a few minutes, she will play up to him, make him feel like she can not go another minute without his profound expertise. At this point, Jim, you need to be walking slowly down the hall. We have matched the Hunt-Fisher security guard uniform, and that's what you'll be wearing. Georgeann, you did a great job. Look, Courtney." He held up the coat that Georgeann had had tailored, and had brought in with her.

"Looks just like what they wear," Courtney said, nodding, admiring the duplicating effort. Turning to her ex-patient, she began clapping. "Let's hear it for Georgeann." The small group applauded appreciatively. Georgeann stood up quickly, smiling, and took a bow.

Nathan resumed his overview. "So, Jim, two things could happen. One is that Short will say to you, 'Hey, Security, could you help escort this patient back to the unit,' a request you will promptly agree to. The other possibility is that he may hesitate. You may need to volunteer to do it. You know, you should say that you overheard Short saying to Courtney that he needed to have Dave escorted back to the unit, you are going that way, can you help? Got it, Jim?"

"I can handle that."

"Good. Courtney, go into Short's office and close the door behind you, okay? He'll understand you need privacy, because you are talking about a patient."

"Will do," Courtney confirmed.

"So, now, the other psych tech there to escort Dave will be somewhere in the area, but probably sitting here," Nathan said, pointing to a crude capital L, meant to be a drawing of a chair near Short's office. "Jim, you should introduce yourself to him and to Dave as he leaves Short's office, in a professional manner. I bought a nametag that is identical to what Security wears. It will say Jim Scott, so you don't get mixed up."

"What makes you think that will make it easier for me to remember?" Jim quipped, drawing laughs from the others.

"Okay, so now Joe, Dave and the tech doing the escorting will walk through this doorway." Nathan showed the spot on the drawing. "The three of you will then turn right, heading through another doorway in the direction of the unit. Now we need to do some stunt work. Georgeann, you will be next to Billy, just beyond the doorway. On my signal—I will be standing here, lurking near the second doorway—Georgeann and Billy will walk into the doorway too, causing a minor collision. Billy, you need to get bumped by the tech from the unit, and then pretend to bump Georgeann. Georgeann you should hang on to Billy and pretend to lose your balance. Billy will drop you down to the rug. A little scene will be created. You guys have to act like it was the tech who caused the collision. Jim, as the tech is leaning over Georgeann, you tell him that you are keeping your eye on Dave, and that you will call down for help. Jim, you'll say to Dave, 'Dave come with me, I'm going to take you back to the unit after I make a call for help to the Security Office.' Dave will say at that point, 'Good, I have group therapy at three o'clock, which I really want to make.' The group meeting is, in fact, on the patients' schedule. I am hoping the tech will feel a need not to hold Dave up in getting to his group session, and he will think that Security has him well under wraps, so he will stay focused on Georgeann. Joe and Dave, you will leave the area, head back toward Short's office supposedly to use the hall phone here"—he pointed to a spot in his drawing across from Short's office—"then you guys will just keep walking out through the exit at the end of the hall, down one flight of stairs and out the door on the ground floor. Georgeann's limo driver will be there, to drive you off the hospital grounds. The limo is great because it has tinted windows, and will keep you guys hidden from Security at the Guard House." Nathan stopped at this point, to assess whether his gang was following along.

Georgeann asked how her part ended. "Okay, I was coming to that. You are not really hurt, but you need to act a bit shook up, to keep the tech engaged there, feeling responsible for what happened. Then you need to get up and act so thankful to the tech for showing so much concern for you. Tell him you know the hospital owner, and you need his name to share with Dr. Hunt. Ask him where he works, how long he has worked there, etcetera, etcetera. The guy will feel like he owes it to you to chat and socialize with you, I hope. Billy, shoot the bull with the guy a little. Take your time, to let Dave and Jim get off the hospital property. Then eventually, you and Georgeann will walk away, saying you are fine. If he tries to stop you, it will be important for you, Billy, to tell him you are with her, and will take responsibility for her. You will need to be assertive. You'll leave at this exit," Nathan said, pointing to a different doorway than Dave and Jim were going to use, "and walk to the north parking lot where we are going to meet earlier, for last minute planning. All of our cars will be parked there. I will come out or be there already to drive Georgeann home."

Nathan looked again at his group for confirmation that they had absorbed the primary aspects of the master plan.

Courtney asked how long she had to stay with Short. "As long as you can tolerate it," Nathan said, laughing. "He will only have about ten minutes, because I'm sure he is probably booked again at three o'clock. At least ten minutes would be great. Walk him slowly back toward his unit, telling him you don't mind, you could use a few more minutes with him as you walk. Try to stall as best you can in the hallway. I assume you can think of a real case to run by him."

"I'll think of something," Courtney assured him.

"By this time," Nathan continued, "Dave will be long gone. And if you can talk Short into taking a different route to the unit, so that you two do not bump into Georgeann and Billy, that would be great."

Georgeann asked if the group could practice the collision. Everyone agreed that would be a good idea. Nathan acted like the tech, pretended to turn a corner, and Billy made the collision happen, holding onto Georgeann and then dropping her down softly to the carpet. Billy got into the acting role he would be assuming. "Are you okay, Mrs. Wagner?" he shouted, then turned to Nathan, still acting, and said, "Hey, watch it, dude, you knocked me into her!" Everyone laughed at his theatrics.

They practiced this over and over, until they felt like they had it right. Georgeann was a trooper, they all agreed, for allowing Billy to gently drop her to the carpet again and again. But she loved playing a crucial role in this ruse, and she turned on a latent histrionic side that Courtney had never witnessed before. Her favorite part was pantomiming dusting herself off and assuring the offending psych tech that she was fine, then finding something creative to say, designed to capture the tech's attention for a critical stretch of time. Everyone laughed harder and harder as she embellished this part, creating different diversionary tactics, like asking the imaginary tech who did his hair, or if he had a girlfriend because she had a granddaughter who was looking, or how he reminded her of a young man whom she had dated in the late 1940's, who had left her because he turned out to be gay. By the end of this practice session, the hilarity of Georgeann's spontaneous creativity had the group gasping for breath to recover from their convulsive laughter. The group broke up feeling amused and well-prepared. Everyone understood their roles. Tomorrow, Nathan reminded the group, they would actually have to execute them.

Georgeann lingered in the Brentwood living room after Nathan, Jim and Billy had left, to chat with Courtney a little longer before heading into the City.

"Why won't you tell me who it is?" Courtney asked her coyly, alluding to the man whose name Georgeann insisted on keeping to herself.

"Because it is my business, not yours," Georgeann replied, invoking the right of a woman her age and status to have her privacy respected, even if Courtney had once been her therapeutic confidante.

"Fair enough," Courtney said with a bemused smile, leaving it alone.

"I met your mother the other day, outside the hospital."

"Really?"

"Yes. She recognized me as I was waiting for Jerry, my driver, to pick me up, after a session with your father, actually. Kind of funny, isn't it? I guess she and I have rubbed elbows somewhere along the line, and she asked me how I was. I said extremely well, thank you, not telling her that my sound health was due primarily to her daughter's and her husband's fine medical care."

"So she doesn't know you are seeing my Dad?"

"No. I am sure she thought I was there to visit someone, or I was on some sort of official business, and did not feel it was her place to ask about it."

Courtney knew her mother had a sixth sense for individuals with high-net-worth. It did not surprise her that Sheila would approach Georgeann if she saw her around town, and was in the process of recruiting eligible patrons for her annual charity extravaganza.

"I'm sure that you two have met before, somewhere along the way. Mother does a lot of fund-raising for the Foundation she leads at Montefiore Medical Center, you know, and she is out at society functions all the time."

"She brought up her Ball, the one coming up pretty soon. She said she was going to send me an invitation. What do you think, Dr. Brentwood, do you think your mother's charity is a legitimate cause worth supporting?"

"It is a legitimate, certainly. Whether it is more worthy than other causes, that is an individual decision. But they do good and important work over there, I'm sure."

"She also asked me if we could have lunch together sometime. I gave her my number. So your father is my therapist, and your mother and I are lunch partners. What do you think of that?"

Courtney only smiled. *I think Mother's after some of your money, that's what I think.*

"Well, I'm off to the City," Georgeann said, getting up to leave. "If all goes well, I will see you tomorrow."

"Have a good time tonight with your mystery date," Courtney said, walking her co-conspirator to the door and then outside.

Before ducking her head to enter the limousine through the door being held open by her chauffeur, Georgeann stopped and smiled a wry grin at Courtney. "I don't think I am going to tell your father about coming over here today," she said, indirectly cementing an unspoken pact between the two of them to keep their respective participation in Nathan's escape plan secret, especially from the mutual authority figure they both shared.

It felt odd, but Courtney suddenly felt a kind of sisterly affection for Georgeann that she did not expect, what with their talk about mystery dates and their shared sense that it was best to keep the old man in the dark about their upcoming escapade.

Georgeann hesitated for a moment, before continuing. "I know this is the right thing to do, though, Dr. Brentwood. I trust Nathan, and I love Dave. I had to help out, once I was asked."

"I wish there was an easier way," Courtney mused, more to herself than to Georgeann. "It is very unprofessional, I know, but, there is no halfway involvement in this project. So, my position now is—let's just get him out of there and move on."

"That's exactly right," Georgeann said, nodding. "Get him out, and move on. I like that attitude. Well, I guess I will see you tomorrow, Dr. Brentwood."

Ducking her head and moving onto the expansive seat inside the limousine, Georgeann waved farewell before raising the tinted window, causing her image to disappear. The chauffeur closed the door behind Georgeann, tipped his hat courteously to his employer's evident ally, before moving into the driver's seat and steering the long black vehicle slowly out of the driveway, down Morningside Lane, and finally out of sight.

Courtney wanted to hang around to see her parents before she headed back to Connecticut. Aaron returned home first, carrying his clubs by the bag handle in one hand and well-cleaned golfing shoes in the other.

"How did you hit 'em, Dad?" she asked as he strode into the kitchen, looking happy and relaxed in a blue sports coat over a red striped golf shirt.

"I did the Brentwoods proud, for a change," he said, beaming, evidently pleased with the opportunity to brag a little. "Shot an eighty-four, which, with my sixteen handicap is a couple under par for me. It's amazing what can happen when you make four and five foot putts all day. I think I may quit medicine and start to practice up for the Senior Tour."

"Wow. You did have a good day," Courtney said in a congratulatory tone. Aaron was not one to aspire to athletic goals. She assumed that Aaron had taken some money from his well-heeled friends, and was riding a wave of nineteenth hole exuberance, as money shuffled his way for a change.

He confirmed as much right away. "I took Jack Andrews for a twenty. It was the first time I've done that in I don't know how long." He came over to give his only daughter a hug, demonstrating an ebullient mood, buoyed by a superior day on the links and evidently by the celebratory drinks that followed.

"Did you eat?" he asked. "Can I buy you dinner?" Courtney declined, knowing he did not want to go out again, and figuring that she could manage to grab something on her way back to the hospital.

"I hope you can wait until your mother gets home," he added.

"Why do you say that?"

Aaron hesitated, before revealing his secret. "I think she wants to tell you she is buying you a pair of tickets to the Foundation Ball. She buys extras every year as a way of adding a little of her own money to the cause, and to give someone she owes a payback. But," he added in a gossipy whisper, "I think she wants to give you an excuse to get out on a date."

"Oh, God," Courtney moaned. "Mother, Mother. She is something." Courtney and her mother had waged many battles of wills over the years, and the conflicts had at times concerned Sheila's unsolicited opinions about the characters in

Courtney's social life. Most often, in Courtney's viewpoint, these exchanges pointed to the relative importance—either high or low—of the respective boy's parents within Scarsdale society. Both of her parents had distrusted the effete and slimy Colin during Courtney's latter years at Cornell, an assessment that turned out to be on target. But now it appeared to Courtney that her parents were tuning into a slight disturbance in her mood, seeing a melancholy side of her that they had never observed before. Courtney did not feel comfortable talking about Jason with either one of them; in fact, Nathan had been the first person with whom she had ever shared her tale of unreciprocated love. *Is it that obvious?* she asked herself. She thought she hid her inner world from her parents better than that.

Aaron chuckled at his daughter's reaction to his wife, remembering how often he had witnessed similar exasperated sounds during his daughter's more contentious adolescent years. "I have to admit, I was all for it," Aaron confessed from the stairway leading to the second floor. "I'm a little worried about you, dear. You seem a bit lonely to me, sometimes. Plus, it will be a lot more fun with you there. Can you think of someone to invite?"

Courtney thought for a moment. Jason came to mind, of course. Certainly, he owed her one, for the late cancellation of the weekend they had planned in Stone Harbor. It was the least he could do for jilting her. Plus, he was always very comfortable assuming the chaperone role with Courtney, since it provided them each with a partner for social events throughout medical school. But Courtney's intentions ran deeper than simply receiving a payback from Jason, or renewing their previous pattern of offering each other neutral company. She was hoping that seeing him again might create an awakening of sorts—not a reversal of feeling, since she knew he was a special man with whom she would want always to remain connected. She just needed to be more practical, and find a way to release the feelings that had overwhelmed her so forcefully earlier in the summer. Up close, in his presence, she would have the opportunity to make a secret emotional surrender—acknowledging to herself that Lara had, and always would have, supremacy over her in Jason's heart. Time spent apart had brought her back to her senses a bit. That, and the disappointment of being forced to defer to Lara's whim to come east for the weekend. Her evening and night spent with Nathan had helped as well. It had gotten her into a place mentally to assess her readiness to move forward with another man in her life. Kissing and snuggling with Nathan had felt very right, very comfortable. They had not consummated the bond with sex, but she had desired him, that was the important thing. For the first time since her breakup with Colin, she had wanted to be with a man, she had wanted to share herself. Except for when Jason was over. She had wanted to be with him, too. But she was beginning to find herself again, moving beyond her melancholy and ambivalence to a place where she felt in more emotional self-control. *I'd like to get Jason up here and see how I handle it. It needs to happen in person—I need to feel it with him here, next to me, and really accept that I want to find someone else to share time and perhaps myself with.*

"Yeah, I think I'll ask my friend Jason, if he is not busy," she said, after a moment of thought. "We always have a good time, and he is not put off by these types of society scenes. He would actually enjoy it, although the fun might be at the expense of some of Mother's friends, who wouldn't even know that they were being ridiculed behind their back." She knew her father shared an innate distaste for the elitist types who frequented these affairs.

But a twinkling in his eye betrayed Aaron's own stake in promoting his wife's matchmaking plot. "Isn't this friend Jason involved with someone else? I don't think that is what Mother has in mind," Aaron pointed out, trying to shift the blame for parental meddling to Sheila.

Courtney read her father's intentions, but she had her own plan, which might achieve the same end for which her parents were aiming. Jason might even create an introduction to someone at the Ball with whom she could connect later. It all made sense: she would use the event to get Jason out of her system, have a good time with a newly reinforced platonic-only friend, and fulfill her pledge to her Mother to attend the event. The whole thing felt right.

"You're right, he is involved with someone," Courtney confirmed to Aaron about Jason. "But it is short notice, and he owes me a favor," she explained. She smiled confidently at her father, to assure him she had things under control. "Don't worry. It will be nice."

Time spent with Jason was always nice.

"Hey, Dad, let me ask you something." Courtney wanted to change the subject.

"Ask away," Aaron said, sitting down to focus his attention fully on what his daughter was about to say.

"Well, I just wanted to know, before you became a Dean and ran the medical affairs at the hospital, when you were more in a peer role with another physician, did you ever challenge another doctor because you thought they were not handling a case properly? And if the doctor did not respond as you hoped, would you do an 'end around' so to speak, to find a way to get the situation dealt with?"

"End around? What do you mean? Like telling a superior, or doing something more directly, like with the patient or the patient's family?"

"I guess either. It is just a hypothetical. Doctors deal with life and death, yet, to me, our profession seems particularly reluctant to challenge each other about what we are doing with our patients. Nurses probably do a better job challenging doctors, but, then again, they can in their supportive role. Am I right about that?"

"Well, the reason I asked what you meant by your end around metaphor is that there is a big difference between going up the ladder in the medical administration hierarchy to challenge someone, which any doctor has the right to do—even though it invites a very contentious process with a lot of down side for doing so. Because, you are right, doctors do not like others telling them how to treat their patients. I don't know if that is particularly idiosyncratic of physicians, though. Judges, teachers, engineers, I don't think any of them do much more in the way of inviting critical feedback from peers. But the more underhanded and more ethically troublesome intervention, speaking or making recommendations directly with the patient or patient's family, on a case in which one is not the physician and does not know all the clinical facts in many cases, that is never defensible. I can not think of an instance when that would ever be the right thing to do. You have a professional responsibility to take a matter you believe strongly in to the right authorities, and prepare yourself to get involved in the fight of your life. But a physician should never do anything that sabotages another doctor's treatment with a patient, in a direct way. It is not right. It is not ethical. It shows contempt for the system that supports your profession. That is how I look at it."

Courtney was aware that her father was looking at her intently, trying to gauge why she was exploring this issue. She would need to dodge him, for now. Surprising herself with the ease with which she was able to do it, she came up with a specious cover for her question.

"It is hard being so inexperienced," she said, as reflectively as she could muster. "I occasionally see other inexperienced PGY1s make mistakes. But I know that I am not the teacher, just the fellow student. I need to let the system work." *Wow. I can be good at this B.S. thing.*

"Want to talk about the situation you are struggling with? What's the other doctor doing that you are so concerned about?"

"No, Dad, I heard what you said, and it makes sense. Hey, I'm just learning, and I need to ask questions, right?" Courtney realized she had lucked out—Aaron had a few drinks in him, and did not have the mental acuity to pick up on the guilty vibes she was manifesting.

"That's right," Aaron agreed. "Ask the questions. But never do anything rash or imprudent with another doctor's case. Especially in your first few years of residency. What a mistake that would be!"

Oh my God, Courtney thought to herself. *What have I gotten myself into?*

Chapter 19

▼

Nathan had the day off on Monday, the day he hoped to get Dave out of Hunt-Fisher and out of Dr. Short's grasp and, in essence, to begin a new chapter in his own life. If all went well, he would be handing in his resignation the next morning. The most important initial variable that needed to fall into place, the variable that would derail the elopement plan before it even started, worked out as planned. Dave called Nathan in the morning excitedly, with the good news: he had been upgraded to Closed Hall-Session Escort status. His effort to be a good boy over the weekend had paid off. In fact, his improved behavior—manifested in his showing great skill in leading an AA meeting on the unit the previous evening—left the staff duly impressed. But the nurse that notified him of his upgraded status also told him that Short was still very concerned about his self-destructive potential. Short had yielded to the nurses' opinion that the status upgrade was warranted, but he was still wary. Dave's status would be reconsidered, in case the patient showed any evidence he could not handle it.

Dave's session off the unit was scheduled for two o'clock. Nathan considered the timing a bit of a mixed blessing: the negative aspect was that there would be more traffic in the hallways as nursing staff rotated shifts at three o'clock, perhaps even staff from the substance abuse unit who might get in the middle of the scene that the group would be creating. Something unplanned, something unaccounted for could occur. On the other hand, the traffic in the halls could be fortuitous, offering Dave and Jim a chance to blend in with others as he was spirited away. *We will just have to go for it, and do our best to avoid the unexpected.*

All the members of the gang needed to be contacted that the plan had a "green light." Nathan reached both Georgeann and Billy, telling them to meet him at the north parking lot at the hospital, no later than two-thirty.

Jim had already called in sick to his job, and was ready to go. He even went for a haircut during the morning, to more fully look the part of the righteous, straight-laced security guard.

Nathan reached Courtney in her office. When he greeted her, she responded without enthusiasm to his voice. He sensed right away that she was having second thoughts. He needed to make a judgment call: should he come on aggressively, pointing out how she had given her word, how all the pieces were in place, how she could not back out now, what with Dave so close to being out of insurance that he was in real danger of a rapid transfer to the State Hospital; or should he coax her back into the team, with assurances that she was doing the right thing, that Short was an ass and she would be saving his friend from Short's cruelty and twisted clinical logic? The intimacy of their night together was still a positive factor, he hoped, but time had elapsed; the further away from their kiss and playfulness in bed, and with greater sobriety playing a moderating factor, the more Nathan understood that her concern was likely to escalate. Nathan, with time only to use intuition, decided the aggressive option would be self-defeating. Bullying Courtney was likely to create a counteroffensive, about how it was her decision, and how her professional career was at stake if somehow it got out that she had collaborated with this scheme. So he took the empathic route.

"You're having second thoughts, aren't you?" he asked.

"How did you know?" Courtney responded, surprised that she had given away her vacillation so easily.

"I expected it," Nathan said. "The closer you get to doing something like this, even if it is the right thing—and it is the right thing, by the way—the harder it gets to pull the trigger, and just do it."

"I feel like such a sneak, Nathan. All day, I play a role that challenges my patients' sneakiness and responsibility-avoidance. And here I am doing what I tell my patients not to. Nathan, please, can't you just do this without me?"

"Not today I can't. We need a way of keeping Short in his office, and you offer the best diversion. Please, Courtney, don't derail this now. It will never come back to you, I promise, even if it gets fouled up somehow. All I ask is that you try. It might not work anyway. Short may be difficult and insist on walking Dave back. I doubt it, but he might. Just bring him a case, a real case you actually could use some advice on. That will keep it real for you. Then, it is up to him, really, whether this works, not you."

"It's just hard for me to actually do this. I know I promised," she acknowledged, but with discouragement.

"You did promise," Nathan countered quickly, playing the guilt card, and ignoring her plea to get baled out of her pledge. "And Georgeann is counting on you, too. Do you think she would do this if it was the wrong thing to do?"

Courtney hesitated, thinking about this question.

"When do you need me there, Nathan?" she asked with resignation in her voice, but showing him that she would follow through on her pledge to participate.

Nathan smiled, and tried to hide his relief that Courtney was not going to throw any last-minute kinks in the plan. "I need you there at two forty-five, in the chair outside Short's office, no later. Thanks, Courtney. I will always owe you for this."

"Good luck, Nathan," Courtney said with a finality that implied an understanding that Nathan's Hunt-Fisher days were just about over.

Jerry, Georgeann's driver, pulled into the parking area where Nathan had arranged for everyone to meet, in a far corner of a lot far out of sight from the main hospital. Nathan and Jim emerged from his Jeep and signaled for other members of the group, already assembled in surrounding cars, to climb into the limo. The shaded windows of the luxury vehicle, he figured, would provide cover for their last-minute planning discussions inside.

Billy had arrived at the hospital early, around two o'clock, since he did not know how long his trip would take from Scarsdale. He had stayed inside his father's Acura, waiting dutifully for the others to arrive. At Nathan's signal, he too climbed into the limo's spacious back seating area. Jim was next to enter Georgeann's vehicle.

Nathan looked around the lot to check for any witnesses to their grouping. No one was in sight. He slipped in last, closing the door behind him. Once inside, he asked for the group's attention. "Now, listen everyone," Nathan said, exerting command of this group whose upcoming actions he had so carefully orchestrated, "this is it." He looked around the car's interior, noting how they were paying full and rapt attention to his words. He was their leader. It was time to rally the troops. "This is going to work," he assured them. "I have a real good feeling about getting Dave out today."

The logistics of the getaway sequence, including how everyone would get off the hospital grounds and then reconvene at a later time, needed final coordination. "Jerry, you should just drive Jim and Dave out to Georgeann's, to get Dave off grounds right away, the sooner the better. Don't wait for Georgeann, okay? Billy or I will drive Georgeann home once the plot has run its course. Everyone agree?"

All heads inside the limo, including Jerry's, responded with a nod.

"Okay, Jim, you need to keep a very low profile while in the hospital, okay? Let's minimize any chance of you being found out by someone who does not recognize you. You might as well fold and carry your coat before you get inside the hospital, so you don't draw any attention outside, at least. And if you see anyone with a similar coat, another security guard, heading your way inside the hospital, do whatever you need to but do not let him see you. That would really screw us up. Got it?"

Jim nodded again, understanding his need to be as inconspicuous as possible.

Still looking at Jim, the most exposed of the group in terms of danger in playing his role, Nathan extended his hand, placing it supportively on his friend's shoulder. "You know where to go, right?" he confirmed with Jim. His roommate nodded. He and Nathan had scoped out the spot outside Short's office the evening before.

"Good. Billy and Georgeann, you need to just saunter around near the area where you will be creating the collision with the psych tech. Take a newspaper, sit and read in the area. Whatever. Talk to each other like you are mother and son."

"Thank you for the compliment," Georgeann said, smiling, acknowledging that her age made her more likely to be Billy's grandmother than his mother. The group understood the wit in her remark, and laughed.

Nathan needed to finish up his planning remarks, as the time for them to get into their respective places was nearing. "Okay. I will be hanging around Short's office, to make sure everything goes as planned." He hesitated again, for effect, looking from one person to the next. They were poised for his signal.

"Let's rock and roll," he said, signaling the escape plan to begin.

The four conspirators baled out of the limousine, and spread out into three separate directions. Billy and Georgeann took a sidewalk path that circled a building next to the parking lot, but headed eventually to the main hospital entrance. Jim headed straight for the doorway he wanted to enter, blue blazer tucked under his armpit. Nathan walked along the access road, which provided a longer route to the same doorway.

At two forty-five, Nathan ambled down the hallway toward Short's office, confidant that Courtney would be there, in a chair just outside the former Chief Resident's door. She was there, in fact, reading through a file, not looking up to acknowledge Nathan at all, playacting superbly.

Down the hallway, Jim stood by a bulletin board. Now in full uniform, he tried to appear occupied, as if he was reading one of the flyers posted there about an upcoming medical education conference. Nathan circled the area, staying in motion, blending in with others walking by Short's office, first going one way and then turning to go by the other way.

Just as he was ready to repeat this circling behavior around Short's office, he noticed a familiar face moving toward him down the hall. It was Cecelia, coming on duty for the evening, but choosing to walk by Short's office, probably for a quick chat, he figured, even though it was well out of her way. Nathan started to panic. She could mess the plan up somehow; he was not sure about the way she would manage to do this, but his gut told him that she represented danger. Cecelia knew Jim, meeting him many times when she slept over at Nathan's house during their romantic period. She knew that Jim worked for a shipping company, not as a security guard at Hunt-Fisher. Cecelia also knew Dave, and could quickly put some clues together about why Jim was there—especially if she spotted Nathan around the area on his day off. Finally, she might be jealous seeing the attractive Courtney outside her boyfriend's door. When jealous emotions run high, paranoid radar would be in full force. Cecelia would be suspicious. *This is not good*, he thought.

Just then, Short's door opened just a crack. The session was ending, but not before a few final words were evidently being exchanged between doctor and patient. Nathan peered around a corner, attentive to Cecelia's body language, trying to gauge the extent of the danger she might pose to his plan. Then he saw her spot Jim. She stopped, doing a double take in Jim's direction. After making this confirming look toward Nathan's roommate, she turned to look at Courtney by her lover's door. Nathan read confusion, and jealousy. Cecelia started to walk toward Jim. Nathan knew she was going to question him about what he was doing there, dressed like a security guard.

Rather than wait, Nathan sprung into action.

Walking quickly toward her, he grabbed her closest upper arm, tightly. "Cecelia, come with me," he said with determination. Startled by his appearance, she acceded to his insistent order initially. But after taking a few steps backwards, with Nathan's hand still trying to force her to follow him, she stopped abruptly.

"Nathan, what are you doing? And what is Jim doing dressed like Security?" she asked, now gaining more control and trying to piece together what was happening.

"You need to follow me," Nathan said, tersely. She did not budge. "Now, Cecelia." He said this as if he was in Jim's role of security guard, looking to coerce a recalcitrant offender of some kind.

"Remove your hand from my arm at once, Nathan. I mean it," she said, angrily, jerking her limb out of Nathan's grasp.

Nathan responded with reciprocal anger. Looking Cecelia in the eye only inches from her face, he pursed his lips and retorted, "No, you need to know what I mean. And what I intend to do if you don't follow me, right now." Cecelia's eyes widened in shock, responding with disbelief to the aggressive, insubordinate manner in which he was speaking to her.

"Listen to me," Nathan whispered to her through gritted teeth. "I don't want you interfering with what I'm doing here. If you don't come with me, now, away from this spot, here is what I am going to do: I am going to turn around and march into Dr. Short's office and tell him all about us, you and me, leaving no information out. He will be interested to learn the details about whom you were fucking right before him, I am sure. Then, I will head down to Ms. Herlihan's office and tender my resignation, saying I could not handle the guilt of breaking the rule about having a relationship with a nurse on my unit, a certain Ms. Cecelia Reade." He hesitated to let his words sink in. Cecelia's jaw dropped, her mouth opened, incredulous at what she was hearing.

"If you back off and come with me, though, I will do neither of these things, ever, I give you my word. What is it going to be, Cecelia?" He re-gripped her arm, and coaxed her away from Short's office. Jim walked by them, as planned, since Short's door was opening wider.

Cecelia astonishment was still very evident. It was a reaction to Nathan's newly assertive manner, as much to the threats he was making, and to his knowledge of her relationship with Short. Then, her face turned to a scowl, a look of pure hatred, for the man she used to cry out to in ecstasy amid their raucous coupling. "You wouldn't do that, Nathan," she said with derision. "You're not going to give up your job. Where will you go?" Nathan saw she was acting instinctively, calling his bluff, unwilling to accept that lowly Nathan Bigelow could bully her in any way.

"C'mon, Cecelia. You have about five seconds to find out if I will do what I said I will do. And I will, believe me. It's not worth it for you to find out, Cecelia. Why blow your relationship with Short, your reputation, and your job here? It's not worth it. Come with me. Just walk away down the hall with me, and in about five minutes this will be all over, and we will just get on with our respective lives."

"Nathan, what are you up to?"

"Five…four…," he counted down quickly. "I'm serious, Cecelia."

Cecelia looked into his eyes, and read his determination. She huffed once, and shook her head in resignation. It was clear that she hated to admit defeat, but the threat to her relationship with Short had obviously hit the mark. "Okay. You win," she said, angrily but quietly.

Nathan escorted her down the hall, and away from the danger zone, saying nothing to her. Cecelia would have blown up the plan, somehow—Nathan was sure of it. She needed to be eliminated from the equation.

Once at a safe distance from Short's office, Nathan released his grip from Cecelia's arm and stopped. They were far enough away from where she could do any damage, and, at that point, Cecelia had been threatened into submission anyway. Nathan was anxious to learn what was happening behind him, a scene he had expected to witness firsthand but one that now had been left to the deceptive skills of his well-trained team. The results would be evident in a few moments.

"Okay, Cecelia, I'll leave you here," he said. "Thanks for not making a fuss. And like I said, let's just let this whole thing go, keep it to ourselves. No one got hurt, neither me nor you. Let's just leave it that way."

By this time, Cecelia was crimson red in anger and frustration. Nathan could tell that she was plotting ways to exact retribution for being coerced like she had just been. If he ever worked with her again, she would punish him, make his job a miserable, psych tech hell. He decided at that point that he would not let that happen. He would quit the next day, and use time he was due in vacation and uncompensated overtime to cover the period required for notice of his resignation. He would tell Emily about his future plans, and she would understand.

Once he decided this, Nathan realized that it might be the last time he would ever see Cecelia. But this was no time for nostalgia. He had to leave her there, and return to the scene of the crime, and assess where things stood. He turned quickly, and began walking away from her. With each step, his pace accelerated. He sensed that while he had been diverting Cecelia, the plan had either succeeded or failed. One way of the other, his time at Hunt-Fisher was coming to an end.

Nathan was practically jogging when he reached the intersection of the two hallways near where Short's office was situated. Then, up ahead, he saw the denouement of his well-conceived conspiracy. Jim and Dave, moving quickly and impassively, were speedily headed through the exit doorway that led to the first floor and on outside. They were so intent on getting away and out of sight that they did not even notice Nathan coming toward them, only a dozen or so steps away.

Nathan stopped, not calling out to them. *Let them get out, into the limo, and off grounds before anyone figures out that Dave is missing.*

It had worked! Dave is free. Nathan was just going to trust that Georgeann and Billy were occupying the victimized psych tech, keeping him away from returning to the unit for a few minutes. Once in the limo, all Jim and Dave needed was about three minutes to get down the access road and off the hospital property.

Nathan stopped, barely believing the success of his plan. He needed to sit for a moment, to absorb it all. Moving to the closest hallway chair he could find, he sat down, leaned back, looking up at the ceiling, collecting himself. It was over, his time at Hunt-Fisher. As crazy and frustrating and tedious and purposeless as his job at Hunt-Fisher had been at times, Nathan could not help feeling positive about the overall experience. He nodded to himself, understanding that sometimes it is best to simply embrace a phase one goes through, when it comes to an end. The skill in doing so involved cultivating gratitude, for the little things one learns, for people one has met along the way, people he would never have otherwise encountered: people like John Bortman, Courtney, Emily, Dominic, Betty and many more.

There are only a few days, Nathan thought as he continued gazing at the ceiling, a handful really, when one's life drastically changes overnight. But one of those major transitions was underway for Nathan at that moment. He was veering rapidly in a different direction, for parts unknown, trusting a friend to make it all work out. After four long years at Hunt-Fisher, he would walk out that door, the same one Jim and Dave had just used for their escape, and not turn back.

Next step: Rhode Island. That's what I am about now.

He glanced back down the hallway toward where he had left Cecelia. Surprisingly, she was still there, standing by herself, staring at him from this distance. Evidently, she was still in shock over what had just transpired. Nathan smiled at her. She was now the one impotently looking at him as he took action. Raising his hand to his brow, he gave her a gentle, informal farewell salute. Nathan sensed that this was a fitting end. He got up from the chair he had dropped into, turned away from Cecelia without checking to see if and how she responded, and walked out of the exit.

It was the final time Nathan Bigelow ever set foot in Hunt-Fisher Hospital.

Chapter 20

In the early afternoon on the day of the Montefiore Foundation Ball, a gala event held in late September at the Hilton in midtown Manhattan, Courtney and Sheila went together to a spa in Scarsdale Village to get their hair and nails done. Courtney was in a festive mood, ready for an elegant evening out in New York. She did not get to do this often—dress up in a sexy evening gown that her mother had bought for her at a boutique on Madison Avenue, mingle with the rich and influential, play the well-connected daughter who can easily mix it up with New York society. Simple partying was one thing: but doing so while wearing a $2,000 Vera Wang gown and special jewelry worth twice that amount—a gift her mother had insisted on buying also, since it accompanied the dress so perfectly—was another. *A girl needs to pamper herself once in awhile*, Courtney thought. *Do the Cinderella thing; become transformed, leave the mundane cottage in the woods and attend the grand Ball, impress her handsome Prince—or maybe some other man in attendance, who is a tad more available.*

Jason would be arriving by train in the mid-afternoon, and he had booked a room at the Hilton for the convenience of being able to get ready for the Ball in the same place as it was being held. The plan was for Courtney and her parents to drive into Manhattan from Scarsdale and meet him in the lobby of the Hilton at six-thirty. She and Jason had spoken directly to each other only once since Jason had agreed to serve as her chaperone to the Ball. During the call, Jason had sounded a little distracted to Courtney, like he was focused elsewhere. She asked him about it, and he owned up to having "a lot going on," about which he would have a chance to tell her more when they were together. Courtney was anxious to hear about it, she told him.

The hair stylist convinced Courtney to try something new, something elegant and flattering for the evening, which involved pulling her hair up and creating an array of curls, complemented by carefully arranged strands descending down below her ears. Sheila supervised the cut and styling, making suggestions and comments throughout. While Courtney bonded often with her father about the trials of post-doctorate residency training and clinical issues in psychiatry, she and her mother had less to work with in terms of generating special daughter-mother moments. But this event offered a wonderful opportunity for the two of them to engage with each other. Sheila's interest was in dressing Courtney up and showing her off to wealthy friends, and Courtney was cooperating fully.

The hair styling effort was deemed a work of art by all: Sheila, Courtney and the stylist herself. Courtney spent the rest of the afternoon protecting the look, especially during a long bath and while making herself up. When she had finished putting on her gown and sleek, high-heeled dress sandals, she called down to her parents who were waiting for her in the living room.

"You ready down there?" she asked, looking to make a grand entrance down the stairway.

"We are," Aaron called back.

When Courtney flowed down the stairs and entered the living room, Aaron was visibly astounded at his daughter's natural beauty and grace. "Wow," Aaron said, smiling proudly. "Wow," he repeated with more emphasis, as Courtney did a model's 360 degree turn to show the strapless gown, cut low in her back, and the special way it billowed from her slim waist to accentuate her trim shape and magnificent legs.

"Like it, Dad?" she asked, knowing the answer already, but being in the mood to hear compliments from a member of the opposite sex, even if it was from a highly biased representative of the male gender.

"There was a time when I would not have let you out in such a dress, Courtney, for fear of the reactions it would cause from boys," he joked. "But my girl has grown up, so what can I do? You look radiant, just splendid, honey. Really, all I can say is, 'wow!'"

Sheila came over, determined to make some minor adjustments to the gown's hem and then to the positioning of the necklace that played an important role in the overall look, since it drew attention to the appeal of bare shoulders and exposed skin from the bust line on up. "There," she said, standing back to admire the end product of the effort and financial resources she had dedicated to this moment. She was pleased. "I love it, everything about it—the dress, the hair, the jewelry, the shoes, the whole package. Now, be careful in the car to make sure you don't wrinkle the gown, Courtney. And be extra careful in New York with that expensive necklace, please."

"Yes, Mother," Courtney replied, playfully, with an adolescent inflection evident, mocking her mother's reflexive need to exert control.

"Shall we go?" Aaron asked.

"Yes, I need to get there early to get things organized," Sheila declared. "We're late already."

The trip into the City was held up only briefly by a long line of cars exiting the Bronx River Parkway onto the Cross County Parkway. But once on the Cross County, it was relatively smooth sailing into Manhattan, with Aaron choosing the West Side Highway since the Hilton was on that side of Manhattan Island.

Courtney was anxious to see Jason. She wondered about the cause of his worry and distraction. He had definitely not been himself on their last call. But he had sounded very enthusiastic about coming up for the Ball. *A chance to separate from the academic process for a couple of days, no doubt.* He probably was overwhelmed with some extra research he had volunteered to do, she thought, or with too much studying, or just with North Philadelphia. So it would be fun for him, she sensed, to get away and enjoy an upscale event in Manhattan. He had seen coastal New England, and now it was time for him to experience another side of the east coast, the style and elegance of a New York society affair. It was not an activity either one of them would want to do with any regularity, certainly not as often as the senior Dr. Brentwoods did; but as a special occasion, it promised to be very entertaining.

Aaron was going first class all the way that evening, so he opted for valet parking at the Hilton. Sheila had already warned his husband and daughter that she would need to separate from them right away, to check in with her event coordinators, making sure that everything was in place. Her role that evening was less focused on managing every event detail—she had ceded that role to her staff. She needed to be out in the crowd, targeting certain existing or would-be large donors with a pitch about how the Foundation desperately needed their ongoing support. But the executive in her needed to be certain that her staff was on top of all the multitudinous minutiae that went into staging such an affair. The moment the car stopped in front of the hotel, she was scurrying out the door and on her way to the Ballroom area, promising to meet up with Aaron and Courtney later.

Coming around the parked car to take his daughter's arm, Aaron escorted Courtney inside to the lobby. Jason was sitting on a chair directly in front of the front door, awaiting his evening's date. As daughter and father approached Jason, Courtney smiled broadly, noting with amusement the funky colored cumber bun he had chosen to accompany his otherwise traditional black evening tuxedo. *God, he is a good looking man,* she thought, once again feeling enraptured by his presence nearby, just as she had when she saw him outside Penn Station in late July.

Jason appeared almost confused as Courtney approached, as if he was not sure it was really her. His eyes widened and his jaw dropped in amazement. He stood up, seemingly transfixed. Aaron nudged his daughter knowingly, as if to say, "See, I told you that you would knock people over tonight."

"Dad, you remember Jason Burke," Courtney declared, looking only at Jason even though technically she had addressed her father. "You met at the graduation, remember? Jason, you met my Dad, Dr. Aaron Brentwood, didn't you?"

Jason did his best to extend a polite greeting to Aaron, but it was obvious he was still recovering from Courtney's entrance. "Yes, hello again Dr. Brentwood," Jason said awkwardly. A silence followed, as Courtney and Jason smiled at each other. Aaron acted quickly on his evident third-wheel status: he sensed there was little likelihood of small talk, at least at this moment.

"Oh my, there is Rick Walters," Aaron exclaimed, looking over at the hotel elevator. "I've been meaning to talk to him. Courtney, Jason, could you please excuse me? I will see you upstairs, okay, honey? Good to see you again, Jason." He hurried off discreetly, leaving his daughter alone with her date.

Once Aaron made his graceful exit, the pair that remained turned to look at each other. "You like?" Courtney asked coyly, twirling again, fishing for compliments as she had done earlier in her parents' living room.

Jason shook his head slowly. "I'm speechless," he said, finally. "Courtney Brentwood, you are a gorgeous thing to behold."

"Thanks," she replied, trying to stay informal with Jason. "I haven't done this in a long time, dressing up and doing the society thing. So my mother and I pulled out all the stops. Check out this necklace. Isn't it amazing?" She acted as if it was not really hers, like it was only on loan for the evening.

"Unbelievable. I'm not going to ask how much it costs; that would be way too uncool when you are mixing with the types we will be around tonight." Then Jason leaned in close to her. "But you'll tell me later, right?" he whispered in her ear.

"Four thousand," she whispered back, before pulling back, smiling and nodding, with her eyebrows raised.

"I have some new socks on," Jason joked. "I just bought them down the street. Spent a lot, too…I think ten dollars for four pair. Does that big spending allow me to hang around with you tonight?"

Courtney laughed, and grabbed his arm to begin leading him toward the upstairs Ballroom. "Thanks again for coming, Jason," she told him. "I think it will be fun. Let's make it fun, anyway."

Jason put his free hand over her hands now grasping his arm, confirming his acceptance of her friendly clutching. He smiled at her, still checking out her new, elegant look, from top to bottom. Then he stopped. "Hey, let's go have a drink at the bar. I checked just a few minutes ago, and there is really no one up there yet for the Ball."

"Great idea," Courtney agreed, remembering that she had arrived a bit early for her mother's sake.

They retraced their steps and found the hotel bar on the main floor. Choosing a spot far away from some smokers who were polluting the air with their cigarette fumes, they sat next to each other at a corner booth. At Jason's insistence, they ordered and began drinking champagne; it only seemed right, given the elegant circumstances.

"So, I've been worried about you," Courtney began, eager to learn what had been on Jason's mind that he alluded to in their most recent conversation. "Is everything all right?"

Jason shook his head. "I don't want to focus on my problems tonight, Court. We are here to have fun."

"Yeah, but I've got to know," she implored. "I won't have fun if I'm just waiting for you to tell me what it is. The suspense will be too distracting."

Jason looked at her warmly. Again, he scoped her out. "Have I told you that you look gorgeous tonight?" he asked. Courtney was aware that his eyes could not avoid wandering down to her bare shoulders and cleavage.

"C'mon, out with it," Courtney insisted, confronting his avoidance.

Jason took a deep breath. He put his hand on his jaw and rubbed it, showing that he was contemplating what he was about to say and how to say it.

"What is it, Jason?" she asked, sensing his discomfort.

"When Lara came to Philly a few weeks ago," he began finally, "it turns out she had a specific agenda. That was why the visit was unexpected."

Courtney gulped visibly, but tried not to appear too shaken. Her intuition told her that the subject of Lara's agenda was to finalize their engagement. Through this anxiety, Courtney was able to maintain steady eye contact, though. She had asked for this, insisting on knowing the source of Jason's distraction, so she needed to role-play the supportive friend all the way through.

Jason continued. "She said that her life was totally changed because of the television show. She said that she wanted me…" He hesitated again, evidently fearful of the impact of the next words he planned to say. He took a deep breath. "She said she wanted me to quit medical school and move back permanently to California."

Courtney's eyes widened in disbelief. "What?" she asked incredulously.

"She said that my being away the whole year frightened her," Jason explained, "because she is already moving around in new circles, feeling distant from me, which she never felt before. She said our relationship, as strong as it has always been, would not survive if I am not around her, not with her. The money she is making is so amazing, she insisted, that there is no real need for me to work, hence no need for me to become a doctor—especially if doing so means that I will need to spend four more years after this one in some kind of intensive training program, as she described it. She said she could not handle that, and that she could provide for both of us, easily, from a financial standpoint. She said she needs to live far more 'in the now'."

At this point, Courtney's face had lost much of its color. She started projecting into the future: Jason heading out west, integrating into the entertainment culture, no longer a party to the bond that the two of them had built, at least in part, on their shared medical profession. In the back of her mind, she knew that soon it would be necessary to start emotionally preparing for his departure to the west coast in the following June. But that was nine months away, giving her plenty of time to work through the impending separation. But this might mean that he would be going far sooner. Maybe even right away. Courtney started to feel a lump in her throat, a product of tension and sadness she was not expecting that evening. But, for the time being, she held her emotional ground.

"Jason, you are in your third year. You can't leave now, can't she understand that? I mean, I suppose you could leave if you had to, but do you have to? It's just not right." Courtney felt a surge of anger at Lara for the selfishness of her position. Jason was a good student, and he would be a great doctor, and Lara wanted him to blow it all up and become her agent or traveling secretary or boy toy or whatever? In a way, Courtney realized, Lara's request showed some insight and self-awareness. Lara was acknowledging that her priorities were changing, and that her relationship needed to adapt to new realities. She was not just an acting student and yoga instructor and medical student's future wife. Courtney assumed she had been tempted by other men, which undoubtedly must be alluring—men who were probably popular leading actors or leading television or movie producers and directors, men whose celebrity and power made them hard to turn down. But it was still a selfish, short-sighted request that she was making. Lara was thinking about Lara, not Jason's needs and interests and long term goals.

"So how did you leave it?" Courtney continued, almost hating to hear the answer.

Jason studied her face again, affectionately. "I'm still in medical school, right?" he answered, smiling. "She visited over three weeks ago, and I am still in medical school. So, if I am voting with my feet, I guess I am resisting this big time." He hesitated, and became more serious. "During her visit," he said, "I sensed things were a little different between us. She seemed a tad more…I don't know…arrogant I guess is the word." Jason stopped to look again at Courtney. Again, he smiled affectionately at her.

"Have I mentioned that you look gorgeous tonight?" he asked again, playfully.

"Three times, I think, but it never gets old," Courtney replied, smiling back. She sensed something was happening between them. Could it be that Lara's demand had raised some doubt in him about their long term plans? Courtney felt like she was being seduced, and it was coming from a welcome source. It was interesting that he had not just complied right away with Lara's request. Or with her demand, was more like it. Courtney hung onto the fact that he was still in school, studying, assumedly putting Lara off.

"What were your most recent conversations like?" Courtney asked.

Jason hesitated. He moved slightly closer to Courtney, lowering his voice for dramatic effect.

"Courtney, I'll be honest with you. I've been a little less than candid. Courtney, here is the truth. I called Lara last week, and I told her I had made up my mind—I'm staying in medical school."

Courtney smiled broadly, tension starting to leave her body. "Yes!" she shouted, loud enough to turn the heads of other hotel guests around them. But Courtney did not care—she was exhilarated that Jason had not succumbed to Lara's ultimatum. She put both of her arms around his shoulders, pulling him toward her, placing her forehead against his, to show how intimately she supported his decision.

"It's the right decision, Jason," she said in close, with a low but confident tone, looking him squarely in the eyes. "Trust me. Things will work out."

As she began to pull away from this physical contact between them, she saw that he was shaking his head.

"What?" she asked, responding to his evident disagreement with the supportive statement she had just made.

"I'm not so sure I want it to work out," he said.

Courtney tried not to overreact. But could it be that the man she had longed for was extricating himself from a relationship that appeared to be as deep and intense as any Courtney had ever witnessed?

"What do you mean, Jason?" she asked softly.

"What do you think I mean?" Jason replied, smiling warmly at her.

"I asked you first," Courtney insisted.

"Okay. Listen, the last three weeks have been a real gut check time for me. A real difficult assessment of what I want. It is a classic case of being at a crossroads, and choosing a direction to go in." He hesitated for a moment, then he pulled her in closer, reaching down to grab her hands with his, entwining his fingers with hers.

Courtney looked at their joined hands, and smiled, thrilled by his effort to bring them together physically.

"Can I share something with you?" he asked.

"Of course."

"Our short weekend in Rhode Island…it stayed with me, Courtney," Jason said, haltingly at first. "It was on my mind a lot, after I left. Did you think about it, too?"

You have no idea, Courtney thought.

"I did," she affirmed, nodding.

Hearing this, Jason smiled, and squeezed her hands. "You asked me a lot of questions about my third year of training, remember?" Courtney nodded. "And you shared what it was like to be a doctor, leading a case. I realized then that I wanted that, what you were doing. Then I realized that I really like what I am doing, studying to be a doctor. I've talked, a little pompously probably, about giving up medicine eventually, but, the field has sucked me in, it has me engaged. I feel a part of it now. I am not just an ambivalent, half-committed participant. I can say it: I want to be a doctor."

Courtney nodded, smiling still, understanding that he had finally surrendered in a sense; he had stopped fighting his physician identity.

"Dr. Sheridan has had a lot to do with it," he went on, explaining his transformation. "I just love this guy. He has changed my attitude about a lot of things. He has challenged me. Before, no one really did that. Now, I feel like I have a purpose in my education, a direction."

Jason hesitated again. Then he inched even closer to Courtney, so that the arm in his coat pressed against her exposed shoulder, warming her. He brought her hands together, and sandwiched them between his.

"Then, I realized, while we were together, after being apart for awhile," he continued, "that I've always felt so comfortable with you, Courtney. But the time we spent together in Norwalk felt different than when we were in Philadelphia together." He leaned toward her, and whispered, "I wanted to stay on Sunday...stay with you. Could you tell?"

Courtney's heart raced. "I wanted you to stay," Courtney whispered back.

Jason smiled. "I sensed that, from you, but I felt the same way. All I could think about on the way back to Philadelphia was you, Courtney, about how I might be missing the chance to be with someone like you. My feelings have been changing since you left Philadelphia. God, do I miss you there. Then after our weekend together, all my supposed priorities started to evaporate. Instead of preparing to become an entrepreneur, I wanted to be a family doctor. Instead of focusing on Lara, all I could think about was you. I sat on it, not sure whether I was going through a stage of some sort, or perhaps I was a little jealous of Lara's success, or something. But I kept thinking about you. Then when Lara called to invite herself to visit, I figured I would deal with it when she got there. But before I could start talking about anything, she gave me her ultimatum of sorts. It was so confusing for a few days, but, you know what? I started to think, maybe she is picking up on how I am changing toward her. Maybe she senses I think about you a lot. Maybe she is saying, 'I feel you pulling away, so let's bring this to a head, because, with my own career taking off like it is, I am feeling more distant from you, too.' It has certainly felt that way, her drifting away from me a bit once she started acting full time. So I admire her, in a way: the only way to save the relationship, she figured, or the only way to give it any hope at all, was to have me with her at all times. Otherwise, it would never work. But I said, 'No.'"

Courtney was tingling. She moved toward him, and they touched foreheads again. But Jason needed to finish explaining himself.

"Once I decided to stay in medical school," he went on, "once and for all, which happened just a few days ago, really, I told Lara that my decision was final. She hung up on me, and I haven't spoken to her since. I should have been crushed. I mean it wasn't pleasant, that's for sure. But quickly, I began thinking about coming up to see you, for the Ball tonight. And now we are here," he said, smiling at her, leaning in to maintain physical contact. "We are together. And, corny as it sounds, there is no place I would rather be."

Courtney's eyes were getting moist. But she needed to hang on just a moment longer, to get a chance to tell him she felt the same, only one hundred times more.

"Jason..." Courtney began, but Jason put his forefinger across her lips.

"I need to finish this, if that is okay," he said. She nodded, easily complying to his request, loving what she was hearing.

"When I saw you a few minutes ago, walking in the door with your father, looking so beautiful, it just confirmed it for me. That I think you are the most wonderful and gorgeous woman I have ever met, and that I am absolutely crazy about you, Courtney."

She remained dutifully silent, waiting until it was clear he had said all he wanted to say. But she could not stem a choking, joyful sob, or the tears that now began to run down her cheeks. "It's true," he confirmed, as if he needed to convince her. "I realize now, Courtney, that when I chose to stay in Philadelphia, it was really a choice to go after what I really want…not just to be a doctor, but to be with you, Courtney. I want you. I came here tonight to beg you to give it a try…to give us a try."

That was it. Courtney could not hold back any longer. She sprung to him, pressing her lips against his with such force that she pushed him back, almost toppling him off his chair. Their kiss was short, owing to their presence in public, but it had such intensity that it left no doubt that they were now lovers.

Finally, she had a chance to tell him what she had told Nathan, and what she had wanted to share with him for at least two months, and probably longer.

"Jason, I love you," she whispered in his ear. "I love you, do you hear? Maybe it wasn't always like that, but I felt the same way about our weekend together in July. You were right to sense it from me. At the very start of that weekend, when I saw you across the street waiting for me in New York, I realized I haven't been myself since I left Philadelphia, and it is because I miss you so much, that I couldn't stand being away from you, that I love you. I couldn't say anything, because I would never want you feeling awkward around me. I've tried to get you out of me, but it was no use. I just never thought you would feel this way about me."

Jason initiated another kiss. "But I do, Courtney. I want us to be together. This feels so right to me."

They sat and looked at each other, smiling, continuing to kiss often.

They finally got up to head toward the Ballroom. At this point, feeling like they did, they needed to touch each other, at all times. So they kept their arms wrapped around each others' waists, or they held hands as they mingled around the Ballroom, occasionally joining slow dances, to wrap themselves around each other and steal more kisses. They tried their best to hold some conversations with a few guests who introduced themselves. But they were aching to be alone together, twelve stories up, in Jason's room 1434 at the Hilton.

Courtney finally could not wait any longer. She decided to sweep by her mother to show that she was still there, hoping that after their conversation Sheila would lose track of her. When Courtney reached her mother, Sheila was talking to two people Courtney knew: Georgeann Wagner, and her date, Dr. Harold Hunt. Courtney said hello to her mother, shook Dr. Hunt's hand, and then hugged Georgeann. Georgeann pulled her aside, causing Courtney to lose physical contact with Jason for the first time since they made their way into the Ball.

"Dr. Brentwood, guess what I just did?" she asked excitedly.

"Never mind that, Georgeann. Dr. Hunt is the one you have been seeing?"

"Yes. There's nothing wrong with that," she added, sheepishly. "He is not my doctor anymore."

Courtney just shook her head, amused by the feisty lady she had treated at Dr. Hunt's institution.

"Anyway, you know what I just did?" Georgeann repeated.

"What did you just did?" Courtney asked playfully.

"I just told your mother that I made a charitable donation deal for her and Montefiore, with my good friends, James and Sylvia Pentchecki. I told James and Sylvia that if they donated a certain seven-figure amount, which I will let them announce, I would add a million. But they had to agree to it right away, otherwise the deal is off. And if they agreed, I'd have your mother announce it right here, tonight, keeping my involvement anonymous. They accepted, just a few moments ago."

"You are a wheeler-dealer, Georgeann. Wow, my mother has been after them for months."

"I know. She told me at lunch one day recently. I told you she invited me, didn't I? Anyway, she asked if I knew them, and I told her that James Pentchicki and John, my late husband, did lots of business deals together. So the bond was already there. I think John would approve of my spending a little of our money this way."

A million is a little money? Wow, this woman is loaded.

"That's great, Georgeann. Good luck with it. Listen I have to talk with my mother, if you will excuse me."

Courtney slid over to Sheila and demanded her attention, as she also grabbed Jason's hand again, missing his touch.

"Mom, great party," she said.

"Thanks, Courtney. Oh, hello Jason," Sheila added, noticing the hand-holding and seeming a bit surprised by the affection it conveyed. Sheila extended her hand to him.

Jason released Courtney's hand and returned the greeting warmly, thanking her for the chance to be part of such an enjoyable event. Sheila turned back to Courtney, giving her a look that read, "So what is going on between the two of you?"

Courtney grasped Jason's hand again with both of hers. "Mother, could you tell Dad that I have made other plans for getting home to Connecticut tonight. Okay? I won't be going home with you guys."

"But, Courtney…," Sheila started to protest.

"Good night, Mother," she said, dismissively, freeing a hand to wave at her. Luckily, Georgeann was bringing another couple to Sheila for an introduction. Halfway to the ballroom door, Courtney sensed her mother's stare on her back. She turned, acknowledged her mother's look, and waved again, grinning mischievously.

Sheila's expression changed. It went from being very puzzled to being extremely pleased.

She waved back, then resumed her networking.

Returns

Chapter 21

Jason needed to return to medical school by Monday morning, and Courtney also needed to be at Hunt-Fisher by then. Otherwise, the two of them might have just stayed at the Hilton for days, rarely leaving the bed where they explored each other's respective bodies and pleasure zones, and enjoyed each other's lovemaking skills. Courtney had some erotic catching up to do, so she crammed as much sex into the day and a half with Jason as he could handle. Jason was a passionate and considerate lover, Courtney learned. But she had expected that.

They ordered room service for occasional nourishment, and Jason had to go out to buy Courtney some things to wear for the trip back to Norwalk, since the gown and a handbag were all she had with her. But otherwise they remained in bed, naked and intimate, until early Monday morning.

In between, they talked about everything—except what would happen next.

Courtney now needed to be with Jason, and he with her; an occasional visit was not going to be acceptable. They had to be with each other, whenever possible.

Courtney foresaw the inevitable; she would need to return to Philadelphia, and often, to see him during any free time she had. But after one month of alternating weekend meetings in Philadelphia and Norwalk, Jason confided in Courtney that he was thinking of staying on at Temple for a residency in family medicine, under Dr. Sheridan's guidance. He knew her feelings about the area, so he wanted to get her reaction, before he made any decisions. Courtney did not hesitate. She would join him there. In fact, she decided to transfer to one of the Philadelphia-based residency programs at semester break, after the Christmas and New Year holidays.

By December, as Courtney made the final arrangements to effect her transfer from Hunt-Fisher to Jefferson Medical College's psychiatric residency program, Jason proposed. A July wedding was planned, after Jason's graduation from medical school. Aaron and Sheila, thrilled with their daughter's engagement and with Jason as a prospective son-in-law, surprised them with an early wedding gift: they bought the couple a house in Blue Bell, well out in the Philadelphia suburbs, near the Wings Field Airport around the Plymouth Meeting Mall. The gift included paying a $150,000 down payment, co-signing for a mortgage of roughly the same amount, along with a pledge to make monthly house payments through the period of the Burkes' respective residencies. Whenever the home was sold, the Burkes would just repay the money they had been loaned, along with ten percent of the profit on the sale over and above the repayment amount. Aaron and Sheila wanted their daughter in a safe and comfortable setting—they could afford it, they wanted to help, and the house was a good investment. Aaron did start another edition of his textbook, though, to begin replenishing his bank account.

After her residency was over, as Jason completed his PGY4, Courtney did some moonlighting at the Temple Public Health Clinic, alongside her old mentor Rolanda James. This yielded a few "I told you so" comments from Rolanda and other Clinic staff, who were nonetheless thrilled with her return.

The couple held off on starting a family until then, during Jason's final year in training. By that time, Aaron and Sheila were nearly demanding a grandchild in return for the financial support they had provided throughout their daughter and son-in-law's medical training.

During Courtney's pregnancy, she received a surprising call from Nathan Bigelow in Rhode Island, with whom she had always stayed in touch and exchanged annual Christmas cards. He encouraged her to apply for a Unit Chief job at Oceanview Hospital in Newport, where he was still serving as Program Director of Residential Services. Nathan had earned his master's degree by this time in counseling psychology from URI, and had married a nurse he had met and begun dating soon after starting with the hospital—one who did not work in the residential program he directed.

Jason became excited about moving to Rhode Island, and he quickly explored family practice opportunities in the area. By the end of his residency, he had three job offers from leading physician groups there. The Burkes sold the house in Blue Bell, repaid Aaron and Sheila, used the rest of the profit as a down payment on a home in Newport, and moved to Rhode Island in 1995.

The Burkes and Bigelows became close friends in Newport. Nathan and his wife Suzy had a baby about the same time that the Burkes had theirs, so the children were constant playmates. By then, Courtney had retold the story many times of duping Short, on the fateful day of Dave's escape. Short had fallen for her request for a medication consult easily. Interestingly, Courtney had actually benefited from his advice that day, in managing a patient she was treating.

The Burkes' favorite television show, Pacific Place, starring Lara King and others, was finally cancelled, after a surprisingly strong six-year run. By then, Lara had starred in three feature films as well, and she was regularly seen on the Hollywood gossip shows, being escorted around L.A. by different leading actors with whom she was rumored to be romantically involved at the time. In one nationally televised interview with Mitt Ciccarone, a prominent reporter from ABC, Lara mentioned how little interest she had at first in becoming an actress—she was going to be a doctor's wife, and together with her husband-to-be, they were planning to become entrepreneurs in the fitness industry. She explained that she had been in a relationship with this guy throughout most of his college and medical school years, almost engaged, but the romance had ended just about the time when Pacific Place was really starting to take off. It was a period, she told her audience, of great emotional upheaval: she had a leading part in a hit television show, but the ending of this relationship nearly broke her heart. But she had pulled it together, channeling her psychic pain into her television role. She learned she really loved acting, and this helped her reframe her goals. In the end, it had all turned out well. Ciccarone amusingly asked if the anonymous medical student needed a doctor himself, for breaking up with such a gorgeous and talented woman. The reporter imagined that this man was no doubt kicking himself now for the stupid choice he had made in letting the relationship end. Courtney pushed Jason off the sofa as they watched this, responding with mock anger to his tongue-in-cheek wholehearted agreement with the reporter's conjecture. It was a reaction he expected, and was looking to playfully provoke from his treasured wife. He milked his implied fame for weeks thereafter, nicknaming himself The Heartbreak Kid, with a feigned braggadocio that Courtney coped with by ignoring it as best she could.

Billy Andrews attended Lehigh in Bethlehem, Pennsylvania, and started at linebacker on the football team for two years. He returned to New York, entered Columbia Business School, and took a job in investment banking on Wall Street. Within a few years, he had bought his own home in Scarsdale, only a mile from his parents' place.

Dave went back to school and graduated from Roger Williams in 1996 with a bachelor's in psychology. By then, he was Program Director of the residential alcohol and drug program at Oceanview, with eight years of solid sobriety. He was particularly adept at marketing his program to referral sources, applying his natural interpersonal gifts. He never saw a psychiatrist again, after John Bortman met with him and said that he need not continue in therapy or with medication, but only needed to immerse himself in his new professional employment opportunity, stay involved in self-help treatment and follow the guidance of Nasty Steve Hirsch. Dave's favorite part in telling his recovery story at open AA meetings was the time he escaped from a mental hospital, with about a week left until his insurance ran out, and facing an imminent transfer to the State Hospital. It was so ironic, he would tell his rapt audiences, because now he oversaw the same kind of locked hospital units himself.

Georgeann married Harold Hunt in 1991. Hunt initiated his marriage proposal quickly since he knew he had limited time left with most of his mental faculties intact, and he wanted to enjoy his time with her while he could. He died in 1998, willing full ownership of Hunt-Fisher Hospital to his wife. Georgeann, now twice widowed, flung herself into the leadership of the hospital, naming herself head of the Board of Trustees. One of her first moves in this role was to gently ask Dr. James Short to leave the hospital and find other employment. Short, who had married Cecelia soon after she got pregnant with their first child, moved to a neighboring hospital and spent much energy trying to compete against Hunt-Fisher for admissions, motivated by revenge against Georgeann. He was finally asked to leave there too, though, when he was discovered having sex on his psychotherapy couch with a nursing student. He and Cecelia divorced soon afterwards, but not before getting embroiled in a bitter child custody battle. She turned in her vanity Connecticut license plates—RNLVSMD—and moved back to Vermont with the children, where she took a job as a head nurse at Mary Hitchcock Memorial Hospital across the river in Hanover, New Hampshire. Short ended up admitting himself to a sex addict's treatment program at Northwestern Institute in Pennsylvania.

Tim Harris was Oceanview Hospital's very first admission, transferred from Norwalk Hospital's inpatient psychiatric unit at his father's insistence, once the senior Mr. Harris found out Nathan worked at a new facility in Rhode Island. Tim also was the very first admission to the residential program Nathan administered. Ultimately, Tim was discharged from Oceanview's longer term residential program, and he took a market research job at General Systems, where his father worked, back in Connecticut. He lived on his own there, and saw a social worker for therapy once a week.

Georgeann called Courtney in 1999 and asked her if she would consider a move back to Norwalk, to become the Director of Resident Education at her hospital. Georgeann did not like John Fencik. After feeling Georgeann's political squeezing, Fencik had resigned, finding a similar job at another teaching hospital in Boston. Courtney declined the offer at first, citing her strong attachment to Newport. But by 2001, Georgeann's persistence paid off. The Burkes moved to Connecticut, and Courtney took charge of the residency education at Hunt-Fisher Hospital. In interviews with new residents, she liked to point to the chair where she too had once sat, in 1990, during her pre-residency meeting with her new colleague Dr. Robert Blakeley and the late Dr. Harold Hunt. It was her way of building a bond with her future trainees, and making them feel more at ease.

Aaron and Sheila played a role in their daughter's decision to accept the position at Hunt-Fisher. They strongly advocated for the move, ostensibly for career-enhancement reasons, but more because their cherished granddaughter Mallory would be less than an hour away as a result, instead of being at a distance of three hours or more. They sweetened their plea to have the Burkes move closer by chipping in on the down payment for an expensive New Canaan home that Courtney and Jason desperately wanted to buy but could not quite afford. Aaron's new textbook was selling well, providing the financial support to help seal the deal.

Mallory Burke and Emily Bigelow, Nathan's child, remained close friends, despite the Burkes' move to Connecticut, because the Burkes kept their promise to her, to visit Newport often and vacation with the Bigelows every summer. On the way to and from Newport, the Burkes always tried to stop at Abigail's restaurant in Mystic.

After these visits, especially those that occurred within a year of the move to Connecticut, Mallory would develop a bad case of homesickness, for Newport and for the close friend that she had left behind. Whenever she became irritable, Mallory would declare that she hated New Canaan—it was the worst place in the world, she insisted.

Courtney, in particular, would say she understood. But she advised her precious daughter that things happen in life, and that this intolerant attitude—while keenly felt—would probably change some day.

Author's Notes

This is a work of fiction. Nothing in this novel actually occurred. Any resemblance to an actual event is completely coincidental. Any resemblance between the characters in this work of fiction and an actual person, living or deceased, is also entirely coincidental.

I would like to thank Mr. David M. Donnenfeld, former CEO at eTherapy.com, for his encouragement and insights through the early stages of my efforts to write this novel.

There have been individuals with whom I worked and from whom I learned a great deal during my years working in and around hospitals, all of whom contributed to my learning about life around medical schools and psych hospitals. It is impossible to name them all. But I'll list a few, apologizing in advance for the many omissions: Pat Weston, Sharon Kennedy, Michael Selzer, Hugni Oskarsson, Mary Ann Hurley, Otto Kernberg, Robert Michels, Richard Munich, John Clarkin, George Alexopoulos, Richard Frances, Valerie Yandow, Mary Lou Stelling, Lou Meisel, Diane Barkeley, Bruno Terrelli, Frank Simon, Joe Sisco, Marcia Case, John and Stacey Caretta, Fran Pasheluk, Art Giordano, Debra Kessler, Mary Ellen Phillips and Richard Jensen.

A special thanks to my close friend Stephen E. Kohn, President of Health & EAP Resources, for his support along the way. And greetings also to all the "Rub" boys, the audience for my earliest works of creative writing, in the letters we exchanged: Keith, John, Peter, George and Joel.

And, of course, to my extended family, now spread widely across the country, from New York to Pennsylvania to Maryland to California.

Les Miserables is the property of Cameron Mackintosh Limited. Lyrics, by Herbert Kretzmer, are published as part of the Original Broadway Cast Recording, Geffen Records, 1987.

0-595-33116-5

Movement Off The Dime

An unlikely pair is conspiring to break a patient out of a locked unit at the famous Hunt-Fisher Hospital. Courtney Brentwood is involved. She is the daughter of two prominent New York physicians, just beginning her own promising career in medicine, and lovesick over a younger fellow medical student she left behind in Philadelphia. Nathan Bigelow, the mastermind behind the plot, is a talented underachiever she meets at the hospital, who cajoles her into abetting a scheme to help out his best friend. *Movement Off The Dime* tells the amusing and entertaining tale of two young people finding themselves, getting untracked in their lives, navigating their way through wide-ranging emotional terrain: career ambivalence, unrequited love, unsatisfied lust, devoted friendship and filial duty.

"I am recommending this engaging story to everyone I know—not just to those who work in and around hospitals or medical schools, but to anyone who enjoys a smart read."
—Susan Tabor, Executive Director of Behavioral Health, Allina Health System.

Photo by Joel Cipes

V. D. O'Connell is a professional writer, content developer and author. This is his second book, and his first work of fiction.

ISBN 0-595-33116-5

X0043QFZ4T
Movement Off The Dime
New

5 U.S.

iUniverse™

www.iuniverse.com